A New York Hold'em

A NEW YORK HOLD'EM

A Novel

William A. Klein

iUniverse, Inc.
New York Lincoln Shanghai

A New York Hold'em

Copyright © 2006, 2007 by William A. Klein

iUniverse books may be ordered through booksellers or by contacting:

iUniverse
2021 Pine Lake Road, Suite 100
Lincoln, NE 68512
www.iuniverse.com
1-800-Authors (1-800-288-4677)

ISBN: 978-0-595-41309-6 (pbk)
ISBN: 978-0-595-67893-8 (cloth)
ISBN: 978-0-595-85664-0 (ebk)

Printed in the United States of America

This book is dedicated to my mother and father. It would take me another novel to thank them for everything that they have done for me. I love the two of you more than words can say.

In Loving Memory
Of
Nicholas Robert Hance
November 26, 2004

-One of God's little angels
May you continue to inspire the ones who love you.

Tom

Thank you for all your hard work, time and effort that you put into making this a better book.

CHAPTER 1

The Deal
(A of Spades, K of Spades)

As Anthony lay in his twin size bed in his little two-room apartment listening to the rain, he couldn't help but think of what his mom-mom used to say: "Rain was God's way of cleaning away the Earth's sins." A smile began to appear on his face. He just had to laugh to himself, thinking if it was only that easy in life to have your sins erased by the gentle fall of the rain. That might have made a six-year-old Catholic school boy with his whole future ahead of him look at the rain differently, but when you are thirty-three and nothing is working out at this point in your life, it is just another autumn rain. This rain wasn't going to wash away his sins. For that matter, he started to think that a priest couldn't do that much better.

Staring aimlessly at the ceiling, the same questions came to him over and over again in his mind, driving him to the point of madness. Why can't I stop? How did it get out of control? How the hell did I lose everything? When will this nightmare end? He knew the situation was beyond help and there wasn't any help out there for him. There were no answers to these questions that would help him deal with the pain or change all his mistakes. Tomorrow sure enough would come, and he needed to find a way out of this mess quickly and time was not on his side.

"Fucking Yankees! How the fuck do you lose the World Series to a fucking franchise team from Arizona?" he screamed. They didn't just lose game seven in the bottom of the ninth. Mariano Rivera didn't just blow his first post season game ever by giving up a punch single to Luis Gonzalez over a drawn in infield. Anthony couldn't get these images out of his head. This was all just a bad dream and he was going to wake up any minute now. But it was much worse than that. This was one of those nightmares that you had as a child that sent you running to your parents' room for safety. But he wasn't a child anymore and this wasn't a dream, this was reality.

These Yankees were supposed to win the World Series for this city and deliver its people out of the pain and misery that they have been suffering with over the last two months. The Yankees were basically playing miracle baseball in games four and five and had a whole city behind them, believing a little more in a God that they thought had abandoned them not too long ago. But in the end they didn't deliver that final cure for these people and while the others would eventually get over it and try to go back to picking up the pieces of what had just happened to them and their city, Anthony just couldn't do that.

"How the hell am I going to get Frankie's fifty g's?" he asked himself out loud. But he knew the answer and it wasn't an answer that would rescue him from this predicament. There wasn't any possible way he could get that kind of money, neither in a week nor, for that matter, in a lifetime. And once again that feeling came, and he ran to the bathroom and threw up. It was only the fourth time in the last hour, but when you are in the kind of trouble that Anthony was in your head just keeps spinning and your stomach won't stop cramping with pain.

Anyone who has ever gambled in their life and won knows how exciting it can be for them. The joy of believing that they beat the house, made money without having to work for it, thinking that luck was on their side. But those little small timers out there who place ten and twenty dollar bets don't know the true excitement of gambling. The true excitement you feel when your thousand dollar reverse you placed with two bets that you knew were locks came through, and now you have four thousand dollars in front of you.

It's an overwhelming joy that you can only share with other gamblers because if you are placing that kind of money on two games, you can't tell your friends and family, because more than likely they have already abandoned you.

Now on the other end of that emotional spectrum is the totally terrorizing feeling of knowing that you have just lost every cent that you own. The only people who could possibly feel the same way are families whose houses had burnt to the ground and they didn't have insurance at the time and they have just lost everything. In cases like this, it was an unforeseen tragedy and you feel sorry for those people. Your heart goes out to them; you say a prayer during

Sunday services or make a donation to help them get back on their feet again. When a man or woman bets everything that they have in the bank on one game or weekend of games and is on the wrong side of those bets, the feeling is sickening. It is ten times worse than a heart attack, the flooding of emotions hits like a tidal wave. Now how could you possibly feel sorry for them? You can't, and Anthony was no exception to this. Anthony was just another lovable loser that you root for; hoping that he finally evens the score on the books. But remember the true meaning of the word loser, and that is all he was and all he would be as long as he continued this life style.

With his head hanging over the bowl, the tears just started coming out again and he couldn't stop them. "Why the hell am I such a loser?" he cried as he picked himself up off the floor. But he also knew the answer to that question and it was one that he had known all his life—he was not meant to be a winner. The world needs both winners and losers—if not it would be an uneven balance and that just can't be.

As he started to go back to the living room the phone rang out, and Anthony just froze. His heart leaped out of his chest because he knew it could only be one person calling him at this, the worst time of his life, and that one person was Bull.

Michael "Bull" Colaiezzi was Frankie's muscle. And if anyone ever fit the nick-name "Bull", it was Michael. He stood about six foot three and weighed two hundred and forty-five pounds and was still in his prime at the age of twenty-nine. He was absolutely the biggest and meanest guy in Frankie's crew. You just didn't want to fuck with this guy because if you did, you weren't going to live to remember it.

Late one Monday afternoon, Daniel Braidwood, a bus driver for the city, found out just how much of a crazy son of a bitch Bull really was. Dan was into Frankie for fourteen hundred dollars and decided that he wasn't going to pay his debt. Frankie determined it was time to get Bull more involved in the collection side of the business.

"Bull, I decided that it is time to let you do what I feel is your calling in our family," Frankie started to explain to him. "One of our regular guys named Dan Braidwood is into us for fourteen hundred, and he feels that he can just disappear without paying off his obligations. I want you to go and convince him otherwise."

Bull had been waiting for this moment for a long time. He had been doing odd jobs for Frankie for years and now he was given a chance to finally do some real work.

"Now I don't want you doing some crazy cowboy stunt to get the money. I think just showing up to this fucking guy's home or work will scare the shit out of him enough that he will pay you something right there on the spot. But if he doesn't, then do what you feel necessary to get it," Frankie told him.

"Uncle Frank, you know I would never let you down and trust me, this fucking douche bag will shell out some money to me before I get through with him," Bull promised him with a kiss on each of Frankie's cheeks.

Bull approached this as his first real test to become a member in his uncle's crew. He didn't want to just show up to this guy's house and beat the money out of him. No, he wanted to make an example out of him. You don't fuck with Frankie Feliciani and get away with it! So after Frankie gave him the okay to go collect the money from this low life, Bull did some research on the guy. Vincent Lusi gave Bull Dan's home address and told him that he was a city bus driver. Dan's route was Broad Street, which was very busy during the day, so Vincent told Bull he might as well just show up at the guy's house while his wife and sixteen year old daughter were home. When a guy comes knocking on your door at ten o'clock at night, you usually were persuaded to give him his money right then and there to avoid any unnecessary consequences.

Instead of doing the obvious like everyone expected Bull to do, he went the way he thought would get the message across to Dan and anyone else who thought that it was okay to fuck Frankie. At three o'clock in the afternoon Bull sat in his 1999 black convertible Corvette outside of St. Mary's High School and waited for Sarah Braidwood to come along. When Sarah walked by his car Bull opened the passenger door and said, "Sarah, hop on in. Your dad asked me to take you to see him."

Sarah approached the car door hesitantly and said, "I'm sorry, but I don't know you and why would my father send someone to see him at work when he is driving a bus downtown?"

"See, that's the problem with you kids nowadays. Always asking too many fucking questions," he told her as he pulled out his 9 mm and pointed it right at her face. "I don't want to hurt you. I swear, just get in the car because I am really going to take you to see your dead beat of a father."

Sarah didn't even have a moment for her mind to register what was happening because Bull had grabbed her by the arm and pulled her into the passenger seat before she could even think.

Twenty minutes had passed and Sarah still didn't understand what was happening to her as they stood on the corner of 7th and Broad Streets waiting for her father's bus. Finally, Bull explained to Sarah that her father was a douche bag who owed his uncle fourteen hundred dollars and he was going to use her to convince him that he should pay off his debts.

"Are you going to be some real tough guy and beat up my dad in front of his passengers? Why did you even bring me down here anyway? Want me to watch?" she asked as she stood there sobbing.

"I think your father will get the message once he sees you with me. Just think, if he had a real job maybe he would have paid off his little problem," he answered her in an unsympathetic voice.

They stood there for the next five minutes in total silence. This was all new to Bull. He had bullied people all his life but he never needed a gun to do it. He was used to getting what he wanted, but if Frankie found out that he got the guy's kid involved that could send the wrong kind of message to the bosses. The repercussions would be deadly for both Frankie and Bull. There were a few golden rules about their business and one of them was never to involve a guy's wife or kids. They weren't the reason why their husbands were in the trouble that they were in, so don't involve them.

But Bull knew that once this guy saw his kid's life in danger he would be scared of Frankie for the rest of his life and he wouldn't be stupid enough to report this to the police. As for the people on the bus, this wouldn't be different than any of the other kind of crazy shit that happens in this city. Bull was now too caught up in the excitement to be worried about Frankie and circumstances. All he wanted was the reward of seeing the guy's face as he watched Bull come up behind his daughter.

As the bus approached he told Sarah, "Just walk up and into the bus and once you say hi, just move a little out of the way and I promise I won't hurt your dad. However, if you yell or scream or do anything stupid I will put so many bullets into your dad's face, you can forget about an open coffin at his viewing. Do we understand each other?" Realizing that this maniac would shoot her father if she tried to be a hero, Sarah decided to do as Bull said and hope for the best.

Bull was like a little kid on Christmas morning. He couldn't control his excitement as the bus opened its' doors in front of them. "Remember to just walk up and give him a kiss hello and move over to the side," he reminded her.

"You just remember what you promised," she turned around and said to him as she readied to enter the bus. The doors opened and to make matters easier for them there were no customers waiting to get off. Sarah walked up the steps with Bull right behind her with one arm around her waist and the other holding the 9 mm in the small of her back.

"Sarah, what a pleasant surprise. What on earth are you doing here?" he questioned her as she kissed him hello.

"I thought it wou..." but before she could finish Bull had pushed her aside and was now standing in front of Dan with his gun jammed right in his belly.

"Hello douche bag," Bull greeted Dan with a smile.

"Jesus Christ, just take the money, it's under the seat, just don't hurt anyone," was the only thing Dan could think to say.

"Shut up, you fucking douche bag and start driving! You owe an acquaintance of mine some money. You do remember your little debt don't you? I thought you might have forgotten so I brought Sarah with me to help remind you of your obligations," Bull explained to him.

"Ah Jesus Christ please don't hurt her, she has nothing to do with this. I swear to God I will get Frankie his money by the end of the week just please don't do anything extreme," he started to cry as he begged Bull.

This feeling of over whelming power was the most unsurpassed rush that Bull had ever felt in his life and a smile now began to appear on his face. The feeling was much different than the feeling he used to get from beating the shit out of some kid in the school bathroom and having them beg for him to stop before he put their head in the toilet. No, this was a totally new nirvana for Bull and he thought he could get used to it.

"Listen to me and listen well, you fucking douche bag. You see that cute little thing standing over there with tears in her eyes? Well if you don't get me Frankie's fourteen hundred dollars by Friday, I promise she won't be cute anymore. Do you understand what I am telling you?" Bull asked him as he kept the gun pointed at his stomach.

"Yeah, I swear to God I will have his money for you on Friday, just please leave her alone," he sobbed.

"Pull the bus over at the next corner," Bull commanded him.

As Dan pulled the bus over to the corner, Bull with one sudden swing landed the butt of the 9 mm right on Dan's nose. Dan never even heard the woman who was sitting directly behind him or Sarah's screams because there was an instant jolt of pain in his face as the blood poured out. Bull swiftly grabbed Dan by his hair and pulled him forward.

"That's for thinking you could just forget about your obligations to Frankie. The next time it won't be your face that gets rearranged," Bull warned him as he opened the door to the bus and let himself out.

Later that night back at *The Club*, Frankie asked Bull how it was going with the fourteen hundred.

"I don't think you need to worry about your money Uncle Frank."

"So you went to Dan's home and convinced him that it would be in his best interest to pay you?" Frankie asked Bull.

"Let's just say I took a bus trip today and the bus driver and I saw eye to eye," Bull said with a hearty laugh.

"Great! So you popped your cherry on the very first guy," Frankie said as he gave Bull a congratulatory kiss on both cheeks.

Bull didn't start off right away as a collector for Frankie. Like everyone else in the crew, he had to work his way up the ranks. But ever since Bull was a teenager he realized that this was what he wanted to do with his life.

He was all city his junior and senior years of high school in both football and wrestling. Four different national colleges wanted to recruit him, but Bull had other ideas for his future and playing college football was not one of them. There was only one future that he wanted and that was to be in his Uncle Frankie's crew.

Before he was sixteen he was hanging around *The Club* doing odd jobs for his Uncle Frankie. When school let out at three o'clock, Frankie would let Bull bar tend and make the guys in the crew lunch. But Bull's favorite job when he was just starting out for Frankie was taking calls on Sundays. This was an extremely important job. Only one other guy in Frankie's crew took the bets on Sundays and that was Vincent Lusi, and he had been with Frankie for over thirty years. But as Frankie's business grew from ten to fifteen customers to twenty or thirty on a steady basis, the calls kept pouring in more and more on Sundays.

Frankie usually got the lines around noon and guys started calling him at ten after. It was a hectic forty five-minutes answering four phone lines and keeping track of all that action. Mistakes would be made and Frankie hated nothing more than mistakes. But what was he going to do? He couldn't start recording the conversations. That's just a ticket straight to prison and no collecting two hundred dollars when passing GO. But he also couldn't blame Vincent; it was just too much for a fifty-five year old man to handle in that short a time.

So Frankie decided to start Bull on the phones so he could acquaint himself with the customers who associated themselves with Frankie. Frankie believed that one day Bull would be his muscle when he needed it and having Bull answer the phones would be a good start to learning the betting habits of his customers.

In the beginning, Bull answered only one of the four phone lines, the line designated for the small players, the ones who usually only bet quarters and halves on any given game. These small players were either the local neighborhood guys that wanted to throw something small on the Sunday games to make them worth watching or the ones who gambled just so they could say to their friends that they knew Frankie or someone else in the crew. And for this second group of betters, it wasn't about winning or losing to them, it was just reward enough to say they dealt with Frankie.

As for Frankie, these gamblers were nothing to him because they were an extremely small percentage of his business. If they went away it would be one less thing for him to worry about. However on some occasions, come Monday nights, these small players would be down five hundred or more, and when that was the case Bull had to give those calls over to Vincent. He was the one who would approve or deny any wagers that they wanted to put in to try to get even. Then, you had to worry about how these guys could pay up if they lost again, because chasing money was time consuming and expensive.

Since this job was not your typical customer service eight hundred number, Bull didn't need to be customer friendly. Who were they going to complain to if Bull mouthed off or belittled them and their little actions on the games? Bull's favorite part of the job was listening to these degenerate gamblers tell him that this was their week. They had locks that couldn't lose and if he was smart, he would throw something on the game for himself.

"So, douche bag, you are going to be a winner this weekend?" he would ask. And the response would always be something like, "You watch. This is the weekend lady luck dances with me!" Sometimes they did get lucky, but ninety percent of the time these same players would be calling Monday night hoping to hit a big reverse to get themselves out of the hole that they dug themselves into on Sunday. Over the four years of answering the phones Bull loved to root against this one degenerate gambler who absolutely couldn't have a winning weekend if his life depended on it. And this poor soul's name was Anthony Albergo.

❦   ❦   ❦

Anthony Albergo was a clean cut kid from the neighborhood. He was the complete opposite of Bull. Anthony was five foot ten inches tall and weighed only one hundred thirty-five pounds in high school. And unlike Bull, he never got involved with Frankie's crew when he was younger. Instead, Anthony went off to college at Syracuse University and was one of the first from his neighborhood to get a degree. Most of the people who knew Anthony were happy for him and glad to see that he was going to do something with his life other than the underworld business that most of his friends ended up doing. However, most things in life never turn out how you expect them and Anthony some how ended up tied to Frankie's crew, but not the way people might have suspected.

Now Frankie would never have Bull check up on a small fish like Anthony because nine out of ten times these guys paid up quickly, and Anthony was no exception to this. But over the years this little fish had grown into a trophy winning marlin. You could say that Anthony had become Frankie's own cash cow in more ways than one, and Anthony had crossed over into the big leagues with his fifty thousand dollars lost. He was now number one on Frankie's books.

Bull's phone call tonight to Anthony wasn't an order from Frankie, but rather it was just for kicks. Usually Bull made the phone calls to guys on Tuesday mornings to make sure they were aware of their situations and that they had until Friday to get Frankie's money. But Bull didn't want to wait until Tuesday morning for this phone call. Screw the protocol, he wanted this pleasure now. Bull had waited years for this call because this call was the call that meant Anthony had gone too far. So far, in fact, that help was out of reach. There would be no more bets from him to try to catch up. He can't get even and since he can't get even, then Bull owns him. And you don't want to become the property of Bull.

Bull absolutely hated Anthony. He hated Anthony because he was a college graduate. He hated the fact that Anthony was the kid from the neighborhood that everyone loved and respected. People never called him Tony for short because it just seemed right to call him Anthony—the more formal of the two names. Bull was envious that Anthony had made something out of his life when most people didn't. Anthony was the lucky one who had married his beautiful college sweetheart and started a family out in the suburbs. He had landed a great job at Merrill Lynch making more money than most adults from the neighborhood.

But what he hated the most about Anthony was the fact that Anthony had become closer to his Uncle Frankie than he was. How could someone from outside the crew be more important to Frankie than the rest of them? Bull didn't understand why Frankie let Anthony in *The Club* to play cards or talk business behind closed doors. He hated to think that he and Anthony were doing some kind of business outside the family. So there was nothing Bull wanted to do more right now than putting a stop to their relationship.

Anthony, still frozen in place, stared as the phone tormented him with its ringing. He had to answer it, because not answering it would only make matters worse. He couldn't let Bull think that he wasn't home. The red flags would go up all over the neighborhood if Bull believed that Anthony had skipped town. Six, seven, eights rings and Anthony had only managed to move three steps. Sweat was building up all over his body and his mouth was completely dry. Finally by the tenth ring, he found the courage and picked up the phone expecting only the worse.

"Douche bag!" Bull cheerfully greeted Anthony with his usual hello.

"Hello Bull." Anthony's response was barely audible.

"Skip the small talk douche bag. Once again you really know how to pick them."

"Well, what can I say Bull? You know me, always on the wrong side of a bet."

"Yeah, and now that makes you on another wrong side, mine. I know there is no possible way an asshole like you is going to raise fifty thousands dollars."

"Who says I need to raise the money Bull? Do you think I would put in the bet with Frankie if I didn't have it? Do you think I want your sorry ass on me?"

"Sorry ass!" Bull screamed. "You better watch it Anthony. Don't start shooting off your mouth to the man who holds your life in his hands. You and I are both aware that you don't have it. You lost your house, you lost your Mercedes and you lost your wife, Sandra, remember her? So, how the fuck are you going to give Frankie fifty g's?"

"Fuck you Bull," Anthony screamed back into the phone. "First off Bull, if you ever mention Sandra to me again, I will kill you. Second, I wasn't disrespecting you, so get over it. And third, you know as well as I do that you shouldn't even be calling me on the night of the game anyway. I have a week to come up with the money, and if Frankie knew you were already harassing one of his favorite business partners, he wouldn't appreciate it."

"Business partner?" Bull was now laughing into the phone. "That's a fucking laugh! Is that what you consider yourself, Anthony? Frankie's little 'financial advisor'?"

"Bull, you are so fucking clueless, it is scary!" Anthony replied back. "I have made Frankie more money legitimately over the last three years than all his organized crime has in a lifetime." And after he said that, Anthony realized it didn't matter if he came up with Frankie's fifty thousand dollars because he was going to be whacked no matter what.

As Anthony waited for Bull's response, he couldn't believe that he had gotten so delirious with rage that it just slipped out. He swore up and down many times to Frankie that he would never let their money matters get back to any of his crew. It was their secret and the one and only reason Frankie made Anthony welcome in his world. And now that trust was broken; their relationship would end.

The awkward silence seemed to last for hours as Bull tried to think of a response to this stunning information. Bull wasn't the brightest of people, but in this line of business he didn't need to be. This had to be a stone cold bluff by Anthony. There was no possible way he could have made Frankie that kind of money. Bull knew Frankie and the crew were small time, but the money had been rolling in over the last couple of years and the bosses were happy. But what if Anthony wasn't lying? Could it be possible somehow that Anthony made Frankie millions legitimately by investing in the stock market? It was possible. Anthony might not know how to pick winners in a football game, but he was a stockbroker at one of the biggest companies in America and that had to count for something. But right now, Bull wanted Anthony to believe that he thought this to be a bluff on his part until he had time to think it totally through.

"That may be true Anthony, but it still doesn't help you now. You are into Frankie for fifty thousand and once Friday comes, you are mine."

"Believe what you want, asshole," Anthony shouted and then he clicked the talk button and threw the phone across the room, where it struck the wall and broke into five or six pieces.

Anthony thought that went as well as it could. "Who am I kidding?" he replied out loud to himself. "I just keep fucking up this situation more and more. Why do I let that asshole get under my skin?" It was true, Bull how gotten to him by hitting a nerve.

❦   ❦   ❦

Everyone has that certain nerve and once that nerve is hit, the mental pain it causes is a thousand times worse than any physical pain that a person could feel. Your mind becomes useless to you because you just can stop all the memories from flooding in all at once, causing the pain to grow even further out of control. You can't think rationally from that point on and every other thought becomes futile. And what was the nerve that Bull had struck which was causing Anthony all this pain? That would be Sandra, his now ex-wife, who was remarried to a doctor and now living up state in their old house that Anthony had paid for with his own money.

Anthony had many loses over the last three years which had cost him thousands of dollars, but money was just money and Sandra was his only love—the loss he couldn't get over. Of course he had been with other women before her, but she was his first true love, the one who knew everything about him. She was the kind of true love that you spent nights in bed telling each other what the future held for the two of you. How could you lose this love? But sadly Anthony knew the answer, which had kept tormenting him over and over every day since she left him two years ago.

"I'm a loser," he screamed out to no one. "Why couldn't I just stop when she asked me to?" Because when you have a gambling problem like Anthony, you don't know just how bad it is until everything you own or love is gone.

Anthony went back to his bed and laid down, hoping that sleep would come and end his misery. Anyone who was in as much trouble as Anthony was in knows that sleep will not rescue him right away. Their mind will continually play the night's events over and over again, until they mentally break down and sleep finally arrives. But on this night, sleep came extremely late and it helped even less.

When the alarm went off at six o'clock, Anthony was barely aware that he was even asleep at the time. Where did the night end and the nightmares begin? Did it really matter? One was just as bad as the other. He did remember the phone call with Bull, but did he talk to Sandra too, or was that a dream? It had to be a dream because he knew that the two of them would never talk on the phone again.

Sandra hated him. She hated how he had let their marriage go to hell and that he had lost all their money, their home and, most of all, how he lost their family. However, Anthony didn't feel the same way she did. He still loved her, wanted her back in his life and wanted to see Kimberly. Kimberly was his angel and he missed her the most. He was her father and Sandra had taken her away from him. But, now was not the time to be thinking of those problems. Today Anthony needed to focus on just one problem, and that one problem was getting fifty thousand dollars for Frankie by Friday.

Anthony rolled over and sat up on the edge of the bed and stared at the clock, which now flashed six-thirty at him. Anthony's head was aching and he needed a cigarette more than ever to focus. He fumbled around the top of the night stand until he found his pack of Marlboros. He took one out and lit it. The taste was worse than it had ever been. Normally Anthony wasn't a smoker, but these times weren't normal and he needed as much help as possible, even if it was a little cigarette to start the morning.

His head was still swarming with the thoughts of last night's game seven disastrous ending. He truly believed he was getting out of this jam. Anthony had all the faith in the world in his beloved Yankees, but they had broken his heart and caused him this horrible mess. They didn't literally cause him this problem. Anthony's lack of control and betting with his heart was what had caused this irreconcilable problem. When he made the wager, he realized his life would be more or less over if it wasn't a winner. And now, since he knew it was impossible to raise that kind of money for Frankie, he was just living on borrowed time. However today was only Monday, and Friday was still five days away, so there was no need to be so pessimistic. He was going to take care of a couple of little problems and then he would focus on the big picture by either getting the money or deriving a plan on how the hell to get out of town alive.

Anthony crushed out his cigarette on the end table, not even bothering to look for the ash tray. He got out of bed and went and got his cell phone to make one of those Monday morning phone calls to his boss; the kind that many gamblers make when they've had an absolutely horrible Sunday and can't understand why they feel too sick physically and mentally to come into work. These phone calls were typical for Anthony over the years. He had made at least three since Labor Day, and it was only the first week in November. Anthony realized the shit he was going to hear from his boss Eric, who was the head Vice President of traders in Anthony's department at Merrill Lynch. Anthony knew he could put up with Eric's bullshit this morning, considering the other people he was going to have to confront later in the day.

Eric Thorne was only thirty-three, which was atypically young for that high of a position at Merrill Lynch. He liked Anthony because they were both the same age and from the city. They shared many interests, but gambling wasn't one of them. Eric's salary was six figures and he didn't see the need for gambling or understand how the rewards of winning outweighed the risks of losing. He made his clients great amounts of money over his seven years at the company and when you make your clients money, you move up the company ladder. Anthony and Eric both entered Merrill around the same time, but the reason Eric was his boss was because Eric's ambition was to get to the top as quickly as possible, while Anthony's was gambling on sports and not the stock market.

Anthony was aware that six-thirty was a little too early for Eric to be in the office, so he would just leave the usual message claiming he had a migraine and would be in the following day, even though he knew that Eric wasn't going to accept his bullshit anymore. He had already confronted Anthony twice about his Monday morning call outs and told Anthony that if it happened again he would have to take serious actions. But the worst that Eric could do would be to fire him, and firing a dead man didn't seem all that bad to Anthony.

On the fourth ring Eric picked up the phone instead of the voice mail that Anthony was expecting. "Hello, this is Eric Thorne. How can I help you?"

This totally threw Anthony off guard because he was only prepared for the voice mail.

"Hey Eric, this is Anthony," he responded in a voice coming from someone who didn't sound like he had a migraine.

"Let me guess Anthony, you are calling me to let me know that you are not coming to work today because you have another migraine," he said in a sarcastic way.

"Actually to tell you the truth Eric, I am completely shit faced and hung over because I drank way too much last night after the game and I just don't feel like getting out of bed."

"Anthony we both know that if you don't come into work today, you might as well not come into work again," Eric said. It was his ultimatum.

Eric hated to say that to him. They weren't close friends, but they were friends enough that Eric didn't want to threaten him with losing his job. Now there were others in the office that he would have loved to have been able to say this to, but Anthony was definitely not one of them. There had been numerous afternoon lunches which they didn't return from because they had made far more than their quotas for the day by then, so why bother going back to the office. A couple of times after work Anthony even invited Eric to join him at Charlie's Dream House to stick some fives down a couple of stripper's g strings, but those days were now long behind them. Anthony's gambling had gotten worse.

"Eric, I know you won't fire me, but you might as well do it to cover your own ass. I wouldn't have come back after Friday anyway," Anthony started to explain to him. "I am looking to start over somewhere else, so you can accept this as my two week notice."

Eric was in total shock at this response. He was expecting Anthony to tell him he would be in after all or maybe that this would be the last time he would call out on Mondays. But this just floored him.

"What do you mean you are leaving? Why the hell would you want to leave Merrill?" Eric asked in an alarmed voice.

"Let's just say I need a change," Anthony answered.

"The job market is horrible right now. Where do you expect to find a job as good as this one?" Eric asked.

"Come Friday a new job is going to be the least of my problems," Anthony explained.

"Talk to me Anthony. Christ, I'm not an idiot. I know that you are having problems. This is the third Monday this fall that you called out and when you come back in the office you are short tempered and miserable the rest of the week."

"It's not easy to explain, Eric. I have gotten myself in some serious trouble with the wrong people. You could say I am in way over my head and I don't know how I am going to get out, so coming into work this week isn't going to help me."

"Let me guess, you are still gambling?" Eric asked.

Anthony really didn't want to get into details about his problem with Eric. Eric wasn't a close friend, not that Anthony had many of those anymore. Actually, he had none. There were only 'associates' that he hung around with at *The Club*. His closest friend and best man at his wedding, Jimmy Conte, had ended their friendship two years before when Anthony couldn't pay back the thousand dollars that he had borrowed to cover God knows what bet that time. But what did Anthony care? He had felt that if Jimmy wanted to end their twelve year friendship over a measly thousand dollars, then fuck him, because obviously he wasn't that close of a friend. But Anthony knew it wasn't the thousand dollars that ended their friendship, it was what he had become due to his gambling problems and Jimmy, along with most of his other friends and his family, was in his past.

Anthony tried to explain his problem as quickly as possible to Eric. "You could say the Yankees cost me more than just a broken heart. If I somehow don't come up with fifty thousand dollars by Friday I will have a lot more than just a broken heart."

Eric flooded Anthony with questions. "Jesus Anthony, you lost fifty thousand dollars? Why the hell did you bet so much on the World Series? Where did you expect to get that kind of money if you lost? When are you going to grow up and take responsibility for your life?"

After this last question from Eric, Anthony answered with one simple response, "Goodbye Eric, it was a pleasure working for you." He hung up the phone and that was the last time Eric ever talked to Anthony.

After a long cold shower to try to clear up his head, Anthony went into the living room and sat down on the couch and tried to get together a plan for the remainder of the day. One thing Anthony needed to do was to go see his parents at their store down in the Italian Market area of the neighborhood, but he was going to put this off until later because he wasn't ready to face them yet. He believed that this would most likely be the last time he would see them and he didn't want to just go down there unprepared. He also knew at some point in the day he had to go see Frankie, and it wouldn't matter how prepared he was when he faced him because Frankie would do all the talking.

Frankie Feliciani was not the typical Hollywood mobster. When you met Frankie for the first time, you would never have believed that he was a mobster boss. He didn't look like an extra on the set of *GoodFellas* or *The Sopranos* and the big reason why he didn't look like a mobster was because he really didn't consider himself one anymore. He looked like most men who were in their mid fifties. Frankie was still in good shape for his age and size and, when he had to, he could intimidate anyone.

Frankie wasn't the biggest of men while he was growing up, but that didn't stop him from making a reputation for himself. Word got out early how he could handle himself on the streets, especially against guys who were older and thought to have been tougher than he was. The old bosses fell in love with him early on as he made his way through the ranks until he eventually became a boss for himself. And with his title and power, he didn't have to worry about proving his toughness anymore.

Even though he was still the head of a crew which was involved with some illegal activities, he was mainly a business owner and that was what he loved the most. He owned a restaurant called *The Club*, which brought in seventy percent of his total legitimate income.

The Club was an extremely successful restaurant because so many people from the neighborhood went there almost every night for dinner and drinks. Frankie didn't want to name it one of the usual Italian names like Palumbo's or Capuano's because he didn't want to draw attention from any tourists who would be looking for a fancy Italian restaurant while visiting the city. It was called *The Club* because that was exactly what it was to Frankie: it was a club and all his customers were members. *The Club* wasn't a huge establishment, but more of a Mom & Pop restaurant and like most Mom & Pop restaurants the food was what drew the customers.

Frankie's wife Ellena Maria and his two daughters Anita and Angela made all the pasta daily from scratch. His mother Elizabeth, who was now eighty-one years old, made the sauce first thing every morning starting around six o'clock, because Frankie only loved his mother's sauce and wouldn't let anyone else make it. The seafood and vegetables were brought in daily at a five finger discount from Charlie Deluca, who was a foreman down at the docks and a member of Frankie's crew. The three waitresses and one bus boy were children of close friends so, all in all, *The Club's* expenses weren't that high.

Frankie didn't believe in charging his customers high prices for their meals. A typical dinner for two with appetizers, wine and a tip usually only cost forty dollars, and for the city that was extremely cheap. Since most of his customers were from the neighborhood and came in two to three times a week, he let them run a tab which they settled up once a week.

Frankie knew ninety-nine percent of his customers on a first name basis because he wanted to promote a family atmosphere for *The Club*. Frankie didn't let members of his crew enter into the back room to hang out until after ten o'clock when all the customers were out of the restaurant. Vincent was the only one allowed back there before ten because he had to answer the phone lines. Since *The Club* didn't have a bar, most of the customers were usually gone by ten anyway. He realized that many of his customers were aware that he was linked to the mob but he tried hard to keep that life outside of the restaurant.

The back room of *The Club* was almost as big as the dinning area. You had to go through the back of the kitchen through double doors that were usually locked until Frankie opened them after ten o'clock. It was a perfect square room that had all the necessities that any typical mob crew would need. When you first walked into the room to your right, there was a ten foot bar that was stocked with all the favorites. If you drank it, Frankie stocked it in his bar. Above the bar was a thirty-two inch television that was hooked up to a satellite, so if there was a game on that night, they could watch it. On the left side of the room was a juke box that didn't have any forty-fives in it recorded after 1975.

Even though it was 2001, most of his crew loved the oldies and why not, considering Bull was the youngest at twenty-nine and most of them were in their mid to late fifties. It was only stocked with their favorites like Dean Martin, Bobby Darin and, of course, the chairman of the board, Frank Sinatra. At the far right of the room was a small closet of a bathroom. In the left hand corner of the room was a table set up with Vincent's four phones and a nice leather chair with wheels so he could move from one phone to another without skipping a beat. Right past the end of the table along the wall was a door that led to Frankie's office. It was just big enough for a small desk and chair for Frankie to run the business end of the restaurant. In the middle of the room were two card tables. One of the tables was for the nightly poker games played amongst the crew while the other usually had a knock rummy game going on with the old timers who just came to *The Club* to play cards and have a drink. The old timers were given the run of the room because if it wasn't for them, Frankie would never have opened *The Club* in the first place.

It was a near perfect room for any man to spend hours and hours in except for one flaw, there was only one window. So if you didn't smoke and hated the smell of cigarettes then this was not the place for you, because by the end of the night if you were sitting at the bar you couldn't see Vincent on the other side of the room through all the smoke.

The Club and its back room was Frankie's little heaven. On most days he was there first thing in the morning at six o'clock when he drove his mother in to start on the sauce, and he was there until everyone was done playing cards, which was usually around two in the morning. So needless to say he was a very busy man who never slept.

Family time was the time spent in the kitchen with Ellena Maria, Elizabeth and the girls while they prepared the food. He made sure that around four o'clock every day they ate dinner together before they opened *The Club* to the public. Frankie knew he wasn't the perfect of fathers or husbands, but he tried his best to give them as much of his time as he could.

Anita was the most important thing in his life because she was his favorite. She wasn't like most kids that have a mobster as a father and knew about it.

Anita was a very plain looking girl. She was only five foot one and her body was nothing to write home about. She didn't dress herself up with brand names clothes and never wore any makeup. She kept her brown hair shoulder length and never changed its style. Anita was never materialistic and didn't even ask Frankie for a car when she got her license.

"Why would I need a car in the city, Daddy?" was what she replied to him when he asked her if she wanted one for her seventeenth birthday. Frankie knew a man like him, who has done so much ill will towards men, should never be blessed with a gift from God like her. Frankie wanted more for her than anything else in life and earlier in the year, when she told him that she had gotten accepted to Cornell and was starting in the fall, he had been thrilled. Not only was Anita going to be the first to attend college in their family, she was going to do it in style. She was going Ivy League and nothing could have made him prouder.

Since *The Club* was doing so well and Anita was off at Cornell, Frankie wanted to cut down on many of his other forms of revenue. He never became a major figure in the under world, and that's just the way he liked it. Over the years he was getting less and less important because he was smart enough not to get involved in too many things at one time. Everyone always thought that being loyal and not ratting your friends out was the way to survive and make it in the mob; but if you asked Frankie, he would tell you that being a small head of a family that didn't get too involved or got too big for themselves was the way to survive.

Frankie never got too greedy. He only wanted to be important enough to have the respect of his crew and the neighborhood. There never was a time when he wanted to climb the organized crime family chart and branch out because this would mean he would have more men under him and once that happens, it brings too much heat not only from the outside world but jealousy from the inside. Frankie had seen enough of his share of hits to realize that the more important you became, the higher the risk you were taking of becoming a target for a hit yourself.

What made Frankie different from most mob members was that he had made more money legitimately than he had ever done through organized crime. Frankie was worth over ten million dollars and most people in the mob didn't know this little fact and he wanted it to stay that way.

The last thing Frankie needed was the wrong people to know he was worth that kind of money because there would be no way of explaining that he made it through the stock market and his restaurant. The higher ups would never believe him and they would suspect one of three things. The first would be that they felt Frankie was expanding his business outside his own neighborhood, which really wouldn't be that bad as long as he wasn't stepping on anyone's toes. But this still meant that he was not reporting to them the extra income and they weren't getting their kick backs. If this was the case, the worst thing to come out of that would be that Frankie would lose some of his millions in a generous gift to make the bosses happy. The second possibility was that Frankie was not being honest with his books, which meant he was tampering with the figures. This was the same as stealing from the bosses and if they felt that Frankie was changing figures and keeping more money for himself, this most certainly would result in Frankie getting whacked. The third would be that they believed Frankie was really being honest and made the money in the stock market and if he did, why didn't he share the information with them? Every boss was looking for a legitimate way to earn money so they could have something to report on their taxes to keep the government boys happy. This would be considered an act of disloyalty to the bosses, which would also end with Frankie being whacked.

No matter which way you looked at it, Frankie didn't need any of the bosses to find out just how well off he was. He didn't think it really would be that hard to keep a low profile because over the last three years he had become such a small figure in their organization that they really didn't pay too much attention to him. When it came to his monthly payments to the bosses, Frankie gave a little more of an increase each month and the reasons he did this were—one, he could afford to and two, it would never bring the bosses down on him. They never bothered with a guy whose books were always raking in more money every month while others go up and down and explanations are in order. Frankie's plan over the next four years while Anita was away at school was to gradually phase out of the 'family' business and once she had graduated he would sell *The Club* and retire somewhere warm with Ellena Maria and his mother and leave this other life behind them.

As Anthony stood in front of *The Club* his heart raced out of control. He realized there wasn't any bullshit that he could sell to Frankie. Frankie had played poker with Anthony enough to know when Anthony was bluffing or when he had the "nuts", and right now anything he would say would be a poor attempt at a bluff. It was only eight-thirty in the morning, so Anthony knew that Frankie would be alone in the restaurant with just his mother and wife. It would be much safer seeing Frankie now than after *The Club* was closed and Frankie's crew was in the back room hanging out. At least now the two of them could talk with out being interrupted, actually without the crew laughing at Anthony trying to squirm his way out of a beating by Bull. Yes, this would be best for Anthony, just him and Frankie without the fear of being whacked from behind by a faceless killer.

"Hi Anthony, what brings you down here so early on a Monday morning?" Ellena Maria asked as he walked into *The Club*.

"Good morning Mrs. Feliciani. I am here to see Frankie," Anthony responded after kissing her on both cheeks.

"How many times must I tell you not to be so formal Anthony? I have known you since you were a teenager, please just stick with Ellena Maria," she lectured him.

"Now you know if my mother ever heard me call you by your first name, I would never be allowed to step foot in her home," he said jokingly.

"You took off of work just to see Frankie? I hope nothing is wrong?" she asked concerned.

"Not in the least bit. I have the day off and I was stopping by to answer a couple of questions Frankie had concerning his retirement in a couple of years. You know how he plans ahead years in advance," Anthony said with a laugh.

"Please, you know my husband will die stirring sauce in that kitchen before he ever decides to walk away from this restaurant," she laughed along with Anthony.

"Yes, you are right. You know Frankie better than he does," Anthony responded laughing out of control and not knowing where he was finding the humor in all of this. The last thing in the world he thought he would be doing today is laughing at some little small talk humor.

"What is all that laughing out there?" Frankie shouted from the kitchen.

"Oh boy, now we set him off again," Ellena Maria said with no hint of humor in her voice anymore.

"Is Frankie not in a good mood?" Anthony asked.

"Well he is upset like everyone else in the city this morning about the Yankees losing last night," she responded. Yeah, I bet he is upset, Anthony thought to himself. The only people in the city this morning who weren't upset were Frankie and every other bookie in town. Not many people bet against the beloved home team so when Arizona won, Frankie just got one step closer to retirement.

"Yeah, I didn't sleep much last night after the game, and I am sure I'm not the only one who called out this morning because they didn't get over the loss well," Anthony said with still a tint of humor in his voice.

"I thought that was your voice I heard, Anthony," Frankie said while standing in the dining area.

"Good morning Frankie. I was just telling Mrs. Feliciani that I was here upon your request to go over those questions you had about your retirement," Anthony replied as he walked to Frankie.

"And I tried to tell Anthony that you will die in that kitchen before you ever retire," Ellena Maria chimed in still standing in the front of the restaurant's door.

"This might be true, but I still have to plan these things out dear, just in case," Frankie replied to her.

"Why don't we go into the back room for some privacy and go over some questions I have, Anthony," Frankie said as he headed back into the kitchen.

"Ok Frankie, if you want privacy from Mrs. Feliciani so she doesn't find out about the boat you are planning on buying," Anthony said to keep the conversation going in a joking manner.

"Boat? He gets a boat after I get my summer home in Boca Raton," Ellena Maria cried.

"You're a funny man Anthony, still quick with the jokes, and I stress joke Hon," Frankie answered as he turned and faced Ellena Maria.

"Enough with the small talk we have to go over my questions before I start the evening specials," Frankie stated to Anthony as the two of them headed into the kitchen and towards the back room.

"Are you hungry Anthony? I can make up some eggs before we head into the back," Frankie stopped and asked as they stood in front of the grill.

Anthony thought that sounded like the best idea so far today. All he had today were three cigarettes, and his stomach was screaming for some food. But, this same stomach would give it right back up five minutes after he ate. Over the last week he and his stomach had not been on the best of terms because of all the stress Anthony has put on it with his gambling. Or should we say all his losses.

"Eggs sound great Frankie. I haven't eaten all morning and two eggs would hit the spot right about now," Anthony replied gratefully.

"Good. Two eggs over easy it is for my skinny friend who looks like a little nigger on one of those commercials for starving kids from Africa with Sally Struthers," Frankie responded with a joke of his own.

"Well, I'm glad to see you are in a happy mood Frankie," Anthony said with a tone of relief in his voice.

"And why wouldn't I be happy today Anthony? I should be the happiest of people after last night. I estimate the Yankees made me close to two hundred thousand richer with the local bettors and another three hundred thousand dollars with Caesars in Vegas," Frankie said in a hearty laughing tone.

"Wow that much?" Anthony questioned.

"Well you take away the games the Yankees won plus game six with Johnson pitching and the whole world betting them to win, I should clear roughly five hundred thousand. You weren't the only one last night taking the Yankees to win. Unfortunately many people hedged their series bets and took Arizona last night, which I tried to get you to do, so that took away from the over all profits," Frankie explained to Anthony.

"Well Frankie, if I ever stop betting with my heart and start using my head maybe one day I will take your advice for future wagers," Anthony answered back.

Frankie flipped both of Anthony's and his own eggs onto two plates and poured them both a cup of coffee. He then turned and handed Anthony his plate and said, "Let's head into the back room and discuss those future wagers of yours." As Anthony took his plate and coffee from Frankie and followed him into the back room, he couldn't help but think that eating these eggs wasn't a good idea because he didn't believe they would stay down for more than five minutes.

"Please close the door behind you and pull up a seat at the bar," Frankie commanded Anthony. "I want this to go as friendly as can be Anthony, because I have known you for too long of a time to hope for this to go any other way," Frankie began.

The last and only time that Anthony ever sat in the back room with Frankie alone was in the summer of '98. Anthony was already starting to get over his head with the gambling problems, but he never had to meet Frankie about them because he always paid off his losses to Bull on time.

On one Friday night Bull got detained with another one of Frankie's customers and he had asked Anthony to drop off the money to someone in the back room of *The Club*. Anthony had never been in the back room of *The Club* only the restaurant part because he wasn't a 'friend' of theirs but he had always wanted to see what the place was like.

He told Bull that he didn't mind dropping off the money and it wouldn't be a problem for him to go down there.

"Bull, who do I ask for when I walk into the restaurant?" he had asked.

"Don't go down there 'til around ten-thirty. When you walk in, go through the kitchen and knock on the back door. Whomever answers just tell them who you are and that you are dropping off money for me," he answered Anthony.

"Alright I'll head down there but please make sure someone knows I am going to be dropping off the money. I don't want someone beating the shit out of me thinking I'm an undercover cop," he said with a laugh.

"I don't think anyone would ever mistake you for a pig, Anthony. A book worm geek maybe, but never a cop," Bull laughed along with him.

Anthony was extremely excited that he was finally going to get a chance to meet the guys in Frankie's crew. Hell, he was finally going to meet Frankie the boss after all these years. As he was driving down to the restaurant, he figured the best thing that was going to happen was that he would knock on the door, someone would answer and ask him, "What the fuck do you want," and then they would take his money and close the door right in his face. But what had actually happened on that fateful night in July changed his and all their lives forever.

Anthony walked right in through the front door of *The Club* even though the sign said closed. The doors were never locked because no one would be stupid enough to try and come in there and rob the place. Everyone in the neighborhood was aware of who owned the place and who he had ties to. Anthony walked by the waitress and bus boy, who were counting their tips for the night in the last booth before the kitchen. Only the bus boy looked up to see Anthony walk by them. Anthony gave him a polite wave and pointed to the kitchen signaling if it was okay to go through. Why he thought he needed to ask the bus boy if it was okay to go back he didn't know, but Anthony was so nervous he didn't even wait for a response.

Now standing nervously in front of the door Anthony took a deep breath and said to himself, "Come on and get it together, you aren't even going to get in the door so calm down". On the second knock Carmine Vitola answered the door and he had a thirty-eight pointed right at Anthony's face.

"Who the fuck are you? You got five seconds to tell me what you are doing here or my fat ugly face will be the last thing you will ever see."

Carmine weighed easily three hundred and twenty pounds. He was a very intimidating figure when he was mad as his face turned a bright red, and that was exactly what Anthony was seeing five inches from his own face. At least ten seconds had passed when Carmine finally started laughing out of control.

"I think he pissed himself. Someone check this guy's pants out. I got fifty saying he definitely pissed himself." Now there was a huge roar from behind Carmine when he moved away from the door and the others got a view of Anthony. Anthony never even had a chance to answer Carmine's first question. He began to realize that Bull had set him up from the beginning.

"You must be Anthony. We were expecting you, but I guess you weren't expecting that kind of greeting when you were knocking on the door?" Carmine had asked after he and the rest of them calmed down from all the laughing.

From over at the poker table Charlie Deluca yelled, "He could definitely be a friend of ours. He didn't crack the fuck up under pressure nor did he piss himself." And with that statement another round of laughter was stirred up in the room. It took Anthony a good minute to realize that it was going to be okay and that these guys weren't going to take him out back and whack him.

Anthony finally got his sense about him as he turned to Carmine and said, "I am here to drop off a package for Bull."

"Yeah, Bull called to let us know you were stopping by, if not, I would have popped two bullets in your face," Carmine replied, with another round of laughter throughout the room.

"You want to go over to that guy by the phones and just give it to him. I promise he won't pull out a gun and stick it in your face." And with that the room was so loud from the laughter that Frankie came bursting in from his office with a bib around his neck.

"What the hell is so damn funny in here that you had to disturb my meal?" Frankie demanded.

"I'm sorry Frankie. I was just having some fun with this delivery guy," Carmine replied.

"I don't recognize you, who the hell are you and why were you let in this room?" Frankie asked Anthony directly, not even bothering to respond to Carmine's answer.

"I'm Anthony Albergo, and I am here to drop off a package for Bull," Anthony answered him in a quiet voice.

"You're Mickey and Erma's kid?" Frankie asked as he approached Anthony, who was still standing in the doorway.

"Yes, they are my parents," Anthony replied back to Frankie as he put his hand out to shake Frankie's hand.

"Well don't just stand there in the door way expecting me to shake your hand. Come over here and show me a little respect in my establishment," Frankie demanded.

"My apologies, Mr. Feliciani but I was in no way showing you disrespect. I didn't want to walk in without being invited."

Craig Rossi from the bar asked, "Can you believe this fucking guy? This kid is too fucking polite for this room. Stop dicking around and just walk over to Frankie and kiss his hand, and apologize for disturbing his meal."

It didn't take Anthony more than a second for that to register in his brain and he went over to where Frankie stood, took his hand and kissed it. "I am so sorry for all of this Mr. Feliciani. I was just stunned that I was allowed in the room," Anthony tried to explain.

"Not a problem Anthony, but if you are going to stay in my room there are a couple of rules. First rule is everyone calls me Frankie. You might not be a member of our little crew but you may still call me Frankie. Mr. Feliciani makes me feel old. Second rule is no one disturbs me when I am in my office. Everyone here obviously doesn't remember that rule or they are just too ignorant to keep it. And the third and final rule is no one cheats during the card games. As long as you respect these rules, you can stick around tonight if you like."

Anthony was in total shock. Did Frankie just invite him to stay in the back room and hang out? No, he had to hear him wrong. Why would Frankie Feliciani invite someone like him to hang out with members of his crew? Anthony didn't even have time to ask if this was an invitation or not because, just that quickly, Frankie was back in his office finishing his plate of raviolis.

"Kid do you have my package or not?" Vincent Lusi had asked from the back of the room.

"Yes sir, I am sorry for keeping you waiting," Anthony replied in an apologetic tone.

Anthony couldn't help being scared out of his mind because one look at Vincent and anyone else would feel the same way. Vincent was an extremely big man and his face had two scars from a knife wound he had received when he was younger. The rest of his face had scars from the severe acne he had during his teenage years. He looked like a guy that you didn't want to fuck with if you could help it.

"I'm expecting six Franklins from you, right?" Vincent questioned him.

"I have six hundred but they're in all denominations. I hope you didn't need six one hundred dollar bills?" Anthony asked.

"Are you being funny kid? Six hundred is six hundred. I don't give a rat's ass what the denominations are that you give me as long as they total your figure in my book," Vincent yelled at him.

"I'm sorry, I didn't know. I was making sure I didn't make it harder on you by giving you tens and twenties," Anthony explained.

"Just don't be a smart-ass kid, because if you are you'll find yourself out in the alley on your ass," Vincent told him.

"Once again, I'm sorry. It's just this is all new to me," Anthony mumbled.

"Jesus Christ kid, enough with the fucking apologizes tonight. Just go over to the bar and ask Joey to give you a seven and seven for me," he requested.

Anthony went to the bar and ordered a seven and seven from Joey. "So, how you feeling now kid?" Joey asked him.

"Man, I don't know how I didn't piss myself yet," Anthony started to explain. "Next time Bull asks me to come down here I might have to think twice about it," Anthony said with a small smile.

"These guys aren't that bad, they just enjoy a good hazing once in a while," Joey told him.

"Well if there ever is a next time I hope that I won't be the one hazed, my heart still hasn't calmed down yet," Anthony said as he patted his chest.

Joey turned around with Vincent's drink and said to Anthony, "Well here's Vincent drink, so go give it to him. If you like poker, pull up a chair and play a couple of hands if you have the funds and the time."

Anthony went back to Vincent with his drink and just put it down next to him, because ever since he went to the bar Vincent had been on the phone with Ritchie matching up the figures that had been brought in so far tonight. Anthony had no desire to stick around. He knew he didn't belong here with these guys. He was out of his element and he just wasn't comfortable here. Anthony felt like he was the sheep and these were the wolves, so he wanted out quickly.

As Anthony approached the door to leave, Charlie Deluca, who was still at the poker table, yelled up at him, "You're not going to take Frankie up on his invitation and stay awhile?"

"I didn't think he was serious about me staying in here with you guys. I know you guys don't want me here disturbing your fun on a Friday night," Anthony responded.

"Don't be such an idiot kid. He meant it, so either pull up a chair and get your ass handed to you in some cards or have a couple at the bar. It's a help-yourself bar, so don't expect anyone here to serve you."

The one thing Anthony wasn't good at was handicapping. He was lousy at trying to pick winners, ever since he was in college. Come Tuesday morning, he was usually in the red on Frankie's book. Now this would be an extremely expensive hobby for most people, but when you could offset it with your card skills, then it was okay.

Anthony was an incredible poker player. He started playing at the age of six with his grandparents. At first it was something fun for them to do together when they were babysitting him, but over the years they started to play for money. And as the years went by, Anthony took quite a bit from them and their friends, who always came around to see if they could beat the kid.

This source of income wasn't just from family members. Ever since the third grade he had started games in the cafeteria at lunchtime or out in the playground at recess. Anthony was even smart enough to know at that age not to have money out in the open. He kept everything written in his notebooks. Before he graduated St. Martin's grade school he had made over two thousand dollars; however, he was also suspended three times. That number could have been a lot higher but he learned at a very early age that teachers are like everyone else and they could be paid off to keep quiet.

When he was in college at Syracuse he basically owned the dorms. If there was a game, he was playing in it and, more than likely, at the end of the night he was one of the winners. There wasn't just one factor that made Anthony such a great poker player. First, he could read people like they were a book, so he rarely bluffed. When he had the weaker hand, he knew it. When it was time to fold, he had no problem with laying down a hand or two to set up the other players for a hand later down the line.

Second, Anthony was also incredible with numbers. He was one of the only people he knew who loved Statistics in college. Taking Statistics was worth more to him than the degree hanging on his wall. It was these statistic courses that made him the complete player.

Anthony was always in a game Monday through Thursday. His grades took a beating, but he wasn't at Syracuse to be an honor roll student. If he was in a game on Monday night, this meant he was trying to make up for his weekend losses to Frankie. Monday nights were the nights Anthony was at his best. He was always looking to make up losses from the weekend, and this made him a dangerous player.

The other kids really weren't a match for him. They either got too drunk before the end of the night, or they were just lousy players to begin with and shouldn't have been at the same table with Anthony. Either way, Anthony usually walked out with their money. Most of them didn't seem to care too much about losing. They would just call home to mom and dad and ask for more money.

Out of the four years at Syracuse, Anthony had only called home twice for money and both times his parents had offered him more money than he needed. They couldn't comprehend how a college student without a job could live away from home for four years and not need money. But like most parents, as long as he wasn't flunking out of school they didn't ask questions.

Right before he graduated, Anthony calculated that he had won over ten thousand dollars in all the games he had played in those four years. Unfortunately for Anthony, he had also lost close to nine thousand dollars in wagers with Frankie. He considered college a success because he had made a profit while getting his degree without ever having to get a part time job.

Now the last thing that Anthony wanted to do tonight was to get himself involved in a poker game with a bunch of wise guys that he had never played with before. He had gone to Atlantic City many times and played with the best down there and had won more than he had lost, but this would be different. These are Frankie's guys playing in their home game with their own rules. The odds weren't in his favor so it would be best not to play and lose more money to Frankie this week, but when you know that you are the best player in the room it is hard to walk away from the action.

Anthony felt this would be the only time that he would get the chance to play cards in this room so he might as well play for an hour or two.

"What's the game tonight fellas?" Anthony asked as he approached the table.

Charlie Deluca, who was only about sixty pounds lighter than Carmine, said, "Tonight's game is 'no limit' Texas Hold'em, ten and twenty betting with a three raise maximum. What you put out on the table is what you play with and once it is gone you can always take out more later."

Texas Hold'em was Anthony's specialty. No other poker game favors the better player more than Hold'em. He took one look around the table and believed it would be easy to come out ahead.

"Do you guys mind an outsider joining you for a couple of hands? I'm really not that familiar with Texas Hold'em and I only have two hundred on me so I doubt that I'll last very long," he claimed as he pulled out one of the two open chairs at the table. Charlie turned to the other five players and asked if anyone objected to Anthony joining them.

Carmine responded, "Easy money is easy money, so pull up a seat kid."

Anthony noticed that so far tonight he has been called kid at least six or seven times. If this kept up, he knew that they were going to take him lightly and he was going to take them to the cleaners. It wasn't going to be if he wins, but what was the limit to his winnings that would be alright with these guys without one of them whacking him afterwards. He couldn't get that thought out of his head the entire night, but it didn't matter because even before he had gotten a chance to deal a hand, he had already won three out of the first four hands and three hundred dollars.

By two o'clock in the morning Anthony had broken Joey, Paulie and Carmine, who Anthony especially enjoyed since Carmine was the first person to ever point a gun at him.

There were only three players left including himself. He had about twelve hundred in front of him while Charlie had about four hundred and Vincent, who had finally joined the game only an hour ago when he got done totaling the figures with Ritchie, had about two hundred and fifty dollars.

"I don't know about anyone else in this room but kid you have had the greatest beginner's luck I have ever seen for someone that never played Texas Hold'em before," Charlie claimed.

"Yeah, I have got to agree with you Charlie. I have seen this kid's numbers in the books for the last six or seven years and he is in the red far more than he is in the black, so it must be beginners luck," Vincent told everyone.

"I hope no one thinks I am sharking you guys, because anyone who knows me knows I rarely ever win when it comes to gambling," Anthony explained to them.

"A card shark in my room? Kid if you are a shark, then I must be the blindest boss in our whole family," Frankie stated from outside his office.

"I have been watching you guys and kid you have done almost everything half-assed backwards. You fold when you should raise, you raise when you should be checking and as for bluffing, you have at least four or five tells that I have picked up," Frankie explained to him.

"I tried to explain to you guys that I'm really not too good at playing cards and I was just happy with you fellas letting me sit down and take in the experience," Anthony responded.

"Well kid I hate to burst your bubble since you have been winning, but now it's about time I teach you a lesson in humility. I think it would be only fair to take back some of my men's money that you have acquired over the last couple of hours," Frankie announced as he pulled out the chair directly across from Anthony.

"I guess there's no chance of me declining this ass-kicking and just getting up and going home?" he asked as Frankie broke out a new deck of cards and flopped a wad of hundreds on the table.

"That would be impolite kid, and if that was the case you could consider yourself banned from this room."

"Well I know I'll never be a member of this crew, but it would be great to be allowed to come back so I guess I will just sit back and let the ass-kicking begin," Anthony said as Frankie dealt the cards to the four of them.

Anthony took it easy for the first hour. He laid down at least two winning hands. On numerous times he didn't raise, which caused the other three to stay in the hand and catch on the river. The set up was going well. Frankie had taken most of the winnings since he sat down. Charlie was down to less than two hundred dollars and Vincent was basically in it for the conversation. Anthony had about nine hundred left, which on any other night was a good night for him, but he wanted it to be a memorable night. He wanted to come into Frankie's establishment and give him a lesson that he would never forget.

Over the years Frankie had taken more money from him in bets than Anthony could ever expect to win in one night of cards. However, poker is a one on one competition, and beating Frankie heads up would erase all those years of lost wagers. In this lifestyle, pride was worth more than money and if Anthony could walk away with a nice chunk of change from Frankie tonight, he would make a name for himself. This would be the first step in the lifestyle that he had been dreaming of ever since he started playing cards.

After two hours of playing, Anthony believed that Frankie was ready for the taking. He was dealt pocket Kings and he decided that this was the hand to break Frankie. Vincent was the first to act and he checked. Charlie who was dealt a Queen-Jack off suit decided to bet fifty. The bet was now to Anthony. He didn't want to raise because he wanted to play it slow and hope that Frankie would be the aggressor, so he just called. Frankie acted just like a man, who was in charge and, to no surprise to Anthony, raised it to a hundred with his Ace-Queen suited. The bet went back to Vincent, who politely told the group to, "Fuck off! I'm tired of these fucking hands. I can't pair up to save my life tonight," as he threw his cards in disgust.

"It wasn't the cards, but the poor player holding them," Charlie turned and told him as he called Frankie's raise. Anthony did like wise. He believed that right now he was holding the strongest hand and he would let Frankie take charge.

The flop came up a rainbow Ace, King, Three. This was huge for Anthony because a rainbow meant no flush draw before the turn card. He had trip Kings plus, if Frankie was holding an Ace, which he believed he was to make that raise, it paired up Frankie to make him want to continue to bet. Anthony was the first to act and bet fifty.

"Kid, it has been a long night, I'm missing the Mrs. and I think it's time we try to end this little get together. I think I will raise it to two hundred," Frankie replied.

"That's good enough for me because I'm tired too, so I'll call your two hundred," Charlie replied.

Anthony hesitated just enough, with a glance back and forth at the both of them, before he said, "I know you two are baiting me, but what the hell I'll see one more card."

The next card that Frankie turned over was the Queen of Diamonds, which was a huge help to Frankie because it gave him two pairs and he believed that was enough to walk away with the pot. Frankie was the first to act.

"Okay I think this went on long enough. I am making the bet an even thousand," he told them.

"You're a real fucking nice guy," Charlie turned to Frankie and told him that as he folded his cards.

"All I have is seven hundred so what do I do if I want to call you?" Anthony asked.

"Well kid you could take a marker out with me and just pay me back the three hundred next week, interest free of course," he replied, which got a couple of laughs from the remaining guys in the room.

"How much of a marker can I take out? What if I want to raise you? Will you give me a bigger mark?"

Frankie believed this was a pure bluff. If Anthony had the better hand he would have bet from the beginning. Frankie felt that the kid was trying to buy the pot.

"How much were you thinking Anthony?"

"Why don't we wait for the last card? You might catch on the river and drown me good. So for now, how about I just call the three hundred," Anthony replied.

"Whatever floats your boat kid? I just hope you don't get in over your head," Frankie said with the confidence that he was going to teach this punk a lesson.

Frankie dealt the river, which was the Seven of Clubs and Frankie believed to be no help for Anthony. The bet was to Anthony and he played it as perfectly as can be.

"I check," he told Frankie. Frankie now believed he couldn't lose. He felt Anthony was holding on for dear life. He was in over his head and Frankie was going to make an example out of him.

"Well kid we really don't check on the river here, so I tell you what I am going to do. If you want to stay in the hand the bet is three thousand dollars," Frankie told Anthony.

"Three thousand dollars? I don't know if I can pay back that kind of money in a week Frankie," Anthony replied.

"Well kid I'll give you three weeks to come up with four thousand, but that means I will also have to black flag you from betting until you are paid up," he explained to Anthony.

Anthony sat back in his chair and acted as calm as could be. He wanted Frankie to gloat a little longer. This was going far better than he could have ever hoped. There was only Charlie, Vincent and Joey still in the back room and all three of them were now standing next to or behind Frankie to intimidate Anthony as much as possible.

"Okay Frankie, I guess I will have to take you up on your marker and I will call the bet."

"Kid, I ain't fucking around with you. You realize you will be in to me for thirty-three hundred dollars if you call this bet and lose?" Frankie asked with a sudden nervousness coming over him.

"Yes, and I said I call you Frankie, so what do you have?" Anthony asked with a grin on his face, which Frankie read as a sign that he knew he had just been played.

"Well kid, you better wiped that smirk off your face because I don't think you are beating my … " and before he could finish his sentence, Anthony finished for him, "Your Aces & Queens?"

"You little fucking cheat! I'll have you fucking whacked for this," Frankie said as he sprung up and leaped at Anthony. Anthony was totally taken by surprise, as Frankie had him pinned to the floor with Vincent standing right beside him with a gun pointed at Anthony's face.

"I'm going to have Vincent here take you outside and put a bullet in your fucking head. You come into my restaurant and try to cheat us," Frankie screamed as he was only inches from his face.

Thoughts were swirling in his head as Anthony tried to think of something to say that would save his life, but before he could even spit out something Frankie had gotten off of him and pulled Anthony off the floor.

"Do you think I didn't know how good of a card player you were, kid? I have been playing cards for roughly forty years and I know who the real players are when I am facing them. I just didn't think you were that good," he began to tell Anthony.

"I'm really not that…"

"Drop the bullshit act kid. The moment Carmine let you in the door you were trying to play us like fools with hopes of us letting you get at the table to win back your football losses," Frankie told him.

"Okay, I guess you are right," Anthony reluctantly answered him.

"You fucking better believe I am right. I wouldn't be in the position that I am in if I wasn't right most of the time. However I don't know if I shouldn't still have Vincent take you out back and explain a few simple rules about playing with wise guys, considering you aren't one of us. I mean it took some kind of balls for you to come in here and try to pull that off, and I respect that," Frankie confessed.

"Actually Frankie, my plan wasn't beating you at cards, that was just a little bonus. What I was really hoping for was a chance to talk to you about a business proposition," Anthony started to explain.

Fifteen minutes later Anthony was now alone with just Frankie and Vincent. If there was business to be discussed, Vincent was always included in the meeting. Not only was he Frankie's right hand man and best friend, but Frankie also respected his opinion. If Vincent told Frankie that the deal didn't sound right to him then Frankie took his advice and passed on the arrangement. So when Anthony, a complete outsider to their business, came to Frankie with an offer, Vincent was right there to hear it.

"Frankie, I know who you are and the power that you have. I'm sure your restaurant brings in a nice sum of money but your other business brings in a great deal more and with that kind of money flow, I'm sure it is hard to hide from the government. I'm sure you can move a good amount of the money through the restaurant and I also know you have people that clean your money, too. However what I'm offering is a chance to invest in a stock that, if it hits its potential, will make sure you never have to worry about money again," Anthony started to explain to them.

"If you let me open an account at Merrill Lynch and let me invest in this stock that I received inside information on, you could stand to make at least two million in about two years and, if that is the case, you never have to worry about having to explain your income to the government again because you will have a perfect legitimate alibi."

"Kid, do you know how many times I have been told about a stock tip that has totally fizzled and cost me money? Do you think a man in my position doesn't have a broker or two handling his money? What would ever possess you to think I would hand my money over to you? I admit you have balls to come in here and do what you did, but kid I don't know you from fucking Adam so why the fuck would I give you my money?" he asked.

Anthony was expecting that kind of response from Frankie. He didn't think Frankie was just going to walk over to a secret safe, open it up and hand him a bag of money. Anthony had done his research first because he had to be absolutely sure that one, the stock was going to be a winner, because his life depended on it and two, he needed facts to impress Frankie.

"Frankie I would never insult your intelligence by expecting a smart business man like yourself to just say, 'hey this kid just took me for four thousand dollars in poker so he must know how to pick stocks. Now why don't I just hand him a bag of money?' I wouldn't be here putting everything on the line if I didn't believe that the inside information I had was gold and it couldn't miss. I also know that your man at Bear Sterns lost you about thirty thousand and, the year before that, the jerk-off from Goldman Sachs lost you roughly twenty-five thousand. I mean it is good to have write-offs now and then, but I think that that is a little too extreme, don't you agree?" he said with the same confidence he had when he beat Frankie in the last hand.

Before Frankie could reply to this little surprise, Vincent jumped into the conversation.

"Can you believe this fucking guy? How the hell do you know about what brokerage firms Frankie goes through and what his portfolios look like? If you ask me kid, that's a pretty good bluff. I think that kind of information is totally confidential and you couldn't possibly know," he claimed.

"Vincent, I'm sure by the look in Frankie's eyes that he knows the information that I just said was accurate. Those dick heads don't know their asses from their faces and you just keep handing them money every year. You already lost over fifty thousand dollars in two years with those so-called professionals, why don't you give me a shot?" Anthony calmly asked.

"Kid you are just one surprise after another tonight. Your information, which I don't know how you got it, is correct about my stock portfolio. But, like you said, everyone needs a couple of write-offs each year and we both know that is not where I get my income. Now here you are in front of me with a can't miss business proposition, so what's the catch? I mean you are risking your balls, kid."

The catch was quite simple. Anthony wanted to belong. He wanted to be one of them with out actually having to become one the traditional way. Anthony was in no way a mobster, but he admired the lifestyle. If Anthony's stock came through, he would be set for life with Frankie. Frankie would give him a free pass into their world. He could go anywhere in the neighborhood and people would look at him differently knowing that he was now with Frankie. He could come and go in *The Club* as he pleased. Anthony would walk in on a Friday or Saturday night and someone would announce, "The kid's here." Everything that he ever wanted would no longer be out of reach. All those dreams that the average man has would come true: like exotic cars, vacations anywhere in the world, two homes—one in the suburbs and one in the Hamptons.

Of course he would have to hide all of this from Sandra. It would be hard to explain the sudden change in his income. She understood that he was a card shark in college, but by no means did she know what kind of gambler he was nowadays. Sandra wasn't your typical wife who didn't have a clue about the family income. She balanced the checkbook every week and always paid the bills on time. All in all, Sandra was the backbone of their business affairs because if it was left up to Anthony to do it, it would never get done. So hiding a sudden change in income would be something that Anthony would have to consider later down the line.

"The only catch, Frankie, is that I get paid for my services. Merrill will pay me on the strength of your portfolio, but I want a bonus commission from you. I truly feel that within two years this stock could reach a hundred, maybe a hundred and fifty. Your initial fifty thousand dollars will buy you roughly sixteen hundred shares. If you keep buying the stock on the way up in five hundred increments, two million would be a feasible target. And for your profit, I expect twenty percent in return. I think that is very reasonable for a man like yourself," Anthony explained his proposition in a cool and methodical way: the same way he would talk to another player at the poker table.

"Kid, I tell you what. I think you got a fucking set of balls on you that I haven't seen from an outsider in years. It looks like you did your homework before you came here and you took one hell of a chance after another all night long, so I will reward you with an answer of yes. However, here is my proposal for you. Let's just say this stock goes the other way and your tip was a bust. Shit happens. However, unlike the other brokerage firms, I will expect my losses to be reimbursed to me."

"What do you mean?" Anthony asked.

"I will treat this like I would treat any other wager. If it loses, you will owe me. And don't think you will just owe me the principal. There will be juice on top of it, let's say a little more than that twenty percent that you are asking from me. Now you can walk out of here right now with fifty large ones or you can go home and think about how much of a lock this tip really is, the call is totally up to you."

Without so much as a slight bit of hesitation, Anthony told Frankie he accepted his terms and assured him that this was the start of a successful business partnership. As he got up and shook Frankie's hand, Frankie took his hand and, with a tighter than usual grip, he explained to Anthony the last part of his proposal.

"Kid, to prove to you all the things that you might have heard about me are true, I want to drive home my point of this little business endeavor. If by chance you can't come up with my money or let's say you might think of skipping out of town or you just have the audacity to say you are not going to pay me my money at all, I'm not going to come after you for my money. That would be too easy, and what would it prove to you or anyone else? To make you realize how serious you are getting yourself in, I might send Bull and Sal down to the village one day to do some grocery shopping, but instead of getting me groceries from the store they get me the whole store instead. Do you understand me? Don't make me have to do something like that kid, okay?"

And once Frankie was finished with his terms, he turned to Vincent and told him to get the kid his money. Vincent handed Anthony an envelope with the fifty thousand in it.

"Kid, like Frankie, I like you and I just hope to God you know what you are getting yourself into. Don't fuck up with Frankie's money."

Anthony took the money from Vincent and was then escorted out the door. No one could have foreseen how all their lives would change once Anthony left *The Club* that night.

On that Monday morning, Anthony went into work with Frankie's fifty thousand and opened up an account in the name of Ellena Maria Feliciani. The first transaction was the purchase of twenty one hundred shares of Tibco Software at twenty three dollars a share; three years and some thirty transactions later, that account was now worth over seven million dollars. Anthony could never have imagined that the stock would ever have reached over two hundred dollars a share. He had made Frankie a millionaire seven times over. Over the last three years, he himself made close to a million dollars in commissions from Frankie alone. Anthony's ultimate dream had come true. He was an honorary member of Frankie's crew. He had everything in life you could have possibly wanted from one incredible stock tip, yet three years later Anthony had managed to piss it all away.

❧   ❧   ❧

Anthony was looking around the room while he ate the breakfast that Frankie had cooked for him and still couldn't believe how things had changed since that July evening. He was so proud of himself that night, striking a deal of the century with the head of the neighborhood family, but that was lifetimes ago and now all he had left was just the memories.

"Are the eggs helping your stomach, Anthony?"

"Have I ever been displeased with anything that you cooked? I can't imagine how much I would weigh if I came here on a daily basis," Anthony answered.

"Well I'm glad that you did the right thing today by coming by and seeing me. There are many people that feel you don't have the money, or that you can't raise what you owe me. So let me hear the truth from you Anthony—should I be concerned?" he asked, while eating the last piece of sausage on his plate.

The one unique thing about Frankie was that nothing could distract him when he was eating. He could be in his office discussing a hit on his own brother with Vincent, and he would go right on eating his lunch without skipping a beat. It was his little way of concentrating on the matter at hand.

"Frankie, have I ever not paid a debt to you in all these years? Friday won't be different than any other time," Anthony tried to reassure him, but he realized that Frankie wasn't going to buy it.

"Anthony over the last two years you have pissed away more money than sixty percent of the people in my books combined. I don't understand you. You were set for life with that stock tip; why the fuck did you keep pissing everything away? I have had more parental talks with you than my own two daughters. I love you like one of my own and I guess I should have beat the living shit out of you to knock some sense into that thick head of yours. However, you are not my kid and I can't protect you from your mistakes," Frankie was now shouting at Anthony the way he would shout at Anita if she came home and told him she was pregnant.

"You have done for me what no one else in my family could have ever done. The money that you have made me will enable me to step out of the 'family' business when Anita graduates in four years."

"Glad I could help," Anthony sarcastically replied.

"Well I'm glad you can still make jokes at a time like this."

"What do you intend to do after she graduates?" Anthony asked.

"I am going to sell *The Club* and the girls and I are going off somewhere to start a new life. For this, I am forever in your gratitude. I also know that you have stayed loyal to me and never let our little business venture out into the open with Bull or any of the other fellows in the crew. I told you when the stock started to take off that under no circumstances were you to speak of this to anyone. If it got out that I was keeping this from the higher ups in the family, I would have certainly been whacked. But unfortunately, your debt is out of my hands."

"After all the money I have made for you, there's nothing you can do for me?"

"You know Bull is now totally in charge of this part of the family business, and I can not just give you a free pass. It would make me look soft and bring down many speculations against me, thus what I want to hear from you is that all of what I just said was meaningless because you have the money and are going to settle up with Bull on Friday night."

Anthony had never felt more hatred for himself in his entire life than he did right now. When Sandra told him she was leaving with Kimberly, he was in more denial of the situation than actual hate for her. She was bluffing, she just had to be. He was a professional at reading people and he knew her too well to believe any differently. He didn't hate himself until days later when reality set in and they were gone, but right here and now he felt like a child who had disappointed their father in the worst of ways.

Frankie had brought him into his world; the world which his real father could not have offered him. His dad Mickey was the typical Italian father who worked eleven hours a day to provide for his family. He never got involved with the Mafia when he needed a loan for the family store. Mickey didn't gamble or play cards, which was the reason why he never really connected with Anthony. He was an old fashioned, straight up Italian father.

On numerous occasions Frankie and Anthony would be in the back room of *The Club* and Frankie would be teaching him the finer points of Poker.

"Kid you are real good and I believe you have great potential of being one of the best players out there if you listen to my advice. Please stick with cards and stop trying to score on betting. The odds aren't in your favor like they are when you sit down at a table," Frankie would always preach to him, but when you are an egotistical person like Anthony, advice was just advice and you were too good to need it.

What could he possibly say to Frankie to make things better? He was above lying and there was no way he would lower himself and beg for the debt to be forgotten. He couldn't even strong-arm Frankie by threatening to go above him with the little information about his net worth. Frankie would just beat him to death right there in the back room. He was going to just come out and tell him he didn't have it and let Bull do whatever he wanted. Yes, that was statistically the best play he had. He had to flat out tell Frankie everyone was right and he didn't have it.

"I could always tell when you weren't holding the winning hand, Anthony. I see it in your eyes. The eyes never lie. You can never look straight at me for more than a second. It was a tell you always had while we played. I guess this means everyone is right and you don't have the money. Didn't you think I knew this already? Sandra has the house. You lost the Mercedes about three months ago and God only knows about your bank accounts. For Christ sakes, Perna's Pawn Shop on 5th Street looks like you personally furnished it. So where else were you going to get the fucking funds? Tell me what the fuck you were thinking?" Frankie asked in a total fit of rage.

"Okay so I am a total fuck-up. Is that what you want to hear? Are you happy I said it? I am a fucking natural born loser who can't pick shit from his own ass. I don't know what else to tell you. I will go to my parents and see if they have it, but I already know that they don't. I really don't know where I could possibly obtain your money," Anthony replied with unexpected tears falling down his face.

Everyone who knows Anthony personally will tell you that it is true that he is a complete loser when it comes to betting. His streak of bad luck is impeccable, however what most people, including Frankie, didn't know about Anthony was that for all the money he had thrown away gambling over the last few years, he had put aside just as much, but none of it was his.

Anthony realized he had a problem ever since he was at Syracuse; he just always believed he could beat it. After his miracle deal with Frankie he knew he had to take care of his future, along with the people he cared for the most. He was a father, a husband and a son and, for some unexplained reason, he believed God was looking down on him when his stock took off. Anthony felt he couldn't slap God in the face by wasting his generous gift, so out of seven hundred thousand dollars he took out over ninety thousand of it and donated it to various charities throughout the city. By doing this he now felt even with the man upstairs, but little did he know that you are never even with the man upstairs because, in the end, you have to keep paying him, one way or another.

Anthony's next step was getting Sandra and Kimberly out of the city and into a single family home in the suburbs. As much as he loved the city and the neighborhood, he didn't want Kimberly growing up in it. Like most caring fathers, he wanted more for her than he had and the first step for this was making sure her childhood surroundings would be the best he could afford.

One of the greatest feelings he had ever had in his life that didn't come from gambling or the birth of his daughter was the day he gave Sandra the biggest surprise of her life. He had come down one Saturday morning to the breakfast table and said it was just too nice to be stuck in the city and that they should take the baby for a nice ride. After about two hours of driving around in some very classy neighborhoods upstate, Anthony pulled up next to this elaborate Victorian style house with a huge yard and a swimming pool in the back. On the front yard there was a 'Just Sold' sign.

"Man I wonder how much a house like this sold for in this classy neighborhood?" he turned and asked Sandra.

"Well it is a lot more than a couple like us could afford, so why even bother thinking about it?" she replied.

"Well, with an attitude like that we will never get one. You need to think more positively. I am going to call the number on the sign and find out what it went for anyway, just to ease my curiosity," he turned to her and said with that look that she was accustomed to seeing when he was up to one of his crazy stunts.

Anthony took his cell phone out of his pocket and dialed the Realtor. "Hi, my name is Anthony Albergo and I am in the drive way of 100 Oakwood Drive. I was wondering how much the new owner paid for this house."

After a couple of nods, Anthony said thank you and hung up the phone.

"Well, what did they say?" Sandra asked knowing that it had to be over a quarter of a million dollars.

After waiting for the moment to build up, Anthony took Sandra's hands in his and said, "The realtor said it was sold to a young couple with a baby girl for a little over four hundred and thirty thousand. Congratulations sweetheart, you are the lucky new owner."

She just stared at him in total shock. She believed Anthony was doing okay at work and he was good at cards, but how in the world could they afford this house?

"The stock market is going great right now and with all my commissions, I thought it was time to get us out of the city and into a nice home while we could. Don't think I just woke up one day and just came out here and bought the house, I did plenty of research about the neighborhood and the schools. It is totally perfect for Kimberly to grow up in, so no need for you to worry," he explained to Sandra.

"Are you sure we can afford it? I know the taxes alone must be outrageous. You swear your commissions are great now, but what about three or four years from now when the market takes a turn the other way, then what are we going to do? Just pack up and go back into the city? I could never go back once I got spoiled living out here. Anthony, are you sure you have all this thought out?" she asked him as she was still looking at him in total disbelief.

"All I can say is stop worrying about our future money problems and just enjoy the moment. We still have to go and pick out new furniture, drapes, colors and everything else that comes with buying your first house."

There were still doubts in her eyes and, no matter what else Anthony would say to reassure her that he had everything under control, she was going to worry. Sandra was the head-strong responsible one out of the two of them, while Anthony was the free spirited and spontaneous one. And why not, he was the gambler and she was the conservative money pincher.

After more reassurance from Anthony, Sandra finally agreed to enjoy the moment and they unbuckled Kimberly from her seat and got out of the car and walked up to their new home. As they got to the front door and Anthony pulled out the key to unlock it, he turned to Sandra and asked, "By any chance do you know how to keep up the maintenance on an in-ground pool?" The two of them were at their peak of happiness, and once you get to the peak there's nowhere to go but down.

Anthony convinced her as best he could that the money for the house was from his commissions at work, which he never really got, and sometimes from those little card games on the side. After that, she was kept in the dark just as planned about his and Frankie's business partnership.

Since he had made more money than he expected, Anthony wanted to make sure that he returned all the time, love and money that his parents given to him throughout his life. Anthony was an only child, and when you don't have any brothers or sisters sharing your parents' love they seem to spoil you a little more than normal. Anthony considered himself very lucky. His parents didn't have a lot of money. When you own a little grocery store in the village the family income just wasn't that high; but, no matter what little money they brought home, they always made sure Anthony had what he needed or wanted.

One night at dinner about four months before he graduated high school, Anthony had told them that he had been accepted to Syracuse, but more than likely he wasn't going to attend because he knew that they couldn't afford to send him. Anthony felt that just getting accepted to Syracuse would be thrilling enough for his parents, since no one in their family had ever gone to college. He explained to them that he was just going to stay home for his first two years and get a part time job somewhere while attending the local community college, until he could raise the money for his last two years and then attend Syracuse.

Unbeknownst to Anthony, Mickey and Erma knew that this day was going to come and had planned for it a long time ago. They saw in Anthony at a very young age what most parents hope to see in their children while they are growing up, and that was how determined he was to become a success. Anthony was too smart to let the street eat him up alive like it did most boys over the years.

Mickey got up from the kitchen table and went to his bedroom. Two minutes later he sat down with an envelope in his hand and handed it to Anthony, who reluctantly took it from his father.

"What's this?" Anthony had asked him, but deep down in his heart he already knew the answer.

"What kind of parents do you think we are Anthony? Did you think we weren't hoping that you would go to college one day? We might not be the smartest or richest of people Anthony, but our love for you is stronger than you can imagine. With tuition as high as it is nowadays this isn't much, but it will start you off in the right direction," Mickey explained to him with as much love as any proud father could possible have at that moment.

Feeling guilty and stupid as ever, Anthony opened the envelope and took out a Chase Bank savings account statement. He knew of course that the name on the statement was going to be Anthony Albergo, but what he was not expecting was the amount in the account. The account's value was a little over twenty-two thousand dollars. His father was right, this wasn't enough to pay his way through college, but for a kid from the streets like Anthony it was enough to get him in the door for a year and enable him to work his way through. And from that moment on Anthony never had to worry about his tuition again. After he graduated Syracuse he only owed about eleven thousand dollars in school loans, which was a lot better than most graduates.

Now it was Anthony's turn to take care of his parents and, just like the night his father gave him that envelope, he wanted this to be a surprise of a lifetime. One day during his lunch, Anthony went down to the bank where his parents had their two mortgages, the one for the store and the one for their little house, and paid both of them off completely. He told the branch manager that he wanted this kept secret from them, so he was to keep the deed and all the paper work in a safety deposit box at the bank. The next step was that the branch manager was to open a new savings account in his parents' name. Anthony made the initial deposit into the account for twenty-two thousand dollars, and he wanted all future mortgage payments that his parents were to make to be deposited into this new account.

Anthony felt he was now squared with God, squared with his wife, and most importantly, he was squared with his parents. He even eventually convinced Sandra to let him take over the handling of their bills. How the hell could he lie to her when there were no more bills being mailed to the house? He finally got her to believe that he was paying them on line from work, and that he kept the bank statements at the office for convenience.

Anthony even paid off his and Sandra's cars, student loans and all the credit cards that they had before they got married. After all of that, Anthony still had over three hundred thousand dollars stored away.

Anthony looked at it as if the rest of the money could be blown. It was easy street from here on out. He could go to *The Club* and play cards any night of the week and not have to worry about the stakes. His usual Saturday and Sunday quarter and half bets were now raised to C notes, and once in a while they became dimes. What did he have to worry about? He and Sandra both had good jobs and all of life's major expenses were paid off. This was just play money to him.

Anthony had one more investment to make before he would have the chance to piss it away. This investment was kept a secret from Sandra too, because it was his gift to their daughter. It was just like the gift his parents gave him when he was ready to go to college, and he didn't want Sandra to know about the surprise. On the same day he went to the bank to pay off his parents' mortgages, Anthony opened a CD for Kimberly in the amount of one hundred and fifty thousand dollars.

Kimberly was only one year old and by the time she would turn eighteen and be heading off to college, this CD would be worth over two hundred and fifty thousand; more than enough to secure all her future hopes and dreams. Everything might be going perfectly well for them now, but he knew how his luck could change and he wanted to be damn sure that Kimberly's future was taken care of before everything else.

🍁   🍁   🍁

"Well Anthony I just don't know what else to say to you. You have never wanted to take my suggestions in the past, so why bother trying now? All I can say to you is have my fucking money for Bull on Friday or God help you, because it will be out of my hands. If you have nothing else to add to this, it's time for you to be leaving. I have many things happening today and I need to get started," Frankie stated as he got up from his stool and headed towards the door.

Anthony realized he was getting off relatively easy today. He felt about as sick as he thought he was going to feel during this visit, however he was relieved that Bull wasn't here, which was a little bonus for him.

As Anthony got up from his seat and walked over to the door, he once again tried to emphasize to Frankie that he was going to have his money for him on Friday. Unlike Sandra, who tried to believe Anthony more often than not, Frankie had heard this a million times over the years. He knew if he could count on a guy giving him his money or not, and right now this was a not if there ever was one. All the assurance in the world wasn't going to change Frankie's mind. Anthony realized it was best to just leave without saying another word, so he gave Frankie a kiss on both cheeks and headed out the door. But little did they know that they would be seeing each other again before Friday night. And their next meeting would not go as smoothly as this one did because the next time they would see each other, Anthony would be looking for revenge for his parents' death.

🍁   🍁   🍁

CHAPTER 2

The Flop
(Queen of Spades, Jack of Spades,
2 of Hearts)

Anthony felt the morning's meeting with Frankie went better than expected. If he was even half as lucky as he had been this morning, his visit with his parents would go as planned. He knew there was no way in this world, after all he had put his parents through with his divorce from Sandra, the loss of his home, and the lack of visitation they had of Kimberly, that he could lower himself to ask them for the money. Anthony had disgraced his family enough over the last couple of years; he couldn't come to them as a way out of his predicament.

The people in the neighborhood were a tight group of people, and talk got out about how Anthony was involved with Frankie. Erma and Mickey weren't as close to their son as they used to be, but they knew he had gotten himself in trouble of late. They felt that their son was never the same after he got out of college. Mickey believed it was four years of education that went in one ear and came out the other. He knew all along that his son wanted the Mafia life style. You can't take the streets out of some kids, even when they have a chance to get away from them. Anthony loved cards and gambling too much to want any other way of life, and this broke their heart.

Anthony realized all along that the real reason he was going to see his parents was to try to set things straight about what happened with him and Sandra. Divorce is a forbidden thing amongst most of the old time Italian

Catholics like Anthony's parents. People don't get divorced, no matter what the circumstances.

In their neighborhood, most of the times it was the death of the husband, who was killed because of what he did for a living that ended the marriage. After thirty or forty years of working in a factory their ticker finally shut down or, if they were in Frankie's line of work, one night someone thought it was finally your time to go and that was that. Either way, they were the more common ways marriages would come to an end in the neighborhood. Most of the old timers were sickened by how their children treated the sacrament of marriage these days. After only a couple of years together when things weren't working out, they would call it quits. And Anthony's parents were no different; they couldn't accept their son's divorce.

When Anthony and Sandra were together, Erma and Mickey saw them a couple times a week and almost every Sunday for dinner. Kimberly was their only grandchild and nothing made them happier than spending time with her. When Anthony hit them with the bomb that he and Sandra were getting a divorce, it just about killed them. Erma could not believe that her son could commit such a sacrilegious act. She took it as a slap in the face and told Anthony from that day on that he was no son of hers, because no son that she raised could do such a thing.

Mickey wasn't as resentful towards Anthony as Erma was because he was aware of how things were in the world today and that most American marriages don't last. What ate at Mickey was the fact that he knew it was completely Anthony's fault. He understood that Anthony's lifestyle was interfering with their home life in one way or another. Mickey didn't think the problem was financial because of their house and cars, but it had to be more about the time he spent away from Sandra and Kimberly.

The other thing that they noticed about Anthony was his short temper with all of them. Like most gamblers, if Anthony had money on a game and it was on TV, he was no Sunday picnic to be around. It wasn't that noticeable in the early years of their relationship because Anthony didn't lay that much money on a game that a night out with Sandra couldn't distract him from it. Later on, when he was dropping a dime or two on the Monday night game, Sandra could have been going down on a hot blonde right in front of him and he wouldn't even want to join in or look twice for that matter. The game and the action on it were all the excitement that he needed on that night.

On one Sunday when they were over at his parents' house for their usual once a week dinner, Anthony was in such seclusion with the Giant's game that he didn't even notice Kimberly when she fell down the steps and split her chin open on the floor no more than four feet from him. Sandra came running in moments later screaming at him when she saw that he was still sitting on the couch oblivious to what was going on around him. She was so upset with him that she took Kimberly to the hospital by herself and left Anthony there at the house to find his own way home.

The only saving grace for Anthony that night was that he was on the winning side of the game and his mind and attitude were in the right place. If he had been on the losing end of that bet, it would have been the main ingredient for one hell of a blow up between the two of them. He still ended up sleeping on the couch that night but, with a 52 inch TV that was airing ESPN's Sunday Night Prime Time, it didn't end that badly for him.

Anthony still kept in touch with his father on a weekly basis to make sure everything was okay with them and the store, but he rarely talked to his mother anymore. She kept her promise and didn't want anything to do with him. The conversations with his father were brief and more business-like than social.

Anthony arrived at his parents' store around one o'clock. The busy times were first thing in the morning, with the old timers getting their fresh fruits and milk for breakfast, and in the evening, with the younger crowd coming in for the necessities for that night's dinner. Mid afternoon was usually quiet time for the store, with just the occasional stragglers here and there. Mickey usually did his inventory and ordering of new food and supplies during this time, so Anthony planned on going through the back door and, hopefully, catching him alone doing one of those two things in the back room. If he could talk to Mickey alone first, it would more than likely alleviate the tension between him and his mother. But, just like most of Anthony's plans of late, this one fell through too.

To Anthony's dismay, the back door was locked when he tried to open it. He thought to himself that they never locked the door before, and this seemed to be a bad omen for him. A true gambler always believed in omens, either good or bad. There was no use in dwelling over the locked door. He knew he had to go through the store's front door like a regular customer and encounter his mother first, because she would be at the register in the front of the store. Anthony just prayed that she wouldn't cause too much of a scene once she saw him.

Anthony stood in front of the door and peered inside hoping that his mother wouldn't be at the register, but, unfortunately, she was there helping a woman with an infant load her groceries into bags. This gave him the chance to walk by her and head to the back to see Mickey without her noticing him. He walked past the store's four aisles and looked down each in case his dad was loading the shelves in one of them, but he was lucky because Mickey was in the back unpacking the morning's deliveries.

Anthony was able to come right up behind his father without being noticed and stood there watching while Mickey went about his business. He couldn't believe how old Mickey looked at this moment. Had he always looked this old? Or was it that he hadn't seen him for so long that it was natural for his dad to look much older to Anthony? But in his heart he knew Mickey was aging badly because of the stress that he has put on their family. It was one thing for Anthony to fuck-up his marriage, but it was a whole different ball game to jeopardize his parent's well-being because of his screw ups. It killed him to see how fragile his dad looked. This was not the last image that he wanted to have of Mickey.

"Hey Dad," was all Anthony could think of to start the conversation.

Turning around and not acting too surprised, Mickey returned the hello. "I was expecting you one day this week. I just wasn't expecting you so soon."

"Why would you expect me to show up at the store, Dad?" Anthony asked.

"Are we going to have a grown up conversation or are you going to pretend that you are still a teenager and that I am the naïve parent, Anthony?"

Anthony realized his dad wasn't a stupid man, but why would he think that out of all the times he could have come to him for money that it would be this week? Mickey walked over to where Anthony took a seat on a food create and sat down next to him.

"In all my years as your father, don't you think I know about your gambling problems Anthony? You were never a good liar, so don't start now. I also know that over the last two years or so you have gotten totally out of control with it. And since I know that the only other true love in your life is the Yankees, I kind of assumed that you took a shelling on the series since it went a full seven games and we were on the losing end. So how far gone are you, five or ten thousand dollars?"

Anthony only stood there with his jaw wide open. He had a hunch that his father had some clue of what was going on, but this blew his mind. Mickey had the situation pegged, except for the fact that he was way off on the figure that he owed. Anthony stood up and took a couple of steps, hoping that he could reach that inner strength inside of him that would enable him to talk to his father man to man and not fuck it up. He knew that, more than likely, this would be the last time they would talk to each other.

"I respect you too much to lie to you Dad, however I won't discuss my financial problems with you either. I am here today just to try to patch up the problems that I have caused between the three of us. You are right to assume that I am a little far gone. In fact, I am more than a little and I believe that I will be going away after Friday. I just want to make things right between all of us if that's possible," Anthony explained to him.

"How the hell can you expect to patch things up Anthony? You took the only pure joy out of our lives. I just can't believe Sandra would punish us for your mistakes. It's not right to keep Kimberly from your mother and me because we didn't do anything wrong. Because she hates you so much and wants to forget about everything, she decided to keep us from seeing Kimberly. She doesn't answer our phone calls, acknowledge the cards and gifts we send Kimberly, nothing! So please tell me, how do you expect us to patch things up, Anthony?"

Anthony was not prepared for this treatment. He believed that Mickey would see that he was serious about the trouble he was in and convince Erma that the three of them could just sit and talk for awhile. Mickey's reaction was a total shock for Anthony, and he wasn't prepared with the answers that Mickey wanted to hear from him.

"Dad, can you just hear me out for a minute before you go off the deep end and make me feel worse than I already do. I just want to...."

But before he could finish Mickey interrupted him. "Feel worse? I don't give a rat's ass how you feel. You brought this upon yourself. You had everything a man could want and you threw it all away for the lifestyle of the neighborhood. I don't care if you are sick in the stomach everyday for the rest of your life, because that pain will never be as great as the pain of losing Kimberly, which is slowly killing your mother and me. Words can not express the amount of pain you have caused us. To think of the potential that you had and see it thrown away is a slap in the face to us," Mickey shouted.

"If that is the way the two of you feel, then you don't have to worry anymore because after today I won't be coming back. I just wanted to make peace with everyone before I left. If you and Mom don't want to talk before I walk out the door, then that's on you. I made an effort. All I ask of you is to go down to your bank whenever you have a free moment and ask them about your mortgages on the house and store. I wasn't a complete fuck-up, Dad; I just made a few mistakes. All in all, I still took care of my loved ones," Anthony tried to justify to him.

"That's your problem Anthony, you think money is the most important thing in the world. Your mother and I never had money, but we are as happy as can be with each other and the store. Love and family makes the world go around. I guess they didn't teach that to you up there in college," Mickey answered back with as much hate that he has ever felt before in his life.

"Well I didn't come here to get the facts of life from you Dad. I just wanted to say goodbye to the two of you. I will save Mom the aggravation and just slip out the back door. Don't forget to go to the bank for me and see what has been going on for the two of you," Anthony said as he turned to head to the back door.

"I'll go to the bank one day, but I could care less as to what I will find there. Money doesn't measure success Anthony, and until you realize that you will never succeed in life."

As Anthony reached the back door, he realized he had forgotten that it was locked as he noticed that the door was dead-bolted. "Why is the back door bolted shut?"

Mickey shook his head as he reached Anthony at the door. "I was expecting you or an acquaintance of yours one day this week so I didn't want any surprises, if you catch my drift. Along with the door, I have also taken a couple other precautions in case you aren't the only visitor I will have this week. Your mother has been through enough lately, and I don't want any more problems," he explained to Anthony.

"I think you are going a little bit overboard on this, Dad. I don't believe anyone who is looking for me gives a crap about your little store. Do you really suppose someone would come here looking for me, or looking for you to have money for me?"

And with that Anthony opened the door and headed out of his parents' lives forever and was unaware that their deaths, and not his ignorance, would be the reason he would never see them again.

The day was still early and Anthony only had to make one more stop before he could reach Atlantic City, his final destination of the day. Anthony was going to the bank to take out the remaining funds in all of his accounts. He was hoping to have at least one thousand in cash. Anthony always left a thousand in one of his savings account for when he was in a crisis and needed funds for a poker game.

Anthony had made plenty of trips to A.C. on a Sunday or Monday night when he was down, and eight out of ten times he would come back with most or all of his football losses. However, the most he ever came home with was seven thousand from a two day poker spree. Fifty thousand was a little too much to be looking for all at once, but if he could at least come home two days from now with ten thousand, it would be a start.

If he gave Frankie the ten before Friday, it would take some of the heat off him. But he knew he would have to go back to A.C. on Friday night for the rest when the big guns were down there spending their money. The weekend was also good for getting easy money from the tourists who watched the movie *Rounders* too many times and thought that they could do the same thing.

Anthony received a nice surprise when Tina, the customer service representative at the branch, told him that he had a little more than twelve hundred dollars left in all his accounts. An extra two hundred would be nice for the gas, tolls, dinners and a room for the night.

Sal Pellegrino was sitting behind the wheel of his Cadillac as he watched Anthony come out the back door of his parents' store.

"Here comes your douche bag," he turned and smiled at Bull.

"Yeah, empty handed and with his head dead. I guess things didn't go too well with mom and dad," he said, with a smile to Sal.

Sal was Bull's best friend in the crew because he was just as big and mean as Bull. When you first looked at them together, you would swear that they were twins. He always accompanied Bull on many of his collecting expeditions. As much as Bull loved to physically collect money from people, Sal was the one who was used to push a guy's button. If Frankie wanted someone to disappear, he would send Sal.

Sal was a complete psycho when it came to whacking guys. Frankie never really told Sal how to get rid of someone, as long as it was done. He was only interested in the bottom line: the problem was solved. Many of the bosses usually told the person who was going handle the hit how they wanted it executed, because the method used was intended to send a message to everyone else—this is what happens to you when you fuck with a boss.

Sal and Bull would usually just take a guy for a long ride to the middle of nowhere and just beat the living shit out of the guy until he was on the verge of passing out. Then Sal would usually put a couple of bullets in the guy's head.

On some occasions, Sal loved to take a guy to an abandoned warehouse and tie him up in a chair and torture the shit out of him first. After he got done torturing them, he would douse them in gasoline and light them on fire. He didn't soak the guy in it, but rather just put enough on them to get the fire going. This took longer to burn the poor son of a bitch, which made his suffering even greater. These occasions were saved for guys who stole from the crew or who were informants for other crews or cops.

For Sal, it didn't make a difference how he whacked a guy, because he loved it any way he did it.

"So where do you think Anthony is going now?" he asked Bull, even though he knew they were taking a trip to Atlantic City.

"My guess is the little douche bag is heading right down to A.C. to try to score fifty thousand. Dumb fuck doesn't realize that he has no chance in hell of winning. I'll call Frankie and see if he wants us to go down or not."

Once they left the bank parking lot Bull took out his cell phone and dialed Frankie to give him the news that he already probably already knew anyway.

"Uncle Frank, it's Bull. The kid just left the bank and we are heading on the parkway as we speak. Do you want us to follow him?"

"If you want to go down, that's fine. He'll stay put there for a day or two once he gets there. Now listen Bull, I don't want you two to fuck with him while he's playing. Wait until Friday night. Do you understand me?" Frankie tried to convey this as strongly as possible.

"Sal and I will give him his space. We'll probably hit the crap tables for awhile and just crash later in a room," he assured Frankie.

"I mean it Bull, leave the kid alone. If I hear otherwise, I won't be happy that you disobeyed my orders," Frankie stated before he hung up the phone.

"You know Frankie is starting to really piss me off. This crew is getting weaker and weaker, and he is doing nothing about it. Why the fuck is he threatening me about this fucking kid?"

"Don't get yourself so worked-up over this punk."

"I should just whack Anthony now and just get it over but before I do that, I swear to you that I am going to get that douche bag to tell me the truth about his business relationship with Frankie. If he made Frankie the money he claims, I am going to confront Frankie about it. I think it is time for someone else to run our crew. All Frankie cares about is his stupid restaurant and not our business. We are the joke of the family, and I want it to change," he conveyed to Sal.

"I don't think it is a fucking good idea to confront Frankie, Bull, you know he would whack you right then and there, nephew or not. Just wait till Friday and once we get Anthony, we'll see what is and what isn't about this whole money thing with the two of them."

"Yeah, I can wait a couple of days until I get what's coming to me. You ready to go play some craps for awhile?"

"You bet Bull. I need a good score myself, after what the fucking Yankees did to me," he said with a huge grin on his face.

❧   ❧   ❧

The trip to A.C. usually took Anthony a little over an hour and a half, but since he was going on a Monday afternoon, he was hoping to be at a table in the Taj Mahal by five o'clock. That gave him plenty of time to get there, check in, grab a bite to eat, shower and get himself in total control before he sat down at a table. Anthony realized that this night would be different than any other night he played. He was chasing more money this time than ever before, and you can't play your best if you have a set figure in your head. His mind needed to be in perfect shape to win the kind of money he had planned. Poker is not always who has the best two cards, but how you play them. He could win with a Two/Seven off-suit if he concentrated on his opponent more than the cards.

The Garden State Parkway was totally clear and Anthony drove most of the ride in silence with no music on the radio. His head was still pounding, and the thoughts from both conversations of the morning kept pulling his mind in a million directions. The one thought that bothered Anthony the most was what his father said about the back door. Did he really believe that someone would show up at their store and try to get money or information about him from his parents?

Anthony has heard the stories about Bull and some of the other guys in Frankie's crew, but he was a part of them and he couldn't imagine any of them wanting to get his family involved. That's just not how it works with these kinds of guys. There were certain rules that they followed, but for some reason he couldn't get it out of his mind that his father might be right about this.

As Anthony reached the Atlantic City expressway his mind started to drift back to reality. He was getting himself into that poker mode. The morning talks were now the farthest thing from his mind. His father basically disowning him happened ten years ago, not this morning, as far as Anthony was concerned.

Many great athletes will tell you that, once the game starts, they are in a totally different world, not aware of anything or anyone around them other than the other players. They are so focused on the game at hand that nothing else exists at that point of time. Anthony reached this point the moment he entered Atlantic City. This was his Disney World, and every time he arrived the excitement was just like it was the first time. Once he reached the city lines, everything else in the world was a blur. He was so focused on poker, his strategies and the players around him, that he could lose track of days at a time and not realize it.

One weekend Anthony sat at a poker table for sixty-seven straight hours, only getting up to use the restroom. Casinos have this magical ability to keep a player at the tables as long as possible with free food and drinks. That Tuesday morning, when he came home from the sixty-seven hour marathon, he had another one of those classic fights between him and Sandra. He didn't have an answer to why he hadn't called or come home for three days, because in his world it wasn't three days. Time lost all meaning to Anthony when he was playing at Atlantic City.

The difference between playing in A.C. and playing with Frankie and the guys down at *The Club* was they stopped playing when it got late. In A.C. it never got late, because someone always replaced the guy that got up. It was a continuous wheel in motion that never ended, and Anthony was just along for the ride.

Anthony pulled into the Valet parking lot and got out of his car, where Louis Rongione the valet greeted him.

"Feeling lucky tonight Anthony?" he asked, hoping to get the usual tip from Anthony in return.

"I don't think that the bitch Lady Luck is on my side anymore, Louis," Anthony said with a smile.

"Just because she abandoned your Yankees doesn't mean she forgot about you. Just play your game and I'm sure she'll be sitting right next to you."

Anthony smiled and handed Louis a twenty and thanked him for the encouragement, but told him to drop dead if he thought that his Yankees were beaten by Lady Luck.

Anthony smelled the excitement in the air when he walked through the front doors. Yes this is his place, he was always a winner and everyone here knew it. For the first time, Anthony actually started to believe that everything would turn out fine. He could win the money back, still continue to work at Merrill Lynch and maybe even patch up things with his parents, but Anthony didn't know how far from the truth he was. The pain he felt once Luis Gonzales got the game winning hit was like a heart attack, but the pain he would later feel tonight and tomorrow morning would be incomparable to anything he had ever felt before.

Anthony wasted no time and headed straight for the cashier, where he got one thousand in chips. He kept the other hundred and sixty-two dollars in his wallet for the room, dinner and gas money for the trip back home. The next thing to do was to scope out a table. Most people just go and sit wherever there's an available seat, but a true professional like Anthony looks for weakness at a table. Where are the usual suspects, the winners, the losers and, of course, the big fish? He needed to find a twenty-five/fifty no limit hold'em table with a couple of big fish looking to lose some money. His plan was to make enough at the lower table, and then proceed to a one hundred—five hundred table that they had in a secluded room for the high rollers.

After waiting about an hour, Anthony found a table that looked ripe for the taking. At this table were a couple of young kids with a thousand in chips each who thought they were the shit. The other three players were an old timer with his "Sands" casino jacket and matching hat, and a couple of women who were waiting for the evening show at eight o'clock and really weren't interested in poker. Anthony picked this table because he only had to really worry about the jackass in the "Sands" outfit. He believed the guy probably got lucky once in awhile, as long as tonight wasn't one of them. He was extremely confident that he would have the two younger guys' money with an hour or two because they played so poorly, and a real player like himself would have no problem figuring out their playing styles. Yes, this was the table where he needed to start his night.

Unlike everything else that happened all day, things finally went the way Anthony planned them. He had broken both kids within two hours and the "Sands" guy left three hours after Anthony sat down. Other people came and went and, since Anthony had gained about three thousand in chips, he was high stack at the table and used this leverage well against all new comers.

It was going on nine o'clock when Anthony actually took notice that he was already up about five thousand dollars. He just couldn't believe he was on such a roll that early. A true gambler never wants to stop and leave a winning table when they are on a streak like this, but Anthony knew that with a streak like this he needed to be at a higher stake table. With that, he signaled the pit boss to come over.

"Yes Mr. Albergo, what can I get you?" Chris Maphis, the head pit boss asked as he approached Anthony.

"Who all is at the high stake table in the back?"

"The usual crowd is back there, Greg Gamble, David Oswald, Tom Brink and a few new faces. Would you like me to move you to that table?" Chris replied.

Anthony had only played at the high stakes table once before. Usually you needed ten thousand just to sit down and have a chance with some of those guys, because, for the most part, these guys are playing with fifty thousand or higher and you don't want to handicap yourself by coming into the game short-stacked.

"What's the average chip count, Chris?" Anthony asked.

"I believe it's not that high right now. I figure maybe fifteen to twenty thousand give or take."

Anthony wanted to ponder this for awhile. He only had roughly six thousand dollars and the night was still young. Also, it was only Monday evening and he had gained five thousand already. He didn't want to be too greedy and try to get it all at once, but when the cards are coming your way it would be nice to be in bigger pots.

"I think it is too early to go back there now Chris, so I think I will stay at this table for awhile. Would it be any trouble for you to order me a nice hot roast beef and gravy on a Kaiser roll?"

"Not a problem Mr. Albergo. I'll keep giving you periodic updates from the back, if you like."

"That would be great Chris," Anthony expressed his gratitude as Chris walked away to put in Anthony's order.

Why ruin a good thing, Anthony thought to himself. I'll just keep myself relaxed, get a sandwich in me and just wait things out. Even if he didn't gain anymore tonight, five thousand was a good way to end one hell of a bad day. He might even get a good night's sleep, which had eluded him for the last four or five nights.

The whole time Anthony was at the table, he never had a clue that Sal and Bull were only five hundred feet behind him at the crap tables having their own lucky streak. If he did, he would not be playing as well as he had been up until then. He looked at his watch and noticed it was going on midnight, which meant that he had been in his seat for close to seven straight hours and was still on his winning streak. After a quick glance at his chips, he guessed he was roughly up eight thousand dollars and he felt it was now time to go to the other table. He had a good amount of chips to play, and the other guys were probably getting tired. With a motion of his hand, Chris came over to collect his chips and bring him over to the other table.

As Anthony reached the table, he noticed that three of the players that Chris told him about were still playing. He was happy about this because he had played against Gamble and Oswald on many occasions and had pretty much owned them in the past, although the two Asian gentlemen at the far end of the table could pose a problem.

Anthony absolutely never played against Asians players because they were just too hard to read and he never had success in beating them. When you look at the people who were successful at the World Series of Poker each year in Vegas, there were always one or two Asians at the final table, which was another reason why Anthony tried to stay away from them. However, tonight he had no choice. He wasn't going to let them intimidate him. He was on a roll, so why let them spook him?

"Gentlemen, how is everyone this evening?" Anthony asked the table.

"Good God, look what the fuck the cat dragged in tonight," Oswald said as he looked up and noticed Anthony.

"Glad to see you are happy to see me Dave," Anthony replied.

"Always happy to see you Anthony, especially when I know you are here chasing your losses," Dave replied back.

"Losses, what losses? I have no idea what you are talking about," Anthony said with a smile.

"If I was you I wouldn't be smiling too much, low stack," Greg Gamble informed him.

"Greg, it's always a pleasure to play at the same table as you. How much have I taken from you over the years, six, maybe seven thousand?"

Greg didn't even bother answering. Over the years of coming to the Taj, Anthony had beaten up on him quite frequently. He just didn't have any luck against Anthony, and Anthony knew it.

Greg was right; Anthony was going to be the short stack at the table. This would make it very hard for him to try to buy pots, and if he expected to win he would need to get the cards early; he could buy some pots later on down the line. The blinds were only two hundred and four hundred, so he had the time to work his way into a good position.

He took a seat next to Tom, because he was another guy from the city. Anthony had a good relationship with him over the last couple of years that they had been playing together.

"So Tom, how are the two guys at the end playing, aggressive or patient? I notice they each have about thirty thousand."

"Well they have been playing very tight, but they sat down with only ten each. I guess they have been picking their spots well. Dave is playing piss poorly tonight, and his tells are obvious. Oh and one last thing, watch out for Gamble, the cards have been his friend all night. He hasn't lost once yet head to head," he informed Anthony.

"Greg is the big winner so far? Man, I guess this is my lucky night," Anthony guaranteed Tom.

Anthony sat back in his chair and thought that this was really his night. Too many things were falling into place. If he didn't let the two Asian guys play mental games with him, he should be able to take down the rest of the players and walk out with half of what he needed.

Anthony played patiently. He didn't play in the first ten or so hands. He just quietly sat back and took in the information he could acquire from the other players. Anthony believed that Tom was right about the two Asian guys and that they were playing tight. They only played in hands when they were dealt a pair or two paint cards, and they didn't bother trying to buy a pot. However, Anthony didn't agree with Tom about Gamble. He was watching him closely and thought that the kid was getting lucky with his betting habits. Anthony felt he saw three hands already that Gamble bought on a bluff. Greg had a particular betting habit over the years, and it hadn't changed tonight as far as Anthony could tell.

Enough was enough, and Anthony was ready to get down to business. He was finally dealt his first pocket pair; Tens. It wasn't the greatest of starting hands, but good enough to see what the others were going to do about him finally playing a hand. After a bet of four hundred in front of him from Dave, Anthony decided to just call it. The flop came up Ten, King, Four and Dave didn't hesitate to bet eight hundred right off the bat.

"I guess you are trying to bully me with your Kings?" Anthony asked Dave.

"If I have them I guess it's not really bullying, now is it Anthony?"

"That's true, but I guess I need to see it for myself," Anthony replied as he called the eight hundred.

The turn was a Three, which was no help to either of them. The bet was to Anthony and he checked. Dave now believed that he had the winning hand with his Kings and bet sixteen hundred.

"I guess this isn't going to be a friendly game tonight," Anthony announced.

"If you want to play checkers, go to the park with the old timers," Dave told Anthony.

This, for some reason, got a laugh out of the Asian gentlemen, who didn't talk to any of the other players the whole night. After waiting a good thirty seconds or so, Anthony called the bet. He felt that if Dave had trip Kings, he would have raised before the flop or at least bet big after flop. Anthony had him figured for Ace/King and hoped for an Ace on the river to get Dave to bet big.

And God gave Anthony his gift from above, as the river card was the Ace of Clubs and like Anthony hoped, Dave bet big. It was a three thousand bet to Anthony.

"With that size bet, I can only assume that you are holding Ace/King and I will now raise. I am going all in," Anthony announced.

Dave sat back and realized he had about a four thousand dollar raise staring at him, and all of a sudden felt that he was being trapped.

"You tripped Tens, didn't you? Playing it nice and slow all along?" he asked Anthony.

Dave already had about five thousand in the pot, but if he called Anthony's raise and lost he would be down to about four thousand left to play with for the rest of the night. There was no way he could lay down top two pair, and he called Anthony's bet hoping that it was a bluff. Unfortunately for Dave, Anthony wasn't bluffing and he was now crippled for the rest of the evening.

The win now put Anthony close to fifteen thousand and in great position to do some damage. He didn't need the cards now; he could play against everyone's emotions. Yes, he felt without a doubt that this was his night and Lady Luck was going to escort him out of his hole.

Bull was the shooter at the table trying to make a hard four, when Sal realized that Anthony had gotten up and left his table. The dice were in the air as Sal tapped Bull on the shoulder and tilted his head over in the direction of Anthony's table.

"The number is seven. New shooter," the dealer announced as Bull looked over and noticed that Anthony wasn't sitting at the table anymore.

Bull and Sal picked up their chips and headed over to the table where Anthony had been sitting. Bull signaled to Chris, who was still standing watch over the table that Anthony had been playing at for most of the night.

"Chris, did you happen to see where the guy who had been sitting here for the last six hours or so went?" Bull asked.

"Yes, Mr. Albergo went into the high stakes room about an hour ago, and he is doing quite well I must say," Chris replied with a ton of glee in his voice.

"How well is the douche bag doing, Chris?" Bull now demanded.

"He went in there with about nine thousand in chips, when he only started out here with a dime. He's about up to sixteen thousand now. The kid is on a real roll tonight," Chris answered.

That's all Bull needed to hear. He relished the thought of Anthony actually getting himself out of his hole. It was only Monday night and Anthony had already made up fifteen of the fifty thousand. It was possible that he could do it.

"If this little douche bag gets out of this, I swear to God I'll kill him anyway just for the aggravation he has caused me," he said.

"Forget about it. There's no possible way an unlucky bastard like him can get himself out of that kind of hole. If he gets close and misses, it's even better," Sal said.

"You're fucking right about that. To get so close and come up short would be the icing on the cake. I'm fucking starving. Let's go check in and order a couple of steaks and a couple of the local bitches for later."

Sal only had to think about it for a second and said, "As long as you are treating, big guy. I never turn down a good steak and some pussy."

It was now nearing one in the morning, and Anthony was starting to feel the wear and tear of his last three long and sleepless nights. His mind was only a little ahead of his tiring body. Anthony was up roughly eighteen thousand at this point; a figure he never imagined he would reach. The thought of retiring for the night kept eating away at him, but he fought it back every time.

Real players just don't walk away from a winning streak until they lose a tough hand or two because these streaks don't come often and when they do, you don't want to insult Lady Luck by calling it an evening and leaving her at the table with someone else.

Anthony decided that he would play for another hour if his chip count stayed about the same or even grew a little. After the hour was up, his chip count had grown about another two thousand, and he continued.

The poker gods must have wanted him to continue, because two hours had passed and Anthony's chip count steadily grew as they passed—and who was he to argue with the gods? A true poker player like Anthony knows a good thing when he sees it, and he had this table confused and off-balanced with his good play. He had bluffed more pots tonight than ever before. He hadn't had the nuts that many times, and when he did he had callers at the end to see his cards and pay him off.

The Asian guys, who had been so patient and doing well before he arrived, were now close to being even for the night. The only other player who was up was Gamble. He was doing just as well as Anthony and even had more money, yet Anthony seemed to be the one in charge of the table. Gamble hadn't lost any heads-up hands to Anthony all night, but the only reason for that was because he didn't get involved in hands against Anthony. He just sat back and watched Anthony play, waiting for his opportunity. How little did he know, his opportunity was only a couple hands away.

When Anthony counted his chips at three o'clock, he noticed that he was actually down for the hour, but he was at a whopping twenty three thousand total. Never in his wildest dreams could he have imagined winning twenty three thousand in one evening of poker. He was a little less than halfway to the magic number, and he still had four days to do it. That was only five thousand a day and, with smart playing at the smaller tables, he could do that in his sleep. If God got him out of this mess, he would never make another bet again with Frankie. He was going to go straight and get his life back in order and stop being a fuck-up, however God, and Lady Luck, had other ideas for him.

Anthony was in the big blind, and he decided that this was his last hand of the night. He watched everyone after the dealer dealt the cards. Tom was the first to act and he folded in disgust. He was down to about three thousand in chips and was going to call it a night very soon. Gamble was the next to act and just limped in by calling the four hundred dollar blind. Dave, who was never the same after that beat down by Anthony, folded and then proceeded to get up from the table.

Dave wished everyone good luck and good night, but he never looked at Anthony as he did. A bad beat was a bad beat no matter how much you try not to let it get to you. The first of the Asian gentleman, Wan Zainal, was next to act and he also called the big blind. The second Asian, Johan Bujang, who was already in the small blind, raised the bet to two thousand.

Anthony had two calls and one raise in front of him. He believed that the two Asians were working together all night and thought the raise was to build up the pot for the other one. They had been signaling between themselves for most of the night. One of them would try to raise the pot with a weak hand to help it grow for the other one, who actually had the better of the hands. This was quite common with friends who played together at the same table and at the end of the night; they would split what they had both won. On most occasions, Anthony would have called it a night and walked away with that kind of action in front of him; but tonight had been a special night, and his suited Ten-Jack of Spades were playable. Gamble and Wan also called, making it four players to the flop.

"Wow, almost a family pot," Gamble proclaimed.

"I don't think our friends at the end of the table will try to make it that way after the flop," Anthony announced. There was no rebuttal from either of the two Asian gentlemen, because like most of the night they weren't much for conversation.

Jack   3   10

This was an incredible flop for Anthony, and the pot already had close to ten thousand in it. He had pegged Gamble for Aces, Kings or Ace/King, and that meant the flop didn't help him at all. As for Wan and Johan, he only needed to figure out who had the real hand, which he believed to definitely be pocket Aces, Kings or Queens. With the Jack being the only paint showing on the flop, Anthony felt he was in total charge and decided to slow play and check. Gamble followed and checked right away, as Anthony knew he would do. Without hesitation, Wan threw in a bet of two thousand that was quickly raised to four thousand by Johan.

"Here comes the fucking oriental express," Anthony announced. "I hate to tell you guys that this is Atlantic City, and we ain't a bunch of wet behind the ears amateurs that you can just sit down and swindle a pot from that easily. I see your four, and raise you another four," Anthony said with that confident grin on his face that had been there all night.

To Anthony's surprise, after a long consideration, Gamble called the eight thousand dollar raise. Realizing his job was done, Wan folded with honorable grace. Playing fast and loose, Johan called the raise.

Jack   3   10   10

Anthony's lottery ticket was just handed to him on the turn. His boat, Jacks over Tens, had just come home to port. The rush was incomprehensible. He was going to be out of the jam just like that. Luis Gonzales's game seven winning RBI hit happened a million years ago. In total awe of the thirty-five thousand dollar pot staring him in the face, Anthony couldn't keep his emotions inside and both Gamble and Johan picked up on his reactions. They knew that Anthony had just made a tremendous hand, yet he checked again.

Once again Gamble wasted no time in checking. Johan realized that his pocket Aces were no longer any good to him even though he had the two highest pairs, because he believed Anthony had trip Tens or better, and decided to check.

Jack   3   10   10   3

Johan didn't even bother to wait for Anthony's bet, because it was very clear that he had the hand to beat.

"Hand didn't go the way you plan, my friend?" Anthony asked with a smirk as big as one could get on his face.

With this ignorance by Anthony, both Johan and Wan got up and excused themselves from the table. After a good night's rest in their suite, both Johan & Wan would take their money to another casino and start all over. With the kind of bank rolls that they had, a night like this, which would cripple most professional players, was just a drop in the bucket to them.

Anthony had a little over twelve thousand dollars left in chips and was trying to think of a reasonable bet to place to see if he could induce Gamble, when he noticed Greg fumbling with his chips. Anthony couldn't figure out why Gamble was even still in the hand, but it didn't stop him from betting seven thousand dollars. After he made the bet, he couldn't help but not like the look on Gamble's face.

"After I call your bet Anthony, I'll still have about five thousand dollars, which is about a thousand more in chips than you. Anthony, I'll tell you what. I am going to do you a favor and I am going to raise you only three thousand. This way, once you call me and lose, you can't say I wasn't fair and left you crippled," he proclaimed to Anthony.

For the first time all night, horror struck in Anthony's heart. He sat back and looked at the cards on the table. No matter how he looked at them, he didn't see where he could be beat. With Wan and Johan betting after Gamble to start the hand, Anthony would have sworn the only two cards Gamble could be holding were Ace/King. There was no way he would have called those bets with just a pocket pair of Threes. He was too tight of a player to make that decision. Anthony felt that Greg was pot committed and was looking for a Queen on the river for a straight, but Greg would have had to know that a straight wasn't good enough for this hand. Unless Greg believed that Anthony was only holding trip Tens, and then the straight would be good enough to beat Anthony. Anthony felt, since the Queen never showed on the river, the only shot Greg had of taking the pot was to try and sell Anthony on the idea that the final Three had just given him four-of-a-kind. And, as for the speech, it was icing on the cake.

Unfortunately for Anthony, the longer he sat back and looked at Greg, he realized he was beaten. This couldn't be happening to him. What kind of a sick fuck was God—to let him get close to being out from under all of his problems, and then taking it away from him at the last instant? And just like that, the emotional roller coaster came crashing back down into the pit of his stomach. This was going to be the worst beat of his life if Greg was really holding those Threes. What does he mean, what if? Anthony was too good to think otherwise.

"Did you fuck me on the river?" Anthony asked.

"I wouldn't say fucked you, Anthony. I believe we both have a boat. Did you really think I would be in this hand without a boat? I could be holding Ten-Jack just like you. That is what you are holding? Maybe I just have the Ten with a Three kicker. The possibilities are endless. You know what I think Anthony? I think you have been playing too long today to think clearly. What if I am holding pocket Threes? Wouldn't that be a hand?"

This speech didn't give Anthony any ill-fated hopes that he could possibly be holding the winning hand. He was beat and it hurt, but he needed to throw in three thousand more to see his fate.

"I just can't lay them down, so I will call your three thousand, and if you are holding pocket Threes more fucking power to you," Anthony told him.

Anthony watched Greg's eyes when he turned over his cards, revealing his boat to Greg. He thought he saw concern in those eyes. Anthony thought to himself that there was a chance that he was holding the better hand. And for one split second, as Greg turned over his cards, Anthony's mind convinced him that he saw a Ten-Three. But reality came back quickly and he saw it wasn't a Ten, but the fourth Three.

"What can I say other than great hand Greg, you finally stuck it to me." In his heart, Anthony couldn't believe the loss. This just didn't happen to him.

Anthony stood up and shook Greg's hand. "Well, this hand did me in for the night."

"Don't be so down on the loss, Anthony. It's not like you ain't going to be back down here next weekend bullying another table like you did tonight," Greg said, trying to console him.

"I think you are wrong about that. This must be a sign to give up cards for awhile. I think it's going to be a long time before you see me here again, but if you do Greg, you better believe I will be gunning for that twenty thousand you took me for tonight."

Anthony excused himself from the table and headed out of the poker room, never to enter another one again.

Anthony had suffered many bad beats in his life. He could recall every football game that he lost on a last second, meaningless, back-door cover touchdown or field goal. There were at least ten to fifteen baseball games where the team he had blew a ninth inning lead, but these were all sports betting. He had never had a devastating beat like this in poker. Anthony had lost numerous hands like everyone else, but he had never been blind-sided like this. He had been caught up in an emotional whirlwind, and he let his guard down. Anthony had no business losing to a player like Gamble considering what was on the line. Anthony's life was at stake and he didn't rise to the occasion.

Over time he had gotten over most of those tough beats, but this time he knew he would never recover. Anthony still had over a thousand dollars, but he had no desire to go through another day and night like this again. The chance to make up Frankie's fifty thousand had slipped out of his hands.

The first thing Anthony was going to do was get a regular room, order some room service, take one long shower and then crash until some time next afternoon. Once he woke up, he was going to start his life over from scratch. This beat was a life changing experience. Obviously, this was a sign to get his life in order.

Anthony was going to go see his father again, and this time he was going to take responsibility for his mistakes. He would convince his parents that he was to blame for everything that had gone wrong over the last two years, and, most importantly, he would amend his problems with Sandra so that his parents could get Kimberly back into their lives. If he could pull that off, time would eventually heal the other wounds between him and his parents.

As for Frankie's fifty thousand, he would swallow his pride and ask his father for the money from the account that Anthony had established for them. He hated to do it, but in the end if he could get all their lives back in order, it would be worth it.

Getting Sandra to meet him would be the biggest obstacle. Her hate for him was too great for him to just call her and expect Sandra to meet with him. Anthony's plan was to surprise her at Kimberly's day care one afternoon and maybe he could get her to talk for a minute or two, which would be enough time to try to convince her that he was going to be a different person and, more importantly, he could persuade her to let his parents see Kimberly.

The plan was in place, but this was all a day away; his head was still spinning and all he wanted to do was get to his room as quickly as possible. Unfortunately for Anthony, his life, and that of everyone in his family, would change, but not the way he had imagined it would.

It was four o'clock in the morning when Sal looked at the clock on the table, as he rolled off the hooker underneath him.

"Do me a favor, honey, and go get me the phone," he told the woman, who he had just fucked. He had no clue as to what her name was, nor did he care.

"What am I, your wife? Go get it yourself," Cindy answered.

But before she could even smile at her smart-ass come back to Sal's request, he had sprung off the bed with a handful of her hair. "When a guy pays you three hundred fucking dollars for a nothing special fuck, you better do everything he tells you," he was now screaming at her while he dragged her across the room to the phone.

Cindy's screams woke up Bull and his entertainment, Brandy, in the other bed.

"Sal, what the fuck are you doing?" Bull demanded to know.

"Well some bitches just don't realize their place in the world, so I am showing this bitch first hand what happens when they don't do what they are told," Sal conveyed to Bull, not caring about the pain he was causing Cindy.

Once he reached the phone, Sal let go of her hair so he could dial the phone. "Now gather your fucking clothes and get the fuck out of here, before I decided to teach you more of life's little secrets," he said, without so much as a glance at her.

Bull got out of his bed and walked over to the chair where his pants hung and took out his wallet. He counted out ten Franklin's and gave them to Brandy, and told her to get Cindy and leave, because he and Sal had business to attend. As the women gathered their things, Sal dialed the front desk. After three rings, the operator came on the line and asked how to direct his call.

"Yeah, connect me to Chris Maphis, the pit boss in the high rollers Texas Hold'em room," Sal demanded.

"Let me connect you to that area, please hold," the voice responded.

Sal was on the edge of going completely out of control with his anger. It wasn't the long wait for someone to pick up the phone or even Cindy's attitude that sent him into this frenzied rage; it was the fact that Anthony was on the verge of winning his debt to Frankie, and that would make Anthony a free man again. This wasn't personal with Sal like it was with Bull; Sal just loved to whack a guy and, since it was up to Bull how it was going to be done, Sal was looking forward to it.

"This is Chris, how can I help you?" the voice on the other end of the phone asked.

Sal was still thinking about Anthony's good fortunes when Chris's voice surprised him. "Yeah, this is Sal. We came over to the Hold'em table earlier tonight looking for Anthony Albergo. Is he still down there playing?"

"I'm sorry, Mr. Albergo left the table about an hour ago and checked into a room," Chris informed him.

"Oh, he checked in? I guess he did pretty well if he is spending the night," Sal stated, hoping that Chris would elaborate on how Anthony's night ended and, not surprisingly, Chris did just that.

"I wouldn't say he did well at all. He was up about twenty-five grand when Greg Gamble busted him all the way down to about a thousand. Anthony didn't bother sticking around after that. He just got up from the table and went to the front desk and requested a room."

Sal cupped the phone and turned to Bull, who was already dressed and waiting to go. "Hot fucking damn, the jerk-off got busted out. He lost it all except for about a thousand. Anthony never even tried to make it up. It's all over, he is completely fucked. Chris said he just got up from the table all dejected and checked into the hotel."

Bull didn't need to respond to this. Sal could see the excitement all over his face. Sal removed his hand from the phone and continued his conversation with Chris.

"Did he say if he was coming back down in the morning?"

"Anthony didn't say either way, but I don't imagine after a beat like that that he would be back anytime soon," Chris replied.

Sal laughed at that response into the phone. "Oh, if you think that was a bad beat, you should see the one he will be getting later in the week. Thanks for the great news, Chris."

Sal hung up the phone and turned to Bull, who still had that look of complete satisfaction on his face, and asked him what they were going to do next.

"I believe our little douche bag will drink himself to sleep tonight and won't get back to the city until sometime tomorrow night. It's still early, I say we head out and grab a quick bite on the way back home. Then it's off to do a little grocery shopping," Bull informed him.

"You know Bull, I couldn't tell you the last time I went grocery shopping, but I think I will enjoy it more than I have ever before," he said, with the biggest of smiles on his face.

Bull was right about Anthony. Anthony had helped himself to a couple of bottles from the mini bar and had passed out about twenty minutes later. He was completely drained and wouldn't wake up from this deep sleep until mid afternoon. By then, everything in his life would be turned upside down.

Bull and Sal pulled up in the alley behind Anthony's parents' store about six-thirty in the morning. Since it was early November, it would still be dark for at least another thirty minutes or so, which was enough time for them to get their business done. At this time in the morning, they didn't have to worry about other customers who might get in the way. The plan was just to put the fear of God into them and send a message to Anthony. Some merchandise would be thrown around, shelves would be knocked over, and glass would be broken, all done with a lot of yelling and screaming.

This was the usual business when they went to go see any store owner who was late with their payments and, like with most plans, the unexpected sometimes happened and fucked-up everything. But, neither one of them could imagine how fucked they would be after this visit.

Bull did most of the talking while they sat in the car.

"I want this to go smoothly, so let's go over a couple of things before we head in there. I'll do most of the talking while you go and turn the place upside down. Remember, this is just a message to Anthony, so don't go overboard with destroying the place. I don't want these people spending weeks cleaning up the disarray that we leave the place in. Understand?"

"Yeah, no problem, you know I don't like messing with older folks who don't have anything to do with us. I ain't a total fucking degenerate. Give me some credit," Sal responded.

"I know how involved in your work you get once you get started, so I am just trying to make myself clear. No physical contact whatsoever, right?"

Sal was now getting a little irritated with Bull. He didn't like being talked down to, but Bull was in charge, so he just kept nodding his head and saying all right.

"Now if we are on the same page, let's get this over with," Bull exclaimed as he opened the door and got out of the car.

Mickey was in the back supply room and never heard the bell when Sal and Bull first came into the store. Erma realized right away that something was not right as they approached her at the register. They had owned the store for over forty years, and not once were they ever robbed. But, robbery was the last thing on Erma's mind, since they were obviously neighborhood guys who weren't trying to conceal themselves. At this point, she wished they were just two punks who were only there to rob them.

"You must be Mrs. Albergo. We are acquaintances of your son. Have you seen the little douche bag lately, because we have been looking for him for days now," Bull informed her as he approached the register.

As Bull was conducting his inquiry with Erma, Sal headed down the first aisle and began his work of implementing their message for Anthony. He was standing in front of at least fifty jars of various spaghetti sauces when he decided that this was as good as any place to start. Sal lunged forward and with one big push, the aisle toppled over in a booming crash. Erma screeched as she jumped back from the register.

"Listen to me, you stupid bitch. Your son has gotten himself in a lot of trouble with the wrong people. You could say he owes these people quite a bit of money. Has he been around asking you for any money? We know that Anthony doesn't have that kind of money anymore, so we figure he might come here looking for some help. Well, what do you say Mrs. Albergo, has Anthony been here lately?" he demanded.

Erma was in complete shock from what was going on. She couldn't think straight. Even if she could, how could she convince these two men that they had cut Anthony out of their lives earlier this year? She now turned her attention to the area where the loud crash had come from, and saw Sal standing in front of what remained of aisle one.

"Hey grand mom, stay with me here," Bull yelled at her as he snapped his fingers in front of her.

"You just pay attention to me and forget about what else is going on in here. The sooner you give me the answers I want to hear, the quicker we get out of your store."

Tears were now streaming down her cheeks. She had never been so frightened in her life and with that fear came the hatred for Anthony, who was the reason why these men were in here destroying their store.

Mickey almost fell off the crate of oranges that he was sitting on when he heard the crash. He had absolutely no idea what could have caused that noise, but he had an idea that something wasn't right, and his hunch was correct once he heard Erma scream. It wasn't the kind of scream made by a sudden and unexpected surprise; it was more of a scream of total horror. Mickey's worse trepidation had come true; the people who were after Anthony had come looking for him or, even worse, maybe they were looking for him and Erma.

Mickey's first reaction was to go running to the front of the store and help Erma. However, something didn't add up. He started to wonder, how long had they been in the store already? It had to be at least five minutes. They wouldn't just come storming in and start knocking over whatever it was that caused that commotion he thought and, if that was the case, then why didn't someone come back here and get him? The answer to this was that they had totally forgotten about Mickey being in the store, which meant that he now had a slight edge.

When Anthony had visited him the other day and questioned why the back door was locked, he had responded that he was preparing for any unexpected visitors that might show up looking for Anthony. Now what he didn't tell Anthony was that he had also brought in a twelve-gauge shot gun, and at this moment he was saying a short prayer of thanks to God that he kept it back here in the supply room rather than in the front behind the counter. He figured if they were going to get a visit, the people wouldn't be foolish enough to come through the front door. Obviously, he gave these guys too much credit because they were arrogant enough to do just that.

*   *   *

"I'm not going to ask you again Mrs. Albergo, has he or has he not been in here asking you for money? We know he was here yesterday. Did he ask you for the money or not?" Bull asked as his patience grew thinner and thinner.

Erma shook her head back and forth as she replied, "I haven't seen or talked to Anthony in months since the divorce."

Bull looked over at Sal and gave him a little nod, and Sal wasted no time heading to the back of the store, where he stopped in front of the glass refrigerators holding the various milks, fruit drinks and sodas.

"Do you want my friend over there to keep having his way in your store? He really enjoys this part of his job. You can say he is like a little kid who can make all the mess that he wants, because he knows no one is going to make him clean it up. Tell me what the fuck Anthony said to you when he was in here yesterday," Bull demanded.

"I swear Anthony wasn't here…." but before she could finish, she was interrupted by the sound of the four glass doors shattering from the baseball bat that Sal had swung into them.

Once again, Erma screamed in terror. She didn't understand why these men thought Anthony was here yesterday.

"Please, I am telling you the truth, he wasn't here yesterday. I swear to God," she cried out to Bull.

Bull gave her his ultimatum. "Lady we can play this game all fucking day, but if you don't give me the fucking details of your conversation, the next thing to be broken won't be anything from the store."

Erma was frozen in place. She didn't have the slightest clue what to say that would satisfy these men and, what was even worse, she didn't know where Mickey was this whole time. Did Mickey slip out the back door to go get help? Because God only knew how much longer she could last under these circumstances. Erma believed that they were going to get physical if she didn't give the right answers.

"You have got to believe me. I haven't talked to him. I don't know who told you that he…." She didn't finish, because out of nowhere there was a sudden loud thud as Sal hit the floor.

Mickey came out from the back room just when Sal had finished breaking the glass and was looking towards the front of the store at Bull for further guidance. Neither one of them saw Mickey approaching, which allowed him to get off a clear swing with the shotgun. The shotgun connected at the base of Sal's neck, and he immediately hit the ground. Before Bull could even comprehend what had just happen; Mickey was just twenty feet away from him with the shotgun pointed straight at his head.

"You must be a real tough guy picking on a defenseless old woman. Makes you feel like a real man does it? Well, let's just see how much of a real man you truly are, tough guy," Mickey yelled at him, as all his rage started to cloud his judgment.

"Now hold on there, Mr. Albergo. All I want to know is where Anthony is, and are you going to give him the fifty thousand that he owes my boss," Bull started to explain.

"I don't give a rat's ass as what you want to know. All I want to know is if you are man enough to get on your knees and beg me and my wife for forgiveness. The way I see it is two guys came into my store, vandalized it, threatened me and my wife with violence, and then tried to take all the money from the register. Now if you ask me, I think any judge in his right mind would rule that I shot you in self defense," he carefully painted the picture for Bull.

"Mickey, where in the world did you get that thing?" she asked as tears continued to fall. "You know how I feel about guns."

"Erma, just relax and pick up the phone and call the police while I finish this nice chat with this fellow."

Unfortunately for Mickey, he was so wrapped up with Bull that he committed the same vital mistake that Bull and Sal made earlier by getting wrapped up in his conversation. He totally forgot about Sal in the back of the store, as they had done with him. The strike to the back of Sal's neck would have been a knock-out blow under normal circumstances, but Mickey was sixty-four years old and his swing didn't pack that much punch. Plus, Sal was a big man like Bull, whose body was that of a NFL line-man. The initial blow had only stunned Sal. He laid there for a couple of moments gathering his thoughts, when he realized that they had forgotten about Mickey in the back room and that it must have been him who came up from behind and struck him on his neck.

Sal couldn't believe that he had let his guard down like that. How could they have made such a critical mistake? With some mistakes came a chance for redemption, and Sal was going to get his redemption in the worst of ways. He had gotten to his feet slowly, trying to keep Mickey in his sights and stay out of Bull's view. If Bull saw Sal get up, his sudden expression might tip off Mickey and cost him any chance of a surprise attack of his own.

Sal slowly came up the third aisle, which appeared to be a blind spot for the three of them in the front of the store. The only way that Mickey or Erma could have noticed Sal was if they looked up into the mirror in the corner of the ceiling. Luckily for Sal, Mickey's total attention was with Bull and as for Erma; she was still in a state of shock from all that was happening. Sal had the baseball bat in both hands as he approached Mickey. Sal was only about five feet from him when Mickey noticed Bull's eyes widen. Mickey turned around just in time to see Sal's bat whisk by, inches from the bridge of his nose, and he pulled the trigger of the shot-gun at the same time.

Mickey hadn't fired a gun since Korea and, unfortunately for him, it hadn't been a shot-gun. The pure force of the gun sent his shot blindly in the air and Mickey to the floor. Since Sal had swung and failed to connect with Mickey's face, the force of his swing sent him sprawling into the shelves and Mickey's shot missed him completely.

The blast from the gun was deafening, and it drowned out Erma's screams of horror. Both Mickey and Sal tried to collect themselves off the floor. Before Mickey could get up in time, Bull was standing over him with his 9mm drawn and pointed right at his head.

"So old man, you had to go out and be a hero, didn't you? You and that bitch wife of yours couldn't just answer my fucking questions. Now what the hell am I supposed to do?" he screamed at Mickey.

Mickey couldn't get his legs under him and laid there totally helpless. Once he realized he wasn't hit from the shot-gun, Sal was up and on his feet.

"Bull, we got to get the fuck out of here. I'm sure someone had to hear that blast, and the cops will be here any minute."

"I'm not leaving until I get what I came here for," he replied to Sal.

"Fuck that shit, I am out of here. It's getting to be daylight out there, and we have to get to the car before someone can id us," Sal tried to convince Bull that his idea was the best plan of action, as he headed back down the aisle and toward the back door.

Bull was now in his own world. He was oblivious to what Sal was trying to convey to him. Bull wasn't great at handling the pressures that occurred when a plan didn't work out.

"I am not going to ask again, what did you and Anthony talk about? Are you giving him the money or not?" he demanded from Mickey, as he pointed the gun right at the center of his face.

Mickey realized it didn't matter what he said to Bull, because he was never going to get up from this spot. Everything had gone wrong for these two guys, and there was no way that they were going to leave him alive. He only prayed that the asshole didn't hurt Erma.

"Does it really matter if I tell you either way? I think you are going to kill me. Nevertheless, I am willing to tell you want you want to hear, as long as you guarantee me that you won't harm my wife."

Bull couldn't believe that this old man was making demands from him as he lay on the floor, looking straight up at a gun pointed at his face. Before Bull could answer him; he heard the faint sound of police sirens approaching.

"You want me to guarantee you that I won't harm that bitch over there?" he asked, as he pointed the gun towards Erma.

Mickey only had the chance to scream no, as Bull turned and shot Erma two times in the chest. She had time to squeal once, but after the second bullet hit her she dropped to the floor in silence.

"After all the shit you have caused me, you want to give me demands? Well old man, you were right, I wasn't going to let you live," Bull told him as he bent down and put the gun right on Mickey's forehead.

"At least you'll be with her again," he told him as he pulled the trigger.

Bull ran for the back door without looking back. When he got into the car, Sal immediately put the car in reverse and drove down the alley.

"I heard four shots, what the fuck did you do in there?" he demanded from Bull.

"What do you mean what did I do? Did you think I was going to leave them alive? You know as well as I do that that wasn't an option."

Sal could only shake his head in disbelief. Everything was totally fucked-up, and he knew it. There was no way that this wasn't going to get back to Frankie. "This is so fucked-up," he cried to Bull. "We are dead, you know that? We are totally dead. Frankie isn't going to think twice about this. Bull, we got to just ride and get the hell out of the city. I can't…" And then there was a sting in his face as Bull slapped him.

"Get a fucking hold of yourself. No one is going to pin this on us. Yeah, I'm sure Frankie will bring some heat on us, but what proof do they have? There are no cameras in the store. Do you think a place like that doesn't get robbed? No one saw us in there. I'm sure the cops will just blame two niggers and that will be that," he explained to Sal, as a father might explain something complex to a ten year old.

"How dumb do you think cops are, Bull? Jesus Christ, you shot and killed two senior citizens in their store. I think there will be a big investigation. I don't think cops are that stupid to just blame some niggers from a gang and act like this is a typical robbery," Sal blurted back. But as he finished, one critical flaw in this story came to his mind. He turned and asked Bull a question that he already knew the answer. "Did you take the money from the register?"

Bull didn't need to answer his question; Sal saw it in his expressions.

Once again they had made a significant mistake. Neither one of them took the money out of the cash register. There was no way in the world anyone would believe that this was a robbery. Two people were gunned down, and no money was taken? It looked more like a hit than a robbery, and who in their right mind places a hit on a couple of seniors?

"Jesus Christ Bull, we are really fucked on this one. We should have just waited for Friday. Man, I can't believe we are really fucked."

Unlike Sal, Bull was not as emotional. He was Frankie's nephew and he believed he could get out of this; he just needed some time to think about it. The first thing they needed to do was to check in with Frankie like normal. The news of their action wouldn't reach Frankie for at least a couple of hours. If they called him about Anthony's night and asked what to do next, it would give them some kind of alibi for now. It wasn't the out he was looking for, but it would buy them some time. In the end he could hold up to Frankie's interrogation, but he didn't have any faith that Sal could. Right now, he just needed to get some composure and think about how calm he needed to be before he talked to Frankie.

To Anthony's surprise, it was only a little after eleven when he looked at the clock. He was wide awake and feeling really good for the first time in months. There were no guarantees that everything was going to work out and things could go back to normal, but his heart kept holding on to that hope. Anthony was never going to get Sandra and Kimberly back, but if he could be involved in Kimberly's life, that was a step in the right direction.

As for his parents, he felt confident that he could get the three of them together again as a family. He would get out of his lease for that shit-hole apartment that he called home and move back in with his parents. The only question left to answer was, what was he going to do about a job? Anthony didn't want to go back to being a trader, because the working environment would be too tempting for him to try and make a quick buck here and there. It would be the same as getting a job as a bartender in a casino. The enticement of money would be too great. Once he paid Frankie, he was sure that Frankie could get him a decent job down at the docks. Hell, he wouldn't even mind working down at the store for his parents to give them some quality time off.

As he rolled over and stared at the ceiling, he believed today was going to be a great day. He decided not to lie around and wait any longer to embark on his new life. The sooner he got to the store to talk to his dad, the quicker every-thing could get back to the way it was before he started his gambling problem. As Anthony walked out of the casino, his outlook on life never seemed brighter. In less than two hours from now, this outlook would all change for the worse.

Bull and Sal pulled into the Golden Eagle Diner parking lot ten minutes after they left the store. In those ten minutes, Bull had gotten himself under control the best that he could.

He turned to Sal as he was turning off the car, and said, "We're going to go inside, order some breakfast, calm the fuck down, and then I am going to call Frankie and give him a heads-up about Anthony's night. You got any problems with that?"

Sal just shook his head and said nothing. In less than twenty minutes, he went from a lieutenant in Frankie's family to a dead man. This in no way should have happened and Bull was going to make it worse for them, but Sal didn't have the slightest idea how to rectify the situation.

"Good, let's get inside and eat, I'm fucking hungry."

Brenda, their waitress, walked them to a booth all the way in the back in the smoking section, because Bull told her they wanted to be away from everyone else. She poured each of them a cup of coffee and left two menus and told them she would be back in five minutes. Bull took out his cell phone and dialed *The Club*. If he was lucky Vincent would answer, because Frankie was always with his mother or Ellena Maria in the kitchen at this time of the day anyway.

After what seemed to be a lifetime to Bull, Vincent finally answered. "Vin-cent, it's Bull, is Frankie there?"

"Nah, he's with his mother in the kitchen. What's up?"

"Just let him know that Anthony didn't score in A.C. last night. The dumb fuck was supposedly up twenty g's, and then got busted out in the high roller's no limit room on one hand. We left after he checked into a room."

"Holy shit, the kid was actually up twenty g's and lost it? What a fucking shame. I'll give Frankie the news. Where are you now?" Vincent asked.

"Sal and I are getting some breakfast. We left A.C. around six o'clock and are starving. After this, I am going home to crash for awhile. Tell Frankie if he needs me I'll be there," he answered, without even a thought that he might be interrogated.

"Alright, I'll give him the message. By the way you know it's only Tuesday, if the kid was up twenty in one day, he still has three days to try to get it to fifty."

"Yeah, yeah, like that will ever happen. Once a loser, always a loser," he replied.

"So what did he say?" Sal asked, with that sickening feeling in his stomach, still eating away at him ever since he heard those four shots.

"Vincent said Frankie was in the kitchen as usual, and I just told him about the kid's misfortunes. No big deal! Now, the sooner you get your mind off of it, the quicker we can collaborate on our story."

Anthony's arrival back to the city took much longer than Bull and Sal's. He was at such inner peace with himself, that he hadn't the slightest idea that he was barely doing sixty the whole way home. He even had the radio on, and was singing along with the songs. You could say that Anthony had found his happy place, but like most places, you eventually have to leave them.

Anthony decided that he was going to go directly to his parents' store before heading home. It was one-thirty, and he figured that he could convince his dad to go get some lunch and talk for awhile. Anthony and his father hadn't gone to lunch with each other since he was a kid.

As Anthony approached the Italian Market, there was traffic and people everywhere. He couldn't turn down the alley that their store backed up to, because two cop cars were blocking it. Three police men were standing in front of the yellow tape and barriers that they had set up. This was extremely strange to Anthony, because in all his life there had never been any police activity down in this area.

He decided to drive down another block to park the car and walk his way back to the store. Anthony couldn't believe that it took him twenty minutes to find a spot. He was a good ten minute walk from the store. While he walked, alarms should have been going off in his head, but today his mind was in a different place and terrible thoughts were not allowed.

When Anthony got to the front of the street, it was blocked-off just like the back alley. There were more cops and cars blocking off the street, and still nothing registered with Anthony. The most obvious sign was the look of the other merchants from the street. Many were crying, while others just stood in shock with their heads down. He was halfway down the street, when an officer grabbed Anthony by the arm and asked, "Where do you think you are going?"

"Ease up there, blue. My name is Anthony Albergo and I am just trying to get to my parents' store, if that's alright with you?" he answered, without the slightest idea that most of these officers were looking for him.

"Did you say Albergo?" the cop asked with the surprise of just being awoken from a dream.

"Yeah, that's right. My name is Anthony. Can I get to my parents' store, or is there a problem somewhere on the street blocking it?"

"Anthony, I want you to turn around, face the car and put your hands on the roof," he directed Anthony like a drill sergeant on the first day at boot camp.

"What? You got to be kidding me? What the hell for?" Anthony demanded.

"Son, if you don't turn around at once, I'm going to put your head through that fucking window. Now do it," he screamed into his face.

Anthony couldn't imagine what was going on. He didn't have the vaguest idea what this officer's problem was with him, or why he wanted to handcuff Anthony. With no other option coming to his mind, Anthony turned around with his back to the officer. Officer Mike Minko had been on the force for over ten years and had seen some of the city's most brutal crimes, none of those could compare to what he saw in that store this morning.

"All I know, son, is there are two people dead in a store down there, and you are the main suspect. An all-out city bulletin was placed on you. So if I was you, I would just relax here until the detectives arrive," he clarified to Anthony.

"What do you mean, two dead bodies? Why the hell would I be a suspect in two murders? Who the hell could I possibly kill?" Anthony demanded to know. But, his question fell on a deaf ear.

Mike was old school and loved to get physical when he could with a suspect. He was an ex-minor league baseball player who had no problems throwing his one hundred and eighty pounds around when he wanted answers. Mike loved the death penalty and if it was up to him, many of America's jail cells would be empty right about now. He also thought that this country had the world's worst judicial system and if he had his say, many of these scumbags wouldn't get their day in court. He saw what a bunch of niggers could do in a high profile case in California, and he didn't want Anthony to get that chance. However this wasn't LA and the people in this city usually came together when it came to putting away scum like him.

Mike clicked the button of his radio and summoned Detective Fishburn.

"Fishburn here," crackled through the radio.

"It's Officer Mike Minko from the 12th precinct. I am four stores away heading south of the crime scene, and I have detained the son," Mike responded back into the radio.

"When did he arrive? Never mind, just keep him there and don't make a scene. I don't need people getting out of control and making this a circus," Fishburn replied back.

"Don't worry I have him cuffed and in my patrol car."

"Why the hell is he cuffed?" Fishburn cried back.

"We were told to detain him no matter what."

"Officer Minko, do you know the difference between detained and hand cuffed? Get him the hell out of those cuffs. I will be down there in a second," he roared. There was now only silence in Minko's radio.

"Jesus Christ! What the fuck is up his ass? I can't believe how lucky you are that I am not in charge of this investigation, son," Mike complained to a still stunned Anthony.

"I still don't know why you have me in cuffs in the first place. I just came down from Atlantic City to see my parents and you stopped me for God knows what reason," he answered back, in a not so amused voice.

This was not the way Anthony had imagined his day starting off. Clearly, this cop had to have the wrong guy. "You're wrong son; God isn't the only one who knows."

Anthony didn't have a chance to think about that last comment, because Detective Joseph Fishburn arrived on the scene.

"Anthony Albergo?" he asked, as he pulled out his badge.

"Yes, I am Anthony. Would you mind telling me what is going on here? It seems to me that this officer wouldn't mind having me alone in a room for five minutes."

Detective Fishburn turned to Officer Minko and asked him, "I guess you didn't take the sympathetic approach? Did you tell him anything, or did you just cuff him and throw him in the car?"

Mike started to get defensive quickly. "No one said we had to baby this guy. He's a big boy and if you want to walk him through this by holding his hand, go for it. As for me, I could care less," Mike answered.

As Officer Minko walked away from the two of them, Detective Fishburn turned back towards Anthony and tried to control the damage that Officer Minko had started to create. "Anthony, my name is detective Joseph Fishburn and this is Detective Engman. I know Officer Minko hasn't been the kindest of people, so I would like you to take a walk with me and Detective Engman."

"I am not going anywhere until you explain to me why that asshole would think that I had something to do with a double homicide," he demanded.

After taking the time to look at Anthony's face, which went from a look of total frustration to a look of utter terror, Joe was certain of two things. The first was that Anthony had no idea that his parents had been murdered and second, he obviously wasn't the murderer. The hard part was now explaining to this poor kid that two or three sick sons of bitches had just murdered his parents in cold blood.

"Anthony, I would really rather we take that walk first and get away from this scene before we go into details of what happened," Joe tried to explain, with that sympathetic tone one would use on someone who knows that you are hiding something horrible from them, and it was too late for that.

It was hard for Joe to pull this off, considering he was an ex-Army ranger who was six two and two hundred and twenty pounds. He still kept his hair in a buzz cut and always wore a short sleeve shirt when he worked to show off his arms and the numerous tattoos on them. Joe didn't come off as a guy who showed a lot of sympathy in his line of work.

Anthony was a pro at reading people, and he realized something was terribly wrong; he could see it on Detective's Fishburn's face. All the signs that weren't registering in Anthony's mind earlier finally started to hit home. The way the people looked at him when he came down the street. The sad and shocked look on the faces of the other merchants who knew his parents and, the most obvious, the way Officer Minko wanted to kill Anthony if he was given the chance to be alone with him. Like a tidal wave crashing on an unexpecting seacoast, the answer finally came to him.

"Oh my God, it's my parents? Someone killed my parents? **NO, NO, NO,** that's impossible. They never did anything wrong to anybody. Why would someone kill them?" he asked these questions to the two detectives, but he already knew the answers.

"Please let me go down there and see them. I want to see them," he demanded at once. "I deserve that right."

Joe walked up to Anthony and put his hands on Anthony's shoulders and told him, "Anthony don't just hear me, but listen to what I am about to tell you. If you really loved your parents and you want to always have beautiful memories to fall back on, please believe me when I tell you that the last thing that you need to do is go into that store and see their bodies. This wasn't just a random shooting. It looks like they were more or less executed."

"Executed? What the hell do you mean executed?"

"I have been a detective for many years and I have seen my share of some horrible and gruesome murders, but this has topped them all. Detective Engman and I once walked into an apartment that a crack whore lived in and discovered a two year old boy that was left handcuffed to a crib for over three weeks before we found him. That was the only time that I actually lost my nerve and threw up at the scene of the crime. You must understand when I tell you that you don't want to have an image worse than that of your parents in your mind forever. There is too much blood and one of them is unrecognizable."

Anthony's heart was beating out of control. He couldn't keep up with the rush of feelings falling over him. Never in his wildest dreams did he imagine Frankie sending someone to kill his parents. This was the last thought that went through his mind, as his body could no longer keep up with his racing heart, and he collapsed in the street.

Frankie was in the kitchen rolling a pile of ground meat into meatballs when Vincent came out of the back room.

"Boss, I think you need to come in here for a second. It looks like we got a big problem." Frankie couldn't imagine what kind of problem would make Vincent look as white as he was at that moment. The only thing that jumped into his mind was that someone in the crew got whacked or pinched; he could live with whacked, a pinch only leads to legal hassles and he doesn't need that bullshit.

"Momma, can you get Ellena to help with the meat balls? I have to tend to some business," he said with a smile that all sons show a mother when they know that the mother would never say no to them. She just looked at him and nodded her head back and forth, then turned and walked out of the kitchen.

Frankie went to the sink and washed the ground meat off his hands and headed to the back room to see what kind of problem was awaiting him on this Tuesday afternoon.

When he entered the room, Vincent was on the phone with Charlie DeLuca.

"Yeah, yeah I know it's a big fucking problem. No, he doesn't know yet. Of course I told him there's a problem, you fucking idiot. Let me go, he just walked into the room."

"Okay that didn't sound good. Would you mind telling me what's going on?" he asked Vincent.

Vincent didn't want to try to explain what he knew; he only pointed to the television above the bar. Frankie turned to see what was on the TV that was causing all the commotion. Channel six was just interrupting *The Young and the Restless* with the breaking news.

A perky little brunette was standing live outside the Italian Market.

"This is Dee Degirmenci reporting live from the Italian Market section of the city, where we have now received confirmation that two people have been brutally murdered. The police believe that this looks like a robbery that had gone badly, and now two innocent people have lost their lives. From the reports that I have received, it looks like two or three perpetrators entered the 'Albergo' family produce store before sunrise and tried to rob the owners. It appears that Mr. Albergo, the storeowner, surprised them with a shotgun. Unfortunately, Mr. Albergo and his wife were not able to defend themselves, and both were slaughtered in cold blood. Police have not determined yet how many people were involved in the break-in, or why these criminals would pick a little produce store like this to burglarize.

Randy, this truly is a senseless crime. Why someone would murder two senior citizens for so little money just makes you wonder what kind of society we live in today. When we get further information we will break in live again. This is Dee Degirmenci for Channel Six news, reporting live from the Italian Market. Now back to you, Randy."

Channel Six's anchorman Randy Moore continued the update from the station's news desk. "Once again, to recap this breaking story, two people have been murdered in their family store early this morning in the Italian Market section of the city while trying to stop a robbery. When we get further information, we will broadcast live from the scene. This is Randy Moore for Channel Six, now back to your local programming."

Needless to say, this was far worse than anything Frankie had expected. He couldn't believe what he had just witnessed. He didn't need to be a detective to know that this wasn't a botched robbery. Frankie realized that he didn't have to think too hard to know who committed these murders and why and if he could, then it wouldn't take the police that much longer. The only question was how much time could he buy himself? A week, more likely less, and if Anthony wanted to have a say in this, he was looking at a maximum of two days, which wasn't enough time to get things organized.

"What the fuck happened?" he turned and asked Vincent.

"I don't know boss. Bull called earlier this morning from a diner on his way home from Atlantic City. He told me that they left as soon as Anthony checked into a room after getting busted out of a high stakes game. The only other thing he said was that they were tired and, after they were done eating, he was going home and crash. I swear Frankie that was all he said."

Frankie was still in disbelief as to how this could happen without his approval. What approval? What kind of fucking monster approves the killing of two senior citizens as a warning to some schmuck to pay off his debt?

"Vincent, I need to know how he sounded. Did he sound unnerved in any way, or did he perhaps sound over-excited about Anthony busting out? Tell me how he sounded," Frankie demanded.

"Boss, nothing sounded out of the ordinary. He was just calling in like normal. I didn't think anything of it at the time. I'm sorry!"

Frankie wouldn't have expected Vincent to pick up anything from the phone call. It wasn't his responsibility. Frankie, on the other hand, would have noticed the slightest change of tones in Bull's voice. This was how he could always tell when someone was lying to him.

One question that was eating at Frankie's mind was why Bull would drive all the way back to the city in the early morning hours, instead of staying in A.C. and celebrating. He knew Bull loved the nightlife in A.C. It didn't make sense for him to come home. Things just weren't adding up and if it was the last thing he ever did, Frankie was going to get to the bottom of this predicament.

"Vincent, God help me if I am right, but you and I both know that no one in their right mind sticks up a family owned produce store. What the fuck were those two thinking?" he asked.

"Come on Frankie, I can't believe Bull and Sal would do something that sick. They know that they would be whacked for it. I mean I know they are a couple of head cases, but fucking killing two civilians is even beyond them," he answered back, confident in his thinking.

"You are right. I don't think that they would have planned on doing something that deranged, but if they went there to get a point across and they were surprised like the news said, then yes I think they could have done it." Frankie went over to the bar and turned off the television. He hadn't felt this disgusted in a long time.

"I want you to get on the phones and get a hold of everyone who we need and have them meet at Tony's Pizza in two hours for an emergency meeting," he commanded.

Tony's was a place they used when they were keeping their meeting a secret from someone in the crew. Vincent usually stayed at *The Club* in case that person would show up looking for everyone. Usually that never was the case, because Frankie would send them on an errand that would take up most of the time of the meeting.

"Make sure under no circumstances do Sal or Bull find out. Am I absolutely clear about this?"

"Yeah, sure thing Frankie, but what are you going to do about the kid? Do you think someone should pick him up?" he inquired.

"It's all over the news, so I am sure he knows about it by now. If he's not home already, he's en route and I think it best to leave him be for now."

Vincent was totally puzzled. Even he knew that the main goal should be to get Anthony before the cops do. If the police got to him first, he would surely lead them to Frankie. "Are you sure Frankie? I mean the kid can totally sink us. He'll lead the police right to you," he explained.

"I have been in this business long enough to know that Anthony won't say anything right away. More than likely, he is in total shock right now and once he starts to think straight, he'll realize that he is just as much a suspect as Bull and Sal. He's not a stupid kid. He'll realize that Bull did this, and it obviously was a mistake."

"Why would you think it was a mistake?"

"Because, if Bull wanted to kill anyone it would have been him, not his parents. When the police find out that he is a regular at *The Club* and he has a gambling problem, they might come to the conclusion that Anthony might have killed his parents for the insurance money and the ownership of the store. It's not like they have been on the greatest of terms lately since the divorce. No, I think we'll be fine leaving him alone for now. As for the other two, I'll make some calls to the guys down at the 12th precinct who are on our payroll to see if they can give us more enlightening information."

"Are you sure you want to wait that long? I mean, the kid isn't even one of us."

"He might not be one of us, but that kid has done a great deal for me and he knows it. I don't want him touched until after our meeting at Tony's. Now get on those phone calls. I need to think over our options before we leave."

♣   ♣   ♣

Anthony's faint lasted less than ten minutes, and when he awoke he discovered himself in Detective Fishburn's car.

"He's coming around," Phil indicated to Joe.

"Are you with us Anthony?" Joe turned around and asked Anthony, who still wasn't all there.

Anthony started to realize that it wasn't a horrible dream that he was waking from, but a horrifying reality. "I guess so. Detective Fishburn and Engman, right?"

The first thought that came to Anthony was how different looking Joe and Phil were from each other. Joe looked like a guy that could kill a man in less than a second while Phil, with his thin, blond hair combed straight back and his spectacle glasses, looked more like a professor from a university than a detective. Phil was barely six foot tall and was extremely thin for his size. He didn't look like he had a mean bone in his body.

"By the look on your face, I guess everything is coming back to you?" Joe asked, as he wondered how long it would be before Anthony could go through all their questions.

Anthony sat back and closed his eyes. It was still too early to try to understand why they killed his parents, but one thing he did know, Frankie wasn't behind it. Frankie would never have allowed this for a lousy fifty thousand dollars considering Anthony had made him millions over the past couple of years. Only one person could have killed his parents, and that animal was Bull.

"Are you taking me back to the station for questioning?" Anthony asked as he opened his eyes.

Phil turned to Joe, who gave him the nodding signal that it was okay for him to answer. It was now Phil's opportunity to turn around and converse with Anthony. "We thought it would be best to take you up a little way to the Golden Eagle Diner, where we could ask you some questions in a nice relaxing atmosphere. Since you aren't a suspect you don't have to agree to this, but right now a lot of things aren't adding up in the murder of your parents and we believe you can help with the investigation," he asserted.

"Why the hell would you think I know the reason why someone killed my parents?" he asked in a defensive tone.

As Joe pulled into the diner parking lot, he didn't bother to turn around before he answered him. "Anthony, why don't we wait until we get inside before we start with the questions?"

"Look, I'll answer whatever questions that you might have, because there is no one else in this world who wants to get to the bottom of this more than me," he replied.

As the three of them entered the diner, not one of them was aware of the sad irony that just thirty minutes earlier, Sal and Bull walked out these same doors.

"I love you, you love me, and we're a happy family…." Barney was singing to Kimberly from the television in front of her. *Barney and Friends* was her favorite television show, and from two to two-thirty she ritually sat on her little chair with her Barney doll singing right along with him. Sadly for Kimberly, her routine was about to be interrupted.

It was a little past two in the afternoon when the Pettyjohn's phone rang. It wasn't until the forth ring that Sandra picked up the phone, because she was in the middle of preparing Kimberly's afternoon snack.

"Hello?"

"Hi Hon, it's me," Chad replied back from the other end of the line.

"What a pleasant surprise. No more patients today?" she asked.

"No, I am in between patients right now and I heard something terrible, and I had to get a hold of you before someone else did. I assume you haven't had the news on yet today?" he asked.

"Now that's a silly question. You know the princess is in front of the TV with her favorite purple dinosaur. Why do you ask? Is there something wrong?"

There was a slight pause before Chad answered. "I don't know how to tell you, so I think it would be best for you to just put on one of the three major news channels. The story is all over the news today," he informed her.

"My God Chad, what's happened?" her voice cracked as she asked him.

"Please, it's best if you see for yourself instead of hearing it over the phone from me. Honey, I am truly sorry! I love you and I'll see you later tonight."

"Wait, please Chad…." but before she could finish, there was only a dial tone on the other end of the line.

Panic started to set into her mind, but the only assuring thing right now was that the two most important people to her in the world were fine, and Chad didn't seem to be that upset. If it were a true emergency, he would have come home instead of calling her on the phone.

Not wanting to wait any longer, Sandra went into the living room where Kimberly was still sitting in awe on her chair, singing along with the purple dinosaur.

"No Mommy, put back on Barney," she started to jump up and down, throwing a fit.

"Honey, Mommy needs to see something real quick. Barney will be right back, okay?"

"No, Mommy, no," she yelled as she ran around the room in a tantrum, but at this point Sandra didn't notice because she was now watching the same emergency news broadcast that Frankie had basically seen over an hour ago.

"Oh my God, this can't be. Why would...." except she couldn't finish her sentence, because she was too choked up. Sandra loved Anthony's parents. The reason that she had kept away from them over the last year or so was to punish Anthony, not them. It was her hope that this might change Anthony. She could never have imagined that they would never see Kimberly again.

"Mommy put back on Barney! You said Barney would be right back."

"Honey, Mommy needs to see this, now stop bugging me or you'll never see that purple thing ever again," she turned and yelled at her.

Sandra turned back to the television, which was showing the scene right outside of her ex-in-laws' store. There were cops everywhere as the camera turned. The report was still the same as the one Frankie had seen. It just stated that the owner and his wife were brutally murdered during a botched robbery attempt this morning.

Sandra had seen enough and, without even realizing it, she turned Barney back on for Kimberly, which delighted her and ended the tantrum right away. Sandra went over to the couch and laid down, where she cried into a pillow for over an hour.

Brenda came over from her station and asked the three of them if they were ready to order as she poured them more coffee. Joe had asked if either of them wanted to order food, and both shook their head no. Anthony was starving, but figured putting food in his stomach right now wouldn't be the smartest of things. He was still feeling the effects of the faint and didn't want to add to it.

"Coffee will be all for today, Brenda," Joe replied with that fake cop smile.

Once Brenda was out of ear range, Joe turned to Anthony to start with the non-formal investigation. "Anthony, I can't imagine what you must be going through right now, so I won't even try to bullshit you on that. What I would like to do is go over some things with you that might help us with some of the loose ends. This is in no way an interrogation, and if there are any questions that you don't want to answer then don't. But if you can be honest with your answers and, more importantly, think long and hard before you answer, this will benefit in the progress of catching these animals. You might not think so, but the simplest little details can lead us in the right direction," he explained.

"I'll answer your questions the best I can."

With Anthony's approval, Joe started his interrogation. "First, let me tell you what we saw and concluded at the crime scene in your parents' store this morning. From what we gathered so far, there is no reason to believe that this was a robbery. Shit, let's not kid ourselves. To put it simply, this was an outright murder, and the perpetrators did a piss poor job trying to conceal it as a botched break in attempt," Joe informed him.

"So you think someone went into my parents' store to deliberately kill them and with no intentions at all of committing a robbery? I'm telling you that it makes absolutely no sense to me. As I have stated before, my parents are in their early sixties. Why would someone want to kill them?" he asked while trying to conceal the fact that he already knew these answers.

It was Phil's turn to jump into the conversation. "Like we said in the beginning, there are many circumstances that don't add up and we would like to go through them with you. The most important was that they didn't take any money from the cash register or the little safe your dad had in the storage room. Even if they were surprised by your father during the robbery, they wouldn't have left without the money, especially after killing both proprietors. Two junkies all juiced up on crack wouldn't have left without the money."

Joe continued from there. "And to top it off, the store itself is all wrong. They wouldn't have picked a produce store that had what, maybe thirty dollars in the register before seven o'clock in the morning. Furthermore, how many botched robberies did you ever hear of that started off with about ten minutes worth of destruction before they even made an attempt for the register. They turned over two whole aisles and broke a couple of glass doors in the back of the store. Why would a couple of petty thugs come into a store to do a quick smash and grab, and then decide to hang around for an extra ten to fifteen minutes to do all that destruction? That just doesn't add up."

Joe just shook his head back and forth.

"The second issue that bothers me is that none of the other merchants are coming forward to say they saw something. In a case of a double homicide that occurs in a public place, someone always comes forward saying they saw what happened, even if they didn't. There was one shot gun blast and at least three or four shots fired from a 9mm. Somebody somewhere had to have heard those shots and come running from their stores to see what caused those shots. Since no one has come forward, this tells us that they knew the suspects and are afraid to be a witness. Let's be honest, if it were a couple of home boys or Ricans, we couldn't keep them from rioting in the streets. There would be a race war in this city like you couldn't imagine. Remember back in the mid nineties in Boston, where that husband killed his pregnant wife in their car and then blamed a black guy? That city was turned upside down for weeks. The blacks still aren't forgetting that one."

Phil chimed back in. "Anthony, this is a close-knit, family owned business district. These people have known each other for decades. They care a lot about each other and their families. These suspects must have put the fear of God into them, for not one of them has come forward with any information, and the only kind of people that can do that is the mob. Another reason that we are leaning towards it being mob related is because your parents were not just murdered, but it looks more like they were executed. To the average person it looks like your mother was killed last for no reason other than not having any witnesses left, but I believe she was killed first and there is a reason behind this assumption. I feel she was killed first out of anger towards your father so he could witness her murder. They found your father on his back in one of the aisles right in view of the front counter, and it was in this aisle that he got off a shot at one of the perpetrators. He must have been knocked down by the second guy and while he was on his back, they shot your mother right in front of him. After they shot her, one of them leaned over your father and shot him point blank in the face and took most of his face off."

Phil stopped to take a sip of his coffee, so Joe decided to continue. "Anthony, most burglars that get surprised while in the middle of a heist, just take off as quickly as possible. If they happen to get into a shoot out, the first person that they would shoot would be the one shooting at them, not an unarmed old lady behind the counter. Have Phil and I painted a good enough picture for you so far?"

Joe paused. "Anthony, do you know how many armed robberies have been committed in the Italian Market over the last year?"

Without even hesitating, Anthony answered, "I'll assume a couple."

"Well you are wrong. There has not been a single one. In fact, there have only been three over the last seven years. This neighborhood is basically protected by the local mob Underboss. No local criminal would be stupid enough to do a robbery in any of these stores, no less a double homicide. Not only would we be looking for them, but so would the mob," Joe explained to him.

Anthony didn't even bother to try to respond to that. You didn't need to be a brain surgeon to realize how this looked, and he didn't want to insult their intelligence or expertise with a ridiculous response. He wasn't going to have to give up Frankie to them, because it would only be a matter of time before they tied the two of them together. Then what was he going to do? Frankie sure as hell would not wait for that to happen.

Anthony figured he had about two days before the police questioned his involvement with Frankie, and maybe even less than that before one of Frankie's gorillas delivered a bullet to the back of his head. If he expected to live past Thursday, he was going to have to meet with Frankie to come to some sort of an agreement. The way he saw it, this looked just as bad for Frankie. One of his crew members flew off the handle and brought some serious unwanted spot light on them and their bosses. Frankie was in as much shit with his boss Pete Ferrigno as Bull and Sal were with him. There might be a little hope for Anthony yet.

Phil saw Anthony start to wander off in thought, so he thought it was the right time to bring Anthony's involvement into question. "Anthony we called your office today and spoke to an Eric Thorne. He told us that you quit unexpectedly yesterday. Can you elaborate on that for us?"

The battle of wits between the three of them was beginning, and Anthony was too good to lose to these guys. Anthony realized that they were now going to bring him into the picture and see if he would slip up. "Yeah, that's right. So what of it? People don't ever quit a shitty job?" he replied.

"I don't know what your definition of shitty is Anthony, but Joe and I are city workers making an abysmal forty thousand a year. There are many risks with fewer rewards, and no one ever appreciates the good that we do for this city every day when we are out there on the streets. Now you, on the other hand, had a nice cushy job in a fancy office making a much higher salary, hardly any risks and endless opportunities for rewards. So enlighten us as to why you would throw that away one day, considering you have to pay rent and child support?" Phil questioned.

"Boy, you guys waste no time in doing your homework. Last time I checked, a basic stock broker brings home just enough to pay rent for a three bedroom apartment in this city, while he can make some fat whale millions for doing nothing other than making a phone call to him. Sure the bonuses are nice, but I guess I started to feel like you guys; unappreciated for all my work that I do for others without getting a kick back from them. They go to their summer homes in the Hamptons for their tans, while I lay on the roof top of my apartment for mine."

One thing Joe and Phil weren't prepared for were quick and logical answers from Anthony. It would be one thing if they were back at the station and he had been sitting in the interrogation room alone with a chance to rehearse his answers, but on the spot like this was different. They couldn't help but start to believe in what this kid had to say; just as Frankie did on the night he met Anthony for the first time.

Joe was the first to respond. "So what were you going to do for money? I mean, I'm sure you're financially covered now, after what occurred this morning." This was his chance to catch Anthony off guard, since Phil's question didn't hit home.

"Since I'm covered? Apparently I was wrong about the two of you doing your home work, because if you had done it as well as I thought, you would be aware that grocery store owners in the Italian Market didn't have much. What fucking kind of money do you think I am inheriting?"

"It's amazing what kind of money can fall into someone's lap when a parent dies," Phil responded.

"Oh I know, maybe they had some ridiculous life insurance policy for millions, because you know companies give them away all the time for high value clients like my parents. My parents didn't have any money and what little life savings they had went to my Syracuse education, so if you are suggesting that I had my parents killed for money then you obviously haven't done the math. In case you weren't aware, my parents and I haven't talked since my divorce. They were devastated when my ex-wife decided to keep them from seeing their grand-daughter. How could I even be sure that I would even be the benefactor if they died? Most likely they would have left everything to Kimberly."

It was Anthony's turn to sit back and analyze his answers. In his mind, he felt he gave cool, calm and collective responses to the two entrapping questions that they fired at him. The only thing he was hoping for was a little more time.

If they didn't buy his answers, more than likely there would be an official inter-rogation downtown tomorrow. But if he was right and they did believe him, it wouldn't be for a couple of days and time was what he needed the most.

It was close to three o'clock when Frankie got the meeting underway at Tony's. Tony's was just your basic pizzeria, but there was a back room just like at *The Club*, but much smaller. There were only two customers in the pizza joint, but once school let out the place would get jam-packed with students from Saint Joseph Prep High School, which was just two blocks over.

Sitting crowded around the small round table were Frankie's three lieuten-ants, Charlie De Luca, Carmine Vitola and Al Mongelli along with his first in command Vincent Lusi.

When Frankie held his special meetings at Tony's, he wasted no time in get-ting to the point because they were extremely important issues and they were usually up against the clock.

"I know everyone here understands why I called this meeting. These horri-ble murders have happened on our territory, and I want answers. Pete has already been notified and he wants someone's head on a fucking platter before the weekend."

Pete was Frankie's boss and he wasn't as merciful as Frankie was when it came to solving problems. He was known by everyone in the underworld as Saint Pete because of the numerous men that had the misfortune of losing their lives directly by him or by an order he gave. However, by looking at him you would never believe that this man could have killed so many people. Pete was only five feet four and very old looking. He was in his seventies with pure white hair that he always has brushed back, and a constant tan which he gets from all the time that he spends in Florida. But he didn't rule the mob all these years because of his strength, he was in charge because he knew how to get things done right and he took whatever means necessary to make that happen.

"He has made it very clear that we are to clear up this mess and not the cops. It would look disgraceful to our family to have the police catch these guys before us. Now I know most of you have either seen or heard the reports already but we can't believe the bullshit that the news is trying to sell to the public. You would think that they are trying to start a riot."

Carmine was the first to speak out. "There's no way that two or three fuck-ing jigs would be stupid enough to come on our turf and hit one of our stores."

This statement got two agreeing nods from Charlie and Al. Vincent Lusi, who already had his talk with Frankie earlier, just sat back and listened.

Al Mongelli, who was extremely street smart and Frankie's choice to replace him once he stepped down, offered his opinion. "Well considering we are short a couple important members of our crew, I'll assume Frankie you already have an idea as to what happened?" he asked.

"Once again Al, you never cease to amaze me with your cunning awareness. Yes, I believe that the two people missing from our meeting played a major role in these murders and if that's true, we are in big trouble. I'm sure that Vincent has informed you by now that the kid was into us for fifty g's and the two people who were murdered today were his parents. It's not hard to put one and one together and if we can add it up, it won't take the police long to either."

"Jesus Christ Frankie, what the hell were Bull & Sal thinking?" Charlie asked.

"That's the problem, I don't think they were thinking. I made some calls down at the station and our man there has informed me that the word out already is that it looked like a hit and not a robbery. I can't even begin to tell you how bad this looks right now and how hard the heat will come down on us for this," he explained.

Vincent, who was still just sitting quietly taking everything in decided it was his turn to be heard. "We need to take action now to stay in good graces with both Pete and the police. We have to clean up this mess quickly. The two of them have to disappear now, no if ands or buts."

"That's fucking easy for you to say. We're not talking about your nephew," Frankie screamed.

"Nephew or no nephew, he and his sick ass side-kick just killed two civilians and it's all over the news. Either they go or it's going to be you and I that will disappear. Pete is looking for someone to pay for this and I ain't picking up the fucking tab," he argued right back at Frankie.

Frankie and Vincent have been together for over forty years and they have been through almost everything that happens when you are involved in organized crime including prison time up state and Frankie knows that Vincent was absolutely one hundred percent right about what needs to be done.

Before things could get out of control and tempers flared, Al made a suggestion that would come from a person who was ready to be in charge. "Frankie, no one is suggesting that you push the button on Bull today, why don't we get him and Sal separated and find out exactly what went down. Don't you have to pick up some winnings in Vegas?"

Al jump started the wheels rolling in Frankie's mind. He had planned to take Ellena on a quick four day vacation in Vegas this weekend to pick up his three hundred thousand but this now gave him the perfect solution with what he can do with Bull. He'll have Bull ordered to *The Club* and tell him in light of the situations that just happened here, he can't go to Vegas and he needs Bull to go and pick up the money. While Bull is out there for three days, they will pay Sal a visit and find out what has happened. Sal wasn't very strong on his own and Frankie realized it wouldn't take much to find the answers. If it was Bull, Frankie would make the call to a friend out there and they will dig a hole in the desert, then Frankie wouldn't have Bull's blood on his hands.

"You just stumbled onto our solution Al. I was going to surprise Ellena with a quick four day get away to Vegas but instead I will send Bull. I'll just tell him with all of what has been happening I can't go and he'll just pick up the money for me. It's not like he hasn't gone to Vegas on errands before and as for Sal staying back, I'll just explain that if we catch the fucking animals I need Sal to handle their disposals. What does everyone think?"

"What about Sal? When do we pay him a visit and who is going to handle it?" Vincent had asked.

"When we get back, get on the phone and have Bull come down to *The Club* tonight. He'll be expecting you to call anyway. When he comes down with Sal, I'll tell him that he goes out first thing in the morning and Sal is to stay at home and wait for the call when we catch the guys. Victor and Al will take Bull to the airport and after his flight takes off they'll hit Sal's place. Once you have him under control, call in and Vincent and I will be right over. We'll have to stay at *The Club* because I'm sure Pete will be checking in on the hour for updates. Everyone understand what the plan is and his role in it? We can't fuck this up boys or it will mean the end for some of us," he declared. It was just that easy; Bull and Sal's fates had been sealed.

Phil believed they had kept Anthony here long enough. It was quite clear that Anthony had nothing to do with the murders of his parents yet he couldn't help sense that Anthony was hiding something. It didn't matter because once they got the papers to bring Anthony in for the official interrogation in that small crammed room with the hot lights and the tape recorder going, he would fold under the pressure.

"Well what do you say Joe? Did you get all you need from Anthony?"

After taking a long look at Anthony he nodded his head and agreed.

"Phil's right, we need to get you out of here so you can start on your parents' arrangements. I'm sure there are many people that you need to call and let know what happened. When my sister passed away, it was hell for three days with all the phone calls to and from relatives plus the calls to the funeral parlor, the church and so on. I truly feel for you Anthony since you are the only child. Do you have anyone that can help you for the next couple of days?" he asked.

"I haven't even given it much thought yet. I have a couple of girl cousins here and there and I'm sure they can lend a hand. I wouldn't even know where to begin other than contacting my parents' church. They were devoted members at St. Martin's so I am sure I can get assistance from one of the nuns or priests. I guess you are never prepared for something like this."

"Well just let us know if you need help in any way coping with this. There are plenty of phone numbers that will get you in contact with the right people that we can give you," Phil informed him.

"Thanks, but everything is so fucked-up, I just want to go home and start the process."

Joe handed the car keys over to Phil and told him, "Why don't you pull the car around because I want to talk to Anthony alone for one more minute if you don't mind."

"Sure, not a problem, I wanted to get a quick smoke anyway," he replied as he got up from the booth and headed towards the door.

After digesting everything that Anthony had told them, Joe felt strongly that Anthony was hiding something. Granted, Anthony wasn't the actual killer nor did he know who was but he sure as hell knew why his parents were killed. It was time to play his trump card. Joe has been involved with this neighborhood for over ten years and if there was one thing that was a given, it was that the mob was involved one way or another when something went down.

"Anthony, you can stay and listen to what I have to say or you can just get up and walk away if you want but trust me I am going to find out one way or another. Phil and I ran a check on you before we even got here. You are as clean as a baby's ass and have never been in any kind of trouble, not even as a kid. That's pretty amazing considering where you come from, no offense but most kids from your neighborhood have done one thing or another in their teenage years. Hell, you even graduated from Syracuse University and that's pretty amazing, so I'll give you your props. Nevertheless, I can't help but think you are lying to us about your involvement with your parents' murders."

Joe sat back in the booth and stared at Anthony waiting to see if there would be just that little reaction in Anthony's face but just like before, Anthony didn't reveal anything. He still showed no emotions when the average person would be fidgeting, looking everywhere other than at Joe or even reaching for a cigarette, anything to draw attention away from them.

Joe was just as impressed with Anthony now as he was after answering all their questions. The kid wouldn't crack and they both knew at this point that he wouldn't. The time to get Anthony to make a mistake had passed and there was nothing Joe could do about it now.

"If you are done putting down my neighborhood I would like to leave now," Anthony replied.

"Don't be so sensitive kid, we are all from this city and when I was in the 5th grade, I got caught stealing five packs of Fleer baseball cards from the corner store. The owner felt that my father would give me the beating of a lifetime if he got the cops involved instead of just calling my dad. Well, he was right, after the cops dropped me off at my house, my father whipped me with his belt for a good ten minutes until I was bleeding from my back, legs and ass. I was just surprised that you don't have a record, even if it was for something stupid like that. Most kids from the city eventually get themselves into trouble. Some get into the kind of trouble that follows them for the rest of their lives."

"You are a neighborhood kid too?" Anthony asked in surprise.

"All my life," he answered. "I became a detective in hopes of changing this city but as you can see after today nothing ever surprises me. I thought 9/11 was going to be a cleansing for this city but I don't believe that anymore. I'm really starting to hate the whole fucking place, you know what I mean?"

Anthony didn't need to sell his answer because it was true and from the heart. This place had gotten the best of him and it was time to check out. "Yeah, I agree with you, this place really sucks. Believe it or not, I was looking to patch things up with my parents and then head off to God knows where to do God knows what just as long as it was away from here. I am sure I would be better off."

There it was; Anthony had made the mistake. He just opened the door and Joe was ready to come on through with his invitation.

"What made you decide to make that kind of life changing decision?" Joe asked hoping that Anthony would now just go ahead and come out with it.

"You're asking a guy, who just quit his job yesterday, has been divorced for over a year, has an ex-wife who was already re-married and up until this morning his parents were mad at him and wanted nothing to do with him. I think that kinds of sums it up don't you?"

"All of this had been bothering you for awhile, why all of a sudden did you decide to do something about it? Come on Anthony, what finally pushed you over the limit to just run away? Or is that it? Yes, that's it, you are running from something. Now what can make you run from everyone and everything that you have known for your whole life? If you ask me it has to be something enormous," Joe enlightened him.

"Running? I don't think so. There is nothing that can scare me that much to alter my life. I am just tired of how things are here and I want something different."

"Who said you are scared? You don't have to be scared to be running from something. Many people run because they don't want to face the consequences if they stayed," Joe answered him back quickly to keep Anthony on the defensive and not on his game.

"Is that a fact? Well I hate to disappoint you detective but I am not running from anyone or anything. I just want a change."

As Anthony finished, Joe noticed Phil had come back in from the car. He made eye contact with him, and Phil went right back outside. This was Joe's show now. Anthony was weak for the first time all morning, and he was vulnerable to opening more doors than just that first one. Without hesitating, Joe dropped the bomb.

"Do you know who Frankie Feliciani is, Anthony? I mean a bright boy like you should know the man that runs this neighborhood. You don't need to answer the question, your face already answered it for you."

Anthony wasn't expecting that question from out of the blue. Why would detective Fishburn ask him that? Christ, he needed to get a hold of himself. He was going to get himself killed if he didn't play this better. If Joe connects Anthony to Frankie this soon, he would end up either in jail or dead, and he wasn't ready for either until he had a chance at Bull.

"I think he is behind your parents killing. Nothing goes down without his consent. The question is why would he want to have your parents killed? We did a search on them too and they seem to be your model citizens, which ruled out that they were involved with Frankie and if they weren't then he killed them to send a message. Who was that message for Anthony? It wouldn't be you, would it?" he asked hoping that Anthony would cooperate so they can bring down Frankie quickly.

"I know who Frankie is and what he means to the neighborhood. I also know that my parents paid him for his protection, which right now looks like he screwed them on that deal. I have no involvement with him. I admit I have been in his restaurant once or twice for dinner but that's about all." Anthony was aware that these answers weren't as convincing as his previous ones but he couldn't regain his composure.

"I can't help but believe that you are hiding something from me Anthony. This is what I think happened. I think Frankie sent in a couple of his goons to scare your parents and something went terribly wrong and the only way to clean up the rest of this mess would be to get rid of you. Does this make sense to you Anthony?"

Anthony couldn't believe how sharp Joe was about all of this. It was like Joe was reading a script to some B rate movie. How the hell could he have put all of this together so soon?

"I appreciate your concern for me detective but I can assure you that in no way am I involved with Frankie Feliciani or anyone in his crew. Now if you don't mind I would like to get going."

"Ok Anthony, we can play it your way. I'll take you back to your car and you can go home to start making your parents arrangements but know this, you won't live long enough to see their funeral. I'm sure Frankie's people are looking for you right now and since you have been here with Phil and me for the last hour or so, he'll put one and one together and he'll know you talked. He won't take any more risks Anthony, you'll disappear before morning. Why don't you just come down to the station, tell us what is really happening here and we can put you into protection. Anthony, not only is this your chance to get out of this alive but it's your only chance to get justice for your parents."

Joe believed that last comment would convince Anthony to talk. If he was right and Anthony was involved with Frankie, Joe was only telling him the facts and not just blowing smoke up his ass.

Anthony hesitated just a second or two before he answered, "Are you done now? I would like to leave."

"Yeah sure, we can go."

Round one went to Anthony. These guys were no match for him.

As Frankie drove himself and Vincent back to the restaurant he wasn't as confident about Anthony anymore. He believed Anthony was going to go to the police because it was the safest play. If he was Anthony he would do the same thing after his parents were just killed. He couldn't possibly believe that he was safe on the streets.

"Vincent, instead of going back to *The Club* I think you and I should go pay Anthony a visit. I think he'll feel more comfortable if it was the two of us instead of Al and Charlie. I need him as relaxed as possible. The kid will believe he won't be in any danger if we go to his place instead of having him sent to us. I need reassurance that he hasn't gone to the cops yet."

"Nah, the kid's head is spinning right now, he wouldn't even have time to weigh all his options," he replied.

"We just need to convince him somehow that it wasn't Bull or Sal that killed his parents. Let's just hope we are right," Frankie said.

Where to begin was the only thought in Anthony's mind as he drove back to his apartment. He had a million phone calls to make but in what order did he make them. There were so many people to inform about what just happened, plus the calls to the different funeral homes and the church for the funeral arrangements. There was also the little phone call to Frankie and he was in no way prepared for it.

Anthony approached his apartment door with the key in his hand, but something didn't look right. When he reached the door, he finally could see for sure what was wrong; the door was already slightly opened. His heart was ahead of the rest of his body and he couldn't help but think that a bullet was going to hit his head at any second. Anthony slowly pushed the door open, still waiting to be shot dead at any time. When the door finally swung all the way opened he could see Frankie and Vincent sitting together on his couch even though the lights weren't on in the apartment.

"Are you going to stand there all day, or all you going to come in and sit down with us?" Frankie had asked from the couch, as he turned on the light from the lamp on the end table.

Anthony was frozen in the door entrance, his legs had quit on him.

"Anthony, stop being a pussy and come inside and sit down with me and Frankie. If we were here to kill you, you would have been dead already. We just want to go over a couple things before you get the wrong idea of what happened this morning," Vincent informed him.

"Kid, why are you so shocked to see us? Don't you think we are just as concerned about what happened today as you and the police? We want to find the animals that did this before they do. This doesn't look good to the bosses when something like this happens in our own backyard," Frankie told Anthony.

"So if you are so concerned with who killed my parents, why are you here in my apartment? This is the last place that the murderers would be."

Right away Vincent stood up. "Don't be such a fucking wise ass to Frankie. Show some respect!"

"Vincent, forget about it. The kid is obviously not himself," Frankie said to Vincent, as he then turned back towards Anthony. "Anthony, come in and take a seat. I just want to get to the bottom of this," he said with the kindness that a father would show towards a child who has just learned that there is no Easter Bunny or Santa Claus.

It took Anthony a moment or two before he walked into the apartment. He realized if they were here to kill him he might as well get it over with, because there was no point in running. Frankie or Vincent could put a couple of bullets in his back before he even made it one step out of the doorway.

"What assurance do I have that you aren't here to kill me?" he asked knowing he wasn't going to get a straight answer back.

"Anthony, if I wanted you dead, Vincent and I wouldn't be the ones here in your apartment, Bull and Sal would and you wouldn't have gotten the front door opened."

"Oh, you mean the same assholes who just slaughtered my parents this morning. None of us here are stupid so let's stop with all the bullshit. We all know that it had to be them. I already sat today with two detectives who believed it was a mob hit and not a botched robbery."

A look of surprise was now on Frankie's face but it wasn't there because he was shocked that Anthony talked to the police already but for the fact that he told Frankie without being asked. There was now no reason for Frankie not to shoot him right here and walk away from this mess. "You spoke to the cops already?"

"I told you Frankie he would run to them if you gave him the chance. Now what the hell do you want to do?" Vincent shouted as he reached in his coat pocket to draw out his gun.

"Settle down," Anthony demanded to the surprise of Frankie and Vincent. "I said to end the bullshitting and I meant it. If I am straight with the two of you I expect to be treated the same. I want answers to what the fuck went down this morning and I want you to tell me all you know. You at least owe me that much before you decide what's going to happen to me. I was ninety-five per-cent sure that someone was going to be in the apartment when I got home today and I can honestly say I am shocked it was the two of you."

Frankie was definitely thrown for a loop with Anthony's brazen attitude. The kid was right, he would have been dead ninety-five percent of the times but Frankie had a gut feeling about all of this and he believed Anthony deserved better.

"Ok, you are either really stupid for telling us that you already spoke to the cops or you truly want to skip all the bullshit and get to the point. If I didn't hold you in high respect Anthony you would have been dead as soon as I heard what happened even though it wasn't your fault. I can't take chances about this but since this was such an awful tragedy I don't want to make any drastic deci-sions until I used all my resources to find out what the hell happened," he assured Anthony.

The room was full of tension from all three of them. Anthony didn't believe he was ever going to leave this apartment alive no matter what was said. The only hope that he was clinging to was that he was going to get a straight answer about his parents before they killed him.

Frankie finally broke the awkward silence. "Tell me what you told the cops this morning and I will tell you all that I know so far," he promised Anthony.

"I guess that is fair enough. I was met by two detectives before I even reached the store."

Before Frankie could get the question out, Anthony already answered it. "Don't bother asking me their names because right now they are my only exit out of this apartment."

Frankie couldn't help thinking how cool this kid always seemed to be no matter how much pressure was on him.

"They told me that my parents had been brutally murdered and as of right now there were no suspects but they had their suspicions. One of the detectives asked me to go for a ride to someplace quiet where they could get away from all of this and talk. He assured me it wasn't a formal interrogation but they thought it could help in the process of finding out who could have done this. So I agreed and we went to "The Golden Eagle Diner". We were there for about an hour and they tried to drill me with all kinds of questions about my relation with you, my finances, and my job. They even asked about my divorce with Sandra."

Anthony stopped and paused for a second and looked at Frankie to see it he could get a read on him. "If I told them anything of relevance do you think I would be back to my apartment so soon? No, I would be at the station right now answering more of their questions on record if I said anything of value to the case. You know as well as I do that if I told them of your involvement that I would never come back to this apartment again. Hell for that matter, don't you think I would want them to put me into witness protection? So stop wasting my time and just tell me what I want to know," he demanded.

"I have to admit kid you do sound convincing. I do believe that you didn't tell them who might have killed your parents but I do know that you told them something important to guarantee your safety."

"I think you can respect my silence on this, Frankie. I didn't drop anyone's name, but I told the detectives that if I came up missing in the next day or two they would know where to go to find the answers to all their questions, if you know what I mean."

At this point, Vincent had lost all of his patience with Anthony. He jumped up from his seat much quicker than Anthony expected for a man his size and age, and had taken out his gun and now had it pointed directly at Anthony's face.

"Listen to me, you little fuck. I am tired of all this bullshit. Who the fuck do you think you are trying to strong arm? I think I will take my chances and just shoot your fucking head right off now then make any deals with you."

"Vincent, calm down and put away the gun. No one is shooting anyone. Did I miss something or am I still head of this family?"

"Frankie, how the hell can you let this pile of shit get away with this? Let's end this here and now."

"Vincent I am not going to repeat myself a second time so put away the fucking gun," he shouted.

As Vincent stared at Anthony for just a moment longer he finally dropped his arm down and put the gun back in his pocket. "Fine, the gun is away but mark my words Frankie. This kid is going to be the end of us. No boss in his right mind would chance everything by keeping this kid alive," he said with disgust.

"No, the end of us is going to be if the two jerk-offs killed Anthony's parents or not. If they did then it doesn't matter if I kill Anthony or not. So do me a favor Vincent, go down stairs and wait in the car. I want to discuss a couple of things with Anthony and since you can't seem to control your emotions right now, I need you to be out of sight."

"Oh, this is just getting fucking better every minute. Next I guess you want to discuss how you two are going to whack me. I can't believe what I am seeing today Frankie. You are slipping and I don't want to be around when you fall," he shouted as he walked toward the door.

Vincent was about to walk out when he turned to Anthony and said, "I don't care what he promises you kid, but if the shit hits the fan, I can guarantee that you will be dead before I ever see a jail cell."

After Vincent was out of the room Frankie felt Anthony would be more at ease and they both could get the answers that they were seeking.

"Ok Anthony, I will be fair and tell you all I know as of right now. For one, I can't promise you but I am almost positive that Bull wasn't involved in your parents' death. He and Sal were at the Taj last night tailing you and he called Vincent early this morning informing us that you crapped out in the high roller room by dropping about twenty g's in one hand. Is this true?"

Total shock filled Anthony's face.

"Jesus Christ, he was there watching me the whole time? I never saw him."

"Of course you didn't see him, he was at the crap tables staying out of sight. So, I am pretty sure it wasn't him but this doesn't mean I won't be questioning him. Now, you let me do what I have to do to get to the bottom of this and just stay put. I have my insiders down at the station giving me hourly reports and I am going to send Bull to Vegas to go pick up my World Series winnings. With Bull away, Vincent and I will have our own interrogation of Sal and see if we can find out if they were involved or not."

"You expect me to just sit here and wait? Jesus Christ Frankie, we both know he was involved in this. I can't just do anything about it."

"You want to become a killer Anthony? Mr. College graduate wants to whack out a mobster to avenge his parents' death. Think about what you are saying and stop being stupid. If you walked out of this room to go to kill Bull, I wouldn't give you a twenty percent chance in hell of pulling it off and even if you got to him I don't think you would have the balls to pull the trigger. Your hesitation is all Bull will need to have enough time to kill you."

"Fine, why don't you take care of this problem for me? You owe me that much."

"Now I am supposed to whack my nephew for some punk who made me a couple of million dollars? You better get that fucking head of yours checked out because you lost your fucking mind," he shouted at Anthony. "Don't assume I won't think twice about putting a bullet in your head before I walk out of this apartment."

Anthony just stood there speechless. He had never seen this side of Frankie. Anthony didn't give himself a forty percent chance of ever leaving this apartment but Frankie started to calm down enough to lessen Anthony's fear. Frankie got up and walked towards Anthony. Once he got to Anthony he took out an envelope from his pocket and handed it to him.

"Now you are going to make all your parents' arrangements in the next couple of days and see to it that they have a beautiful funeral. This should cover everything. If you need any help with phone calls or meeting with the proper church officials let me know and I will have Ellena help you. Please accept my deepest apologies Anthony but whatever happened this morning was not done by Bull or someone else in my crew."

Anthony stood there staring at the envelope dumbfounded. Why was Frankie giving him money? He owed the man fifty thousand dollars.

"Frankie, what's this? You know I can't take money from you, Christ I owe you fifty thousand."

"Yeah, I almost forgot about that. I am going to push your date back for now. You still have to pay off your debt but I am going to extend your period for another three weeks by then all of this will have blown over. I'm sure in that time, you will have received the insurance money or have sold the store, either way, have the money to me by then. Don't worry about Bull hassling you for it because he will have more important things to worry about if you are right. Now if you'll excuse me, I have to go back to *The Club* to start making some of my own phone calls."

Frankie gave him a short hug and a kiss on both cheeks and was already out the door before Anthony even had a chance to say thank you.

Anthony finally sat down but he still wasn't clear as to what had just happened. The apartment had fallen to a dead silence except for the slow drum of the refrigerator in the kitchen. He just sat there moving Frankie's envelope from one hand to the other. This was crazy he had to open and see how much Frankie gave him. After tearing the top of the envelope, he turned it upside down in his hand and one hundred one hundred dollar bills came out with a note attached to one of them, "I know it's not much but it should cover most of the expenses for the funeral" signed F.

Anthony was now sitting with ten thousand dollars in his lap. Why would Frankie do that for him? He wasn't family or a member of his crew. If it wasn't for the situation that they were both in, Anthony might have expected help from Frankie but he would never have expected anything after what went down today.

Anthony looked up at the clock and realized that half the day was already gone. He had so much more to do, but his head was pounding and all he wanted to do was just to lay down for an hour or two and hope that when he woke up, that all of this was just some horrible dream. Instead, he got up to get the phone and start working on those phone calls. He had to make as many as he could before most of his relatives had to hear about what happened to his parents from the news instead of him. Anthony pulled out the cell phone, but decided the nap was more important to him because he was never going to get through the rest of the day with his head aching like it was.

❦   ❦   ❦

"So how was I in there?" Vincent asked as Frankie got into the Cadillac.

"Well I don't think Tom Hanks has to worry about you winning any Oscars in the near future but I think it worked. Anthony has been put at ease for now and with the money I just gave him for the funeral I think we don't have to worry about him anymore."

"I can't believe you gave the kid ten dimes. Who's to say he ain't going to pack up and go somewhere with it and that'll be that?"

Frankie reached into his jacket to grab a smoke. After taking one out and lighting it he took a deep drag and closed his eyes and laid his head back. "And what would be so bad about that? Just think about it. How bad could it be to lose sixty thousand to this kid compared to having him sink the whole crew or maybe worse the family but I don't think he's going to skip. Anthony has too much morals to leave town without paying. I told him I would give him extra time to payoff the debt until after he received the insurance money however my fear is that he'll do something stupid and try to be a Charles Bronson and go after Bull."

"Christ, the kid is as clean as a whistle other than his gambling problems. Forget about it. He wouldn't be that stupid. I mean he would be signing his own death certificate," Vincent explained.

"At this point Vincent, I don't think the kid is worried about dying. After this morning he has been left with nothing. No family, an ex who don't want anything to do with him, a daughter he isn't allowed to see, no job and a debt of fifty thousand dollars. I think that constitutes a man who has nothing to lose don't you?"

Vincent kept looking straight as he drove them back to *The Club*. He didn't need to look at Frankie to realize that he was absolutely right about that. The kid was a loose cannon and was ready to go off at any moment.

"So, what do you want to do Frankie?"

Frankie opened his eyes again and opened the window to throw out the cigarette.

"I think we stick with the plan. Bull is going out to Vegas and Sal is going to have a visit. With Bull and Sal out of the way, Anthony can't get himself in any trouble and once the deaths sink in and he starts on all the arrangements, his mind will be occupied with more important things. Now just get me back to *The Club* I'm sure there are many messages waiting for me."

Not even twenty minutes into his sleep Anthony rose up drastically. An idea had hit him all of a sudden as he dreamed. It was a crazy half-assed idea, but if he thought it through he just might able to pull it off. The only question he had to ask himself was he really that crazy to do it? There was no time to lie in bed and think about that question, he needed to get a hold of his cousin Kevin and start working on his idea that can get him even with the house.

Kevin Pelino was Anthony's cousin on his mother's side. He lived at his parents' home with his younger sister Tami. His parents had died tragically two years earlier in a car accident returning from a trip from the Poconos, and he decided to move back home to take care of Tami. Kevin was twenty-nine and living an entertaining bachelor's life when they died.

Since he was six foot one and two hundred and ten pounds and good looking, he had no trouble finding company for the night. The thought of settling down and doing the whole married life never even crossed his mind. Kevin was all about Kevin and no one else.

Unlike Anthony, Kevin didn't go to college. He was as blue-collared as they came. He started working at Nick's Auto Body Shop when he was eighteen, and now he managed the place. Nick's business was doing so well he opened a second shop and decided to let Kevin run the old place. Most of his regular customers only kept coming back because of Kevin's work anyway, so the least Nick could do was to give Kevin the position.

With all his street smarts and right connections, Kevin was aware of how to make the most profit on the cars that came into the shop. He had various acquaintances with different chop shops all around the city. He would get most of his parts at a discount from them and turn around and charge his customer for a factory made brand new part. Who was going to question him? Hundreds of shops all over the city did this and most customers were clueless.

All in all, Kevin was doing rather well for himself and since his parents' house was paid off after the accident, he didn't have a worry in the world other than Tami going off to school and getting her degree. However, all of this was about to change after Anthony's visit.

❦   ❦   ❦

Bull didn't show up at *The Club* until the dinner rush was over. Frankie was in the kitchen helping Ellena with the last of the entrées when Bull walked in through the doors. "Making anything special, Aunt Ellena?" he asked as he gave her a kiss hello.

"Michael, what a nice surprise, we are just working on the last two orders of tonight's special, raviolis and stuffed peppers. Would you like a quick dish for dinner?"

"If Uncle Frank doesn't mind waiting for me to have a plate I would love to," he replied back.

But Frankie did mind because he was in no mood for small talk and wanted to get the meeting over as quickly as possible. "Where's Sal? I thought Vincent told you to bring down Sal?"

"When I called he wasn't feeling that great. Told me it was the last time he was going to eat that diner crap after a night of drinking. If you want I can call him again and tell him to get his ass down here."

"That's fine, you can fill him in on what's going down after you leave here. Now do me a favor and head into the back, Vincent is in there waiting for you. I'll be back in a minute after I wash up."

"Frankie, give Michael a break and let the poor kid have a nice cooked meal. You know these young kids don't eat right, always in a rush and never bothering to take the time to sit down and eat a healthy meal."

Frankie turned and gave Ellena a harsh look. She hadn't seen that kind of rage in his eyes in such a long time.

"I'll tell you what Aunt Ellena, you wrap me up a plate to go and I will eat it as soon as I get home. I am here on business and Uncle Frankie is a busy man so I shouldn't be keeping him waiting."

After Bull went into the back room, Frankie walked over to Ellena and took her hands into his. "Honey, never ever confront me in front of someone. When I tell a person to do something, I expect them to do it. Even though Michael is your nephew he is still an employee of mine and never question my authority in front of him. It's not good for business."

Frankie had never disciplined Ellena before. She was a great wife and a perfect mother. She had never questioned Frankie about his other business. Ellena believed the less she knew about it, the less she would have to worry. She had more to worry about with Anita now away in college than Frankie's Mafia life.

"I hate to have to say that to you Hon, but after this morning with Anthony's parents' death, many people around here are expecting me to find out who was responsible since the police were useless. I am just under a lot of strain right now and I need Michael to fully concentrate on the seriousness of the situation and not about getting a plate of raviolis and stuffed peppers. So, I'm sorry," he said as he kissed her forehead.

As Frankie entered the back room he saw that Vincent was on the phone and Bull was at the bar helping himself to a Bud.

"Vincent, you mind hanging up so we can get this started with." Vincent gave him a nod as he finished up with his call.

Frankie went around to the other side of the bar and made himself a seven and seven as Vincent pulled up a stool next to Bull. "Want me to make you one?"

"No thanks Frankie, I think I have had enough already today."

Like with everything else when it came to business, Frankie wasted no time getting started. "I am sure you are aware by now what happened this morning in the Italian Market area."

"When I woke up this afternoon I heard it on the news. You can't miss it, it's on everywhere."

"I realize it was a stupid question, but do you know who the two people were that got murdered?"

"No Uncle Frank, I didn't pay that close attention to the names of the victims."

This response made Vincent shift a little on his stool. Almost everyone in the crew and the whole neighborhood knew who they were, so of course he had to have known.

"Then I guess this will come as a real surprise to you. The people who were murdered were Anthony's parents," Frankie informed him.

"The kid's parents?" Bull asked surprised.

"Yeah, his parents, and the word out on the streets is that it doesn't look like a typical hold up. I have made a few calls down to our friends in blue and they have informed me that it looks more like a hit than a hold up gone wrong."

"What, you think I had something to do with this? Sal and I were in A.C. last night and most of the morning watching him. How the hell could we have done it? Ask Vincent, I called in early this morning from the diner."

"No one is saying that you two had anything to do with it. That is not why I had you come here tonight. Michael, if I thought for one second that you were behind this, the three of us wouldn't be having this meeting."

Frankie took a long gulp of his drink, put it back down on the counter and poured himself another one. "What I think happened is after the kid went broke last night, he stopped by his parents' place to ask for the money and when they said no, he must have panicked and things got out of control and he killed them. I'm not sure if he did it out of rage of being rejected or in the hopes that he would score on an insurance policy."

"I told you that kid was a fucking loser, Uncle Frank. Why you even let him in here always puzzled me."

"I don't have all the facts yet, so I'm not a hundred percent sure he did it. Until I do know, he is off limits to everyone including you. You are not to go near him until I give you the word. Pete has given the orders and there's nothing I can do about it."

"What, the kid is going to get a pass? We ain't going to get the money? I can't believe this shit."

Vincent had enough of sitting silent. He had heard enough to know that Bull and Sal were to blame. "Did your uncle say he was getting a pass? Until we get through with our investigation or by some dumb luck the police find out something on their own, we are not to touch him. If Anthony was behind this, you will be the one who can fix the problem, but until then nothing happens to him, *capiche*?"

"Fine, I give you my word, I won't go near him."

"I know you won't because you aren't going to be around to have the opportunity to do something. I am sending you out to Vegas tomorrow morning to go collect my World Series winnings at Caesars. I was going to go with your Aunt for a nice short vacation, but Pete has made it quite clear that I am to stay put until this problem has been resolved. So I thought what better person to go for me than you? This way I can be at peace knowing that you won't bother Anthony, and Anthony won't bother you."

"What do you mean, Anthony bother me? Why should I be worried about Anthony looking for me?" Bull asked in a pissed off manner as he got up from his stool.

"You said it yourself, Bull," Vincent explained.

"You thought that maybe we believed you had something to with the murders, and if we considered this what the hell do you think the kid has already done? Right now there are three logical possibilities floating out there that happened this morning. The first, a couple of real fucking morons held up a store in our neighborhood. The second, Anthony did it and the last, you and Sal did it and that is Anthony's assumption."

"Vincent and I, along with almost everyone else, believe that Anthony went out of his fucking mind and crossed the line into insanity. However to protect everyone involved, I would like you to do me this favor and go to Vegas, pick up my money, spend an extra day relaxing and when you come back, this all should be over and things can get back to normal. If you ask me that's a sweet deal," Frankie conveyed to him.

"I can't believe you are sending me out to Vegas for my protection. Even if Anthony thought I killed his parents, do you think I would be afraid of him looking for revenge? Give me a break, the kid probably hasn't been in a fight in his entire life, let alone killed anyone. Why the hell are you sending me away? Send Al, Victor or Charlie. I want to be here if this douche bag comes after me."

"Shut the fuck up and listen to me before I do something I am going to regret. You are going to Vegas and that's final. You have no say in the matter, so just accept it and enjoy the time away."

"Fine," Bull replied.

"Let's say it was Anthony and he does come after you and you were dumb enough to do something about it. Guess who the cops come looking for next? See, that is your problem Bull and one reason you will never run your own crew. You don't think and you let this macho bullshit of yours get in the way of your brain. I have other people besides you who I am protecting and if you happen to bring heat down on this whole organization, I won't be able to protect you."

"Protect me from who?" he asked.

"Pete. He is already pissed enough that something like this has happened on our territory and he wants someone's head for it. Now that head could be Anthony's or yours—take your pick. Because all I know is that it won't be mine or Vincent's, so get it through that head of yours that you are taking this trip because I am the boss and I am the one you report to, do you understand?"

Bull now realized the significance of the situation. If Frankie did think he was responsible, he wouldn't be here right now arguing about a trip to Vegas.

He needed to calm down and get the hell out of here before he said something stupid to bring more heat on himself.

"You are right Uncle Frank. I let my emotions get the best of me, but it's hard for me to let go about that loser having the balls to come at me and you wanting me to just walk away. It makes me think you have no confidence in me."

"Michael, I am only thinking about the best for not just a member my crew, but for my nephew. Take the two days vacation, spend some of my money and be back on Friday night to pick up the rest of my winnings from our books. We are looking at around a hundred and fifty thousand and I want you here to be involved in the collecting. That's a lot of money to be picked up and I don't want to send just anyone. Another reason you are going to Vegas is to pick up three hundred big ones for me. I want to make sure that it is coming home. So yes, I do have confidence in you. You are in charge of collecting close to half a million of our money, so don't let me down."

"I'd never let you or the crew down Uncle Frank. So what time are Sal and I heading out tomorrow?"

Frankie was in the middle of pouring his third drink when he glanced over at Vincent. Vincent realizing that as his signal stood up. "You are going alone on this one. We need Sal here. Both of our muscles can't be away at a time like this. If it turns out to be the first scenario and it was two fucking idiots, we need Sal available to get to them before the police. We can't let Sal miss out on the fun of punishing them now can we? Your uncle and I realize that this is a slight possibility, but we need to be prepared if it is true. Now let's go over your flight and hotel reservations that we booked for you."

As Anthony sat in his car out front of Kevin's house, the radio clock flashed eight-twenty. He had been in his car for over thirty minutes without even realizing that he had already gone through seven cigarettes. If Anthony's plan didn't work, he was going to be in worse trouble than just owing Frankie the fifty thousand. This would seal his death, but he believed for the plan to work he was going to need help and that's where Kevin came into play. But how do you ask your cousin to risk his life for you on some half-assed scheme? Kevin had responsibilities. He had to look out for Tami now that their parents had passed away and Anthony didn't what to be selfish and jeopardize this. Fuck it, what's the worse that Kevin is going to say, "Fuck you for asking me to do something like that, now get out of my home?" Anthony had nothing to lose other than time so he crushed out the last of his cigarette and headed for the front door.

It took Tami no more than ten seconds to answer the door after Anthony rang the door bell. Once she realized who was standing in front of her on the other side of door, she couldn't help but run into his arms and cry. Anthony couldn't make out what she was saying as she sobbed into his chest other than, "I am so sorry about Aunt Erma and Uncle Mickey."

This lasted for at least two minutes until Kevin started yelling from upstairs at Tami, "Who's at the door Tami?"

Anthony was the first to break away. "God, you have gotten so big. You have become such a young lady since the last time I saw you."

"Thanks. It has been at least three years since your wedding. Oh, God I'm sorry to mention that. That was really stupid of me."

"You don't need to apologize for that. It doesn't bother me and I have so much more on my mind right now even if it did, so no harm no foul. Do you mind if I come in? I need to talk to you and Kevin."

"Don't be so ridiculous, get your back side in here. I'm sure you have a lot on your mind to talk about," she said as she led him to the living room.

Tami yelled for Kevin to come down. "Anthony, have a seat on the couch. Do you want anything to eat or drink?"

"You know I would love some ice tea if you have any."

"Okay, I'll bring you a glass." As Tami left the room, Anthony could hear Kevin coming down the steps. He got up from the couch and faced the stairs.

"Jesus Christ Anthony, how are you?" he asked. "Why didn't you tell me sooner it was Anthony?" he yelled into the kitchen at Tami.

He walked over and gave Anthony a huge hug and told him how sorry he was for his parents' death. "How are you holding up? I wanted to call, but the only number we have is your old house and I wasn't going to call her. If we didn't hear from you we were going to get your parents' arrangements from the paper. I can't believe something like that could happen in that part of the city. It had to be a bunch of fucking crack heads looking for money. I just hope the local protection finds them before the cops do, if you catch my drift. They'll send the perfect message that things like this don't happen in our neighborhood. So what are you doing here? Do you need help with something? Because Tami and I are here for you," he informed Anthony.

"Yes, I could really use your help but I will wait for Tami to come back in with my ice tea."

"Hey, you name it, we're here for you."

Anthony was surprised to hear that. When Kevin's parents had died, Anthony was nowhere to be found. He had felt too ashamed at the time to see everyone in his family because of the divorce, and he had never shown up for the funeral. Anthony didn't want to go through hearing the whispering and seeing the looks from everyone. That day wasn't supposed to be about him so he stayed away instead of becoming a distraction; however he knew that this still wasn't a justifiable excuse.

Tami came back into the living room with Anthony's ice tea and the three of them sat down. Tami sat next to Anthony and Kevin was in the recliner across from them. Anthony thought to himself that some things never change, and it seemed to him that Tami still had a crush on her cousin. Another thing Anthony couldn't help but notice was how beautiful Tami was. She had grown into such an attractive young lady. She had an olive complexion, long, wavy brown hair and a very nice figure that was going to make it difficult for Kevin to keep the boys from coming to the house looking to date her.

"I feel like a complete jackass asking you guys for your help with my parents' funeral considering I didn't even attend your parents', and there is no excuse I could ever give you for that. Unfortunately since this is a murder case, the police will be hounding me every waking chance they get. I don't think I am going to have the time to get everything that needs to be done accomplished. Tami, I would be forever grateful to you if you could possibly help with the phone calls. I know almost everyone has heard it already on the news so I don't need you to call anyone about what happened, but I will still need to have all the arrangements made."

Anthony took out Frankie's envelope and handed Tami the ten thousand dollars.

"Here's ten thousand dollars. This should cover all the expenses and whatever is left over, you can keep it for all your hard work," he told her.

"Jesus Anthony, what are you doing walking around with ten thousand dollars in your pockets? Why don't you just give Tami one of your credit cards?"

"I never found the need for one after Sandra and I got divorced. I cut up all of our old cards and never bothered getting new ones," he answered. "What do you say Tami, you think you can squeeze in the time between your school work and social life?"

"Anthony, you don't have to apologize for not coming to my parents' funeral. We received your Mass card and flowers before the funeral and neither Kevin nor I expected you there because of what was going on in your life, but you had us in your thoughts and that is all that counts. I would love to help you."

"Great. I know nowadays most of you high school kids have cell phones so I imagine you can make numerous calls during school breaks and lunch. I will have my cell phone on in case you have any questions or if someone would need to get a hold of me about certain arrangements that you have selected. My parents had already bought plots so that part is done and the Church, of course, is St. Martin of Tours, so basically all you really need to do are all the little things. I will write a list for you before I leave tonight with any questions that I think you might have. I figure the viewing will be Friday night and the mass and burial will be Saturday morning. You think you could handle this for me? Think of it a quick part time job before college next year," he told her with a smile on his face.

"Of course I can. Don't be silly."

"Tami, I can't thank you enough for this. I will write the obituary for the newspaper tonight and drop it off at Kevin's shop tomorrow. Everything else that you will need, I will give you before I leave tonight," he told her as he got up to give her a hug.

As Anthony hugged her he whispered into her ear, "I will take care of you for this," and then they both sat back down.

"Tami, I'm sure I interrupted either your homework or phone calls to your girlfriends. I know how senior year can be, so why don't you go upstairs because I still have a lot of issues I need to go over with Kevin."

"Oh, ok. A girl can take a hint when she isn't needed anymore. I will leave you two men alone. I'm sure I can go upstairs and get in a chat room some-where. Just remember to leave me all the numbers and instructions before you leave Anthony," she stated as she made her overly dramatic exit up the stairs.

Once Tami was out of ear shot Kevin turned and asked, "How the hell could something like this happen? I am still in total shock and I can't imagine what is going through your mind."

"Needless to say it hasn't fully hit me yet, but I have ridden the emotional wave all day today. The time this morning with the cops didn't help matters."

"Tell me, do they believe the bullshit that the news is putting out or do they know what really went on? I for the life of me can't imagine your parents being on the wrong side of the mob. Uncle Mickey and Aunt Erma were the ideal cit-izens in this neighborhood. So, who the hell could have done this to them?" he asked while he shook his head in disbelief.

"Kevin, I didn't just come here to ask for Tami's help. I could have just easily called a number of other relatives. The reason I came all the way out here was to try to convince you in doing an absolutely crazy and life threatening mission of some sort."

Kevin stared at him for no more than two seconds. "Jesus Christ, you know who did this? How do you know who did it? It wasn't Uncle Mickey and Aunt Erma that was in trouble, was it? You were the one they were after?"

"Settle down and don't jump to conclusions so fast. I have been involved with Frankie Feliciani for awhile and my gambling had gotten out of hand and what happened this morning was totally unexpected. Fortunately for me he had nothing to do with it. On the other hand it was his nephew, Bull that killed my parents without Frankie being aware of it."

"I thought that asshole was working for him."

"You know Bull?"

"Yeah, I have had to deal with him once in awhile down at the shop. He has brought his Vette to the shop a couple of times acting like the typical jerk-off who was connected to the mob."

"Not only is he Frankie's nephew, but he is also his muscle. Frankie told me this morning that Bull was down at A.C. last night following me around and that he couldn't have gotten home in time to do it. I'm not a detective, but there couldn't be anyone else who would do it."

"How much do you owe? What kind of figure are we talking about that would make Bull whack your parents?" Kevin asked with that stunned look on his face.

This was Anthony he was talking to, the college graduate, and he couldn't picture him being involved with those kinds of people. "After the World Series the other night, I am into him for fifty thousand."

"Holy shit Anthony, fifty g's? How the hell did you get that far in the hole?"

"I don't think that is relevant at this point. However, what I do think is relevant is that I believe Bull was in A.C. watching me last night and when he saw me get busted out from the high stakes no limit poker game, he came home and paid my parents a visit. Unfortunately for all three of them, it got totally out of control and he ended up killing them."

Kevin was still on the edge of the couch with his hands on top of his knees as he tried to comprehend what Anthony had told him. He had a hard time believing his story because this all seemed too crazy to be true. This was something out of a movie and, from what he knew about Anthony and his parents, their lives were far from that of a movie. They were your average Italian family with little or no excitement in their lives. Yet as he sat there looking at Anthony, he saw in Anthony's eyes that he was telling the truth about what happened to his parents.

"If all of what you say is true, what do you intend to do about it Anthony? I don't think you have the ability to go after Bull and if you did, Frankie would put an end to you if you succeeded or not. If you don't do anything and the police somehow incarcerate Bull, Frankie would have you killed before it could go to trial. I don't really see any options for you other than packing up your things and getting the hell out of this city once you bury your parents and never look back. Other than never seeing Kimberly again, what else do you have here that is worth staying for? The way I see it, just leave for good on Saturday and fuck Frankie's fifty thousand."

"I know leaving would be the easiest path to choose, but I am not a quitter. The last thing that I want to live with for the rest of my life is knowing that I had a chance to settle the score and I took the coward's way out."

"Anthony, you might say that now, but think about what you are saying. Have you ever killed anyone before? And don't answer that because we both know you haven't. Let's say you do somehow kill Bull; that is the easy part. The hard part will be living the rest of your life always looking over your shoulder for Frankie because, make no mistakes about it, he will come for you. And when he catches you, do you think it is going to be a quick and simple death? You could only pray that it would be a bullet to the back of the head. No, it's going to be one long and agonizing painful death. I'm telling you, it's not worth it to be tortured to death just to get the man who killed your parents. If it was some punk from the streets, yeah I would be behind you one hundred percent, but you are talking about the Mafia, hit-men and made people. You are out of your league."

"What if I told you something even crazier than everything you have heard so far? I believe I have come up with a plan to get Bull, and it won't even be me to pull the trigger."

Kevin had heard enough. He couldn't sit on the couch a moment longer without going over to Anthony and smacking him in the face. "You must be one fucking idiot if you are thinking about hiring someone for a hit on Bull. Who the hell are you going to find in this city that would do it knowing who he is without turning you over to Frankie? What the hell happened to you after college Anthony? You seem to have gotten stupid real fast."

"Listen Kevin, I know this all sounds completely crazy but please sit down and hear me out. After I am done explaining my plan if you still think it is a suicide mission, then I will do what you suggested and walk away forever. Please sit down and give me just ten more minutes of your time to hear me out."

Kevin walked into the dining room where there was a cabinet full of many different kinds of liquors and he pulled out the bottle of Southern Comfort. He took out three ice cubes from the ice bucket and dropped them into the tallest glass he had in the cabinet and filled it to the top. After taking a good size gulp, he topped off his glass and headed back towards the living room where Anthony sat, waiting and wondering how much of his plan he was going to be able to tell Kevin before he thought it was a ridiculous idea and asked him to leave.

"Anthony I'm not kidding. I have enough crap in my life going on right now to be worrying about a cousin getting himself killed. It is bad enough I lost my parents and an aunt and uncle over the last year. I don't want to keep adding on to these losses. If your plan isn't fool proof, which I can't imagine it is, I am going to tell you to walk away, but the floor is all yours, hit me with your plan."

Anthony realized at this moment that if he sold Kevin on his plan, that all three of their lives would be changed forever.

"Kevin, no plan is fool proof, but I am confident enough in my plan that I am willing to stake my life on it. I don't intend to have a hit put out on Bull, instead, I am going to have him set up and Frankie will kill him for me. I feel safe in assuming that Frankie is pretty sure that Bull murdered my parents. He told me today that to insure that neither one of us ran into each other, he was sending Bull to Vegas to pick up his World Series winnings."

"What does this trip have to do with anything?" Kevin asked.

"Why would Frankie care about us running into each other unless he was convinced that Bull did it? I think Frankie is sending him out to Vegas to get him out of the way until he decides how he is going to fix the whole mess. I know I'm not in the Mafia but I'm pretty sure that to clear this mess up, Frankie's boss is going to want Bull to disappear and that's just for starters. If this ever got leaked out by the news, Frankie and his whole crew could disappear. No matter which one of these scenarios pans out, either way I know I am a dead man."

After a pause, Anthony got up and asked Kevin if he could get himself a drink from the cabinet. Anthony didn't really want a drink, but his body needed one to get through this speech. He believed he was doing well and he had Kevin's full attention, but he could feel the start of his nerves slipping and he didn't want to lose this only chance he had of getting Kevin's help. When he returned with his drink, he sat down on the couch and took a sip of his Ama-retto and started right back up with his pitch without skipping a beat.

"For the last three hours I have tried to put myself in both Bull and Frankie's shoes. What would I do next if I was them? Even as dumb as both you and I know Bull is, I'm sure he has to be suspicious of his trip to Vegas. Maybe he thinks he isn't coming back from this trip. If he felt that way, what could he do to ensure his safety? Perhaps he would act first by going to the cops and plea bargain a deal to give up Frankie for his freedom. I know if I was in his shoes, I would do something. But other than sending Frankie away, what else could he do?"

"Anthony, you think he is going to whack Frankie? He wouldn't be that stupid. Where the hell could he possibly go after doing something like that? The whole underworld would be looking for him."

"Correct, killing Frankie isn't an option either. What if I told you a third option that Bull has that would serve him better that putting Frankie away or whacking him?"

"Ok, I am listening," Kevin replied.

"Frankie is sending Bull to Vegas to pick up three hundred thousand dollars. What if Bull doesn't come back with the money?"

"What, you think Bull might take the money and vanish somewhere?"

"No, Bull isn't bright enough to do that and I'm sure the thought never crossed his mind. But what if he doesn't come back and Frankie thinks he kept the money?"

"Is your plan to go to Vegas and settle up with Bull after he collects Frankie's money and you intend to keep the money? That is one fucking stupid plan Anthony. You really gave that one a lot of thought didn't you? How the hell are you going to sneak off to Vegas without Frankie knowing? I'm sure he is keeping an eye on you."

"Wait a second. I never said that was my plan. All I said was what if Bull didn't come back? Everyone would suspect him of double crossing Frankie."

Kevin was now getting frustrated with all these questions and what ifs. Anthony was beating around the bush with his point and he was exhausted and a little drunk. He was tired of just sitting here and listening.

"Anthony, I have no idea what you are getting at. You don't plan on going out there to take care of Bull and steal the money. You don't think Bull will double cross Frankie and steal the money and all you keep saying is what if Bull doesn't come back. Am I missing the picture that you are trying to paint me or am I just too drunk to understand what you are saying, because at this point I don't know what to think."

"I know you are getting frustrated and I haven't really made my point clear. So I will cut to the chase and tell you what I have planned, and then tell me what you think. Is that fair enough?"

"Well, my patience and time is running low. Therefore please get to the point or go home, either one is fine with me."

"My plan is to set up Bull when he gets back Friday night. Frankie settles up with all his books on Fridays, and this Friday he told me he was roughly looking at around two hundred thousand dollars. For an astronomical amount like that, Bull would be the pick up guy. Now what I plan on doing is having Bull detained at the airport when he arrives home so he can never make that pick up."

"How the hell do you plan on having him detained at the airport?"

"I admit this is the only real snag I have right now. I have a college buddy, Phillip Olsen, who is now a big wig for USAir over at JFK. I bailed his ass out plenty of times in college when he got carried away with his betting. It's been a couple of years, but he should still be able to lend a hand especially when I tell him who is involved in this favor. I think Frankie has about five thousand of his parents' hard earned money that should have gone to his tuition."

"Anthony, that's a real stretch, relying on some college buddy to be able to pull some strings and get a guy like Bull detained at the airport."

"Are you kidding me Kevin? After what just happened last month on 9/11, security is tighter than ever. Bull will be in line just like the rest of the cattle trying to pick up their luggage at the baggage claim area. Phillip should be able to get his flight information and, once his plane comes in, he can have someone plant a metal object of some sort like a pizza cutter or a knife in his bag, which would require the police to detain him for a couple of hours to answer some annoying questions. I got to believe that would hold him up for at least three hours or so, which is plenty of time for us to get in and out with the money."

"Whoa, what do you mean "us"? There is no "us" in this. I would consider helping in someway, but you must be out of your fucking mind if you think I am going to stick up someone from Frankie's crew. How the hell do you expect us to get the money from them without using guns and killing them? Do you seriously think these guys would just surrender that kind of money to us? Anthony you are really fucking stupid you know that? I really think it is time for you to go home. I will make sure that Tami helps with the funeral arrangements but if you come back here or contact me again about this, I swear to God, I'll kill you myself before they do."

Anthony wasn't surprised at Kevin's answer. He realized it would have been a miracle to get Kevin to go along with a crazy idea that involved jeopardizing both their lives. Anthony stood up and started to head towards the door when he turned to face Kevin one last time. "I just want you to remember one thing, Kevin. When your parents were killed in that accident and the police fucked-up their reports with the information from the breathalyzer test on that guy, who already had two other DUI citations, who did you call when you wanted restitution? Was it a good lawyer to try to get a case on the guy to go to trial? No, you called one of Frankie's men and asked if they could have something done about it."

"You heard?" he asked.

"What, you think I didn't hear about this? Oh, I heard and I was also informed that you chickened out and had nothing done to him and that son of a bitch was still on the road driving as of that day. And guess what, I don't know if you were aware of it or not but three months later he was involved in another accident and this time he killed a couple of high school girls. I believe they were seventeen and eighteen, that's Tami's age right?"

Kevin could only lower his head as he replied. "Yes, I know he did."

"Well, the cops didn't fuck up the reports this time and they convicted him on two accounts of first degree murder and he'll never see the light of day as a free man again, but I think it's a little too late. How do you sleep at night Kevin? Do you look into Tami's room at night when she is asleep and thank God that it wasn't her in that car? I don't know about you, but I couldn't live with myself knowing that the person who killed my parents was out there a free man and then killed again when I could have done something about it but I guess that's where you and I differ. I have the balls to do something about it and you don't but it's ok. I guess I'll just see you Friday at the viewing."

Anthony was at the front door when Kevin yelled at him, "Fuck you Anthony! This is totally different and you know it. It would have been at best a seventy-five percent speculation that that guy was drunk when he killed my parents and I couldn't live with the fact that I had an innocent man killed for revenge."

"Don't kid yourself Kevin, the odds were better than that."

"Whatever, but you on the other hand killed your parents because you got yourself in a jam and they paid the ultimate price for it. This is all on you! So when you go to sleep every night for the rest of your life remember no one else killed them but you. You might not have been the one who pulled the trigger but you might as well have been."

"Kevin, you still could have made a difference and those girls would still be alive today."

"And to answer your question, yes, I thank God every night that I have Tami and I ask him for forgiveness for the deaths of those girls. It wasn't till after the fact that I know I made the wrong decision and should have had something done about that guy but I didn't; case closed. I was a coward and he was a drunk and because of me, he got the chance to kill again. I get to live with that for the rest of my life and yeah it hurts."

Anthony played this to perfection. He had Kevin exactly where he wanted him. This could be Kevin's atonement for the death of those two girls.

"Kevin, this is your chance to exorcise those demons. There is nothing you can do to bring back those two girls but you can at least help me make Bull pay for killing my parents. I can't guarantee this will work or that we will walk away from this when it is all over, but I am very confident that it will work. With two full days before Friday night, we can work out the bugs in my plan. So what do you say?"

"You know Tami is graduating in the spring and then it's off to college for her. She's never been away from home and now with my parents gone it's only me here to make sure everything is alright for her. What happens to her if something goes wrong and I don't make it back? I just don't know if I can jeopardize her future," he said to Anthony shaking his head.

"I can't tell you to what to do but I can promise you this: tomorrow morning when I meet with my parents' attorney, I will sign over everything to Tami in the event of my death. So if I fuck this up and neither of us makes it back at least Tami will be set for life. Between my parents' store and the insurance money, she can go to any university that she wants and have enough money for a home one day."

"You'd do that for her? Anthony, I need the peace of mind that she'll be taken care of if all hell breaks loose."

Anthony put his hands on Kevin's shoulders and said, "God forbid something goes wrong and I only make it, I'll take her someplace where no one will ever be able to find us. I always wanted to go south and live in a little town with nice warm weather and forget about this fucking city. Just do me a favor and send Tami somewhere safe after the funeral Saturday. Make sure no one knows where she's going just in case."

"Why, do you honestly think that they would come after her? If there's even a remote chance of that happening, you can just forget this whole crazy idea," Kevin said as he shook Anthony's hands off his shoulders.

"Kevin, that's not even an issue but I want to play it one hundred percent safe. Don't you want that piece of mind? Just send her to a girl friend's house. I'm sure it won't be too hard to convince her to spend the night over at a friend's house."

Kevin headed back to the couch and picked up his drink. His nerves were totally shot and the nightmares of those two girls were already in his mind. Anthony stayed where he was standing as he watched Kevin pound down the last of his drink. He thought to himself that Kevin was going to have one hell of a hangover just like he had yesterday morning and felt sorry for him because he was sure that Kevin never imagine his evening would turn out like this.

"Well I think I have given you enough excitement for one night so I am going to head out. Do you think you can get out for a couple of hours tomorrow night to go over some of the details about Friday? I figure we can meet somewhere in the city for a night cap and go over what needs to be done."

"Yeah, I think I can get away for a couple of hours but not to late because I don't want to leave Tami alone that long on a school night."

Anthony turned around as he got to the door. "Oh, two quick questions for you, do you think you can get a hold of a Corvette or Trans Am for Friday night? It doesn't matter the color or the year as long as it sounds good it won't matter because we only need it for sound effects anyway."

"I'll have to make some calls to other shops but I think I can get one from somewhere."

"Great, we'll only need it for the night and you can return it the next day."

"What's your second question?"

"Do you have any young kids working at your shop or running errands for you? And before you answer, I need someone that can pull off being a college kid at Cornell, look attractive enough and has the ability to use his charms on the young freshmen."

"What does this have to do with Friday night? Do you need him to drive the car, because Dale from the shop is a god behind the wheel of a car? If we need someone to get us out of there in a hurry, he's our man."

"No, we don't need a driver. If all goes to plan, we won't have to worry about getting out quick. This is going to be a surprise attack and if it doesn't work, we won't make it back to the car anyway. What I am looking for is a little insurance, you can call it leverage for afterwards. I can't explain it now but do you think you can get a kid good enough to do the job that can spare the weekend upstate?"

"Man, I don't know Anthony. Charlie Hance down at the shop has a younger brother Nicky. He always brags how well his brother scores with the older girls. I think he is a freshman here at the community college so fitting in the college scene shouldn't be a problem."

"Ok, talk to Charlie tomorrow and see if we can meet his brother either tomorrow or Thursday. I need to be sure of him before I send him up to Cornell on Friday."

"Yeah, no problem, I'll talk to him tomorrow."

Anthony felt a lot better now than when he first came to their house, and decided to call it a night and head home. He was tired and still hung-over from all that had happened to him today and from the looks of it, Kevin was looking a lot worse than him. "I'm going to head out because from the looks of us, we both need to get some sleep. Thanks for deciding to go through with this."

"I can't say you're welcome because I think that was a fucking shitty thing to do to me by bringing up those two girls. But I can't blame you, because I would have done the same thing."

"I'll call your shop some time tomorrow and we'll set up a time and place for tomorrow night."

"No problem. I'll be there all day."

After he closed the door behind Anthony, Kevin went back to the couch and sat down and laid his head back. He was starting to feel the effects of the Southern Comfort. He was aware that it would be a long time before sleep would come to him and start his date with the two high school girls that he had been having in his dreams over and over for the past year.

❦   ❦   ❦

CHAPTER 3

*The Turn
(7 of Hearts)*

When Frankie woke up Wednesday morning he had re-thought his plans for Sal. He was going to send Victor and Al to pick up Sal first and then head over to Bull's to take him to the airport. This way Sal would feel more at ease. Once they dropped Bull off, Victor and Al would bring him down to the railroad tracks where many homeless guys and drug addicts live. Al would tell Sal that Frankie had gotten a tip that one of the guys had been pinched many times and he's been seen down at the tracks before.

Frankie hated planning a hit on someone in his own crew. In all his years as a boss he only had to do it three times, but the situation that he was in called for it. It didn't matter what Sal was going to try to say to the guys to save his life, he was going to die in one of those empty box cars and that was the cruel reality of the business they chose.

The alarm clock was buzzing but Bull was already awake. He had been up since six o'clock. He didn't sleep much because he just couldn't get over the feeling that something wasn't right about this whole trip to Vegas. Maybe Frankie did just want him to get away from the city and get some sun and fun but there should be no reason that Sal couldn't come.

Sal was going to be Bull's right hand man one day when it was his turn to run the crew. There hadn't been an errand for Frankie in the last two years that they didn't do together. The excuse of needing Sal here in case they found the guys who killed Anthony's parents just didn't sit right with him. Yes, Sal was the sickest bastard in the crew and if you wanted a guy to suffer a long and painful death, he was the man, no argument there. Bull just didn't like the fact that he was being sent alone to Vegas.

Bull sat on the edge of the bed with his phone in his hand desperately wanting to call Sal for some reassurance. He didn't want Sal to think he was in trouble because he might go to Frankie first and explain the whole thing and sell out Bull. If he did that, they both would end up dead. He had to just trust Frankie and believe that he was really going to Vegas to pick up his money. He would call Sal tonight from Vegas; if Sal answered and things were fine back at home then he had nothing to worry about. However if he called Sal and couldn't get a hold of him, then his trip to Vegas was a one way trip, he was sent because he was going to be whacked. Either way he would find out in less than twelve hours what the future held for him.

Unlike Bull, Sal was in a deep sleep when his phone rang at six-thirty. Once he got home yesterday and saw the continuous news coverage of the murders on the television he sat in his living room and drank himself to sleep. The phone was on it's forth ring before Sal got his mind to focus and realize that he wasn't dreaming and it was the phone in his house that had just woken him up. The events of yesterday were still a blur when he answered the phone, "Yeah?"

Al was on the other end of the line. "Didn't Bull tell you we were coming to pick you up this morning?"

"Bull?" Sal answered puzzled and still too drunk to comprehend what was happening.

"What are you fucking drunk, stupid? Yeah, Bull. He was supposed to tell you that we were coming by to pick you up at seven. He has a nine o'clock flight to Vegas and you, Victor and I are taking him. Get yourself ready, we'll be over in less than half an hour."

"Sure, sure, I'll be ready…" but Sal was talking into a dead line because Al had hung up before he could answer.

Everything was all cloudy to him. He couldn't remember talking to Bull last night but that wasn't important right now. Sal needed a shower to help him sober up before Al got there.

As he stood in the shower with the water hitting him square in the face, yesterday's events were coming back to him. Bull had just killed two innocent people. No, killed wasn't the correct term; executed was the better choice of words for what he did. He was only there to scare the Albergo's for information on Anthony but Bull pulled a *One Flew over the Cuckoo's Nest* and things got out of control while he sat in the car. It wasn't until Bull got back to the car that he found out that there were two bodies back there. The only thought that wasn't clear in his head was how the hell he was going to get out of it. He didn't have the answer yet, but he needed to start focusing on what he was going to say to Frankie when he got questioned about what happened yesterday.

Anthony never even made it home from Kevin's. He found himself driving aimlessly on the Garden State Parkway just thinking about how he and Kevin were going to pull off Friday night without either of them getting killed. For Anthony, driving always cleared his mind. He could become so relaxed behind the wheel of a car that he could drive from point A to point B without realizing he had reached his destination until he was there. It's amazing how the mind can free itself from all worries when it is behind the wheel of a car driving on an empty highway at two o'clock in the morning. At this moment all of the days' events were miles behind him and the only thoughts that were going through his mind were the arrangements he had to make for Friday.

Anthony came out of his trance when he drove by a road sign reading "Dunkin Donuts" this exit. His mind and stomach at that instant got on the same page. Anthony was starving. Three apple and spice donuts and a cup of coffee were all he could think about. He needed food in the worst way.

After Anthony got back into his car, he put his coffee down in the cheap plastic cup holder and ripped opened the bag with the donuts in them. The first one went down in two big bites. The second one only took him three bites to finish. His body had been craving that sugar rush for hours. He was riding on pure adrenaline since the diner that morning. Anthony felt spent but there was too much business to take care of before Friday and he didn't have time to stop and sleep. He picked up the coffee out of the cup holder and took a nice long swallow. When he was finished he put his head back and didn't wake up until two hours later.

Anthony had no clue where he was or why he was sitting in his car but he somehow had the awareness to know that there was a cup of coffee in his hand. His head was throbbing and his neck and back were on fire but other than that he had no other complaints. He looked at the clock on the dashboard in front of him and it read six-forty five. It was already getting too late in the morning and since he didn't recognize the "Dunkin Donuts" parking lot, Anthony knew that he was far from where he wanted to be.

Anthony needed to get back to the city as soon as possible. There just wasn't enough time in the day to meet the four people that he had to see and time was already slipping away.

As he pulled back onto the Parkway, Anthony's visions of how Friday night's events would unfold came back to him. The further he drove, the stronger the images became and the stronger they became, the more confident he was of them pulling it off. Getting Kevin to feel the same was going to be a challenge, but he was the last person that Anthony needed to see before the end of the day so he had time to work on his sales speech.

The challenge at hand that Anthony had to work on was the order in which he was going to see the other three people on his list for today. He dreaded having to see all three of them, especially Sandra, who he wouldn't know what kind of reaction to expect. It had been over a year since he had seen her in person and they hadn't talked since she'd told him that she was getting remarried.

Another one of the people that he had to see was Larry Perna, who now owned almost all of Anthony's assets down at his pawnshop on the corner of 5th and Market, including his wedding band. It was always a pleasant experience walking into Perna's shop. He didn't know what he hated most about it. Was it the fact that he had to look at all his old possessions spread through out the shop or was it having to talk to that fat obnoxious bastard. It didn't matter what time of the day he would go there, Larry would always be puffing on a stub of a cigar, which most likely had been in his mouth for at least three days.

The last person on the list was Father John Jordan. Anthony hadn't seen him since the divorce because going to church wasn't a high priority anymore. He was sure Father John would have some harsh words for him about that and, of course, the divorce.

He tried to come up with an order to see them in by their availability in their day. Sandra would be home all day with Kimberly so he had at least until five o'clock before Chad got home. Father John usually did morning Mass and helped with the afternoon confessions so that left early evening for him. This left Perna, who lived in an apartment above the store and was always there. Oh well he thought, might as well get the least appealing one out of the way first.

Sal was standing in front of the mirror in the foyer practicing what he was going to say to Frankie when he heard the blast from the Cadillac outside. With one last look in the mirror he said to himself, "This is what separates the boys from the men."

Al hit the horn a second time as Sal was just coming out of the house. "Hurry the fuck up. We still have to pick up Bull and get to JFK by eight o'clock."

"Don't worry about it, we got plenty of time," Sal said as he jogged to the car.

"Well after 9/11 it takes forever to get through security and I don't feel like sticking around the airport all day waiting with Bull for the next available flight," he answered back as he opened the front passenger door.

Sal didn't notice that Victor Sosa was sitting behind Al as they pulled away.

"Morning Sal, heard you were a little under the weather."

"Holy shit, I never even noticed you back there. Yeah, something didn't agree with me yesterday. It was either that all you can eat seafood buffet at the Taj or that cheap ass greasy diner breakfast. Hell I could have gotten a bug from the bitch I was with for the night down in A.C."

"Now that wouldn't surprise me," Al said with a laugh.

"I don't understand why you two still pay for bitches," Victor complained.

"I never had to pay for a whore in my life, if anything, they should have been paying me."

Al looked in the rear view mirror and said, "That would have been the day to see some dumb bitch pay you money for thirty seconds worth of action."

Al and Sal both roared with laughter.

"That's the trouble with your fucking generation, always got something insulting to say. You two fucking numb nuts would never have scored like I did back in the seventies when everyone was basically giving it away."

"Ok dad, settle down back there. I didn't mean anything by it," Al said as he still couldn't get himself under control.

"You dad me one more time, and those won't be tears of joy you little fuck."

"Alright, alright, just shut the fuck up so I can get us to Bull's on time," he said still laughing a little.

Sal was feeling pretty at ease by the way the conversations were going. Usually if something was going down, it would have been a more somber mood in the car.

"So, how long is Bull going to Vegas?" he asked the both of them.

"Frankie wants him to pick up his World Series winnings at Caesars, so I don't think more than two days. He has to back in time for Friday night's book pick ups. We cleaned house so I'm sure Frankie wants the four of us to go get it," Al replied.

"Frankie told me we have to pick him up at eight o'clock Friday night after we leave the viewing," Victor chimed in from the back seat.

"Who's viewing?" Sal asked trying to sound surprised.

Al hesitated a moment before he looked over and answered Sal. "The kid's parents' viewing is Friday evening."

"I'm just surprised Frankie is sending you guys to the viewing."

"No one said anything about being sent. We are going out of respect to Anthony. He might not be a true member of ours, but he is still one of us and a straight up guy. So if I was you I would highly consider getting one of your suits ready for Friday night because you will be coming with us," Victor said.

"I didn't mean anything by it. I am just surprised with all that's going on and all that we will be dealing with that there should be more concern with finding the guys who did this."

"I don't think we have to worry about them. Frankie made some calls last night and got a lead from our friends down at the station. From what they tell us, one of the two guys left prints all over the counter top and they match them to some crack head nigger that has a huge sheet for the last several years."

"Typical low lives, leaving finger prints," Sal responded.

"Yeah, the police are getting the warrants written up this morning but it doesn't matter, they won't need them anyway. Frankie got the guy's home address and go figure, it is one of those fucking project buildings on the north side. We're heading there after the airport. Are you ready to fuck up a low life nigger?" Al asked.

"What kind of stupid question is that? You know I am always up for that, especially the way I am feeling this morning it would be nice to spread the joy if you know what I mean."

"So what does Frankie want us to do with them?" Sal asked.

"Because of the pressure Pete is putting on him, he wants them gone as quickly as possible. There's no fun involved with this visit. We are to go to the address and make sure they both are there and unload a clip into each of them. Of course you can aim anywhere you want but the last two go to the head. He wants the bodies left there for the police to find."

"We aren't going to dump them?" Sal asked.

"No, our guy down at the station promises to make it look like the two got double-crossed on a drug deal. He's going to plant some needles, vials of crack and a bag of cocaine. It will make them look like heroes with the media and the citizens and it will take the pressure off of us. Everyone goes home happy from this except for Anthony of course. Kid loses his parents and still owes Frankie fifty big ones. Kind of fucked-up if you ask me, but things are the way they are and that's that," Victor explained to Sal.

"How sure is Frankie that this cop isn't going to screw us and have a couple of undercovers waiting for us outside after we walk out of the building? I mean they can easily turn around and pin this on us and claim we were there plant-ing evidence on these guys to cover our asses saying it was mob related the whole time."

"Now why would they want to do that?" Victor asked.

"I don't know, you tell me. What's the bigger prize? Nailing a couple of crack heads, which are a dime a dozen or a head mob boss and a couple of his crew that have been running things for years? I hope Frankie has a lot of confi-dence in this guy. I never killed a cop before but I'm telling you this, if I walk out of that fucking project building and there are a couple waiting for us, my guns are a blazing."

"What do you think Al? You think Sal got a point?"

"Of course I got a point. I trust a cop about as much as I trust a nigger."

"Just settle the Christ down. I'm sure Frankie's guy has been checked out. Do you think it is the first time that we used him? And if he would even be dumb enough to double cross us, he would be dead before he could reap his rewards. We haven't even dealt with the airport bullshit yet and the two of yous got me so worked up. I swear to God I might end up shooting the both of yous before the day is over," Victor told them.

Anthony couldn't believe he was standing in front of Perna's shop again. He swore that no matter how bad things got he would never be in this place again to do business. But this time he was making a withdrawal instead of a deposit. It was just before eight o'clock and even though the sign read the store hours were Monday through Friday ten am. till six pm., Anthony knew Larry was in there. The man basically lived his life in this little shit-hole of a store and why not, he had everything a single guy could want at his disposal.

He tapped on the glass of the front door for about a minute before he saw Larry emerge from the back room.

"Fuck off, I ain't open yet, can't you read the sign on the door," he yelled from the counter.

Anthony was persistent and kept knocking and once Larry was close enough to see who had disturbed him from his stroke magazine he immediately changed his tone and rushed over to unlock the front door.

"Well if it ain't my favorite customer. Step right on in and let's do some business. Can't say I am surprised to see you Ant man. I figured your team broke your heart and your bank account again, so what are you handing over this time?"

Anthony was disgusted as soon as he saw Larry. Larry looked no better than most homeless men. His clothes were always dirty. No matter what shirt he had on, it never could keep his belly from sticking out. Larry shaved maybe once every two weeks and he probably showered even less than that, which would explain the smell that seemed to follow him.

With great reluctance, Anthony entered the shop. "I see you're still the same old piece of shit Perna, it's just a different day."

"Flattery ain't going to get you a better deal so save your breath kid. What did you bring me today?"

"I hate to disappoint you asshole but I came here to buy something."

"Are you shitting me? You had the Diamondbacks? There's no way you bet against your beloved Yankees. Even you aren't that stupid enough to get lucky. All kidding aside, what do you want to pawn?"

Anthony was in no mood to have a conversation with this low life. He wanted to be out of this store as soon as he could so he reached over and grabbed Larry with both hands by his collar and forced him face down against the front counter top.

"Listen to me you fucking scum of the earth, I want to go about our business as quickly as possible so shut the fuck up and listen to me and don't say a fucking word until I tell you, understand me?"

Larry was totally taken by surprise. Anthony had come to his shop at least thirty times over the last three years and he wouldn't be lying if he said

Anthony was his best customer. If Anthony had the time to look around him he would see many of his old belongings. Larry actually had Anthony's TV, couch, recliner, stereo system and entertainment center all together on the one side of the store almost set up exactly how Anthony had it in his first apartment after the divorce.

"I don't know who the fuck you think you are talking to, but this is my store and if you don't get your fucking hands off me, the cops will be picking pieces of you off the walls, floor, and ceiling if you catch my drift."

"Actually, it's you who doesn't have a clue who you are talking to. Do you know who I am with, asshole? If I let that someone know that you are a fucking sick child molester, they'll be finding pieces of your body all over this city, understand what I am saying?"

"Wait just a minute, I don't know what you been told but that's total bullshit and you know it. I never touched any kids before you little fuck," he screamed as the sweat started to trickle down the sides of his head.

"That's funny, I could have sworn that I read somewhere this summer that the police had you in for some questioning about having some grade schools boys in your shop."

"You asshole, it was all bullshit. One of their fathers was into someone for a lot of money and when he came down here and tried to dump some of his things, I wouldn't give him enough so that he could get even and what does he do? He goes to the police saying I lured his boy and a friend in here. The charges were never brought up because there wasn't any evidence. He didn't have a leg to stand on so don't even try to pull any shit with me kid. In fact get the fuck out of my store before I call the cops."

One of the first things Anthony had noticed about Larry this morning was how he looked much more like a slob than he was used to seeing. His shirt was hanging out as usual because it was too small to be tucked in over that fat belly and as for his pants; the crotch area was sticking out a little too far. Anthony didn't need to guess at what Larry was doing before he answered the door.

Anthony let go of Larry and started to head to the back room where he had emerged just five minutes ago.

"Where the fuck do you think you are going? You can't go back there."

But Larry's cries fell on deaf ears. Anthony went into the back room and stumbled onto what he was hoping to find. In the room were a small TV and a couch with a coffee table between them. Playing on the television was a foreign X-rated movie with two naked teen boys doing unspeakable things on a bed. On the coffee table were a couple of magazines that looked to be filled with the same disgusting things that was happening in the movie. Anthony bent over and picked up the magazine and went back to where he left Perna.

To Anthony's surprise, Larry had a twelve—gauge shotgun in his hands and it was aimed right at his head.

"Go ahead and try to walk out of here with that and see just how sick I really am." But to Larry's utter horror, Anthony kept right on walking toward him. Somewhere in the back of his mind, Anthony believed that this sick asshole would never pull the trigger.

"I don't quite think you understand the severity of this situation. I am walking out of here today with what I came for and you are going to give it to me free of charge. If you decide to shoot me, and I highly doubt a low life motherfucker like yourself has the balls to pull the trigger, my acquaintance will send a couple of his people over here."

"Who the fuck are you trying to bullshit? You don't have that kind of power."

"Actually, yes I do Larry. See, first they will work you over for kicks. Sort of like the kicks you get when you watch one of the movies back there. Then they are going to burn this shit-hole to the ground while you beg them to stop hurting you and finally, they'll kill you by either cutting or shooting off your balls and watching you bleed to death. I guess it just depends on if they are wearing gloves or not because I wouldn't recommend touching those things without them. Did I paint you a fair picture or not?" Anthony calmly asked.

"You don't scare me you little piss ant. You don't have that kind of pull and you know it. I ain't giving you shit, so fuck off and get out of here," he yelled back as he started to lower the shotgun.

"Larry, let's not be stupid, I came in here for one thing and I am either leaving here with it or you are going to shoot me. You don't want to call my bluff because I do have that clout with Frankie and he will have people over here in less than twenty-four hours to do what I said they would do. Did you really think I took a guess that those magazines and movies would be back there? To almost everyone, you are the worst kind of criminal, you are a sick shit that needs to be flushed away if you catch my drift."

Realizing that Anthony wasn't kidding about his intentions and he could no longer keep up any kind of front that he would shoot Anthony, Larry decided to cave in and ask him what he came in here for in the first place. "What the fuck do you want from me?" he asked with hardly the same tough guy tone in his voice that was there a few moments ago.

"I'm sure you have at least one or two of want I need. I am looking for a 9mm, do you got one?"

"The kid is finally playing in the big leagues. Yeah, I actually have one left and two or three clips to go with it."

"That's fine. I won't need that much ammo anyway, one clip will do."

Larry went over to a glass case next to the counter and took out the last 9 mm he had left with the two clips of bullets and brought them back to the counter and laid them down on it.

"I will go far enough as to sell you this gun but I will be damned if I am letting you walk out of here with out paying for it. I don't run no charity around here and I sure as hell wouldn't start by letting you be the first."

"I had no intentions of paying you," Anthony replied back as he already had the gun in his hand and the first clip installed.

Anthony had the gun pointed at Perna's face. "Don't like it much do you? I should just do the world a favor and kill you now but that's not on my agenda today. But I will promise you two things Larry: first, I'm not giving you a fucking cent for this gun, and be happy with that because that's my final offer. And second, and pay attention because this is important, if anyone happens to come by here and ask if I have been in your store recently, no matter what answer you give them, they are still going to kill you. If I were you, I would close the shop for a couple of weeks and take a trip to one of those Asian countries, where they tolerate the sick shit that you like to do."

Anthony headed towards the front door and for the first time he left this place feeling happy.

"You'll be back you little piss ant and when you do I promise you that things won't turn out the same next time," Larry yelled from the counter.

Anthony opened the door and turned around with a smile on his face. "The next time you see me Perna, it'll be in hell and you'll have been there a long time waiting for me."

That was the last time Anthony saw or talked to Larry Perna because someone else was going to pay Larry a visit this week and they weren't going to be as friendly as Anthony.

Bull was standing at the curb when Al pulled the Cadillac up next to him. Sal got out and opened the right rear passenger door and met Bull about three feet from the door.

"I heard you are getting to go to Sin City for two days."

"Yeah, I guess. Frankie wants me out of sight for a while until things blow over. No matter what, don't be stupid and say anything. No one likes a rat, just remember that."

"See that Vic, our Bull is a smart guy. He knows he's only going to be gone for two days so all he's got with him is a carry on bag now we don't have to worry about checking in any luggage at the front counter. If he would be bringing a woman with him, forget about it, three fucking bags and an hour headache at the check in counter," Al said as Victor and Sal laughed at that.

"I would bring the bags on the plane and check the bitch instead," Bull replied. This got even more of a roar from Al and Victor.

"So you ready for a little sun and fun for a couple of days?" Victor turned and asked Bull.

"Yeah, after thinking it over last night, why the fuck do I want to hang around here with a bunch of wise guys like yous in this city in the cold of November? I would rather be lying in a lounge chair pool side watching the young girls greasing themselves up with tanning lotion."

"See that Sal, you keep hanging out with this guy and you'll learn something. He ain't stupid. He knows it would be much better out trying to fuck some bitch than sticking around here killing a couple of niggers," Al said while heading onto the expressway ramp to JFK.

Bull leaned over the front seat and asked Al, "What did you mean about that?"

"Didn't Frankie tell you? One of our men down at the station said they got some prints from the counter top at the store and it turned out to be some crack head nigger that had a huge wrap sheet. He gave us an address and we're heading there after we drop you off."

"They came back with prints that quickly?" Bull asked in a stunned voice.

Victor responded to him before Al could. "In a high profile case like this, they want to give the public the felons as quickly as possible, even if it isn't the right guys, just as long as someone fries for it. Frankie doesn't care if they did or didn't, if the cops are pinning it on this guy and his friend that's good enough for him so it's good enough for us as well. We're going to head to the projects, knock on the guy's apartment door and when he answers, we're to put a full clip into him and anyone else that might be in there. Frankie was promised that our man had a unit waiting to head inside after we were done and they were going to make sure that there were drugs and other incriminating evidence in the apartment. So hopefully everyone will be happy and this will all be over with shortly."

"My uncle never misses a beat. I knew he would get to the bottom of this without a hitch."

Al looked into the rear view mirror and made eye contact with Bull. "Let's not go celebrating already. We haven't nailed the fucker yet and we won't know if this is going to look real or not when it's all said and done. My main concern is when this is all over that Pete doesn't want any retribution for what happened in our own territory. Just say a prayer that he looks the other way on this and we all walk away clean. If not, God only knows who he wants to take the blame for this, including your uncle."

Bull decided not to comment on this and the last ten minutes of the ride to the airport they all sat in silence. Al was thinking to himself that he and Victor had done the job that Frankie had asked of them; keep Bull and Sal relaxed and sell the bullshit story of the two niggers. He could see that Sal was totally relaxed and had no idea what was in store for him once they got to the projects.

It was just after eleven when Anthony pulled up across the street from the front of his old home. The house still looked the same other than the name on the mailbox. God, he couldn't believe how much he missed this place and Sandra. This was his dream that he started for them and now he wasn't a part of it at all.

He couldn't muster up the courage to get out yet. He didn't need any courage this morning when he went to Perna's. Anthony was quite confident of what the outcome was going to be before he arrived at the store. When it came to dealing with Sandra, he had no clue as to what to expect from her, not even a gut intuition. All Anthony was hoping for was that they could talk like two rational adults and that she would let him have some time with Kimberly.

Anthony killed the engine and sat there for a few moments in silence. All at once a little nostalgia came to him and he opened the glove compartment looking to see if he still had his cassette tapes in there. He was rummaging through all the vehicle papers, expired parking tickets, that he was never going to have to worry about and some old pictures when he found the cassette holder.

He only had three or four in there. Like everyone else in the world, he had converted his music collection to cds but he still had a couple of tapes left because his car didn't have a cd player. He took out the holder and unzipped it and to his amazement the tape that he wanted was still in there. Without even thinking twice he took the tape out and put it into the player and pushed play.

It didn't take long for the acoustic guitar, piano and flute to flow through the speakers of his car. A moment later the soulful voice of Van Morrison was singing Tupelo Honey.

Anthony had already drifted off before the second verse began. He was back to their second year of dating, their last year of college when he had taken her on the date that would seal their marriage.

It was a Saturday in late October and it was an unexpected warm and beautiful day. They were in her dorm room and she was studying hard for a marketing test on Monday and he was just going over the last of his morning bets when he asked her what she wanted to do today.

"Anthony, you know I have this marketing test on Monday and I need to get in as much studying as possible this weekend."

"Come on Sandi, it's too nice to be stuck in all day plus I have a great idea anyway. I'll let you study for a couple more hours but when I come back I want you to be showered and ready to go out. Dress casual, but pack an overnight bag and make sure you bring the nicest formal dress that you have for later tonight."

"Are you serious? Where are we going that I need a formal dress? Anthony, you know it will take me at least a couple of hours to get ready if we are going somewhere nice and I really don't the time to prepare myself."

"You can get ready in the car because it will be at least a couple hour drive. Just continue to study and I will be back later this afternoon."

Anthony kept his promise and was back in three hours. Sandra was just finishing throwing the last of her personal items in her duffel bag.

"So are you ready to get out of here for the night?" he asked her as she was running back and forth from her bedroom to the bathroom grabbing items that she needed.

"Anthony, I really have to be back early tomorrow because I really need to finish studying for my test."

"It's really no big deal. I just thought a nice ride along the country side would do the both of us some good. You'll stop agonizing about your schoolwork and I won't worry about a score board for a change. See, we'll both get something out of it. I'll have you home nice and early tomorrow morning. So what do you say, are you ready to take a nice ride and have a fun evening?"

"I guess you're right. I can use a night out because I am stressing myself out way too much about this test."

They had driven for over two hours in relative silence except for a few comments here and there. They were both soaking in the sun's rays and taking in the beauty of the day. You can tell when you share something special with someone when you can be in their presence and not have to say anything to each other. You know they are there because the moment wouldn't be perfect without them being with you to share in it.

Anthony pulled the car into Marion Caterers just as the sun was setting. It was a little after seven o'clock and there were fifty to sixty cars in the parking lot along with four limousines. The big sign out front in the parking lot had read "Congratulations on your marriage Christopher and Patricia."

Sandra had straightened up in her seat and was no longer totally relaxed. "I can't believe you didn't tell me you were bringing me to a wedding. Is this wedding for someone in your family? My God Anthony, I can't see your family like this without my hair being properly done. Please, you can't make me go in there. I will be devastated," she said as she started to cry.

"Why are you getting yourself all worked up? I don't know who Chris and Patricia are and we weren't invited to their wedding so why are you having a nervous breakdown?" he asked as he held her hand.

"I don't know, I saw the sign and remembered my dress and your suit in back of the car and put two and two together."

"If we weren't invited why are we here?" she asked stunned.

"I said we weren't invited and I didn't know who they were but we are here to go to their wedding. Didn't you ever crash a wedding before?"

Sandra sat there totally shocked. This was not her at all. She wasn't spontaneous and carefree. There was a risk involved and Sandra never took chances. If they got caught, she would be embarrassed for life. "Anthony, there is no way you are getting me in that wedding. Are you out of your mind? What if we get caught? Do you know how embarrassed I will be? Let's just call it a day and head back to school and you can crash in my dorm and I'll make it exciting."

But Anthony was all ready out of the car and changing as she was speaking to him. "Sandra, that's the problem about your plan, it isn't exciting. I mean don't get me wrong, I love the whole exciting part of your plan but where's the adventure in it? There are no tangibles involved. Everything with you is always planned out so where's the unexpected surprise? You have five minutes to get dressed right here in the car and come with me or you can sit in the car until I decide I have had enough fun with Chris and Trisha and decide to come back out."

"You have got to be kidding. You expect me to just change right here next to the car where people can see me?"

"It's dark out and everyone is inside. Who is going to see you? Will you just stop worrying about consequences for once and live outside the lines for a change."

When she got out of the car, Anthony already was dressed except for his suit coat. It was amazing to her how he got dressed that fast outside next to a car without even looking in a mirror.

"Good, I'm glad you decided to join me on this little adventure into the unknown," he said as he walked over to her side of the car.

"Now I'll stand in front of you so don't worry about someone watching you. Just get your clothes off and throw on the dress and you can do your hair inside if you want or you can take my word that you look beautiful enough and we'll head right into the reception."

It didn't take Sandra long to decide. Before she even realized what she was doing her jeans were around her ankles. Next she took off her sweatshirt and grabbed the dress from the back seat. She slipped it on, took out some deodorant and perfume from her bag and did a little touching up here and there. She fished around in the bag for her make up mirror and applied the finishing touches. When she was satisfied she put everything back in the bag and shut the door.

"Well, what do you think?" she asked as she stood in front of him awaiting approval.

Anthony could only stand there staring at her. Sandra looked like everyone's girl next door. She was just five foot five with sandy blonde hair and an incredible figure, which her dress complimented. Looking at her at that moment, Anthony believed she could be on the cover of any magazine she wanted.

"See that, I knew you had it in you to go through with it. You look absolutely stunning," he replied as he kissed her gently on the lips.

"Promise we won't be long?"

He took her hand and led her to the entrance of the place. "Here's the plan. We walk in and go right to the table with the invitations, we find out where there are empty seats and then we walk right to the bar. Its eight o'clock now, so dinner should be over and the dancing and other activities will be in full force. Most people are going to be either at the bar or on the dance floor as the bride and groom start to walk around, saying their hellos and collecting the envelopes. We are going to blend right in with everyone else. We'll have a couple of drinks. Have one or two dances and head out. Does that sound okay with you?"

"I can't believe I am going to crash a wedding. I never even went to a party in high school if I wasn't invited. How do you just find the courage to do these things Anthony? I could never have done something crazy like this."

"That's the problem Sandra. You think this is a crazy stunt. We are only walking into someone's wedding uninvited. What's the big deal if we get caught? They are merely going to ask us to leave. You only live once and you need to start living a little more. Throw some thrill into your life. We are graduating this year and then what? Starting our careers and maybe a family one-day? Who even knows if you and I will be together then so for now, let's just have a little fun tonight."

Anthony was right about what was going on. Almost everyone was on the dance floor doing the chicken dance, a dance he absolutely hated from all the Italian weddings that he had been to, or standing around the bar.

"You've got to love an open bar wedding," he said as he handed Sandra her drink.

"Ok, I have to admit this is really cool. We can keep a low profile and hang out here for a little while."

"I hate to tell you, but I am heading onto the floor when they announce all the single bachelors out there for the garter throw."

"Well, depending how you make out I might just find the courage to go out there to catch the bouquet," she said with that smile that just always stopped his heart.

"How funny do you think it is going to be three weeks from now when Chris and Patricia are looking through the video and photo albums and there we are on the dance floor for both events. Who do you think will say they know who we are to the other first?" he said laughingly.

"I bet it will be him because the girl always knows who is on the guest list," she answered.

After her second drink, Sandra was starting to really enjoy herself. They stood by the bar for awhile just talking and drinking and watching people they never met make complete jackasses out of themselves on the dance floor.

"Isn't it great when you can stand back and make fun of complete strangers?"

"Anthony, this was such a great idea. I am so happy that you convinced me to "live your life the right way" by Anthony Albergo."

Anthony laughed at her comment as he put his empty glass on the bar. "I'll be right back. I have to head to the little boy's room because the drinks are going through me too quick."

"Hey, don't you leave me here too long."

"I swear. I'll be back in a second. It doesn't take that long you know," he replied with a smile as he walked away.

On his way back from the men's room he made a quick u-turn to the deejay table.

"Yo buddy, I need you to do me a favor," Anthony yelled to try to be heard over the music.

"What's up?"

"I need you to play a song for me," he responded.

The deejay threw him a look before he answered. "Dude, you must be kidding me. Do you see that list over there on top of the records? Well, that's the list of songs everyone wants me to play tonight and that isn't even the bride and groom's personal list that I have in front of me. So unless your song happens to be on their list, I think you are shit out of luck," he said as he continued his work on the turntables.

Anthony thought to himself that he was obviously dealing with an amateur. He worked his way around all the albums and speakers to get behind the table next to the deejay. The deejay had headphones on and was listening for the moment to start the next song when Anthony tapped him on the shoulder.

"I don't think you understood what I said back there. I want you to play a song for me next and I want you to announce a dedication before you play it," Anthony told him as he handed him a C note.

"Are you shitting me? You are going to give me a hundred dollars just to play a song for you?"

"No, I am giving you a hundred dollars for you to play a song for me and make a dedication to my girlfriend before you do it."

"Look, I am only making two hundred and fifty for this five-hour reception, this is one hell of a tip you are giving me."

"I know, so please put this tape in your tape deck and just push play. It is already set at the spot of the song."

Anthony handed the deejay the tape along with a note with what he was to say before he played the song.

"Okay it will be on after the next song," he promised Anthony as he returned to his duty of playing the next record on the list.

Anthony walked across the dance floor to the bar where he saw Sandra looking around for him impatiently. "Did you miss me?"

"Where the heck have you been?" she asked in a frustrated tone.

"I ran into the bride and groom on my way back and I offered them my blessings."

"Are you serious? What did they say?"

"The usual, thank you for coming to our wedding and sharing this special day and so on and so on."

As Anthony was finishing his explanation the deejay came on the microphone. "Okay, it's time to slow the pace down a little. All you love birds out there, including the married ones, these next three songs are for you guys. I want to see some real close slow dancing going on out there. The first song is especially dedicated to Sandra from Anthony. Thank you for taking a chance and seeking some excitement for once in your life."

Sandra didn't have a clue as to what was happening as Anthony led her onto the dance floor while the deejay started the song. "Anthony, I can't believe you actually dedicated a song for me. How on earth are we going to dance with all these people looking at us and not one of them know who we are?"

"Just go with the flow and don't think about it," he answered.

Van Morrison's *Tupelo Honey* played, while Anthony and Sandra danced together in the middle of the dance floor with only four other couples dancing along with them. Sandra had her head on Anthony's shoulder and he had his against hers.

What they were doing could hardly be called slow dancing rather than just two people becoming one with each other in a slow movement to the rhythm of a song. They never once kissed or looked at each other during the playing of the song. There was no need for any for that; it went perfect without needing to express their love in any other way. For them, it was that one special moment in time that all lovers seek to experience with their soul mate but only a few actually succeed.

When the song was over, Sandra lifted her head and had tears streaming down her face. "That was the most beautiful experience of my life Anthony. I was actually lost somewhere that whole time yet I wasn't because I was here with you. I don't know if I could ever feel that special again."

"Sandra, I can't promise you wealth, I can't promise you all the things a girl wants in life but the only promise I can offer you is that I will always love you," he replied to her as he slipped an engagement ring on her finger.

"I guess I was wrong. I feel even more special," she said as she started to tremble. "I will marry you one day and I know you will make me happy for the rest of my life."

Al pulled up to the USAir gate. There were policemen everywhere. After 9/11, cars weren't permitted to park in the drop off lanes for a long period of time. "Go have yourself some fun, don't fuck up bringing back Frankie's money and what ever you do, don't miss your flight back because we need you for Friday night," Al lectured him.

"Stop being a fucking douche bag. When have I ever fucked-up a pick up for Frankie? Tell him I'll call in after I get the money."

As Bull was exiting the car, Victor got out from the back, "Hey, don't forget to call Al's cell phone Friday night when you get off the plane because we'll be parked on the exit ramp like everyone else. Once we get the call, we'll pick you up at the curb."

"No problem," he said as he leaned in the window and said goodbye to everyone not realizing that this was the last time he would see any of them again.

Anthony snapped out of his day dream before the song was over. He didn't know what he was trying to accomplish by playing that song. It only brought him great sorrow whenever he heard it, but he was trying to find their happy place before he got out of the car to face Sandra. He got out of the car and without realizing he was doing it, Anthony picked up the 9 mm that was lying on the passenger seat and stuck it in the back of his waist band.

He couldn't believe he was standing in front of a home that he owned and was ringing the doorbell to get inside. It only took Chad about five seconds to open the door after Anthony rang the bell.

"What are you doing here Anthony? You know she doesn't want to see you."

"Chad, can you please just go get her for a second. I'm not sure you have been paying attention to the current events in the news but I just lost my parents and she just lost her ex-in-laws."

"We both feel sorry about your loss, but that still doesn't change the fact that she doesn't want to see you and even if she did, I wouldn't allow it. So do me a favor and get back into that little piece of shit car and get the hell out of here before I call the cops," he said as he closed the door on Anthony's face.

It took Anthony only a few moments to register what just happened to him. His ex-wife's new husband basically told him to fuck off and then finished the deal by closing the door in his face. Anthony rang the doorbell again. Chad, who never moved from the other side of the door, opened it swiftly.

"I thought I told you to get the…." but before he could finish his sentence he realized that he had a gun pointing right in his face.

"Chad, I'm not sure but I really don't think you understood what I asked you a second ago. I want to see Sandra for a minute or two and I will be damned if I let her new husband, who is living in a home that I bought, tell me to fuck off."

"Oh, I understood what you said and it still doesn't change anything."

"Seeing as I have the gun and you aren't man enough to do anything about it, you will allow me inside while you go get Sandra for me. One more thing Chad, if you are stupid enough to try something funny, I'm going to blow your fucking face off, because to be honest, I never liked the fact that my ex-wife married a guy like you. To me, you're nothing but a common thief. I mean you prey on a naive woman, who was going through a divorce, and when you find out she is getting a nice home from the settlement, you make sure you marry her. Yep, you're one hell of a guy Chad."

"Anthony, don't be stupid and put away the gun before you do something you are going to regret."

"See, there's where you are wrong Chad. I won't regret shooting you in the face. In case you aren't keeping score, but I am sure you are, you must know that a lot hasn't been going right lately for me, so what the hell do I care if I spend the rest of my life in jail for killing the asshole that married my ex-wife?"

"Fine, just put away the gun once I let you in here. I don't want you scaring Sandra and Kimberly."

"Don't you worry about that asshole. I'm just here to say goodbye to them and what the hell are you doing here anyway, shouldn't you be at your office?"

"Well I figured you would eventually be around today or tomorrow so I wanted to be here to make sure she didn't talk to you," he replied.

"So the good doctor wanted to be a tough guy. Wanted to be the big hero for his little wife and step daughter? I guess you don't realize the kind of people I associate with Chad. Do you really think I would let you tell me to take a hike? You must really be fucking stupid. If I wanted to see my daughter for one last time, neither you nor anyone else would be able to stop me."

Chad took two steps back and gave Anthony room to enter. Anthony let Chad lead the way into the kitchen and when they got there he called Sandra. But what neither one of them was aware that Sandra had been standing in the dining room holding Kimberly the whole time the two of them were at the door.

"Hello Anthony. I guess you still haven't changed. In fact, I think you actually got worse. How dare you point a gun at Chad? What on earth were you thinking? He's my husband for God sake's. I have no idea what you want to talk about but I have nothing to say to you. I am truly sorry about your parents' death. I even had all the intentions in the world of going to the funeral, but after that display how could you expect me to go now?" she asked as she started to weep.

"Sandi, please listen to me for a second. All I came up here for was to say goodbye to Kimberly. I'm leaving the city for good after the funeral Saturday and I just wanted to see her one last time. Can we just go into the family room for a minute and talk? If you give me that I promise I will be out of your lives forever."

"You expect me to believe that you are just up and leaving and we're never going to hear from you again?"

"Yes, after today I can promise you that I'll be out of your life for one reason or another."

"You're in that much trouble Anthony?"

"Not as much now as I will be come Friday, so please let me talk to you for a couple of minutes. I want to go over some paper work for Kimberly's future."

"Okay, you can stay for twenty minutes and then you'll have to go. It's already Kimberly's nap time and I don't want to throw her off her schedule. She's really cranky when she doesn't get her sleep."

"Hum, I wonder who she got that from."

"I'll leave you two alone and head back upstairs to my office. I've got a lot of paperwork that I have to get back to before you came and interrupted."

"I think I want you right there sitting at the kitchen table where I can see you. In fact before you sit down, why don't you put on a pot of coffee? I know I can go for some," he answered back to Chad.

"What do you think I would be stupid enough to call the police and endanger my wife and daughter?"

"The question really isn't if you are that stupid enough, I already know you are an idiot, but if you would be chicken shit enough to actually sneak out of here and abandon your wife and step daughter if I gave you the chance?" Anthony answered.

"Anthony, if you expect me to talk to you, you are not to use that kind of language in front of Kimberly. You are sitting with your daughter, not your Mafia friends."

"You are absolutely right and I apologize, it won't happen again. Now can we go sit and talk?"

"Does everyone know what they have to do?" Al asked as they approached the project building.

"Yeah, you and I are going to knock on the door and when the guy answers, I am to hit the door with all I got and you are going to take the first shots. Victor stays back and keeps guard in the hallway. I am to look around to make sure he is alone and after I secure the place, we sit him down on the couch and ask who was with him yesterday. After we get what we want, I will unload my clip into him and we will exit this dump. Victor will be the first to go down to the car and make sure everything is on the up and up and then we are gone."

"Glad to see we are all on the same page. I don't want to go busting in there with my pants down and my dick in my hands if you don't know what to do," Al replied.

"Forget about it, you don't have to worry about me. You're acting like this is the first hit that Frankie sent me on."

"No, this isn't your first hit for Frankie, but it is the most important one. All of our lives are depending on this going right. We can't afford any fuck-ups," Victor leaned over from the back seat and replied.

Al pulled the Cadillac up in the back alley of the building. The three of them got out together and went in through the back entrance of the projects.

"What apartment is our guy's?" Sal asked.

Al took out a piece of paper that had the name Tyrone Willis apartment 15C, 8th floor written on it. "Our boy Tyrone lives on the 8th floor in apartment 15C," he answered.

"Jesus Christ you expect me to walk up eight fucking flights of stairs?" Victor cried in anguish.

"Oh, stop your bitching old man. If you didn't smoke and eat like you do, eight flights of stairs would be a piece of cake. I bet you're going to tell a story how back in the day, you could do twenty flights of stairs, beat the shit out of some mark and still had enough energy once you got home to go two rounds in bed with the Mrs."

"Watch your mouth or I might forget to get your back if things don't go right."

"If things go wrong in there, I think your old ass would be my last choice for back up," Al said laughing as they continued up the flight of stairs.

"Like the elevator would still be here. I bet these niggers took it out and sold it on the streets for some crack," Sal responded laughingly.

Unfortunately for Victor, they had to take the stairs because three white men standing in the lobby of a project building waiting for the elevator would have looked out of place. It would have made it easier for any witness to remember the three of them when the authorities showed up asking questions.

Al looked at both of them as he had his gun out, "Is everyone ready?" He looked at Victor, who nodded, and then over to Sal. He could see why Sal was always sent on jobs like this. The guy had a look of a Green Beret ready to attack an enemy base in the middle of the night. His face was stone cold and colorless but his eyes were full of a blazing rage. It was eerie to Al just how intense Sal became before they entered the apartment. Al had committed hits for Frankie before, but he treated it as a job because that's all it was to him. Sal seemed to get passionate about it.

"Sal, are you still with us?" Al asked.

"Yeah, I'm ready, just give the signal."

"So, what kind of trouble are you in Anthony? Does it have anything to do with your parents' death? It is, isn't it? I just don't understand you anymore. You're not the person who swept me off my feet back in college. You never realized it was time to grow up and take responsibility for your actions and your parents had to pay with their lives for your lack of maturity," she said to him as she continued to cry.

Anthony was listening to her, but he was more interested in watching Kimberly color with her crayons on a big Barney poster.

"Will you look at that, she's doing a really good job staying in the lines and she's not even three yet. God, I hope she takes after you and doesn't turn out like me. Please promise me you will be a great mother and guide her in making the right decisions."

"Did you even listen to a word I said Anthony? I'm not interested in your concern about Kimberly. I want to know the truth about your parents and what is going on with you," she demanded.

"Look at you finally taking charge of a situation for a change. Well good for you Sandra. I hope you don't let people push you around anymore, especially that asshole you married."

"You leave Chad out of this, our marriage is no concern of yours."

"Listen, we are obviously getting off on the wrong foot and this is not what I want. I don't have much time today to sit here and go over our past problems and how you feel that I destroyed our marriage and myself. I just want to tell you about a couple of things and then I need to ask you for a big favor. If you let me down on this favor, you won't be letting just me down, but my parents too and I know you wouldn't want to do that."

"That's a laugh, don't even try to spin this around on me you asshole. I loved your parents and I will not let you try to put a guilt trip on me. There's no favor I could possibly do for you that would have any bearing on them," she cried back.

"Sandra, please just hear me out. If you want closure on us, let me speak and then I'll be out of your life forever."

"One, two, three," Al said as Sal busted through the door. The apartment's living room area was empty as they entered. Sal immediately ran through the living room and kicked opened the first door he saw. After hearing the first crash made by the front door, Tyrone sprang off his bed and reached for the baseball bat under the bed. He got within three feet of the bedroom door before Sal came crashing in and shot him in the leg. Tyrone dropped to the floor clutching his leg and wailing in pain two feet in front of Sal.

"Jesus Christ motherfucker, what the hell do you want?" he cried.

"Time to pay the devil you low life nigger," Sal replied as he grabbed Tyrone by the hair and dragged him out into the living room knocking over a table and a lamp as he went through the hall.

"Throw him onto the couch," Al yelled over to him from the other side of the room.

"What the fuck do you two want from me?" Tyrone demanded to know. "If Bobby wants his money, I'm good for it. I don't know why he sent you two fucks down here to get it. Shit man, I was going to have it for him on Friday."

Sal kicked him in the chest as they reached the couch.

"Just shut the fuck up asshole. We weren't sent by Bobby, who ever the fuck that is, we're here for retribution for the two people you axed yesterday in the Italian village."

"What people? I wasn't at no village yesterday. You got the wrong brother, I swear to God it wasn't me," he cried.

Al walked over to Tyrone and slapped him across the face. "I think you better start telling us what happened yesterday or you are going to have more than just that one hole in your leg Tyrone."

"Please man, you got to believes me when I say, it wasn't me. I was with Maurice all day on errands for Bobby, you can check with him, he'll tell you. Man, just pick up the phone and calls him."

Al looked at Sal and just that quickly another bullet went into Tyrone's other leg. There was a loud scream but in the projects, there are always loud screams that go unheard. Though gunshots were just as common as screams in this building, Sal's gun had a silencer on it because he intended to fire many shots before leaving the apartment, and too many shots might bring the police.

Victor came in through the front door and said, "You better put something in his mouth. I don't know what it will take for one of these neighbors to finally call the cops so put a muzzle on him."

Tyrone was screaming in agony as he rocked back and forth on the couch with both hands on his leg as he laid there in a fetal position. Al walked past Sal and headed into the kitchen where he grabbed a towel from the sink and brought it back over to where Tyrone was and rammed it halfway down his throat. He began to rock fiercely back and forth because the towel was blocking his airway and he was choking on his own mucous.

Al sat Tyrone straight up in the center of the couch. His body began to tremble out of control as Al slapped him a couple of times to try to settle him down.

"I'm going to ask you one more time Tyrone and I want the truth and if you don't give it to me, my friend over there is going to put another bullet into you. The next one might be to the knee or maybe even worse, how about that big dick of yours? I don't think you'll need it again anyway."

"I doubt highly that he will need it again. Maybe I'll practice my aim and shoot for the center," Sal chimed in from the other side of the room.

Tyrone shook his head violently back and forth pleading with them as the tears rolled down his face. He was trying to scream something, but the towel muffled any words that he might have been trying to say.

"Tyrone, look at me. Look at me you piece of shit," Al yelled at him. Tyrone immediately looked over and nodded his head yes. "Now Tyrone, why did you execute those people yesterday?"

He could only cry and bounce up and down profoundly and shake his head back and forth but it was to no avail because before he could finish trying to scream words through the towel there was a massive sting where his penis and balls used to be. There was a sudden warm flow gushing out from the center of his pants after the bullet went through him. The initial sting immediately intensified into a massive pain and after Tyrone realized that he was shot a third time he had passed out from the excruciating pain that he was suffering.

"I wasn't directly involved with my parents' death Sandra. One of Frankie's men took his job too far and got out of control and killed them. I lost fifty thousand in the World Series to Frankie, and his collector didn't think I was good for the money. He went to pay my parents a visit to convince them to pay my debt."

"Jesus Anthony, how the hell could you have possibly bet fifty thousand dollars? Where did you expect to get that kind of money?"

"What kind of question is that? Who the hell paid for this house? I guess the lawyers didn't tell you it was already paid off? I guess you didn't know that my parents' store doesn't have a mortgage either? I'm not this big loser that everyone would like to believe. I'm going to tell you something that only one other person is aware of and Sandra, this is the kind of information that can get you killed, so before I go on do you want to know the whole truth or not?"

Sandra couldn't believe this was happening to her now. Before yesterday morning her life was all roses. She had Kimberly and Chad and everything was perfect. She hadn't thought of Anthony in months, maybe even a year. That part of her life had been closed until today. Anthony's visit not only reopened it but he was going to control her again.

"Anthony, I don't know what I want from you. I know our whole marriage was based on lies. I know you were a faithful husband but other than that I don't know what other horrible things that you did. You were spending more time with the wrong crowd than you were with your family."

"Sandi, what kind of horrible things do you think I did?" he asked.

"Oh, I heard the stories that were going around about you. Do you think I was stupid? I knew about Frankie and who he was but I didn't believe people when they said you were with him. How deep are you with these people Anthony? What did you do for them?" she begged him to answer her as tears started to pour down her face again.

"Please tell me you haven't killed anyone. Anthony, if you killed someone I could never look at you again as a person. You would be nothing more than an animal and I will never let you near me or your daughter again if you answer yes to that question."

"Do you want to wake him up before I waste him or should I just finish the job?" Sal turned and asked Al.

"I think he suffered enough and we're pressed for time. I just need to take care of something first," he answered.

Al took out a pair of gloves and moved Tyrone's body into a sitting position again. He was still alive but that would soon change. Al looked down at the couch to make sure he wasn't about to sit in a pool of blood. He crouched down as close to the couch as he could and then opened his jacket and took out a 9mm and aimed it at Sal. "You might want to move a little unless you want to get hit."

"Whoa, what the fuck are you doing Al?"

Al paid him no mind and fired two shots to the left of Sal and into the kitchen.

"Why did you do that?" Sal demanded.

"You think it will look real if this guy didn't put up some kind of fight. He just shot two people yesterday with a 9mm, you think he wouldn't be ready for the cops or us without be armed?"

"You're right, but shouldn't you have put it in his hands first before you fired it? There are no prints on the gun."

"Jesus Christ what the fuck was I thinking. I swear to God I act like such an amateur some times when it comes to this stuff. I've been doing this so long, you would think that I would be good at this shit by now."

He placed the gun in Tyrone's right hand and placed his index finger on the trigger. Al motioned to Sal with Tyrone's hand and the gun. "You might want to move back to the middle of the room. I can't shoot in the same spot again. Now it will look like he was shooting all over the place."

Sal went back to where he was standing when he shot Tyrone.

"This fine?" he asked.

"Yeah, perfect," Al replied as he aimed the gun back at Sal and then shot him twice in the stomach.

Sal dropped his gun and immediately hit the floor. His was clutching his stomach wailing and howling in pain. "Al, what the fuck are you doing? Jesus Christ, you shot me. You fucking shot me Al," he cried over and over.

"It's time to pay for Anthony's parents Sal. We can make this quick and end your pain or you can suffer worse than our boy Tyrone."

"I swear Al it was Bull! I didn't have any part in it," he cried as he started to cough up blood.

"You know a gut shot is one of the most painful places to take a bullet. They say the pain is a hundred times worse than when a woman gives birth. Now since I never experienced either one of these events I can't say, but I'm sure you could voice an opinion. I'm not going to ask you again Sal, what happened yesterday and why did you guys kill his parents?"

Sal couldn't remember the last time he actually cried in front of someone but right now that was the furthest thing from his mind. He realized there was no way he was leaving this apartment alive, but he at least wanted to die with dignity and to make sure that Bull took the fall and suffered a worse death.

Sal started to try to sit up but the pain was too intense and his coughing was getting worse. Blood was spraying everywhere from his mouth with each cough.

"Bull wanted to go down to the store after Anthony crapped out Monday. When we got to the store, it was only his mother at the counter."

Sal took a moment because the coughing was getting out of hand. He tried once again to sit up hoping it would stop the coughing. Sal managed to get into a sitting position and went on with the story.

"Bull was just being Bull and tried to scare the woman to make sure Anthony paid his debt. I was going down the aisles knocking things over and I even broke a couple of glass refrigerator windows in the back. We both forgot about the old man being there and he snuck up behind me and clubbed me with his shotgun. I was out for awhile and when I came to, he had the gun pointed at Bull."

Sal struggled to get up but it was no use, he could feel all the energy escape him and he was getting cold. He was aware that he was running out of time and didn't have much longer to tell Al everything.

"I manage to return the favor and sneak up on the old man and he got off one shot before I got him to the ground. Bull told me to get the car ready because he believed someone had to have heard the shot. That's it, end of story. I walked out and waited for Bull in the car," he said and blood continuously poured from his mouth.

"You're telling me that you didn't lay a finger on either of them? I find that fucking hard to believe Sal. You didn't touch or shoot either one?"

"I swear to God on my mother's grave I didn't."

"Well I'm sorry to hear that Sal," he said as he shot another bullet into Sal's left knee.

The screams were deafening. Sal rolled back and forth with both of his hands clutching his knee. He was screaming and crying like an infant, begging Al to end his pain.

"Do you want to change anything about your story Sal? This is your last chance to end your pain."

"Jesus Christ, Jesus fucking Christ Al, it was all Bull. I wasn't in the store at the time. He came to the car and told me…" but Sal started to fade out from the loss of blood.

His blood was everywhere. Sal was a big guy and it was quickly flowing out of him. He wouldn't last more than ten minutes; but Al's orders from Frankie were to make sure he was aware of every last minute before he died.

Al bent down and slapped Sal's face a couple of times. "Don't you die on me sweetheart, it's time to wake up."

Sal started to come around and noticed Al standing over him with Victor behind him. He started to mumble something to Victor but there was just too much blood in his mouth and his was losing conscience again. This time Al kicked him in his wounded knee and the pain shot a sudden jolt through him and he rolled on his side and started to scream again.

"Sleeping Beauty is with us again," Al said to Victor.

Victor was now bending down on the other side of Sal. "Sal, be a good boy and tell us what we want to know and I promise I'll put one right through the center of your head. Try dying with some dignity. You crying like a little girl and telling lies about Bull is really disappointing me."

"Please Vic," he started to say but he couldn't finish, his mind was giving out on him as he passed out again.

"Are you satisfied enough yet or do you want to wake him again?" Al turned to Victor. "I told you all along that it was the other fucking maniac that killed the kid's parents. Frankie just better let me take care of Bull the same way. He was there alright, but I don't think he had any hand in what went down other than what he told us."

"Hey, what the fuck do you want from me? Orders are orders and this is what we do. This wasn't some fucking angel we just whacked, so let it go. Now finish what you were supposed to finish and let's get the fuck out of here," he told Al.

Al put the 9mm in Sal's mouth and pulled the trigger. There was blood and teeth everywhere, including on Al's pants and shoes. He then walked over to where Sal's gun lay and picked it up and turned to finish off Tyrone.

To his surprise Tyrone's eyes were open and he had witnessed what Al did to Sal. Al could really care less about that and stood about the same spot as where Sal had been and unloaded the remaining rounds into various parts of Tyrone's body other than his head. When he was finished he threw the gun onto Sal's body and followed Victor out the door.

Waiting on the other side of the door was a can of gas that Victor went back to the car to get as Al and Sal were torturing Tyrone. He brought it into the apartment and poured half of the can on Tyrone and then walked over to Sal's body.

To his amazement Sal was still alive, but just barely. He tried to shake his head no, but it was all in vain. Al stood over him and emptied the remainder of the gasoline onto Sal. His body started to go into spasms at once but it didn't stop Al. Once he got outside he took out his cigarettes from his pocket and lit one. He took one long drag and then threw the cigarette at Tyrone's dead body. Within an instant the whole apartment went up in flames and Al turned around and followed Victor back down the stairs and to the car.

"Sandra, I'm not like them. Growing up in my neighborhood that's what all the kids wanted to be. We idolized those guys, but I never wanted to be one of them. It wasn't until later that I wanted to live their lifestyle. That was it, I just hung around and became a part of their lives without actually becoming one of them. I could never be a gangster and to finally answer your question, no, I have never killed anyone. Are you satisfied?" he asked.

"Do you swear Anthony? Do you swear on your parents' grave?"

"Sandra, I never lied to you, I just never gave you the whole story when you asked about my personal life."

Anthony got off the couch and sat down next to Kimberly. "Hi sweetheart, what are you coloring?" he asked her as he kissed her on the head.

"I'm coloring my purple dinosaur, see?"

"Gosh, you are doing such a good job honey. What's your dinosaur's name?"

"His name is Barney and he's the bestest thing in the whole wide world," she replied as she stretched her arms as far apart as she could to show Anthony how much.

"Wow, that's a lot. I guess you really love him."

"Yep, he's my favorite."

Anthony returned to the couch where Sandra was watching them. "Does she remember me?" He paused. "Has she ever asked about me?"

"Since we are being honest with each other, the truth is no, she doesn't remember you. She never mentions you Anthony and I can only assume that she has forgotten all about you. I'm sorry, but it's the truth."

"You don't need to apologize for that. It's my fault and that's one of the consequences that I have to live with for the rest of my life."

Anthony had to take a second to regain his composure. "Oh well, back to my story. One day after we were first married I was sitting at work and got the call that changed all of our lives forever. Nick Kitchens, from Goldman Sachs called me with a stock tip that he guaranteed was a sure thing.

"The one who stopped over a couple times while we were married?" she asked.

"Yes, that guy. We had been sharing inside information for each other for awhile and he always came through with winners. Nick went into his sales pitch and told me this was the one that was going to make him Vice President and set his clients for life. I did a little research and it was supposed to be the next high tech stock, so I called most of my clients and got them into it, but I wanted more. I wanted to be done with having to worry about work, our mortgage, college loans and most of all I wanted Kimberly's future secured. I was given the opportunity to meet Frankie Feliciani one night and I took a chance."

"You just went to a major crime boss with a stock tip and he took it from you?" she asked surprised.

"Of course not, the first night that I was in *The Club*, I took him for about four thousand dollars at poker. He wasn't thrilled about it but I gained his respect. I stayed there after everyone else left and sold him my sale's pitch. He opened up an account down at Merrill and ever since, he has made millions. I guess you can say, I made him more money than his business and restaurant did together. After that I became his adopted son with a pass to his place any-time I wanted to use it."

"This is crazy. You mean to tell me you made Frankie Feliciani millions of dollars on a stock tip?" she asked as she shook her head back and forth. "I find that absolutely absurd. What the hell did you get out of it if you made him that kind of money? You don't look like you have been rewarded for your services if you ask me, Anthony. Don't get me wrong, I know you put down money on this house, but what else? After the divorce, you went from one apartment to the next, each one getting worse as you moved. And to top it all off, you come here today and tell me the reason why your parents were murdered was because you owed Frankie fifty thousand dollars? How can you possibly owe him anything at all? I'm sorry if I'm not following your story correctly, but something here isn't adding up."

Anthony realized Sandra was getting frustrated. He even understood why. He sat there and placed himself in her shoes and yes, the story did seem very far-fetched and he just wasn't in the mood to try to sell it. Anthony couldn't waste any more time here and he still didn't trust Chad, who was sitting quietly in the kitchen.

"What I got out of it was like I said before. Our home, two cars and two college loans were paid off along with my parents' store. Have I ever missed sending you child support even though, by law, I don't have to since you are re-married?"

"Anthony, I never touched that money. It is sitting in a box in our bedroom and when Kimberly is old enough, I will tell her it was from you for her college tuition. I know you weren't obligated to send money, I just figured this was your way of staying in her life and I wasn't going to take that from you."

"Speaking of which, that brings up the other topic I wanted to discuss," he told her as he reached in his jacket pocket and took out two envelopes. "I have here two envelopes as you can see. They are both for Kimberly when she is ready to enter college. I want you to put them in a safety deposit box in your bank in case anything ever happens to you. I don't want Chad to know about these envelopes and you getting a safety deposit box will at least assure me that Kimberly gets them. The first envelope has a CD in it in Kimberly's name worth one hundred and fifty thousand dollars which she can only cash if she proves to the bank that she has been accepted to a college. That should take care of her tuition, books and housing and enough for her to pursue her dreams."

He took a moment to gain his composure, and then he took Sandra's hands into his. "Please promise me that you will see to it that she gets the second envelope. This one is more important to me than the one with the CD in it. This envelope contains a letter to her that I wrote awhile ago. It has a little of everything in it. There's the detail of how you and I met and what happened to us. I explained why I wasn't a part of her childhood and asked her for her forgiveness. The conclusion of the letter is what a father would tell his daughter who is ready to leave home for college and ready to start her journey into adulthood. Sandi, promise me, that you will do this for me."

"I don't know what to say Anthony. You let me think that you were such a screw up all these years. Why would you let me and your family go on thinking that? Jesus Anthony, if you would have just said something, we could have saved our marriage," she said as fresh tears were now coming down her face.

"That's the problem Sandra, I was never going to change. I am too selfish of a person and the two of you are a lot better off with me out of your lives. I want you to know that I did try to reconcile with my parents before their deaths and my apology went on deaf ears and I wasn't going to let that happen between us."

"You should have asked for help. Why did you have to continue to gamble if you already made so much money? From what I hear, most people with gambling problems bet because they need money. You already had it so why did you continue?" she demanded to know.

"It's not that easy Sandra. I loved the lifestyle of being a big shot with Frankie. Unless you grew up in my neighborhood, you couldn't possibly understand the lure of the lifestyle. I didn't realize just how far gone financially I was until I reached rock bottom."

Anthony noticed the box of tissues on the end table and got up and took two out and handed them to Sandra. "Do you mind if I go into the kitchen and grab a drink?" he asked Sandra.

"No, go help yourself."

Anthony walked by Chad and went to the sink and poured himself a drink of water.

"So Chad, are you enjoying your day off?"

"You know, you might be a big man with that gun but I would have loved for you to have tried this little stunt of yours without it, then we would really see how much of a loser you are Anthony."

"Now Chad, we both know that gun or no gun, there wasn't anything you could have done to stop me because I would have just beaten the living shit out of you. The gun saved you from that embarrassment and made this visit a peaceful one so don't go ruining it for everyone," he replied.

"We'll see how tough you are after you leave here because I am eventually going to call the cops and I promise, I'll be down at that station waiting for your entrance to press charges," Chad had threatened.

"You just don't get it do you? Let me fill you in on a little secret. The one thing I do well is read people. I can meet anyone for the first time and after being in their company for only a short time, I could tell you more about them than they knew about themselves. Call it a gift. That's why I hardly ever lose at poker. You don't need the knowledge of the game to win, rather than the personalities of the people you are playing against. I am going to tell you two things that I have gathered from this brief meeting today. The first is that you are a little chicken shit. I bet you have never even been in a fight in your entire life. Am I right? You don't need to answer because your eyes already have."

Anthony put his glass down onto the kitchen table and walked right up to Chad to get into his face. "You don't have the fucking balls to call the cops once I leave here and you know it. When I walk out that door, you are going to thank God that I left and nothing happened because that's the kind of person you are."

"What makes you so damn sure about that?" Chad asked.

"You know as well as I do that if you called the cops, you would be dead before the night is over. If I get arrested for kidnapping, my phone call wouldn't be to a lawyer but to Frankie to tell him who put me here. That one phone call will make you disappear forever. Oh, and the second thing Chad, in the little time that I have just spent with your wife, I already know that she doesn't love you because she's not over me yet."

As Al got to the car he noticed the unmarked police car heading towards him. When the car pulled up along side of him, the window rolled down and Lieutenant Joseph Brown sitting in the passenger seat asked, "So how did it go in there?"

"Everything went fine, but you better call the Fire Company down here, the apartment went up quick," he answered.

"Ah, who gives a shit if this whole place burns to the ground it would just save us a lot of time and money from busting most of them anyway. For the most part they are just low life rats living above ground instead of in the sewers."

"I can see you're a man with a warm heart, Lieutenant."

"No, just a man who is tired of the trash that continues to come out of these places. I have a warm heart. Didn't I just do your boss a favor? Now where's my compensation for my services?" Lieutenant Brown asked as he reached out his hand to Al.

Al reached in his coat pocket and took out the envelope and handed it to Lieutenant Brown.

"I assume there's no need for me to count this?" he questioned Al as he took it.

"Actually Frankie threw in an extra two grand if you hurry the information along and it makes the noon news."

"Don't you worry about that, I told Frankie this morning that everyone is going to get what they wanted after this is all over. He knows I always keep up my end of the bargain."

"Frankie knows you have always been helpful in the past so I'm sure you'll see this through and that will be that."

Tyrone Willis was on the right track about who sent the men to his apartment this morning to kill him. The Bobby he was referring to was Robert Stefanik, who was an arch rival drug pusher. They were both small time hoods but Tyrone was making a name for himself lately by killing some of the more important competition in the neighborhood and there was tension growing between the two of them.

Frankie had decided to change his plans a second time before Al got to Sal's house. If he had just had them kill Sal down at the railroad tracks and left his body undiscovered that wouldn't solve any of their problems, other than the in-house one. The police still would search endlessly for the real killers because the media and the public wouldn't go away. Ever since 9/11, the people in this city wanted justice, you could say there was more demand for "an eye for and eye" than ever before. Someone was going to have to take the fall for this, but it didn't necessarily have to be one of his own. Frankie was going to take care of that, but he needed someone to satisfy the public.

As crazy as it would sound to someone who lived outside of this city, a mob boss was still held in high esteem to most of the people who lived in their neighborhoods. These citizens looked to them for protection; to make sure the neighborhood didn't turn bad and most of all, that it was safe for their children to grow up there. So if it got out that a member of a mob crew went off and murdered two innocent elderly shop owners, this would be too damaging to their image to overcome.

When he got off the phone with Al the first time, Frankie made a call down to his inside man, Lieutenant Joseph Brown, down at the 12th precinct. Joe had done plenty of small jobs and one important one in the past for Frankie and he was always rewarded generously. It was after that one important job that Frankie made a couple of phone calls to the local city council men that he knew well through various ways and, a week later, Joe was made a Lieutenant. From that day on, their relationship went to that next level, the one that you can't come back from if you wanted out and Joseph Brown was now officially owned by Frankie Feliciani.

After the second ring, Joe answered the phone. "Lieutenant Brown, how can I help you?"

The voice on the other end replied back, "Joe, your friend needs a favor this morning, are you available to help?"

"I was expecting your call, but we haven't gotten anything back from the lab yet and I do have a rush on for those results."

"No, that's not why I am calling. I already have an idea what those results are going to show and I want you to make sure they either get lost or you match them up with someone else if you understand what I am saying."

"Frankie before I can do anything you got to let me know what's going on. It's not that easy this time around because The Mayor wants someone's head on a platter for these murders. There are way too many people involved on this case right now for me to get access to the lab work or the crime scene," he explained to Frankie.

"Now Lieutenant, it is Lieutenant, Right? I think you have some major pull over there, do you not? Now the only thing that I am going to tell you is that unfortunately one of my own went loose cannon on me and killed those people. I know it was very unfortunate for those two people, but I can not allow this information to get out to the public. If it gets out there, many people are going to take the fall on this, from Mob bosses to dirty cops if you catch my drift. Do we understand each other?"

"Frankie, I would never say no to you. All I am trying to explain is that it is going to be difficult to cover this mess up. There are too many hands involved, so what do you expect me to do to get you out of this?"

"I need a fall guy that the people can accept and this will all go away once you have him. So look around your office in those folders and pick someone who you wouldn't mind seeing disappear and get me a name and an address quickly."

"There are one or two guys I would like to see off the streets right about now, but how do you expect me to make a connection between them and the killings yesterday?" he questioned Frankie.

"Are these guys big timers yet or just small fish? Are they involved together or are they competition for one another?"

"No, neither one of them is big time yet but they are rivals and I'm sure if you take down one, the other's members will take revenge of the killing and start a war amongst themselves, which would do me just fine."

"Good, give me the name and address of the bigger guy because there's more of a guarantee that his people will go out looking for revenge."

Joe turned around in his chair and rolled over to the file cabinet and took out Tyrone Willis's folder. "I got a guy for you so how do you want to play this?" he asked Frankie.

"I am sending a couple of my men to this guy's house to take care of your drug problems and once they are done with that, my dirty laundry will be left behind to be cleaned and that will take care of my problem. Before they leave they will torch the place and by the time the investigation is done, there will be no way to trace this back to me and my people. Now do you understand what I need done, because time is really against me and I don't want to waste any more of it going over the details?"

"Yeah Frankie, I understand what you need done and I will take care of the prints from the lab to make sure they match those of our man. The guy you want to go after is Tyrone Willis and he lives is the projects on the West side in apartment 15C on the 8th floor. Are you familiar with them?"

"No it's not a regular hang out of ours, but I'm sure my guy can find the place."

"I'll send a car to be there outside to scare off any unwanted witnesses that might be there looking for trouble. Their kind usually goes scurrying back into their holes once a blue drives by," he promised him.

"Joseph, I want you there. I don't want some regular screwing this up for us. I mean if my men come out of there and all of a sudden one of your boys wants to be a hero. You would hate to see something like that happen wouldn't you Joe?"

"No, Frankie, I wouldn't," Joe reluctantly answered back.

"Good, then you are to be there to assure me that nothing goes wrong."

Joe looked at the clock on the wall and realized that he had a full plate today and didn't have the time to spare with this unexpected business. He tried to think of how he was going to get away from the office for at least two hours and what excuse he was going to come up with once he was back but this was the least of his worries. If this got botched, it wasn't the shame and embarrassment of losing his job and career; it was the loss of his life that concerned him the most. This was the kind of shit that he knew he was going to face one day ever since he was on Frankie's payroll. It's true what the other cops had told him; once you are in, there was no way out.

"That's not a problem Frankie. I'll be there in the back alley waiting for them. I'll make sure that my presence is known and they should have no problems."

"They'll have your envelope when the job is completed and they are safely back at the car and since this is a huge favor and short notice, I've double my usually gratuity. So don't fuck this up for me," he said and then hung up the phone.

❧   ❧   ❧

Anthony let go of Chad and picked up his glass from the table and headed back into the family room to continue his conversation with Sandra, which was taking longer than he wanted.

"Sandra, I still need to talk to you about the favor that I need of you and I am really running behind right now so I am just going to come out and ask. I need you and Kimberly at the viewing Friday night and the gathering at my parents' house after. Do you think you can do that for me?"

"Anthony, did you honestly think I wouldn't have come? I had all the intentions in the world of showing up, so don't worry about that."

That was a huge load lifted off Anthony's chest. Sandra committing to come to the viewing Friday night was essential to his plans. She and Kimberly were going to be his alibi.

"That's great, but there is one more catch. I need you to spend the night there, and this is really more important to me than just you showing up."

"Anthony, there's no way in this world that we can do that. That would be totally unfair to Chad and I could never even ask that of him. I have to say no. I'm sorry, but it's just too unreasonable to ask."

Anthony sat there for a moment shaking his head. "Jesus Christ Sandi, do you think I am asking to sleep with you? What the hell are you thinking? I just need certain people to see that you spent the night there."

"Why?" she asked.

"I can't really get into it right now but it is extremely important to me that you do. My plan is to have you at the gathering and when it gets late and Kimberly is ready for bed, you and I will walk up the stairs together and we will put her to bed. You will stay with her in my parents' room until morning and as for me, I will stay in my old room. Sandra, out of everything I have ever asked of you before, this favor I can't accept no for an answer. There is too much riding on this, including some people's lives. Please just do this for me. After everything I have revealed to you today, I think you owe me that much," he expressed to her.

"You are right Anthony, I am truly grateful for everything that you have done for Kimberly, but I don't know if I can. Do you know what kind of strain this is going to put on my marriage? How do you expect Chad to handle this? What if you were in his shoes? How would you act if your wife dropped a bomb shell on you that she was going to spend the night with her ex-husband in his parents' home? Anthony, I really don't think you understand what you are asking me to do."

"Please believe me when I say yes, I do understand. I am asking others to do a great deal more for me on that same night and they are putting their lives on the line for me. You, on the other hand, are worrying about a little fight with your husband that will last a couple of days at best. Can we get serious for just one second?"

Anthony got off the couch and kneeled in front of Sandra on both knees and took her hands in his for the second time that afternoon.

"Sandi, look at me and tell me that that is your excuse, that you are really worried about what this will do to your relationship with Chad? Have you forgotten who you are talking to right now? Sweetheart, you know that reading people is one of my gifts. With everything that has gone on this afternoon in here, if he truly loved you, he would have tried to do something about it, gun or no gun. Look me in my eyes and tell me that you love him? You can't lie to me because the eyes are the windows to the soul, and I don't see love for him in them."

With that, he got up and kissed Sandra on her forehead and said, "I'll see the two of you Friday night and don't forget to pack a bag."

He went over to where Kimberly had fallen asleep without the two of them realizing it and knelt down and kissed her goodbye.

"You don't need to get up, I'll have Chad see me out. Thank you again for your time today, it meant a lot to me."

As he walked into the kitchen, Anthony suggested to Chad that he see him out. Once they got to the door, Anthony turned around and spoke to Chad for the last time.

"Eventually Sandra, like the good wife that she is, is going to come to you with a favor that I have requested of her. You are not going to give her any shit about it and allow her to do this for me."

"And why the hell should I do that?" he asked.

"All I can promise is that nothing will come of this. I am a man of my word and I assure you that as of today, I am out of the three of your lives forever. Please be a good sport about all of this and everything will all be over after Friday night. If you don't want to work together, I'm sure I can find some ways to influence a couple of your patients to come up with horrible allegations against you. It's your choice, cooperate and play ball and everyone walks away from this happy or be an asshole and risk everything in your life, including Sandra. The choice is yours and I'm confident that you will make the right one."

Anthony walked back to his car and he never had to deal with Chad Pettyjohn again.

♣   ♣   ♣

Vincent walked into the kitchen where Frankie was slicing some vegetables with his mother.

"Frankie, can I see you for a second?"

Frankie excused himself to his mother and stepped into the back room with Vincent.

"That thing we discussed; it was taken care of?" he asked Vincent.

"Yeah, you can say it isn't a burning issue anymore," he said with a smile. "However, there is something you should know."

"What's that?" Frankie asked.

"Al wanted me to tell you one thing. He says that Sal went until the very end swearing up and down that it was only Bull. I mean if you ask me, you put a bullet in a guy's stomach and he continues to lie, he's got some balls. But if you shoot him a third time and he still sticks with his story, then both you and I know he isn't lying. Al gave him the chance to end the pain, but Sal stuck with his story that Bull went crazy and shot the kid's parents while he was in the car. So, what do you think?"

Frankie could only put his head down into his hand and shake it back and forth. "Shit, I was afraid of this. I'm not naive, I was aware that Bull did it, but I was still certain Sal had helped. Sal never made a move without Bull giving him the go. What the fuck was Bull thinking?"

"Don't beat yourself to death about this. You did what you had to do about Sal and I hope you realize that Bull has got to go. If he doesn't, it ain't going to look good with Pete."

"This isn't that easy you know. How the hell am I going to look into Ellena's eyes for the rest of my life knowing that I killed her sister's kid? I know he's got to go. What do you think is going to happen when he tries to contact Sal from Vegas?" Frankie asked.

"You think he might panic and run? It's not like he can hide forever. We'll eventually find him," Vincent replied.

"No, I don't think he'll run, it's not his style. He'll want revenge for Sal and then he'll try to disappear. You know he's not the brightest one of the bunch."

Frankie walked into his office and sat down and picked up the phone.

"Who are you calling?" Vincent asked as he followed Frankie.

"I was going to call the Maciocha brothers to handle our problem on Friday."

"You think that's necessary Frankie?" Vincent asked.

"Yes, because if I get someone on the outside to take care of this at least my hands will be clean of it. I'll have them waiting at the pick up spot Friday night and once the drop off is complete, they'll take care of Bull and I can just explain to Ellena that he was shot during a routine job for me. They can leave his body right there in the alley with his wallet missing. It will look like he was there waiting for someone and was shot during a mugging. This shit happens all the time. I don't think it will be hard for us to come up with a story for the police."

"Do you think you can get the Maciocha brothers on that short of notice? You know how they are used only for special hits. They plan everything to the very last detail. Frankie, I don't think they'll like the idea of just showing up on Friday night waiting in the alley to hit a guy for us."

"Well let's just see about that," he replied as the phone rang.

It didn't take long for Teddy to pick up the phone. "Yeah?"

"Teddy, it's Frankie Feliciani, how are you guys doing over there?"

"Frankie, I can't say that I am surprised to hear from you after everything that I have seen on TV and read in the news papers. So, you have a problem that needs to be fixed?" he asked.

"Man, I haven't heard that line today. Actually after this morning, most of our problems over here have been fixed. I only have one more issue that needs to be cleaned up."

"Frankie, I've known you for about ten years and have done some jobs for you over that time, and I knew that there was no way you were going to take out your own nephew. I mean family is family, and you do have your wife to worry about. When you are married that long, you have to worry about them too and killing her nephew wouldn't sit well on your conscience now, would it?"

"Teddy, I always believed you were the best in the business, but how did you know it was my nephew?" Frankie questioned him.

"You wouldn't be calling an outsider to kill one of your own unless it was an extremely delicate issue and there are only two people in your crew that would make this a sensitive issue for you, Vincent or Bull. And we both know Vincent wouldn't have done something like that."

Frankie took a moment to gather his thoughts and he looked over at Vincent, who could only shrug his hands in a gesture of "what is he saying?"

"Hey, I didn't mean to offend you, but you don't know what the hell I have gone through for the last two days and I'm still not sure if this will be all over even after we get rid of Bull. I'm more worried about what Pete is going to do about all of this. Hell for all I know, he already called you and you are holding a contract on me."

"For what it's worth Frankie, I personally haven't heard from Pete nor have I heard any word on the street about your problem, but if I was you, would I believe this?"

"If the situation was turned around I wouldn't believe it either, however I still need your services if you and your brothers are available. What do you say? Would any of you take the job?"

There was a little hesitation of the other end of the line as Frankie waited for an answer.

"I had already talked to Michael and Jeff about it and Michael is going out of the city this weekend with his wife for their anniversary. Jeff said he would do it, but I am skeptical of this job and I don't want my youngest brother doing a big job like that alone and walking into a surprise. Frankie, I have been thinking about this since Tuesday night because I knew sooner or later either you or Pete or for that matter both of you were going to call me. And you are right, who's to say he didn't call me already?"

Teddy paused for a minute to let Frankie consider that. "What's your angle? I mean other than not having Bull's blood on your hands, what's in it for you? I know if I was you, my play would be to do it myself, that way Pete realized you could handle the issue even if it meant taking out your own blood. Let me talk to Jeff again now that you have called and go over a couple of things. Where are you now?"

"I'm in my office," Frankie answered.

"Fine give me about twenty minutes and I will call you right back," Teddy replied as he hung up the phone.

Frankie was sitting with the phone still in his hand when he looked at Vincent again. "I didn't like how that just went. I think Pete might have called Teddy already and no matter what we do on our end, Pete has already made up his mind as to what he has planned for us."

Vincent had never seen Frankie this flustered. There were reasons why he was the boss and being level headed and always in control of the situation were just a few, but this time it was much different. Their problem was more than just business, it had gotten personal and that was the worst thing that could happen in their line of work.

"What do you want to do? Do you think you can trust Teddy and his brothers or do you want Al or Victor to do it?" he asked Frankie.

"We can't take the offer off the table now. We will need everyone that will be in that car Friday night to just be ready for anything. After they are done Friday night, everyone is going to meet back here and I'll hold an emergency meeting concerning the future of our crew. I think it is time that we really think about it," he said as he put the phone back down.

Frankie didn't need to wait long for Teddy's call. In less than ten minutes he was on the phone again making a deal to take care of his nephew.

"Jeff and I will do it but there will be guide lines that will need to be followed or the deal is off."

Frankie was waiting to hear the right combination of words, the tone change in Teddy's voice or the unusual request to give away that Pete already had him on the job and he was going to double cross Frankie but none of those things happened. His requests were reasonable and Frankie was almost positive that Teddy was on the up and up.

"So what did you have in mind Frankie?"

"Al, Victor and Craig are going to pick up Bull from the airport on Friday night and head for the usual pick up spot in the back alley of 6th and Walnut around eleven o'clock. Bull will be in the front passenger seat and he'll get out and take the money from Daniel Rodenhausen. They'll probably bullshit for a minute or two and that's where I want you to drive up and shoot Bull as many times as you can, grab the bag and be sure to take a couple of shots at both cars too. I want this to look like someone tried to steal from me and not a hit. I don't want Dan's people thinking this was a planned hit on Bull."

"I don't want to have three or four guys firing back at Jeff and me. If I just shoot Bull, Dan's people are going to fire at us."

"Teddy, no one besides Bull and Dan are going to be out of the two cars. This is a routine pick-up and they have been meeting each other at the same spot for over a year. There would be no reason why anyone else would be out of the cars and before Dan's people even know what had just happened, you will be more than half way down the alley and out of sight."

"What about Dan's men?" Teddy asked.

"He'll have no more than two guys with him and when they hear the shots, their first instinct will be to duck. Al and Victor will fire a couple of shots in the air, and then they will get back in the car and take off after you. I can guarantee that Dan's men won't get a single shot off. This isn't a drug deal between a couple of Jamaicans and Colombians trying to see who is the toughest kid on the block by taking out all their guns and firing until only one is left standing. Relax, no one other than Bull is going to get hurt," he tried to convince Teddy.

"God help you Frankie if something happens to Jeff because Pete will be the least of your worries. You might be a mob boss, but we all know that I am the one that has more power when it comes to creating pain and suffering for someone, so don't make me prove that to you. We wouldn't want to see something happen to a loved one now, would we?" he asked.

"No Teddy, we wouldn't, but let me tell you one thing. You might be one of the best cleaners in the business and are backed by some of the most influential bosses in this city, but never threaten me because I can get to you and your brothers, so don't threaten me."

There was silence for a moment and Frankie actually thought this deal just went terribly wrong and he was now going to have Teddy against him, which would be one problem that he couldn't afford at this point. All Frankie wanted was to get through Friday night and collect both of his winnings and get Ellena, his mother and himself as far away from this city as possible. He would also have to break it to Anita that she was done at Cornell and would have to get an education somewhere else but that was still a long time away.

"Frankie, I think we are getting off the topic here with these ridiculous threats. Jeff and I will take care of Bull on Friday night. We will be there in plenty of time to scope the alley and make sure everything is legit and when the time comes, Bull will be gone. The price for this little job is fifty thousand dollars and it isn't negotiable. Now I know it is a lot more than the normal asking price but let's not kid ourselves, there isn't anything normal about this problem, is there? I will take my cut out from the bag and will return the rest to Al at a designated location. Sound fair to you?" he asked.

"I wouldn't go as far as to say fair, but it's not like I have a lot of people to call to compare prices, now do I?"

"No, you don't. If you want your problem fixed, you know I am the only man in this city that is a guarantee to get it done. Oh, Frankie, one more thing for you to think about before we end this conversation. A loss of a close brother in this line of work is painful, however a loss of an innocent daughter, who is in the prime of her life, would be much greater especially if you had something to do with it. We can end our conversation on that note," he told Frankie as he hung up the phone.

Anthony stood outside of St. Martin of Tours Church and was dreading going inside. This was the church that he visited every Sunday ever since he was fours years old, but hadn't been back to since his wedding. St. Martin's was one of the oldest and nicest churches in the city. Anthony was baptized, received his First Holy Communion, Confirmed and graduated from its school yet he refused to step inside after his divorce.

Religion was one of the subjects that he and Sandra never brought up. They were both Catholics, but neither one was a steady practicing one. Sandra had asked him once if they could start going to mass when Kimberly had gotten older, but Anthony said he wasn't interested in going back and she never pursued the issue again.

It only took him a couple of years to be back standing in front of its doors. Out of the four people that Anthony had to meet today, Father John Jordan was the one who he was scared to see. Anthony was always a good kid and that is how Father John would remember Anthony, but after today, Anthony wasn't so sure of that.

Anthony had many issues with God that he wanted to get off his chest with Father John and he also needed his confession heard, which would be the first time in years. But the most important reason Anthony was there was to explain to Father John what happened to his parents and what he had to do to rectify the situation.

Anthony couldn't wait any longer, he was being a child by just standing outside the door waiting to find the courage to step inside and face his demons. Father John was not as powerful as Frankie, but Anthony feared him more.

Anthony entered the church and dipped his hand in the holy water bowl to his right, making the Sign of the Cross after doing so. He walked down the center aisle of the church and saw at least twelve people in the various pews, praying, saying the rosary or just sitting there with their thoughts. When he reached the end and was standing in front of the altar, he genuflected and made the sign of the cross. He made a right and headed into the back toward the sacristy. When he got there, he knocked on the door and heard from the other side, "Enter".

The last time he was standing in front of this door was twenty-five years ago when he was an altar boy, living his life according to the ways of his religion, and fearing the worse for his soul if he didn't. Catholic schools had that influence on many of their students at that age, yet here he was twenty-five years later fearing the same repercussions for his soul. Saving his soul wasn't the real reason he was here today; he was here to end the nightmares that continued to haunt him about his grandparents' death.

Anthony's mom-mom and pop-pop were extreme devoted Catholics and before their deaths they managed to go to church everyday. Most Catholics that Anthony knew couldn't make it to church every Sunday, yet his mom-mom and pop-pop went everyday like clock work. To Anthony, it seemed normal for people their age to make their peace with God and to go the extra step knowing that they will be seeing their creator shortly. However, as devoted that they were, God decided to test their faith one more time before his mom-mom's death.

One Saturday in July of '91, Anthony had plans to go to a friend's house for a birthday party. As he was walking out the door to go to the party, his mother asked him to go and see his mom-mom on the way home because she hadn't been feeling well for the last couple of days. Anthony knew that this would be a big burden to him because it meant that he had to watch how much he drank and he couldn't stay as long as he would like at the party. However, Anthony was her favorite and he wasn't going to tell his mother "no" and ruin his day with an argument with her before it even began. So he said he would stop by on the way home.

Anthony looked at his watch: it was already a quarter after five and he had about four or five beers already. He realized that he had to get over to see her before she would turn in for the night. When he reached their home, she was still up and they were both watching TV in their robes and she insisted on making him something to eat.

"Mom-Mom, just sit down and relax. I really can't stay too long and I am just here to check up on you. Mom said you have been under the weather lately so I decided to stop by and see how you are feeling," he told her as he sat down between them on the couch.

His pop-pop, who thought everyone in the world was out to get him, answered for her. "Your mom-mom is fine, she just has a summer cold and those damn doctors want to test her for every damn thing they can think of just so they can make money. They don't give a shit about anyone nor how those tests make people feel after they are finished. Money is the only thing that they care about. Every one of them sons of bitches should die a long horrible death from a dreaded disease and let's see how they feel being on the other end."

"I'm sure they have their reasons Pop to ask Mom-Mom to take certain tests," he answered but this only added fuel to the fire.

His pop-pop threw up his hands in the air and walked to the kitchen to get himself a beer. Once he was out of the room Anthony took her hand in his. Anthony was nineteen at the time and never really noticed the progression of his mom-mom's aging but at this particular moment she looked much older than he could remember. It was the first time in his life that he realized that they were old and the whole cycle of life process was taking place.

"Now that the lunatic is gone, tell me seriously, how do you feel?"

"I'm okay, it's just a little cold, and that's all. Your pop-pop is right, doctors nowadays want to send you to the hospital every chance they can. I'll be fine in another day or so, now stop worrying about me. Are you sure I can't fix you something to eat?"

He could only look at her and wonder how his mom-mom had gotten old on him all of a sudden. "No, really Mom-Mom it's okay. I just came from a birthday party and I had too much to drink and I should be getting back before it gets dark. You know I hate to drive at night to begin with and having a few beers in me doesn't help. I'll take a rain check on that dinner for one night next week when you are feeling better. How does that sound?" he asked as he got up to head out the door.

"I'll be fine by Monday. Why don't you stop by with your girlfriend and I will cook the both of you a nice dinner."

"That sounds great. I'll call you on Monday and set up a night for next week. Tell Pop I said good bye. I don't want to bother him anymore since I got him all rattled up about the doctors," he told her as he kissed her goodbye.

"You drive safe Anthony and ring the house once you get home." Anthony waved back to acknowledge her and turned back towards his car.

He was the last person to speak to her other than her husband. She had a major stroke later that night and never came out of the coma until her death seven years later.

Almost every adult wishes that they could go back in time and have the opportunity to live one moment over again; to have the chance to alter an event that would change their lives to the way they wished it could be, instead of the way it was. For Anthony, that Saturday in July was the defining moment in his life. You could say that day changed the way he lived and looked at life in general.

He became a selfish person and his values and views on life and religion changed forever. How could God, who he was taught about for twelve years of Catholic school, let his mom-mom live in a coma for seven years? This was not the way things were supposed to work out. Yes, people get old and die, but a person as devoted and caring as she was wasn't supposed to suffer a long and painful death for their services towards Him.

Anthony wasn't here today to seek penance for the sins that he had committed, or for the great sin that he had planned for Friday night. He wasn't here to explain to Father John why he hadn't been back to church since his wedding, or why he and Sandra got divorced and didn't save their marriage. No, Anthony was here today for the sole purpose of seeking answers from this priest that he had looked up to his entire life, and he wasn't leaving until he achieved satisfaction and relief.

Now that he felt more anger than fear, Anthony opened the door and prepared himself for his biggest confrontation of the day.

"Dear Lord, is that Anthony Albergo I see standing before me?"

"Hi Father. Yes, it's really me."

Bull looked at his wristwatch and saw it was five o'clock. As he threw his bag down on the floor of the hotel room he realized it was still too early to call home and check in on Sal. They were probably still taking care of the body and once that was done they would probably meet back at *The Club*. During the whole plane ride to Vegas, he couldn't get a feel from the conversation in the car ride to the airport. The cops could have had prints already, but they weren't going to be his because he wore gloves. Which made him wonder, whose prints did they have, or were they just giving Frankie a couple of guys that they wanted off the streets?

Cops had funny ways of doing business with the mob. Most people watch too many movies and believe that the mob runs the police, who do them all the favors, when in reality the mob does most of the favors and dirty work for the police and politicians.

No matter what scenario Bull played in his head, something was always missing. It just didn't seem right to him that they were going to pin this on some low lives from the projects, when most people wouldn't believe that these two men would ever step foot in that neighborhood.

The longer Bull sat in his room the more he tortured himself about the conversation. He needed to get out and just relax for a little while. When he got back to his room, he would call Sal. Once he got him on the phone, he could put his mind at ease. Tomorrow night he would pick up Frankie's money and then take in the Vegas nightlife for one more night before heading home the next day. He just needed to listen to everyone and take it easy for a couple of days. "God, I need to just relax, go to the bar for a couple of drinks, shoot some dice for awhile and maybe pick up a bitch," he said to himself.

Christie Brady was laying on her bed in her freshman dorm reading her Introduction to American History book and listening to U2's latest CD which was blaring on her radio. American history was boring to her and she couldn't study without the help of the music. Christie was second generation to attend Cornell but, unlike her father, she was going to find it extremely hard to stay there. Even though she always had good grades her whole life, she had no desire to be here at Cornell. All her friends from home stayed local and went to West Virginia University. This wasn't what she wanted in life, but she had to make an effort for her father because it was a big deal for their entire family.

She never heard Anita walk into the room.

"Chris, can you turn that down? Hello, Chris? Please turn that down."

Christie looked up and jumped back when she saw Anita standing there in front of her. "Damn, you scared the hell at of me. How long have you been standing there?" she asked Anita as she turned off the radio.

"I just walked in about ten seconds ago. How can you possibly read and listen to the music at the same time? I need total silence to read."

"Well, when you share a house with six brothers and sisters your whole life, you get used to not having silence when you study. This room is too quiet when I am all alone, so I put on the radio to concentrate. I guess old routines are hard to break. So, where have you been?"

Anita took out her French Literature book from her backpack that she had been reading over in the library and threw it on the bed. "I was over in the library studying for my French Literature quiz on Friday. I don't even know why I took this course. I really hate myself sometimes because I had a total of six years of Spanish between grade school and high school and I speak fluent Italian. But, I decided to challenge myself and try something new with this French thing. Boy, am I ever regretting it."

"You? I am regretting coming to this school in the first place. I left all my friends and family back in West Virginia just to please my father and come here to follow in his footsteps. Talk about bad choices we make."

Anita was sitting on her bed facing Christie with her French Literature book in her lap. "Just be glad that your father only pressured you to go to the school where he was an alumnus. I'd be happy to trade places with you if you wanted," Anita said as she closed her book, because she couldn't remember what she had been reading anyway.

"Why, what school did your dad go to?"

"My father didn't go to college. The streets were where my father learned how to be successful in his line of work."

"Really, what does your dad do? Does he own a business or something?"

"I don't think you would believe me if I told you, and I really never discuss it with strangers anyway."

Christie sprang from her bed and ran across the room and jumped in bed next to Anita. "Oh, you aren't getting off that easy. We aren't going to be roommates for a year and hold secrets from each other. You tell me what your dad does, and I'll answer any question that you might have about me. I have no problems answering any questions that you want to know. Why live in the dark and have skeletons in your closet I always say."

Anita shook her head back and forth. "It's not that easy. You wouldn't understand. I came here to get away from him and our lifestyle. I just want to find myself while I am here and, when I graduate, I expect to move far away from him. I don't want to be dependent on him anymore."

"Wow, sounds like you've got some big skeletons in your closet, city girl. We country girls really have nothing to hide. In fact our secrets are too small for closets, more like little boxes," she said while laughing.

Anita smiled back. She never really had close friends in high school. Everyone there knew who she was and they or their parents were afraid of her. One way or another, most people left her alone. Her high school years were very lonely, which left only her mother for friendship and guidance, and how much guidance could you possibly get from your mother? She didn't have a best friend to share her secrets with or to talk about boys, even though she had never been on a date with one. Finding friends was one thing, but trying to find a guy to ask her out was a whole different ball game.

Anita's senior prom date was Joey Tucci, who her father had chosen for her because Frankie was working on a business deal with Joey's father Paul. Even though she hated her father for using her as a negotiating tool for a business deal, the prom turned out to be a really nice time and she ended up getting her first real kiss goodnight.

Christie was the complete opposite of Anita. She was blond, beautiful and had all the confidence and outgoing personality that came with her looks. Christie had many boyfriends throughout high school and had numerous offers already since she got to campus. Christie and Anita were a modern day version of 'The Odd Couple'.

"If I tell you, Chris, you promise not to draw conclusions about me? You don't know what high school was like for me. I look over at your part of the room and I see hundreds of pictures of you and all your friends. You don't see any on my side do you? I was an outcast for the most part in my high school years because the other kids knew about my father and they feared getting involved with me. And my main goal for attending college was escaping and starting a new life and creating friendships that I can take with me forever, and I would really like to start with you."

"Talk about the drama queen type. I don't know how bad you had it before you got here, but you can count on me to be the first close friend you make at Cornell. To prove to you that you can trust me, I will tell you something about myself that only my best friend Nicole knows. If I tell you my story are you going to tell me who your dad is and why it's such a big deal?"

Anita started to fill with excitement as her eyes opened slightly wider just like a little girl at her first slumber party. "Okay, but your story better be good or I'm not going to tell you about my dad."

"It's a deal," Christie said as she stuck out her hand to seal their deal.

"When I was sixteen I lost my virginity to one of my dad's colleagues from his law firm. My dad was having one of those stupid dinner parties and I was forced to attend and put on a pleasant face and serve drinks and hors d' oeuvres to all the guests. Well needless to say I was drinking more than I was serving and I got pretty wasted. I ended up puking my brains out in the upstairs bathroom. Afterwards when I came out, Henry was on the other side of the door waiting to use the bathroom. I guess he heard me the whole time and asked if I was all right. I said I just had a little too much to drink, but before I could finish I got sick again and ran back to the toilet and threw up in front of him."

Anita's jaw dropped wide open, as she didn't know what to think of the beginning of Christie's story.

"Now, I know what you are thinking, this is a typical romantic story, but it does get better."

"I should hope so," Anita said, "Because this is nothing like one of those trashy novels that I like to read," she replied and started to laugh.

"Oh, just shut up. I don't think you can top this story with any of those trashy novels."

"No, you are right about that," Anita said and at once stopped laughing.

"As I was praying to the porcelain god, Henry followed me in and was keeping my hair back so it wouldn't get in my face as I spilled out everything I had consumed. After I was finally done I went to the sink to throw water over my face and as I was doing that Henry asked if I mind if he took a leak because he said he had been waiting a long time. I shook my head no because at the time I never even gave it a thought. After I was done rinsing my face, I couldn't help notice him as he went. It was the first time I saw a man's penis, and it was bigger than I had thought. I was so stunned that I didn't notice Henry was watching me as I watched him. 'Does this bother you Christie?' he asked.

I shook my head no. I believe I had to be blushing pretty good by then.

'Have you ever seen a guy before Christie?' he asked me as he turned to zip up and to make sure I got a better look. I didn't know what to say, and I just shook my head no again. All at once I wasn't feeling sick anymore, but excited. I had been going through those teenage changes already, but I hadn't experimented yet with any boys my own age. I had let one boy get to second base but that was it, and I never touched him because I just hadn't felt the urge yet. But here I was, in my bathroom, with a man in his thirties standing in front of me about to zip up his pants. I asked him to wait one second, and I went over to the door and locked it. After that, I went to the sink and quickly rinsed my mouth out. If I bothered to brush my teeth I might have lost the nerve to go through with what I wanted to do."

"Oh my God," Anita said, "You gave a thirty-something year old man a blow job in your bathroom after throwing up just five minutes earlier? How didn't you get sick again while doing it?" Anita asked, as she was totally involved in Christie's story.

"Girl, are you going to finish the story for me or do you want me to tell you what happened?" Christie asked as she saw how hooked Anita was on her story.

"I'm sorry, but this is the most fascinating thing I ever heard. Then again, I have no other story to compare it to," Anita replied.

"Okay then, I'll be nice and finish it." Christie got herself more comfortable on the bed and finished her story.

"So, when I turned around after wiping my mouth on one of the towels hanging from the rack, his pants were unbuttoned and his penis was erect and standing straight out. 'So, what would you like to do Christie?' he asked me. This was all new to me, but I'm sure not to him. The only thing I could think to say was 'can I touch it?' as I walked over to him. He took my hand and put it on it and stroked my hand back and forth. It was like nothing I ever felt before. I was getting so aroused that I wanted more than just this. 'How about we try something different,' he said. 'Okay, what did you want to do?' He reached into the back pockets of his pants and retrieved his wallet and took out a condom. 'How about I put this on and we see what happens from there.' I really didn't want to loose my virginity this way: to someone I hardly knew, who was twice my age, and in a bathroom of all places, but I was too far into it to stop."

Anita was too far into the story to want Christie to stop. This was the greatest story that she had ever heard.

"He pulled down his pants and put both toilet seats down and pulled me over to him as he sat. We started to make out for a little while and then he started to grope me down there. I was so turned on by then that I didn't realize that he already had my panties down around my ankles. I just went with the flow and stepped out of them and then he picked me up and placed me on top of him. At first it really hurt but it eventually stopped and then it started to feel really good. I don't know how long he lasted but all of a sudden there was a knock at the door and we didn't know what to do. I yelled 'Wait a minute, I'm in here and I don't feel so good, please go use the bathroom downstairs.' Henry never even stopped. He kept pushing me up and down until he finally got off."

Anita just stared back at Christie in total astonishment.

"To this day, I never talked to Henry again nor did I ever find out who was knocking on the door. Now, close your mouth, wipe the droll from your face, and tell me what your dad does for a living."

Anita felt like she had been in a deep dream the whole time Christie told her story.

"My father?" she asked with a hoarse voice.

"Yeah, your father, you were going to discuss what your father did for a living, remember?"

"Of course I remember, I was just fooling around," Anita replied. "Like I said, this isn't easy for me to talk about, nevertheless, you did share that outrageous story, so I guess I will keep up my end of the bargain and tell you what he does for a living."

After pausing a little longer, Anita finally caved and told Christie.

"My dad is a head of a Mafia family in the city. I don't know how big, but I know he must be powerful because we are extremely well off and he has eight or ten men report directly to him. I see them come in and out of our restaurant on a daily basis. Please don't ask me all the details about him, I really try not to get involved. I only know what I hear at the restaurant and of course the stories that get passed around the neighborhood and in my school."

"That's it? You are making such a big deal about your father being a mob boss? I told you an incredible, one of a kind story and you are making such a big deal about your dad's occupation? I kind of figured that out on my own before you told me. I mean, a nice Italian girl from the big city, what else would she be hiding?" she said as she began to laugh.

"Please don't laugh at me. I am too sensitive about this. I opened up and shared my problems with you."

Christie put her arms around her. "Look, I'm not laughing at you, but with you. This is Cornell University. You are going to meet all walks of life around here. Do you think you are the only one with problems? Even though I would love to have your problems because my dad is only a small time lawyer in our town, you don't realize how lucky you are. Forget about your dad and let's go get something to eat. We'll talk about what we are going to wear to Friday's big party at The Phi Kappa Sigma's house."

"Oh, I don't think I am ready for a Fraternity party just yet," Anita replied. "I wouldn't fit in. Once we got there, you would leave me to the wolves, and then what would I do?"

"Come on, this is your chance to break out of your shell and meet people. Listen if you promise me that you'll go, I'll tell you one more secret before we go get a bite to eat. What do you say?"

Anita thought about it for a moment before she answered. "I don't know if your next secret is worth promising you that I will go to that party on Friday night. The risk isn't worth the reward if you ask me," she replied back to Christie.

"What if I treat to dinner tonight too? Then will you go Friday night?"

"Dinner tonight and a party Friday night, you really know how to treat your ladies don't you?" Anita responded.

"Does that mean we have a deal?"

"Yes, but first tell me another one of your secrets before we go," Anita demanded.

"Right, I almost forgot." Christie got off the bed and went over to her side of the room. She bent down in front of her dresser and opened the bottom drawer, took out a magazine and then came back over to where Anita was sitting on the bed and handed her the magazine.

To Anita's surprise it was this month's Penthouse. "Oh my God, is this yours?" Anita asked.

"Yeah, it's mine. I have a confession to tell you. I like to masturbate to the stories and sometimes even to the pictures. No, I'm not a lesbian before you ask. Since you liked my story so much, you can borrow the magazine anytime you want. I took it from page twelve. I can't believe you thought I actually did that with one of my dad's co-workers. I mean I love sex and all, but please, the first time at the age of sixteen with a guy in his thirties in our bathroom? What kind of freak do you think I am?"

For the second time in less than ten minutes Christie had Anita speechless. "I can't believe you made up that story just to get me to tell you about my father. You are such a shithead," Anita said in anger as she got off the bed.

"First of all, I didn't make up the story, I just memorized it from the magazine and second, I did tell you a secret about myself, I told you I masturbated to guy magazines. Come on, that was worth something. I bet you never told anyone something like that. Let's just go get a bite to eat and we can goof off some more when we get back."

Anita was more ashamed than angry with Christie. She couldn't believe how gullible she was to the ways of people her own age. She was way behind sexually compared to the other girls and wondered if what Christie did was common for girls her age?

"I couldn't tell you something like that because I never did that before. I am very boring and I couldn't imagine ever doing that to myself."

"Listen Anita, eighty percent of all kids our age, both guys and girls, has masturbated once before the age of eighteen, and the other twenty percent lied about it. So when you are ready to try it, you know where I keep the magazines. Now let's get out of here, all this talk about sex has made me hungry."

It had been about twenty minutes since Frankie hung up the phone with Teddy and he and Vincent were still sitting in his office.

"Do you think Bull is going to call Sal?" Vincent asked Frankie.

"Of course he is going to call. He probably tried once already and he is going to call at least two more times before the night is over and when Sal doesn't answer the phone, Bull will get suspicious."

"Do you think he is going to take the money and run? I mean if I was him, that's what I would do. I would take my chances and not come back."

"All these years Vincent and you still don't think. Bull knows we can get him out there just as quick as we could here. He also knows that this would be better for us because if someone else whacked him it would solve our problem for us."

Frankie sat back in his chair and closed his eyes for a moment. He had been thinking of another way out of this while assuring himself that he could get Bull to come back home without a hitch.

"What I was thinking over the last twenty minutes was what if we call him first and tell him what really happened? Al, Victor and Sal went to the projects and got double-crossed by Lieutenant Joseph Brown. I'll make the call in the middle of the night tonight while he is more than likely half bagged and exhausted from his date. I'll break it to him that Sal was killed and Al was shot in the set up. I'll just say it looked like Lieutenant Brown was aiming for the bigger score by taking down a couple of mob guys. When he calms down, I'll explain that Pete called an emergency meeting earlier tonight and he made it quite clear that we are to get even with this Lieutenant. What do you think?" he asked Vincent.

"I don't think it's too far fetched for Bull to believe. I guess it's all up to you Frankie and how you relay the story to him. You have to be convincing and sound angry. And you want to get Bull to feel that same anger so that he'll want to get his ass on that plane and come home. So yeah, I think it could work, but are we still going through with Teddy?"

Frankie got up and walked around Vincent and headed to the bar. He poured two seven and sevens. He handed Vincent his glass. "Of course we are going to use Teddy. When Victor and Craig Rossi pick Bull up from the airport on Friday night, he will be so wound-up and ready to go that he won't have his mind focused right during the pick up. He'll be an easy target and that will be the end of that."

"Why are you sending Craig and not Al?" Vincent asked seeming a little confused.

"Because Al was shot yesterday, so he can't be there, now can he?"

"Jesus Frankie, I'm sorry, I just totally forgot what you just said back there."

"You know, maybe you are right, I should send Al too, with his arm in a sling to make it look good. He can be in the car feeding Bull some bullshit story about what took place in that apartment and get him even more fired up. See that Vincent? There are no stupid questions, just stupid people."

"Whatever you say Frankie," Vincent answered.

❧   ❧   ❧

"What do I owe for the pleasure of this unexpected visit Anthony?" Father John asked as he got up to shake Anthony's hand.

"How have you been Father?"

"Same old thing, just a different day, but what else can an old priest say about his life? From the looks of you Anthony, I am guessing small talk isn't the reason that you are here today. Why don't you have a seat and let's talk."

Anthony sat in one of the two chairs in front of the couch where Father John sat. "I really don't know where to begin. I have a lot on my mind right now and I am running around on fumes so if I start to babble, I apologize in advance," he replied.

"I have to believe the main reason that you are here is to discuss the arrangements for your parents' deaths. I can not express enough sympathy towards you for their death. The whole congregation was in shock when we heard the news. A tragedy involving two senseless deaths always puts your faith in God to the test, but you must be strong in knowing that your parents are up in heaven right now, enjoying eternity with God."

"It's funny Father, how you can make it sound that easy for me to let go of what has happened and take comfort that they are at peace with God. We are talking about my parents, the two people who have been there for me every day since I was born, having their lives brutally ended for no good reason. You now expect me to feel at ease knowing that they are in heaven?"

"Anthony, I know you are grieving, but you must believe that they are in a better place now."

"I hate to be the one to give you the news flash Father, but we are talking about dying in a gruesome way. No growing old together. No dying of a natural death later in life. No, we are talking about two people getting their heads blown off and the police needing their fingerprints to make a positive identification. I can't bring myself to come to peace with this as easily as you can."

"Anthony it is not our place in life to question God. You must be strong with your faith and accept what happens and be grateful that we possess the knowledge that there is a heaven waiting for us. Not to get off the subject because I'm sure you want to talk more about it, but I just wanted to let you know that we have talked to Tami and most of the arrangements have gone smoothly. The viewing will be Friday night as you requested, and the Mass will be Saturday morning at nine o'clock, with the burial around eleven-thirty at Oakland Cemetery. Are there any other requests that you can think of while I have you here?"

"No, everything sounds fine. I knew I could count on Tami. She has been making numerous phone calls for me and I don't know what I would have done without her help."

"See, there is hope for the next generation after all. Every time people complain to me about teenagers and how bad they are, I can always find someone like Tami to make them see differently. She is something special," Father John replied.

"Listen Father, as I am sure you are aware, I have a million things to get done by Friday and I would like to get started if you don't mind."

"So, what's on your mind, my son?"

"I know you haven't seen me around here in years, and I have many sins I would like to confess if you have the time to listen to my confession," Anthony explained.

Anthony confessed all the sins he could think of right up to waving a gun at Chad's face this morning. He felt that a great burden had been lifted from his chest when he was done, but he still wasn't at peace yet.

"Father John, there is one more thing that I need to confess but I haven't actually committed the sin yet. Can I confess to you a sin that I know I am going to commit even though I won't be remorseful after I have done it?"

"Anthony, the object of confession is to be sorry for what sins you have committed against God and his church. If you intend to commit a sin knowing that it is wrong and not being apologetic for it, how can you repent for it? That is the complete contradictory of a confession. What sin do you intend to commit that you can't find in your heart to be sorry for if you go through with it?"

"I know who killed my parents and I know how to even the score. I won't be involved in the actual event of revenge itself, but the actions that I take will see to it that this person will be killed for what he has done. I know we are supposed to turn the other cheek and all, but I am a firm believer in "an eye for an eye" and I want to even the score and make things right."

"Anthony, "an eye for an eye" is never the right way. You are old enough to know that two wrongs don't make a right, so why would you want to risk your soul over another senseless killing? All sins are equal in God's eyes no matter how great or small they are. Think about what you are planning to do. Can you live with yourself for the rest of your life knowing that you had someone killed because of your actions? You are obviously not the same boy that I watched grow up. Where did that boy go, Anthony?"

"It's funny, Father, that you ask me that question. That little boy died the day his mom-mom went into a coma. He woke up and realized that life is some sick joke that God is playing on us. He's just up there in heaven pulling on our strings and performing our lives like some kind of demented puppet show. There isn't a day that goes by that I don't think of her and how she looked all those years as a vegetable on that hospital bed in the nursing home. You tell me not to question God and his plans for everyone because everything happens for a reason. Well I say that's total bullshit and I'm not buying it."

Anthony got up from his chair as his anger continued to grow. He had kept this all bottled up for years. Sandra knew about his mom-mom, but she wasn't aware of the whole story and the great impact that it had on Anthony. This was his demon that he had inside of him that was waiting for years to come out, and today was the time.

"Anthony, please sit down," Father John insisted as he stood up and took Anthony by the shoulders. Anthony was already gone. His emotions and tears poured out of control.

"Father, do you have any clue what that is like, to watch the person, who loved you the most, other than your mother waste away for seven years? You haven't a vague idea the damage that does to a person. I can't escape the nightmares. I see her all the time in my dreams and it hurts too much. Do you know I was the last person to talk to her other than my pop-pop before she went into the coma? And you want to hear something even funnier? I don't remember what we talked about because I was pretty liquored up during my visit with her."

Anthony was sitting again and he was crying out of control. He was finally able to relinquish all that built up anger that he had inside of him. Father John took the opportunity to get up and bring Anthony the box of tissues that were on his desk. Anthony took it and continued to cry for a couple more minutes before he took one to clean himself up.

"You are right Anthony, I don't know what that must feel like. Both my parents and all my grandparents were gone now, and all their deaths were expected and easier to accept. I would be a hypocrite to tell you anything else, but you still need to realize that God is good and right now the four people you love the most are together in heaven looking down upon you. Do you want them watching you as you go through with your plans Anthony? I'm sure all of them want to see you again, but that won't be possible if you renounce your beliefs and commit this sin. Your soul will be condemned to hell if you never confess your sorrow for this sin. Is it really worth that to you Anthony?"

Anthony finally had himself under control again and was ready to finish his conversation with Father John. "I guess we are at a stand-still Father. I lost my wife and kid because of my immaturity and lack of discipline and nothing I do is going to change that. My parents are dead because of me, but I have the opportunity to rectify the situation by taking actions to make sure that the correct justice will be served. And I won't let this opportunity pass by."

Anthony got up from his chair and went over and gave Father John a long hug. "Thank you for listening to me and letting me get all that built up grief off my chest. It's hard going through life without a shoulder to lean on once in awhile. I know you can't forgive me for what I have to do but at least say a prayer for me and ask God to guide me through this and that no one else gets hurt."

"Anthony, I have always kept you in my prayers and asked God to guide you back to me and this church. I will pray for your safety and the safety of all that are involved in what you must do but in return, I would like one favor from you. When this is all done and over with, I want you to come back for another confession and start attending my Sunday services. Can you promise at least that to me?"

Anthony was at the door when he turned around with a smile on his face when he answered Father John. "I'm sorry Father, but this was a one time visit. If everything goes right Friday night, I'll see you at my parents' mass on Saturday and then I am out of this city forever. I will send you a post card and tell you the name of the parish that I will start to visit on Sundays. However, if things go the other way Friday, hopefully you will be wrong and I will be somewhere with my family again."

As Anthony turned to walk out the door Father John yelled out to him, "Please reconsider what you are planning to do and come to your senses. Don't go through with it."

Anthony stopped in his tracks and turned to face Father John. "Father if you were me and not a man of the cloth, you would do the same thing. Trust me, if you didn't, you couldn't live with yourself. Guilt is one tough son of a bitch to live with," he said and then walked out of the sacristy and headed out of St. Martin's, where he returned Saturday for his parents' mass.

❧   ❧   ❧

Dinner at the Pettyjohn's that night was far from the usual. Sandra and Chad sat in complete silence for the first time since they had been married. Neither one of them bothered to pay attention to Kimberly as she played with her food; half of which ended up on the floor. Twenty minutes was long enough for Chad. He had enough of Sandra's silent treatment. He wasn't the one who brought this problem into their lives; it was that fuck-up of an ex-husband of hers.

"I can't believe that you allowed him into our home. Why the hell didn't you tell him to get out and stay out of your life? Oh, do I need to mention that he had a gun? He brought a fucking gun in our home and waved it around at me in front of Kimberly. I guess you must have forgotten your spousal and parental obligations during that whole incident. You have no idea how pissed I am and if you want to see me go on a tirade, go ahead and ask me about Friday. See what I'll do," he threatened her.

"See what you'll do? Just like today, Chad? You were always such a little coward. Anthony might have his problems but at least he stood up for what he wanted and believed in. I guess you can't say the same. I wasn't the one who allowed him in our home today, now was I? I believe you answered the door."

"And what the hell was I supposed to do? He pointed a fucking gun at me," he roared back at her.

"In case you have forgotten, our daughter is sitting five feet from you, so stop the cursing," she told him.

Sandra picked up her glass of wine and finished it. She very rarely drank after Kimberly was born but tonight called for it because today was one of those special occasions where you needed a drink to get by.

"Do you really think he would have shot you in our home in front of his daughter? He was testing you and he was right. He was confident that you wouldn't have the balls to do anything about it."

"Have the balls to do something about it? You stupid fucking bitch, he's the main suspect of a double homicide in the murder of his own parents and what the hell would stop him from killing his ex-wife's new husband? I'm glad you think it would have been that easy to tell him to fuck off and get out of here," he screamed at her.

Out of the two years that they have been together, Sandra had never seen him like this before. Chad was a doctor and never really showed a temper because he never had reason for it. They never fought about anything that most couples fight about. When she and Anthony were together, their fights were always about money or his gambling. It got to the point where there was no need to fight anymore. He would never change and they were never going to have money, so she left.

Chad was just a quick rebound for her. She met him one night while she and Kimberly were at a restaurant having dinner. He was sitting at a table alone and he and Kimberly were making eye contact and smiling back and forth. Sandra decided to ask him if he would like to join the two of them since Kimberly seemed to like him. After that, they only dated a few times before the ball got rolling out of control and they ended up married. Because Chad was a doctor, he was never around, but that never bothered her because she married him for security, not companionship. Kimberly was all she needed for that. No, Chad was her financial security blanket and there would be no more arguments as long as she was content with her marriage.

Arguing was something new in their relationship, but it wasn't new for Sandra; she had enough experience with Anthony to make her an expert. Chad was too much of an easygoing guy and was totally out of his league to come out the winner tonight.

Sandra got up from the table and went over to the sink and grabbed a wash cloth and went back over to Kimberly and wiped her hands and face. When Kimberly was cleaned up, Sandra placed her in the family room in front of the TV, which would entertain her until her bedtime. Now she could go back into the kitchen and finish this argument that Chad foolishly started.

"Let's get a couple of things straight before we end this little discussion. First of all, Kimberly and I are going to that viewing Friday night and we are spending the night there. If you are too insecure to accept that, then that's on you. Second, get it through that arrogant head of yours that you are not the boss of me. You might be a doctor and I am just a housewife, but I have a degree too and was working full time until we got married. We both agreed that I should stay home with Kimberly, so don't think that you are better than me," she explained to him.

"I'll tell you something that you should know. If you spend Friday night there then we are through. I'll meet with my lawyers Monday to work on the divorce papers. Let's not kid ourselves, you don't love me any more than I love you. Oh, don't look at me like that. I might not be street smart like your loser ex-husband, but I'm not too naive to see that you are still in love with him and never will be with me. Fine, I can live with that. I married you because of the house and you married me for the financial security a doctor brings. We both got what we wanted out of this, a convenient marriage."

Sandra walked over to the table and poured herself another glass of wine. After a long swallow, she was ready to end this argument. This had gotten out of control and she didn't want it ending like her last fight with Anthony, in a divorce. Sandra realized she was never going to find true love in this marriage but he was right, they both needed each other for the security that wasn't in their lives before they met.

"You are right. I used you and you sure as hell used me. I can still live with that if you can. I was never looking for the fairy tale marriage. That's just something that little girls dream about. Kimberly and I are going Friday night because whatever happened to Anthony's parents, he needs us there to help him make things right. Neither one of us has any intentions of doing anything that shouldn't happen. Just swallow your pride again and just let me do what I have to do. After the funeral Saturday, you can believe Anthony when he said that he is out of our lives forever. If you are smart and concede defeat, I'll go up stairs right now and do whatever you want. You can even ask me to do a little experimenting."

Chad understood that she had the upper hand. What good would come out of this if he continued to fight this lost cause? He was never going to get Anthony or their past out of their lives unless he agreed to her proposition. Neither one of them were fools. She knew he wasn't going to throw away a home and she wasn't going to throw away a husband who was a doctor. They were in a mutual arrangement which neither one wanted to jeopardize. So for the second time in less than five hours, Chad had to swallow his pride and give in to her demands. But, he would make her pay for it when they got up to the bedroom by taking her up on her offer of experimenting.

It was around eight o'clock when Anthony finally caught up with Kevin at Palumbo's. Anthony suggested a crowded place because he still wasn't entirely sure that it was safe for him to be out in public. During all three stops that he made today, he never feared that he was being followed. But, ever since he left Sandra's this afternoon; he had a strange feeling that he was being trailed. Twice he pulled over to allow the flow of traffic to go past him and waited for awhile before he continued. Kevin was already at a booth and drinking his ice tea when Anthony sat down.

"Thanks for meeting me tonight Kevin. Is Tami all right at home by herself?"

"Her friend Sydney Collins is over helping her with the rest of your phone calls. What the hell could I do about it anyway? If she wants to have someone over, she is going to with or without my permission. It's not like she doesn't have the opportunities. She's alone there all afternoon before I get home from the shop."

"Is she seeing anyone?" Anthony asked.

"She hasn't been seeing anyone steadily this year. She is too involved with her schoolwork and reading all those college brochures that she picked up from her guidance counselor. Tami is really determined to get into a good college next year."

"You should be happy that she even wants to go to college."

"It scares the hell out of me, but I know she wants to get out of this city and not come back. I believe she has felt that way for a long while, even before my parents' death. Christ, I feel like a father instead of a big brother. That's why I must be a complete asshole to agree to go through with your half-assed idea."

"I know Tami is the most important thing in your life Kevin and if you want out, please say so. I don't want this on my conscience if you did this only because of the guilt and nothing more. Either way I am still going to go through with it. Having you makes my alibi that much better," Anthony explained.

"I said I was in and I'm not going to change my mind."

"Hi guys, are you ready to order yet?" Gloriana their over perky waitress asked.

"I don't know about you Kevin, but I haven't eaten all day and I am ready to eat."

Anthony didn't even open his menu before he ordered. "I'll take the linguine and clams in a white sauce with a plate of mussels for an appetizer, a salad with house dressing and an ice tea to wash it down."

"And what would you like, sir?" she asked Kevin.

"I'll just take a plate of ravioli in meat sauce and another ice tea," he replied as he handed her his menu and thanked her.

"How did you make out today with all your plans?" Kevin asked after Gloriana had walked away with their orders.

"Actually, I think I did quite well today. I got the gun that we are going to need for Friday, very easily I might add. I met with Father John at St. Martin's to go over my parents' viewing and mass. Oh, he said he had already talked to Tami earlier in the day and said she was a great kid. I thought you might like to know that. And lastly, I met with Sandra to make sure that she and Kimberly were coming Friday night. I have a feeling that I am going to need her as another alibi."

The first part of Anthony's sentence just registered in Kevin's head. "Whoa whoa whoa," Kevin jumped in abruptly before Anthony could say anymore. "Wait just a minute. You never said anything about a gun. Why the hell do we need a gun?"

"Don't worry I will go over everything before we leave here tonight. Trust me, you will be up to full speed with everything. After you leave here you can go home and work on my plan and if anything doesn't seem right, let me know."

Kevin didn't like the way this sounded already. He thought that he must be a complete jackass to be here with Anthony tonight.

"Kevin, the real question that you will have to ask yourself later tonight is: can you go through with it or not? What I plan to ask of you tonight is outright ludicrous. It involves you using a gun, sticking up a mob crew and walking away with over two hundred thousand dollars without having to kill anyone in the process. This is the kind of shit that only happens in the movies or on TV, and I don't need to tell you what happens if something goes wrong. Neither one of us will walk away from this alive if we are caught and our deaths won't be simple and quick. You have a lot of thinking to do later because you have much more to lose than I do."

The one great thing about coming to a place like Palumbo's, it doesn't take long for the food to be delivered. Gloriana had brought back their salads and drinks along with Anthony's mussels. After she walked away Anthony suggested that they wait to continue their talk until after he had a chance to get some of this food into his stomach.

Detective Engman was sitting at his desk eating his McDonald's Quarter Pounder and cold fries when Detective Fishburn came running into the office.

"Did you hear about the fire down at the projects earlier today?"

Finishing his mouthful of burger, Phil answered, "Yeah, what about it?"

"I guess you didn't hear who they pulled out of the apartment?" Joe replied.

"I haven't heard the official results yet because I have been sitting here working on the Albergo's double homicide. You remember them, the old couple slaughtered in their store yesterday?"

"See, that's what I love about you Phil. Your banter is far more entertaining than any other detective in this office. Let me help with the Albergo case by filling you in on that little fire today. It seems that they pulled out two bodies from that apartment, and both of them had a lot of bullet holes in them."

"What's so surprising about that? Sounds like a typical drug deal gone wrong and someone was covering it up. What's your point?" Phil asked.

Joe sat down in a chair across from Phil's desk. He rolled himself over into arms length of Phil's fries and took three off of the hamburger wrapper that Phil had laid out over his paper work. "Man you really need to start eating better. If you don't get killed on the job, this shit will catch up to you and give you a massive heart attack before you have the chance to retire," he said sarcastically.

"Are you kidding me, what I eat is the least thing that I fear that can kill me," Phil responded.

"Now what I was trying to explain to you before you so eagerly dismissed what I was saying was that one of the bodies was a black male and the other was an extremely well built white guy. Word is that the apartment belonged to the black guy, of course, and forensics won't have a positive id on either of them for at least another day or two. Have our three tails called in yet today with any useful information?"

Phil was taking in the information that Joe gave him as he reached for his notebook, which was lying next to the phone, "A car picked up Sal and Bull early this morning and they dropped Bull off at the airport. He was seen getting on a flight to Vegas. I can only assume that Frankie Feliciani sent him for a couple of days until the other bosses had time to think over this problem. But they lost them once they left the airport. The unit at Sal's house said he hasn't been back since this morning and Ronald Dawson, who has been out front of *The Club* all day, just called about half an hour ago and the only people there are Frankie and Vincent Lusi."

"What about Anthony?" Joe asked.

"Detective Jamie Casey has called in three times so far today. It seems Anthony has been very busy today. He started his morning off at Larry Perna's pawnshop, which I can only assume was to get some of the pay off money. Once he left there he went to his ex-wife's house. This sent up a red flag for me. He said it himself—he hasn't seen her since the divorce, so why would he go there unless he was worried that something bad was going to happen to him?"

"You think he went to see his kid?" Joe interrupted.

"Well it sure as hell wasn't to talk to his ex-wife."

"You think he's planning to run?" Joe asked.

Phil took the last two bites of his hamburger and, once he was finished, he replied, "I believe he is doing one of two things. He is either going on the run and never coming back, or worse, he is considering some sort of retaliation and knows he might not succeed. Either way, he is getting his goodbyes in while he has the chance."

"I don't know Phil, Anthony doesn't seem the type to have the balls or the sources to mastermind some kind of revenge against the likes of Frankie and his two goons. Do you really think he would try something like that?" Joe asked.

"Do you want to take a guess at the third place Anthony went today?" Phil asked in return.

"Okay, I'll bite. Where else did he go today?"

"Anthony went to St. Martin of Tours Church for over an hour. That's his old grade school parish and where his parents continued to go to church every Sunday."

Joe sat back in his chair and wrote something down in his own notebook. "Why does this surprise you Phil? If it was his parents' parish, he was probably there making arrangement for the services later this week. A church isn't like reception halls where you just pick up the phone and say 'Hey I want to have a little get together Friday night because my parents were just murdered.' There are a lot of details, including paying for it. He was probably there talking with whichever priest knew his parents the most and was going over all the details. I'm sure the two had a lot to talk about. It's not like it is an easy topic to have a conversation about."

"That is all true, but from what I gathered so far about Anthony, I think it would have been a lot easier on him to just make the phone call. We found out that Anthony hasn't been to his old church in years. Why would he want to subject himself to a priest's questions face to face when it would be so much easier to do it over the phone? No, I think he went there for the purpose of seeing a priest one on one to make himself square with the big guy in case things didn't go as planned."

"You really believe that he went there to discuss more than just his parents' arrangements? What, you think he was looking to receive absolution for something he did?"

"No Joe, not what he did, what he intends to do. My gut is telling me that he is planning to do both. I think he has all the intentions in the world to avenge his parents' deaths and then disappear and start fresh somewhere else. And whose advice is better to seek if you had any doubts about going through with something like that than a priest?"

Before Joe could answer him the phone rang.

"Engman here. Yeah. What time was that? No just go back to his place and wait there. Alright, check in when he gets back. Joe and I will stop there in the morning," he told the voice on the other end before he hung up the phone.

"That was Jamie, he lost him late this afternoon after Anthony left the church. I told him to just wait at his place until he comes home. You and I will pay him a visit nice and early tomorrow morning. Let's call it a night and get some rest."

🍁   🍁   🍁

With their plates empty and their stomachs full, Kevin was sitting back smoking a cigarette when Anthony decided to finish filling him in with his plans for Friday night. "Kevin, before I go into full detail about Friday night, I just want you to realize that you will be the one taking most of the risks and firing the gun that I told you about earlier. Let me make one thing clear: my plans don't have you killing anyone, but you will need to shoot someone in an arm or leg to attain the maximum effect. Have you ever fired one before?"

"You are a fucking piece of work Anthony. Yes, I have fired a gun before, but never at anyone. Now, where do you intend to be hiding while my ass is on the line?" he demanded to know.

"You know that one of us has to be waiting in the car. If you let me finish, it will all make sense to you," Anthony responded. "As long as you are familiar with firing a gun you shouldn't have any problems. The plan is really quite simple. It doesn't have a lot of details. I feel simplicity is the best way to go with a plan like this. After a major sporting event like the Superbowl or the World Series, Frankie has Bull meet Dan Rodenhausen at the usual place, in the alley at 6th and Walnut Streets. They have never changed the spot or the people that were involved since I have been hanging at *The Club*."

"How do you know all of this?" Kevin asked.

"Obviously I have never been on one of these runs, but I have been in *The Club* many times playing cards when they returned from their errands. Bull usually takes the same three guys with him; Sal, Al, and either Vincent or Charlie, whoever of the two that wanted to take the ride, I guess. Al is always the driver and Bull is the only one who handles the money. If Frankie sends the same people every time, then the people that take the money should be the same too. I don't see why they would be different if Frankie's people were the same every time. Now pay attention because this is the key for the plan to work. Bull never counts the money in front of them."

"Why not, what's the big deal?"

"It's that whole 'trust and proper business ethics between the crews' thing. What usually happens is that Bull takes the money and counts it in the car and while he is doing that, Dan and his men leave. Most of the time it usually takes five minutes or so, but this week's payoff is huge. Frankie was looking at two hundred thousand give or take, and whoever decides to take Bull's place when he doesn't come out of the airport will take even more time to make sure that all the money is there."

"Yeah, especially since they probably aren't used to counting money under pressure like that," Kevin replied.

"I know if I was responsible for taking that money, I would be damn sure to take my time and count it correctly. I wouldn't want to be accused of coming up short if you know what I mean."

Kevin felt even worse about this plan than he did the other night now that he had heard Anthony explain it out loud. "Damn it Anthony, most of your plan is based on assumptions that this and that will happen. None of it is concrete. First of all, how the hell do you know that you can get Bull detained at the airport? Did you get a hold of your friend Phillip?"

"Yes, I talked to him today. He will be at the airport from noon to ten. I gave him Bull's full name and told him he should be arriving sometime on Friday. He checked and told me that Bull's flight was due to land at seven on Friday night. He assures me that if Bull has luggage, one of the baggage handlers can put a switch blade in his suitcase and if he doesn't have checked luggage, Phillip will personally be there at the ramp and he will put it on Bull's carry on bag as he walks by."

"Are you sure that Phillip is going to be able to get to his luggage or even him?"

"I can't see how Bull wouldn't have luggage because his carry on bag will be the three hundred thousand dollars. He ain't letting go of the bag for anybody. Even a person as disgusting as Bull has to bring at least one bag with him. He has to have at least one clean pair of underwear."

"And what if he doesn't?" Kevin asked.

"Then I guess I have to rely on Phillip getting the job done. Either way, he will call my cell phone once Bull is detained or if he walks out without an incident. If he walks out, we forget the whole thing and I leave the city Saturday after the burial. But you need to have faith Kevin."

"I think you need to sound more convincing before I put my faith in you."

"Fine, fair enough," Anthony responded. "Anyway, with all the security issues at the airport after 9/11, they will keep him there for hours and forget about him having a phone call, he'll be detained for awhile in a small little room getting the shit kicked out of him. He won't be able to call Frankie for at least three hours, maybe even longer. The local boys will work on him before they bring in the Feds. And once they run Bull's name through their computer, forget about it."

"You think they will keep him that long for just a couple of little objects in his luggage?" Kevin asked.

"Don't forget about having to explain the large amount of money that he will have on him. It's all legal, but I'm sure they'll want to call the casino to verify his receipt. I'm telling you he's there for hours and by the time he gets out of there and calls Frankie, it will be too late for him," he tried to assure Kevin the best he could.

"Okay let's say your friend Phillip does keep his end of the bargain up and it works. This doesn't explain why Al and the rest of them would leave without Bull. The whole reason why they are there is to pick him up, right?" Kevin asked.

"Because if I am right, they already took care of Sal and they might expect Bull to stay in Vegas and run. If he doesn't come out within an hour or two, they'll call Frankie and he'll tell them to leave and head for the pick up."

"What if someone goes inside and looks for him?"

"Frankie will want them to keep to their schedule and get his two hundred thousand because that will be more important to him than getting Bull. He'll deal with Bull after they come back with his money. And after they don't come back with his money, Bull will be as good as dead when he arrives back at *The Club*."

"Let me make sure I am following your plan correctly. First, we are hoping that your friend Phillip is correct and Bull will be on that plane Friday, and that he is going to be able to put a switchblade in his bag and have him detained. Then, we are expecting Frankie's men to just leave without Bull. That is the plan so far, right?" he asked sarcastically.

Anthony realized it wasn't going to be easy to convince Kevin. Kevin's patience was running short, and he was getting more frustrated as Anthony explained his plan to him. His hopes that Kevin would be more at ease after a good meal clearly weren't working out the way he hoped it would. "Kevin I know you are a man who needs concrete proof when it comes to believing in something. Hell, I bet you think Oswald acted alone since they haven't pinned Kennedy's murder on anyone else. Yet, you feel strongly that OJ murdered Nicole and Ronald and why is that?"

"What do you mean, why is that? Because for one, it is in all the history books that Lee Harvey Oswald killed JFK and I don't think all those books would be wrong. As for the other, don't even get me started. Everyone knows that son of a bitch killed those two people and if it weren't for those eight or nine racist jurors, he would be on death row. So don't go telling me different about that," he warned Anthony.

"Thank you for proving my point. You believe in the first because that's what everyone has been putting in your mind since you were a kid and as for the second, that's what you want to believe because you are thinking with your heart and not your head. Kevin, I know this seems so far-fetched right now, but I know these guys and their routines. I have been hanging around with this crew for the last four years and I know how they think and what actions they will take when they are faced with certain circumstances. They are like a children's book. You can't misread them."

"Anthony, it's not the same," Kevin replied.

"Yes it is Kevin. As strongly as you feel about the OJ disaster, I feel the same way about what will happen if Phillip comes through for us. Then, the dominos will fall into place with Bull going down last."

Gloriana came back to their table and wanted to know if they wanted dessert or coffee. Anthony thought that he might not have many more chances at a fresh piece of cake. He decided to order the cheese cake with cherries on top and a coffee. There was still more planning to do tonight, and he figured he might as well load up on the coffee now instead of later.

"When do they normally schedule their pick ups?" he asked Anthony.

"Normally they meet around eleven o'clock. It should be close to that time, especially if Bull gets in around eight or eight-thirty, because they usually go to Tony's for some pizza or subs before they head out. But don't worry about that, we will be there around ten waiting for them to get there. We won't miss them," he guaranteed.

"Anthony, I think you are forgetting what is already happening Friday night. Your parents' viewing, remember?"

"No, I haven't forgotten and that is where Sandra will come into play. The viewing is from six to eight o'clock and right back at my parents' house afterwards with a small gathering of friends and family for some sandwiches and drinks. If I know Frankie, he will show up along with Vincent to say some words and then leave. I'm sure he'll have people outside, too. But, before he leaves I am going to take Sandra and Kimberly upstairs to bed and not come down. I make a little announcement thanking everyone before we go up and I'll put my Aunt Marian in charge of seeing people out. That won't be too hard to sell to anyone who might want to know where I was from nine until midnight, if you know what I mean."

"So how do you plan on getting out of the house? Where the hell am I going to be this whole time?"

Anthony laughed as he was finishing a huge piece of his cheese cake. "Kevin, are you serious? I grew up in this house. Do you know how many times I snuck out of there during my high school years? That's not a problem. As for you, once the viewing is over bring Tami to my house and head back to your shop and pick up the car. Then, meet me on Terrace Avenue two streets behind mine. I'll cut through the alleys and meet you at the corner. I doubt highly that anyone will be watching the back of the house."

"You're not a teenager anymore, do you really think you can get out and then back into the house again?" he asked, sounding unsure that Anthony really could.

"Please, even at my age I can still do it. I have done it so many times it's like riding a bike, you never forget how to do these things. I don't think I will run into any problems with getting back inside," he assured Kevin.

Kevin sat there shaking his head as he watched Anthony finish the last of his cake. Anthony's whole proposal was absurd. There were no tangible scenarios to Anthony's scheme, it was all based on chances and Kevin was not one for taking too many risks, especially if it involved putting his life on the line.

"Kevin, at anytime if one of the chain of events does not occur the way it should go, then we will back out of it. Everything that I have said up until now we can walk away from without consequence. We haven't even come to the part of getting the money, and you have questioned everything I've said so far. Just relax. I haven't brought up anything yet that will put you in harm. Right now the only person who is taking an enormous risk is my friend Phillip, because if he botches his end of the arrangement, not only does he have to worry about Bull and Frankie, but the locals and the feds and his career. If I knew you were going to be such a little girl about this, I wouldn't have asked you."

Anthony always knew the right words to say to push someone's buttons and Kevin's was just pushed to the edge.

"Listen to me, you little fuck! I have no problem with doing any of this, but I would have a little more confidence in your whole idea if it wasn't put together half-assed. Christ, did you see this done in a movie or read about it in a comic book before? Because to me, those are the only two places that this idea of yours would work," he informed Anthony.

"It's not based on absurd calculations. I have thought this through based on what I know about these people. Everything up to this point has about an eighty percent success rate. As long as Bull is on that plane and doesn't make it out of that airport, everything will fall right into place," he assured Kevin.

"I forgot to ask, how did you make out getting that kid for Friday night?"

"I talked to his brother and he said Nicholas will do it, but he wants the whole evening to be paid for before he agrees to do it. And what exactly is he doing for you? For God's sake, I don't want to involve some kid in all of this."

"Nicholas is going to be our insurance card for walking away from all of this if something goes wrong and we are confronted by Frankie," Anthony explained as he reached into his pocket. He took out a photo of him, Frankie, Ellena and Anita and handed it to Kevin.

"What kind of insurance can Nicholas possibly buy us?" Kevin asked.

"He is going to go up to Cornell on Friday and find Anita. He'll make sure she has a nice night, and keep her out until sometime Saturday afternoon. He'll have my cell phone number to call once he finds her, and the rest is up to him and his charm. Don't get the wrong idea, I don't want him to do anything other than keeping her from going back to her dorm until late Saturday. This way if Frankie feels the need to call her dorm room on Saturday morning, Anita's roommate will tell him that she hasn't come home yet from the night before. And what do you think he is going to assume?"

"What kind of crazy shit is that Anthony? You want a guy like Frankie thinking his daughter has been kidnapped? Do you know what he'll do to us? Oh Christ man, this is totally out of control. I can't believe you are talking about getting his daughter involved in all of this!" he screamed out in a fury.

"Kevin, no one is talking about kidnapping, or getting Anita involved in this. Nicholas is going up there to take her out for a night and have a good time, within reason. The only thing I want to happen is to have that thought in Frankie's mind. If our backs are to the wall, we can count on her not answering her dorm room phone. For all we know, this could be one of the nicest nights out for her."

"A nice night for her, you must be kidding me," Kevin said.

"Who knows, maybe they hit it off and start dating, good for them if it happens. I know she never had a real boyfriend and sure as hell could use one in her life. This is only a last resort, a bluff and nothing else. More than likely this will never come out in the open."

"Anthony, you know my situation with Tami and do you know how I would react if this involved her? I would kill the motherfucker, that's what I would do. I just want you to know where I stand on the issue. I think we are crossing the line by bringing his daughter into it."

"I totally understand Kevin and like I said, she won't be involved in any way. I am just making sure she won't be home to answer that call, if it comes. Stop worrying about it. Nicholas is going to get out of the city for a night on us with a young beautiful girl if he can find her. If not, I'm sure he'll have a good time at one of those parties because there are plenty of women up there. I'm sure on a Friday night they'll be a party or two on campus and it won't be too difficult to find them. If she's at one of them, hopefully he can work his magic. If he succeeds, great, if not, no big loss to us other than the hundred dollars that I am going to pay him for his effort," Anthony explained.

"You're the poker player, do you even have the slightest clue what the odds are of Nicholas finding Anita and hooking up with her long enough to keep her out all night? You are really crazy if you think that's going to happen."

"If Nicholas can find her at a party then the odds of him working his charm on her are very reasonable. This isn't your typical freshman college girl from the big city with a lot of experience when it comes to boys. I have known her for the last three years and she never dated anyone that I was aware of, and I know her prom date was set up by Frankie as a business proposition. She is a very shy girl and if she happens to actually find the nerve to go to a party, it won't be that difficult for him to work his magnetism on her. But I want to talk to him before he leaves. I want to make sure we are on the same page about this. He is only there to talk to her and hang out. I don't want him trying anything on her," he insisted.

"Do you want me to have Nicholas come down to the shop tomorrow and you can talk to him there?" Kevin asked.

"No, I don't want to come to the shop at all. I told you earlier that I thought I was being followed, so I don't want to take any risks by going down there. Why don't you have him come down to the shop? You can give him the picture, the hundred dollars and my cell phone number and have him call me later in the night."

"That shouldn't be a problem. When Charlie gets into work, I'll have him tell Nicholas to come over after his classes," he informed Anthony.

"That works. Ok, let's get back to our business. After you pick me up, we'll head right to the alley. I will drop you off somewhere in the middle of Walnut Street and then you will walk to the back alley, where there is a huge green dumpster half way down. You can stand behind it and there is no way that they could possibly see you. The alley isn't long, so you should be able to see everything from there and once Dan's car leaves, then it's show time."

"Showtime? What exactly are you expecting me to do?" he asked Anthony.

"This is the serious part of the plan and that is why I want you to listen to everything first before you ask questions. If for some reason things don't go right in that alley, it's your life and no one else's that is at risk. I will be across the street inside the car observing, and if something goes wrong I am leaving and going straight to where Tami is and heading right out of town. But I know it won't come to that because you can get through this without a glitch," he replied.

"Yeah, that seems fair. It's my head out there on the chopping block while you're across the street. Why can't I be across the street and you be in the alley if you are so confident that nothing is going to go wrong?"

"Because out of the two of us, who do you think will come off looking like Bull under a ski mask in the darkness of an alley?" Anthony asked back.

"Kevin, I thought you were following along with me. I need you in that alley to come out of nowhere and surprise them while they are in the car counting the money."

"I have been following you. Don't you know sarcasm when you hear it? I just think it is ironic that you are the one in trouble here and it's my neck that's on the line. Does it seem fair to you?" he asked.

"No, it doesn't, so stop with the fucking sarcasm. This is no time to be fooling around. I need to feel secure that I have everything in order before we head out Friday night because we only have one shot at this."

"Fine, I was trying to relax and make you calmer. If you were me and could see your face right now Anthony, you wouldn't agree to this. Your sales pitch isn't the greatest and no, I don't have total confidence in you. But, if I can make a joke in spite of everything, that's one less moment that I wouldn't be thinking of kicking your ass for putting me in this situation."

"I guess that's fair enough," Anthony replied.

"But you need to pay complete attention to the rest of this, all right?"

"Like I said, stop worrying about me and just focus on your plan," Kevin responded back.

"Good, now let me finish. We will make an early run tomorrow night to the alley to map it out but I am relatively sure that from where the dumpster is located in the alley you will be behind them. Two cars can fit side by side only to a certain point in that alley and the dumpster is beyond that point. This means everything is going to take place in front of you. When you see Dan's car pull out of the alley, wait about a minute and then go into action."

Anthony hesitated just a moment to make sure he had Kevin's full attention.

"I want you to stay low and along the wall as you approach the car and once you get to it, you need to hit the front side passenger's window with a crow bar and bust it in. I've got to believe a guy with your strength can do that."

"Trust me, I can break a fucking car window."

"Good because the moment that window shatters, it will be total chaos in that car. You need to act right away, and under no circumstances can you give them a chance to react. Surprise and fear are your advantage, but if you freeze and don't take out that gun right away and put it in the passenger's face then they'll have an opportunity to re-organize. If you allow that to happen, you won't stand a chance of getting out of there. But if you stay on top of them the whole time and have that gun out waving in their faces, then they will do whatever you ask."

"You actually think they are going to give over close to two hundred thousand dollars to me without pulling out a gun and killing me first?" he questioned.

"Anthony, there is no way in this world that they'll just hand me the money and walk out of that alley. Frankie will have their heads once they reported back to him. There is nothing that you can tell me to convince me otherwise. That's not how these guys handle certain situations."

"You are right Kevin, they would never give up that kind of money without a fight. Being shot would be a lot better fate than what Frankie would have in store for them, unless they knew who took it and that they could get it back," Anthony started to explain.

"There are a couple of details that I left out. Unfortunately you don't have a choice about the first one. You are going to have to shoot the driver and whoever is in the back at least once in the leg or arm—whatever you can manage to hit. You need to persuade these guys that you mean business."

"You expect me to just shoot these guys, just like that?"

"Yes, I do. And once you shoot the two of them, the passenger will hand you the money without hesitation. By shooting the driver, this will give us a huge head start on escaping, because they will have to get him out of the driver seat and someone else in his place to drive. Like I said, it will be total chaos and you shooting one or two of them will only add to it. Kevin, under no circumstances can you loose your nerve and not shoot them. If you don't, no one would believe it was a heist and it also strengthens our chances of getting out of there without them being able to follow us."

"Jesus Anthony, what if I kill him or worse what if whoever is in the back seat gets off a shot at me and I have to end up shooting him a second or third time and he ends up dead? There's a difference between stealing dirty money from these guys and murder. I just don't know if I could live with myself if I killed someone Anthony."

"Kevin, I highly doubt that it will come down to you having to kill anyone because the second detail that I have neglected to tell you should help ease your mind. The reason why they won't put up any kind of a fight once you shoot the driver is because you are going to say the words 'douche bag' at least five or six times."

"What the Christ do the words 'douche bag' have to do with them shooting back at me?" he shouted at Anthony.

"Because Kevin, once you break in the window and yell, "Hand me the fucking money douche bag", you'll add to the confusion that is already going through their heads. They are going to be frozen in place once they hear those words."

"What's so special about those words?" he asked Anthony.

"They are the most frequently used words in Bull's vocabulary. Believe me I should know, he constantly uses them on me. In the dark and under a ski mask they'll believe it is him the whole time and someone is bound to ask, "What the fuck are you doing Bull?" that's when you shoot the driver. It will be pure pandemonium and trust me, they'll do nothing about it until they get back to Frankie with this information."

"You really think they will register douche bag with Bull?" he asked.

"You better believe they will," Anthony assured him.

"And as for the last little detail from my plan, once you come out of the alley, I will be waiting at the entrance. When I floor it and we burn rubber and screech away, they'll hear it and assume it was Bull's 'Vette. As you can testify, a 'Vette has that magical sound only it can make."

"That it does."

"Now tell me, other than having to shoot one of them, what do you think? And don't lie. If you don't think this can work, then I don't want you going through with it because I can take my chances on the run from Frankie for the rest of my life. It just would be so much more rewarding if I could be doing it with over a hundred thousand dollars in my hands."

"I thought you said that there would be over two hundred thousand in the bag?" he questioned Anthony.

"I did, but did you think I was keeping it all to myself? This is a fifty-fifty deal. Once we come out of that alley with the money, it gets split equally. Of course I will have to stash the money and have you send it to me at a later time, just in case Frankie wants to check my place or my parents' house on Saturday. I don't want the money anywhere near me. I just haven't decided on a good location yet."

"You are planning on giving me over a hundred thousand dollars? That's a lot of money for me to hide, Anthony. How could I explain if someone asked where that money came from?"

"Well keep it hidden until Tami is ready for college. Open up a safety deposit box in Tami's name at a bank other than the one you use now. It is important to have it in a different bank in case someone comes looking for it. Pick some small little mom and pop bank in the city that hardly does any business, but just make sure that Tami is aware and has the second key."

"Man, I can't say that I couldn't use that kind of money, Anthony, but I still don't know if this is such a good idea. I mean, I know you put your heart and soul into this and really believe that it is going to work, but in your mind and in reality are two different things. Forget about the airport part and Nicholas as insurance, we can prepare all we want the next two days, but when the time comes and I am standing there with a gun in my hand, I just don't know if I can pull that trigger," he confessed.

"I assume your instinct will kick in and you won't find it difficult to pull the trigger. We aren't talking about innocent, law-abiding citizens here. Everyone who will be in that car has killed more than once or twice in his lifetime, so etch that into your memory bank for Friday night. These guys are total animals who would kill you, me, Tami, Sandra and even Kimberly without blinking an eye, and if you don't pull that trigger they will," he informed him.

"You have sprung a lot of shit on me tonight and I need to go home and think this through. I assume you have gone over this in your head numerous times to come up with the different situations that can happen if things don't go according to plan, but I need to go over them for myself. I'm going to get out of here, go home and grab a drink or two and run your idea over and over again in my head until I believe it will work. Or that it is just too fucking crazy, but either way I will make up my mind tonight. Where can I reach you tomorrow morning?"

"I am heading over to my parents' house to crash. More than likely I will be there in morning, if not reach me on the cell phone. I haven't been in the house since the murders and I need to check to make sure the place is okay. If the cops didn't feed the cat when they were over there investigating, I know that Nova more than likely tore the place up looking for food."

"Alright, I'll call you there in the morning and I'll tell you where we stand on Friday night." Kevin got up and put his jacket on and was about to walk away before Anthony stopped him.

"Hey Kevin, can I ask you two things?"

"Yeah sure, why not, what else could you possibly ask me to make this evening worse?"

"One, can you please make sure to thank Tami for me and let her know what I said about the priest?"

"Yeah sure, no problem, but I think it would be nicer if she heard it from you."

"Great, it means a lot to me that she knows I value her help with everything. It's not easy for a girl her age to dedicate her time to a family member, especially under these circumstances," he informed Kevin.

"Don't worry I'll tell her, but why don't you give her a call tomorrow in the afternoon to check up on her and then you can tell her yourself? What else did you want to ask me? Because I am tired and I want to get the hell home to those drinks."

"When the demons come to visit you in your sleep, what do you fear the most about the encounter? Is it looking into their faces and seeing their pain? Or is it the sound from the crash of metal against metal that you hear right before their screams? What exactly do you dread the most about those dreams?"

"What kind of fucking question is that to ask me? Why do you think those two girls haunt my dreams? I never brought that up to you."

"You didn't have to. I saw it in your eyes the other night at your house. I saw the horror in your eyes when I brought up the accident and I was just wondering what the worst part about it was for you."

Kevin didn't even know where to begin with his answer. He had never mentioned the dream of the girls to anyone before.

"Do you have any idea what it is like for me every night, knowing I have them to look forward to when I sleep? I thought about going to seek help for it, but I don't see what good would have come out of it. There was nothing he was going to tell me that could bring those girls back from the dead. What would be the best he could tell me, 'Don't beat yourself to death over this, Kevin? There was no proof that this guy was a three-time DUI loser. What could you have done? You didn't botch the police report. That wasn't your responsibility. You need to let it go and move on with your life.' Anthony, regret is one fucking burden to live with and that is why I can't make the same mistake twice.

You just better make sure that you go over your plan some more before we meet tomorrow night."

"Don't worry about me Kevin, just go home and get some rest. When this is all over and you have hopefully exorcised your demons, I will tell you about mine, which no one else knows about."

"Anthony, when this is all over with, I don't expect to see you again," he replied as he walked away from the table and out the door.

Neither one of them realized that after Saturday, Anthony would never get a chance to tell Kevin about his demons, because Kevin would be dead.

It was around six-thirty Vegas time when Bull's cell phone went off in his pocket as he was standing at the craps table. "What's up?" he answered.

"Bull, this is Frankie. How's the trip going?"

"The trip is going just fine. I am up about a dime on the crap tables and you kind of caught me in the middle of my streak. Is this important, or can I call you back later on tonight?" he asked.

"Who am I to get in the way of a man's good streak? Just do me a favor and make sure you call me back tonight no matter what time you get back to your room. I will be at *The Club* for the night anyway and I do need to go over some things with you."

"Hey Uncle, if it is important I can stop playing and talk. What's going on at home?"

"Hey, listen. Enjoy yourself and don't worry about it. I will inform you later, so just keep winning and don't use any of my fucking money if you start to lose," he demanded.

"I haven't picked it up yet. I'm not leaving that kind of money in my room and I don't trust these douche bags with it in their safes. I had planned on getting it tomorrow night after I hit the town."

"Smart thinking because, no offense, I wouldn't trust you with that kind of money in your possession for two days," Frankie answered back.

"That hurts. Listen, the dice are one shooter away and I got to go. I'll call you as soon as I go upstairs for the night, just give me a couple of hours."

"Yeah, no problem and oh, by the way, learn how to walk away when the table turns on you," Frankie warned him before he hung up.

"I always do," Bull answered but the line was already dead.

Frankie sat back in his chair and was glad to hear relaxation in Bull's tone of voice. It's not hard to be that way when you are winning big at the tables, and it was also taking his mind off of what was happening at home. The more comfortable Bull was, the easier it was going to be to spring the news on him later tonight. Frankie just hoped that Bull wasn't going to be stupid, piss away his winnings and have his mood change before he got the chance to talk to him.

Kevin walked in the door around ten o'clock. He could hear the music blaring from Tami's room upstairs, which meant that Sydney was still over and was going to spend the night. He had hoped that she had gone home already and that Tami had crashed in her room for the night, but he was not that lucky. So the best he could do was to make himself a couple of stiff drinks and collapse on the couch and think about Anthony's plan for Friday night. Kevin was emotionally drained from his dinner with Anthony and he couldn't believe he had put himself in this predicament. His life was good, and things were great at the shop. The only major concern for Kevin was where Tami was going to go to school next year. But, that all changed yesterday when Anthony showed up and fucked everything up.

After pouring his drink, Kevin took the afghan from the recliner and went back to the couch where he propped up two pillows, and laid down. He never even finished his drink before sleep finally took over him and he forgot all about Anthony's plan.

Everything in the living room seemed to be the same as Anthony remembered it from the last time he was here. His parents had left all the photos of him, Sandra and Kimberly up on the mantel, which didn't surprise him except for the wedding picture. He guessed that was his mother's doing because she was one for holding on to lost hope. As he stood there and looked at all of their old pictures, Nova came scurrying from the upstairs. And just as he had thought, the police hadn't bothered feeding her.

Anthony went to the kitchen to get Nova's food. When he walked in he had realized nothing in here had changed. Dishes were set on the table for that's night dinner. The pictures of Kimberly were still on the refrigerator. The dreaded big wooden spoon and fork were still hanging on the wall above the table and the morning's dishes from Tuesday were washed and on the drain board on the kitchen counter. Erma was not one for letting housework wait. She would never allow herself to leave the house to go to work for the day knowing that there were dishes waiting for her when she got home to be washed.

He went over to the kitchen closet and grabbed the cat food bag and poured out enough food to last the cat for three days. Now that the cat was taken care of, Anthony went to the refrigerator to see about a little late night snack. When he opened the door he was not surprised to see last night's dinner sitting waiting to be cooked. Erma had placed two steaks in the refrigerator that were marinating in her homemade sauce. Anthony guessed he would cook them for himself for dinner tomorrow night.

After looking around and not being able to find anything worth taking, Anthony decided to just pour himself a glass of milk and call it a night. He hadn't anticipated the approach of sleep like this in a long time. All he wanted was to just jump in his old bed and close his eyes and sleep until early afternoon.

As he stood in the doorway after turning on the lights, he saw that his room was exactly as he had left it before he went away to college. His mother and father never put away his trophies or took down any of his posters. Nothing had been moved or put away. Unlike most parents who relish the opportunity of having a new bedroom to use for storage and closet space, Anthony's never touched his and left it as is.

He went over to his bureau and turned on the lamp, which immediately shown on the pictures he had placed between the dresser mirror a long time ago. There were a couple of him and Jimmy from Little League, and there was one of him and Gina from his junior prom. But the one that hit home the most was of him standing between his parents at his high school graduation. He took that one off the mirror and sat on the edge of the bed and looked at it closely.

Anthony lost control of his emotions and the tears began to build up in his eyes. The reality of his parents' death had finally hit him. He had lived these last two days basically in the future with no thought about the present. His only concern had been Friday night, and this had helped him block away the fact that his parents were killed. The sad reality for Anthony was pictures and memories were all he had left of his parents no matter what happened Friday night. Friday night could only bring him justice; it was never going to bring them back.

And just like Kevin, sleep caught up to Anthony quickly and he had no chance to think about his plan anymore that night. He had cried himself to sleep thinking about his parents with their picture in his hands.

❧   ❧   ❧

It was just after eleven o'clock local time when Bull did just as Frankie had predicted and had given back all of his winnings. Drunk and totally pissed off, Bull had come back to his room to have a couple of night caps, watch some porn and go to bed. It wasn't until after his third bottle from the mini bar that he remembered to call Frankie. Without even thinking, he picked up the hotel's phone instead of getting his cellular and called Frankie.

Frankie and Vincent were still in his office going over the details about Friday night, as well as what they planned on doing if the heat came down from Pete, when the phone rang. "Yeah," he answered on the third ring.

"Uncle Frank, its Bull," the voice on the other end replied.

"You sound drunk, Bull. Did you have a rough evening after we talked?"

"I hate this fucking place, the house always win. That's why I'd rather stay at home and just go down to A.C. Why fly all this way to give these douche bags my money?" he slurred his question.

"I told you to walk away while you were ahead, but of course you young guys never listen. Now you are too drunk to listen to what I have to say. Go get some rest and call me when you wake up tomorrow morning and I'll go over this thing with you then," he told Bull.

Bull started to get in his usual defensive mode. "I'm not drunk," he shouted into the phone. "Really, I'm fine. I'm more pissed about the money than I am drunk. What's this thing you need to discuss? Obviously it's important if you want to make sure I'm sober enough to know what you're saying."

"Bull, what I have to say is very important and I need you to be totally focused when I tell you what I got to tell you. So, do what I say and get some sleep and we'll talk in the morning. If I don't hear from you by noon your time, I'll call your cell," Frankie told him as he said good night and hung up the phone.

"Uncle Frankie, I'm fine. Tell me now," he answered into a dead line. "Fuck!" he screamed as he slammed down the phone into the table, breaking it into two pieces.

❧   ❧   ❧

Anthony almost got his wish of sleeping until noon. It was just after eleven when he was awoken by the knocking on the front door. It took him a couple of seconds to realize where he was and what the noise was before he got out of bed to go answer the door. He didn't need to get dressed since he fell asleep in his clothes, but he still wasn't getting to the door quick enough for the persistent knocker on the other side of the door. Anthony was halfway down the steps when he yelled, "Hold your fucking horses! I'm coming." But that didn't deter the persistent knocker.

"What the fuck is the rush?" Anthony asked while he opened the door.

"Well, good morning sunshine," Detective Joe Fishburn replied.

"We tried to get you at your apartment and when you didn't answer the door, we figured you were here. I mean, why sleep in a shit-hole apartment when you can spend the night in a nice house instead?" Detective Engman replied.

"And what do I owe for this pleasant visit this morning?" Anthony asked.

"Oh, come now Anthony, you don't know why we would be at your door first thing this morning?" Joe asked.

"No, but I guess you are dying to tell me."

"Why don't you put some coffee on and we'll go over a couple of things," Phil replied.

"Do I have a choice in the matter?" Anthony asked knowing it was a stupid question.

"I'm not even going to answer that question. How about you step aside and let us in anyway," Phil answered.

Anthony's day wasn't as busy as yesterday, but he still didn't have time for any of their bullshit. However, he still needed to go over the details of Friday night, call Tami to see how she was making out, and talk to Nicholas. Plus, there was the trial run that he and Kevin had to do tonight to scope out the alley and see if his plan was realistic or not. And if he was feeling up to it after all of that, he was going to call Sandra later in the night to make sure she was still going to be there for him.

Anthony led them into the kitchen and started a pot of coffee while the two detectives sat down at the kitchen table.

"Planning on company for dinner tonight?" Joe asked as he noticed the plate settings on the table.

"My mother had a habit of setting the table every morning before they went to the store. If you noticed the morning dishes from Tuesday are still sitting on the drying rack. She wasn't one for putting off work until she came home, knowing that she still had to cook their dinner and do the dishes afterwards."

Feeling awkwardly stupid for his comment Joe answered, "Your mom sounds like she was a great wife Anthony."

"She was the typical Italian wife. She was aware of her place in the marriage and never complained about it. You can't say that these days. The first thing a wife doesn't like about the relationship, bam! She's divorcing you and taking half of everything you got."

"Was that the case with you and Sandra, Anthony?" Phil asked.

Anthony was finishing filling the coffee maker when that nerve in the back of his mind was touched again. "No, what happened between Sandra and I was the fact that I was a selfish prick who really stopped caring about everyone else in my life other than me. I wasn't a good husband and I was going to be an even worse father. I was hardly around, and when I was I was more interested in whatever game I had money on at the time instead of them. So no, that's not what happened. She was smarter than me, decided that she had had enough and left without taking anything that wasn't hers. I gave her the house without a fight and she got more than a fair share when it came to her alimony payments and Kimberly's child support."

"You don't hear many husbands saying something like that," Joe replied.

"Well that's because many husbands don't take the time to pay attention to what the problems are in their relationships. If they did, most divorces could be avoided, unless of course the bitch was going around fucking his best friend," Anthony responded.

Both Phil and Joe laughed at that, which lightened the mood a little. Anthony couldn't afford any set backs this morning so the more at ease everyone was, the better off he would be.

"I think the three of us know that you aren't sitting at my parents' kitchen table to discuss my ex-wife, so why are you here?"

"Another keen observation on your part," Joe replied.

"Considering how long it took you to get to the door this morning, I think it is safe to assume that you haven't heard the morning news?" he questioned Anthony.

"I came home from dinner last night and went right to bed around ten o'clock. I never even turned on the television. Why, did the news put out some information about my parents' death?"

Phil looked over at the coffee maker and saw that the pot was full. "Why don't you pour the three of us some coffee and we'll talk about what we have heard so far. I want mine black with a lot of sugar, how about you Joe?"

"Jesus Christ, how many years have we been together and you need to ask me how I take my coffee?" He turned to Anthony and said, "Make mine with some cream and two teaspoons of sugar. Thanks," Joe replied.

Anthony didn't even notice the coffee was done. He went over to the cupboard and took out three cups. His mother still had the very small tea cups that they received as a wedding gift so many years ago.

"I hope you don't mind but my parents only have tea cups, no mugs. You'll need to help yourselves to your next cup because I only do the host thing once," he said as he brought the three cups over to the table.

"I didn't see you take out any papers when I answered the door, so I know you aren't here to bring me down to the station and arrest me. So what news did you guys come across that brought you knocking at my door so early in the morning?"

Phil put down his cup, looked over at Joe and then turned and answered Anthony. "After speaking with you yesterday Anthony, we are pretty certain that you are involved with Frankie Feliciani, but if you want to deny that for now that is your choice. However, we wanted to give you a heads up of what took place yesterday in one of those project apartments on the other side of town. It seems that a drug deal went amiss and two burnt bodies were discovered. The guys down in forensics came back with an ID on the body that didn't live in the apartment, and guess what Anthony, it was Sal Pellegrino, one of Frankie's muscle boys. I find that quite strange—that Sal Pellegrino would be doing a drug deal for Frankie in the projects, don't you?"

"I'm not sure I know or care about Sal being at a drug deal," Anthony answered.

"Of course you do. Now, what do you think he was really doing there? Joe and I believe he was being set up for the murder of your parents. And what convinces us even more is the fact that Michael "Bull" Colaiezzi wasn't with him because he was on a plane to Vegas yesterday morning. I find that very convenient that Bull would be in Vegas while his best friend was murdered in a crack house apartment, don't you? From the look on your face Anthony, I think you are following along just fine. Do you want to tell us anything about all of this?" he asked.

"Like I said yesterday, I know who Frankie Feliciani is and certain people that are in his crew, but that doesn't mean that I am involved with them or that they had anything to do with my parents' death. If your guys in forensics can come up with proof that Frankie or any of his men had something to do with their murders than that would be great. I could have closure on the issue, and I would even be willing to cooperate with you in getting a conviction. Otherwise, I am not going to say one word unless you take me down to the station and arrest me," he informed them.

"Anthony, Phil and I believe that Sal and Bull were the ones that killed your parents. However, we know that Frankie has certain people on his payroll and once this story comes out on the news later today, the drug addict will be the fall guy for your parents' deaths, and Frankie's man was there to take vengeance for them. Of course no one can prove that Frankie did any of this, but it won't matter because the locals will make him a hero. These are all assumptions for now, but Phil and I have been detectives long enough to know how things work, and trust me, that is exactly how it will turn out."

"That's not my problem. As long as you guys can come to me later on and guarantee me that it was Bull and Sal who killed my parents, I don't give a shit who the news pins it on or what becomes of Frankie. Because like I said, after Saturday, I am out of here to start a new life and I could care less about this city and the neighborhood. Once I get settled, I'll call the realtor and have them sell the store. After, of course, your people are done with their investigation and the place gets cleaned up. And once that is done, all I'll have left of my parents and the store are pictures and memories," he explained to them.

"Well here's the little problem with that scenario," Joe began to explain to Anthony as he got up from the table to get himself another cup of coffee. "If Frankie had sent Sal to that apartment for an ambush, and he sent Bull to Vegas on a trip that both Joe and I believe he isn't coming back from, then what reason does he have for keeping you alive?"

"I don't know, you tell me," Anthony replied.

"I mean, what sense would it make to keep the last piece of the puzzle alive in case one day you might want to bring this all down on Frankie? Now with that all being said, are you sure you don't want to tell us anything about your involvement? We can promise you full protection and full immunity for your cooperation. What do you say? Want to play ball with us or take your chances out there alone?"

"Trust me, I have no concerns about Frankie or anyone else in his crew looking to come after me. I don't have anything that he wants, nor did I have any involvement in my parents' murder that would concern him. If Bull and Sal did kill my parents like you said, then that's between Frankie and them. I had nothing to do with it, nor do I have any intentions on doing something about it on my own. How crazy do you think I am to go after Frankie Feliciani or Michael "Bull" Colaiezzi? Last time I checked, I was a law-abiding citizen without any past record. What makes you think that I would have the balls to try to do something as crazy as that?"

"Some people might want to get closure on matters like these."

"The only concern that I have is that I want closure on this whole mess before I leave on Saturday, and that's where the two of you come into the picture. Find me the true killers and then I could start the process of putting this whole tragedy behind me. Now unless you guys have anything else to say to me, I really have to get going. I have a million things to do today and this is putting me behind. I have to go back to St. Martin's and finish making arrangements with Father John, I still need to pick out caskets and Mass cards for them and there are still numerous phone calls to be made. And I am spending the next two nights here to go through my parents' belongings to see what I will keep and what I will donate to charity. This was more work than I had imagined it would be."

"Phil and I totally understand, and we'll get out of your way and let you get back to your business. Did you contact anyone to help you out with all of this?" Joe asked.

"Actually, yes I did. One of my younger cousins is taking time out of her day when she is done school to make a lot of the phone calls and emails. She also has called the florist to order the flowers for the church and the funeral parlor. Today she is going to buy a new dress for my mom and a suit for my dad. As for all of the other work, I need to personally do it. I owe them that much."

"Thanks for letting us in this morning and for the coffee, Anthony," Phil said as he rose up and shook his hand. "I do wish you luck with everything, and I hope that you have other family members that can comfort you in this time of need. Joe and I will leave you to your work. Like I said, please call us if you think you can help us any further with this investigation," Phil told Anthony.

Anthony led them out of the kitchen through the foyer and to the front door. As they were walking out, Joe turned to Anthony and said, "Just so you know, for the next two days there will be a unmarked car following you wherever you go, and one stationed either here or at your place depending on where you intend to spend the night. We already have one outside of your apartment building making sure no one goes in or out that doesn't belong there. It has nothing to do with us not trusting you Anthony; it's more that we don't trust certain people who might want to do something to you.

"Now I have to worry about your men following me? You know I don't have the time to deal with this bullshit."

"I'm sure with your busy schedule the next two days, you won't even notice them. As for the viewing tomorrow night, they won't get in the way of anyone who is trying to get into the funeral parlor. They are only there to make sure that Frankie and his men don't get inside," Joe said as he shook Anthony's hand.

Round two went to Anthony as well, but could he win the all important third, and final, round?

Bull woke up feeling the same way he went to bed, totally pissed off, but hung over instead of drunk. He had a monster of a headache, and his stomach wasn't the greatest. All he wanted to do was take a long shower, grab some breakfast and lay at the pool for the rest of the afternoon. He was in no mood to try and even the score with the hotel by doing any more gambling. Why make this trip even worse, he thought. It was time to just relax, get some good food and maybe get a girl for later tonight. Then, first thing tomorrow morning he was going to pick up Frankie's money and get the hell out of this town.

He had just gotten up from the bed and was halfway to the shower when his cell phone went off in his pants' pocket. It dawned on him that he was supposed to call Frankie this morning. Bull walked over and grabbed his phone and, before he answered it, he noticed that the time on the phone was two-thirty.

"Morning Frankie," he answered.

"Just getting up sleeping beauty? You realize that it is almost two thirty here?" Frankie asked.

"What can I say, it was a long night," Bull responded.

"Well I was trying to call your room but the operator said it was busy. What did you do take the phone off the hook?"

"You could say that," Bull answered.

"I haven't got all day because we are extremely busy over here and I need to talk to you now. You feeling better than you did last night?"

"Yeah, I'm fine and I was fine last night too, so I don't understand why you didn't just tell me last night."

Frankie was in no mood to be questioned, especially by Bull. He was going to have to try really hard to keep his emotions under control, because he believed that Bull was going to lose his and it wouldn't benefit either of them if they weren't stable.

"The reason I didn't tell you last night, and why I want to make sure that I have your undivided attention today, is because what I have to say is tremendously important. Are you ready to talk?" Frankie asked.

"Yeah, just give me a minute."

Bull went over to his bag and took out a bottle of Excedrin. He popped out three and walked back over to the bed and laid down again. He swallowed the three pills with a half of bottle of vodka that he had left on the table the night before. His head was pounding something fierce, and from Frankie's tone he didn't think it was going to get any better.

"Alright I'm ready, so what's going on at home?" Bull asked.

"I really hate having to tell you this over the phone and not in person considering you are half way across the country, but I got some fucked-up news and I need you back here tomorrow night to help the family get through this problem."

Bull didn't even need to ask what had happened because he already knew what Frankie was going to tell him. Frankie was going to say that Sal had been killed and there was nothing they could do about it. And once he would tell him that, he believed he was next. He didn't even think he was going to make it back home. If Frankie had placed a hit on him, it would be much more convenient to have him killed out here and placed in a hole in the middle of the desert than trying to get rid of him in the city. This is exactly what he feared when Frankie first told him that he was being sent to Vegas.

"You don't need to sugar coat this for Christ sake. What the fuck happened?" Bull demanded.

"Listen to me Michael, I need you under control, because if you're not then you won't be any help to me. Now get your emotions under control and listen to me. We were set up yesterday. Do you know our guy Lieutenant Brown from the 12th precinct that's on our payroll?"

"Yeah, he's the guy you always use."

"Well, he really fucked us yesterday. He gave us a false tip on the killers of Anthony's parents. I sent Al, Victor and Sal there yesterday to check out the place and pay the guy a visit. Needless to say they were waiting for them to come in and they shot Al and Sal."

"How bad were they shot?" Bull asked. Already knowing what Frankie was going to say. He would inform him that Al was injured and Sal was dead.

"Al took one in the shoulder and he is over at Our Lady of Lourdes. Unfortunately, Sal wasn't that lucky. He was shot in the face, and to make matters worse the apartment caught fire and they couldn't get Sal out of there in time. His body was unrecognizable and they had to use his dental records for the ID."

"But Al got out?" he questioned. What a surprise, he thought.

"Yeah, he did. We are pretty sure that Lieutenant Brown's intention was to frame us for Anthony's parents' murders and to bring the heat on the family. It would look much better on his permanent record to bring down a mob boss, rather than some drug addicts. Things are really bad right now. Pete called a meeting last night. First, I just want to say I'm sorry about Sal's death and second, we are going to strike back quickly to get us even with that dumb, fucking back-stabber."

"Where was Victor the whole time this happened?" Bull asked.

"Sal rushed into the apartment first and was shot right away in the face. Al didn't even make it into the apartment when he said the third shot got him in the shoulder and Victor was behind both of them. Al managed to get off two shots and he said he hit the first gunman that he saw. Next thing he knew Victor was pulling him back and out of the doorway. It wasn't until Victor had Al on the ground that they noticed the smoke billowing out the door."

"How the hell did a fire break out?"

"They don't know how the fire started, but maybe one of Al's bullets hit a kerosene heater or a gas line. You know those places are nothing but fire hazards to begin with. There was nothing they could have done for Sal. The place was totally consumed by flames within a minute. However before they left, they noticed an unmarked car across the street. Neither one was quite sure if Brown was in the car or not, but I am pretty confident that he was. The motherfucker hasn't returned my calls yet."

"Frankie, why the fuck did those two douche bags leave Sal's body behind? Neither one of them could have gotten his body out of there? When was the last time we lost someone during a job and their body was left behind? That doesn't happen and you know it," he said.

"Michael, I wasn't there but I have seen Al and he's wasn't in the greatest shape. How the hell do you expect a man Victor's age to be able to drag a man Sal's size out of a burning apartment not knowing if there is someone on the other side still ready to shoot at him? Come on, think with your head instead of your heart. Do you really think they did that intentionally? For Christ sake, it's the fact that they had to leave his body that is going to bring the heat down on us."

"I can't believe those two assholes ran out of there and left his body at a murder scene."

"Without his body at the scene, we wouldn't be tied to what happened in that apartment and at Anthony's parents' store on Tuesday. It's only a matter of time before the police announce the guy from the apartment's prints were found at the store and it was Sal's intention to go to the apartment for a little payback. Pete is fucking pissed and wants someone's head. Vincent and I agree that Pete is going to take some serious actions, but I want to make sure we make the first move. We are dead if we sit and wait."

"What do you want from me? You want me to come home tonight? I'm not sure I can catch a flight back on such short notice," he replied.

"No, we need to stick with the initial plan. Vincent and I need to come up with a way to get rid of this piece of trash. We can't just execute a lieutenant on the police force like he was a regular person. Besides, I figured you would want the honor. I owe you at least that much. If for some reason you don't trust me and you think things aren't making sense, you could always stay out there. I will understand your decision if you elect to stay out there and not come home if you think that's what's best for you. But if you decide to stay out there, just have the hotel wire the money to my checking account."

"Uncle Frank, why wouldn't I trust you? People in our line of work die all the time. I don't doubt that they were set up. And you are right, I want to be the one who settles up with this cop."

"Bull, I think you should take the rest of the day to really think about every-thing that I have told you before making your decision. However, I can't prom-ise what Pete has in mind for any of us. Christ, before tomorrow night is over, we all could be with Sal. It's hard to say, things have really gotten fucked-up and Pete isn't one for any bullshit. I have already started to make arrangements for myself and the girls."

"You really think that things are that bad, Uncle Frank?"

"It's hard to say right now. I guess it all depends on what gets out in the news. But one thing is for certain, as of this moment, we are not in control," Frankie informed him.

"What about that little douche bag Anthony, do you think he was involved in any of this?"

"How the hell could Anthony get involved in this Michael? This was one cop trying to look like a hero and better his position on the force. The city is dying for answers about his parents' deaths. Whoever gives them the killers will be worshiped and rewarded for a very long time. I can understand why he did it, but the reward will not be greater than the risk, I can promise you that."

For the first time, Bull didn't notice his headache anymore. The anger and rage had taken over his mind. He wanted to be home at this very moment and doing something about his best friend's murder. Sitting in this hotel two thousand miles away was the last place he wanted to be.

There was no need to take Frankie's advice and to think this all through. He had already made up his mind. They had killed Sal and he was next. Frankie wanted him to stay in Vegas so someone could dispose of him in a hole in the middle of the desert, of that he was certain.

The best thing he could do to fuck up their plans was to come home. Once he was home, he was going to end all of this with a one on one with his uncle. He had the whole day today and the plane ride tomorrow to come up with a plan to take care of Frankie and anyone else who might get in his way. There was also the problem of where he was going to go once this was all over with, but he would have three hundred thousand dollars to help him find a place to hide.

"No I don't need to think it over. I'll be home tomorrow night. Who is going to pick me up?"

"Al is being released later tonight and if he is up to it he will, along with Victor and maybe Charlie Deluca. I haven't really thought about it. I guess it really depends on what transpires over the next thirty hours or so. But no matter who picks you up, you are to immediately go get my money from Dan. Like I said, I want to have all my arrangements in place in case Pete comes down on us. Do you have any money stashed away in case you have to up and disappear after tomorrow?" Frankie asked him.

"I have some, but not enough to go into hiding for a year or two."

"That's the problem with your generation—none of you think about tomorrow. I can give you a descent amount to at least get you started somewhere else. And you do realize if you go into hiding, you will need to get a legitimate job somewhere? You are going to have to lay low and not get yourself into any kind of trouble. If you ever got picked up by the cops, anyone who was looking for you will know where they can find you."

"What are you going to do if the shit really hits the fan?" Bull asked.

"The girls and I will have to leave everything behind us, including the restaurant. I always had a contingency plan in place in case the heat was coming down on us, or if I didn't come home for some reason. Ellena has an envelope with all the bank account numbers, passwords and a list of instructions on what to do and where to go."

There was a long hesitation before Bull answered. "I'm sure you'll be fine. As for me, I don't care about anything after Friday as long as I have my payback for Sal. Plan or no plan, I am going after Lieutenant Brown and his whole fucking family. These douche bags have got to realize that you don't double cross our kind. So fuck them and fuck the consequences, I don't give a rat's ass. I am taking my revenge with or without your permission Uncle," Bull advised him.

"We'll discuss this once you are home and back at *The Club*. I guess that's the good thing about you being out there, I don't need to worry about you flying off the handle. Try to relax and let me do what I have to do over here and I promise you that I will come up with something. Lieutenant Brown will suffer for his disloyalty."

Bull was no longer in control of his emotions. He hated being lied to and what was worse: he knew that he was being betrayed by his own family. Listening to this crap was making his headache come back and all he wanted to do was kill someone, and that someone was Frankie. But first, he had to be one hundred percent positive it was Frankie that gave the orders for Sal's death and not Lieutenant Brown. He couldn't just whack Frankie. He would be as good as dead within twenty-four hours. However, if Frankie was being honest with him and his story really wasn't that far fetched, they were all in deep shit with Pete and the police. Either way he looked at it, no matter what, Friday night was going to be one fucked-up night for everybody.

"I guess you have those thirty hours to come up with a plan because once I land and get your money and bring it back to *The Club*, I am heading out looking for Lieutenant Brown and his family."

And this time it was Bull who got the last word in as he hit the end button on his cell phone and powered it off. He put the phone down on the night stand and closed his eyes for a minute. He wasn't tired anymore, but between his original headache and all the news that Frankie had just sprung on him, he was going to need some time to sort all this out.

❦   ❦   ❦

It was around two o'clock when Kevin had a chance to take a break for lunch. He was unexpectedly busy for a Thursday, but he didn't mind because it took his mind off of tomorrow night. It wasn't until he was in his office eating his usual Italian hoagie for lunch that he thought about Anthony's plan for the first time. It didn't take him long to lose interest in his lunch. His stomach was a mess all day and he had chalked it up to hunger, but now he realized that it was his nerves and the pressure that was building up inside him.

Kevin wasn't a very educated man, but he didn't have to be to understand that he was absolutely crazy to go through with Anthony's scheme. But he was still willing to go to the alley with Anthony tonight to see if the plan could work. If it couldn't, then he was going to tell Anthony that he was pulling out. Anthony wouldn't give him a hard time about it because if it looked bad, he wouldn't expect him to go through with it and risk jeopardizing Tami's future. Anthony was a father and would understand his decision.

Just as Kevin started to feel a little better about the situation, there was a knock on his door.

"Hey Kevin, my brother Nick is here, you want him to come in or should I have him stay out in the waiting room?" Chuck asked.

"No, don't be a fool. Have him come on back. I'll only need him for five minutes. Thanks," Kevin answered.

Kevin was starting to clear his lunch off the top of his desk when Nicholas knocked on the door. "Come on in Nicholas," Kevin answered.

"Please, call me Nick. Everyone else does."

"Ok, no problem, Nick it is. Have yourself a seat and I will make this as quick as possible. I know a kid your age doesn't want to be stuck in here during his afternoons."

"Chuck told me that you had a job that you wanted me to do tomorrow night. I need to warn you that I am not very good with cars, but if you need me to run an errand for you, that's fine."

"Ha, no it isn't for a job here at the shop. I have enough useless help as it is right now. What my cousin and I need is a young guy like you to take a trip for us tomorrow night up to Cornell to meet someone. Do you think you would be interested in taking a trip up there?"

"Am I meeting this someone to pick up or drop off anything that is illegal, because I have to tell you I can't jeopardize my future to do something like that," Nicholas replied.

Kevin sat back in his chair and laughed. If this kid only knew what kind of shit him and Anthony had planned for tomorrow night, he would have thought the question to be relevant.

"No, no, nothing like that. What kind of business do you think we run here at the shop? What we need from you is for you to try to find a girl that we know who is a freshman at the school and take her out for the night. But here's the catch: she can't know that you were sent by us. The hard part will be finding her first, but there should be a party somewhere on campus."

"What do you want me to do once I find her?" Nicholas asked curiously.

"Before you get any ideas, no, that is not what we mean by keeping her out all night. I want you to use that charm that your brother is always bragging about and get her to leave the party and take her somewhere to get breakfast. Maybe if things are going well, you can go watch the sunrise, who knows, all we need is to make sure that she doesn't go back to her dorm the next morning, not until later in the day. I personally don't think you will find her, but my cousin is confident that you will."

"It does sound unrealistic," Nicholas told him.

"Here is a hundred dollars and a picture of what she looks like. The hundred is for gas and food. It should be plenty and whatever you don't spend, consider it pay for your efforts. Is this something that you might be interested in doing?" Kevin asked.

"Let me get his straight. You want me to drive all the way up to Cornell University tomorrow afternoon and search for the girl in this picture. Once I do, you want me to try to keep her out for the night without even trying to sleep with her?"

"I know what you are thinking—your brother's boss is crazy. Nonetheless we still need you to try and accomplish this."

"Where the heck is Cornell anyway? Is it a long ride?" Nicholas asked.

"Cornell is located upstate in Ithaca, which is only two hours away. If you leave after your last class tomorrow you should be up there by six o'clock. That's plenty of time for you to walk around campus and look for flyers or go down fraternity row and find out where the parties are going to be. If you happen to find her that would be great. If you are able to keep her out for the night and away from her dorm room that would be even better. If you can't accomplish either of the two just call the cell phone number on the back of the picture and let us know. It is really a simple proposition, just a little far-fetched. Well, what do you say?"

"Can I bring a friend along for the ride?" Nicholas asked.

"Absolutely not, it's a solo trip."

"Who is the girl?"

"Her name is Anita Feliciani. Do you know her or recognize her name?"

"No, I have never met her. Should I know her?"

"She went to Little Flower High School, so I doubt that you would have known her, but her name doesn't ring a bell with you?" Kevin questioned him.

"I know I have heard the name before, but nothing is coming to me. Is it a name I should be familiar with?"

"No kid, you shouldn't and just leave it at that. And whatever you do, don't go asking around about her after you leave here. Don't even mention it to Charlie. Trust me, the less you know the better off you'll be."

Nicholas sat there in his chair for a moment. The idea seemed like a waste of time, but a free night out of the city to go to a real fraternity party on a major college campus like Cornell was a different story. If he didn't find their girl, there would be plenty of other choices for him at one of those parties. He was tired of the local neighborhood sluts with no brains or money. It was time for him to find himself an upper class Ivy League girl.

"Alright I'll do it, but I want more than a hundred dollars. Gas alone is going to cost me close to forty bucks. I want two hundred if I find the girl and get the job done, but if I don't succeed then we can stick to the original hundred. Deal?" he asked.

Kevin looked at him and thought, this kid definitely has what it takes to win Anita over. He was one confident young bastard with great looks and an athletic body and Kevin admired him for it. "That's fine with me, but I'm not the one in charge of the funds for your trip. When you get home today call the cell phone number on the back of the picture because my cousin Anthony wants to talk to you and make sure you are on the same page with what I conveyed to you. When you call him you can ask him about the extra money. I can't see him saying no to you, but don't try to be a dick about it and ask for more than two hundred, we don't need you that much," Kevin informed him.

"Great. I'll call Anthony when I get home. You do realize this is a total shot in the dark. I mean what the hell are the odds of me finding one girl on a campus of that size at a party?"

"I couldn't tell you. But if you really want to know, Anthony has probably already calculated it. He's the professional gambler."

Nicholas got up and shook Kevin's hand and thanked him for the job and then he turned to let himself out.

"Hey Nicholas, remember what I said. I don't want you saying a word about who you are going to meet tomorrow night, especially to your brother you got me? If I find out you did, and trust me I would, I'll fire Charlie Monday morning and I know you don't want that to happen, right?"

"Sure no problem, I won't say a word to anyone," Nicholas replied.

And that was the last time Kevin ever saw Nicholas. He never found out if Nicholas succeeded in finding Anita.

❧   ❧   ❧

"Hey Tami, it's Anthony, how are you doing with all the phone calls and arrangements?"

"Hi Anthony, everything is going as well as can be expected, I guess. I called almost everyone on your list and asked them to spread the word around. The church and the service are taken care of and will be Saturday morning at ten o'clock. I called Garzone Funeral Home and the viewing is set for Friday night starting at six o'clock and lasting until eight o'clock. I have to go over today and make a deposit on the caskets. I figured you would want to go over there with me and pick them out," she said.

"Actually, I really don't have the time. I hate to put you in this spot but just pick out two basic caskets. They wouldn't want to be buried in anything too elaborate. Can you order a head stone for them or is that done someplace totally separate?" he asked.

"No, it's separate. I found a couple of places on line and in the yellow book and took their numbers down for you. You can call and set up an appointment with them or go on line and browse through their catalogs," Tami explained.

"Why don't you give Kevin all of that tonight and I will look through them when I get home. What about Oakland Cemetery? They didn't give you a hard time about Saturday did they?"

"Not really. I called and told them who I was and who your parents were. Just like everyone else I spoke to today, they were more than willing to go the extra step for me because of what happened to your parents. They assured me the grave site will be ready for Saturday morning."

Anthony couldn't believe how mature and responsible Tami had become. She was handling all this like she was a professional secretary and not a senior in high school. He was quite confident that whatever career she chose to follow, she was going to be great at it. Kevin didn't have to worry about her. Tami was going to make him and their parents very proud.

"Do you still have enough money or do you need more from me?"

"Well, that depends. The caskets alone are going to take up most of the money, unless you want me to just make a down payment."

"Yeah, put down the minimum that they require and I'll pay off the balance at a later date. Did you order all the flowers for both the funeral home and the church?"

"Yes, all the flowers are taken care of and will be sent directly to both places. But there are a couple of things that I am going to need your help with, because these are decisions that I shouldn't be making for you," she advised him.

"Okay, what do you need from me?"

"Well you are going to need to see the mortician about how you want your mom's face to be made up, and you need to pick out clothes that you want them buried in. I don't know if you have a suit and dress picked out already. Did you plan on going out and buying them something nice?"

"I figured that I would come by now and pick you up. We can go buy my mother a new dress and I'll even let you pick out some nice make-up for her. My father has his favorite suit and we promised that when he died we were going to bury him in it."

"Did you have anything special that you want to put in their coffins? I put my favorite watch on my mom's wrist during her viewing so that every time I look at my watch, I can't help but think of her. Think about it, how many times a day does a person look at their watch?"

"Wow that was a really nice idea for you and your mother."

"When do you want to go shopping?" she asked.

"It will have to be now because I have a very tight schedule and Kevin and I have to go out later tonight. How about I pick you up in about twenty minutes and we'll get a bite to eat after we're done. We should get back to your house around the same time as Kevin."

"Ok, I'll be waiting," she replied and hung up the phone.

Frankie told Vincent that he looked like shit and should go home for the rest of the day. They both didn't get much rest at *The Club,* and sleeping on that couch wasn't the greatest for his back. Frankie was drained and exhausted from all that had taken place over the last couple of days, and he realized things were going to get worse before they would get better. If Friday night didn't go as planned, it would clearly mark the end of his reign as head of his crew. Even if Teddy and his brother Jeff did get the job done, there were no guarantees that Pete was going to let this mishap go unpunished. But there was nothing more he could do now other than wait, so he was going to go home, shower and take one long nap before tonight's meeting with everyone.

"Before you leave Vincent, I want you to get a hold of Al, Charlie Deluca, Victor Sosa and Craig Rossi and have them all here by eleven o'clock tonight. I have to discuss what needs to be done for tomorrow night and what they are to expect. This has got to go as planned or we're all in deep shit. So no excuses, everyone needs to be here tonight. I am heading home and getting some rest and a shower. I recommend you doing the same," he told Vincent as he got up from his desk.

"Frankie, do you think this is the end of everything or do you think we are going to get out of this mess? I mean if Joe comes through for us and puts that guy Tyrone on the news as one of the two killers things still might work out for the best, don't you think?"

"I think we might come out of this alright if a couple of things go our way. First, Teddy and his brother need to get the job done without any problems. Second, I think we might be able to put a twist on what happened in the apartment yesterday."

"What do you mean?" Vincent asked.

"If the news mentions Sal's name, it won't take them long to connect him to our family, and that might actually be a good thing. With our help and the citizen's crazy love for their Mafia, the news might just make Sal a hero. Think about this for a front page story: "Local mob soldier takes action in own hands and dies while trying to avenge loss of two elderly citizens." The way this city has suffered through tragedy over the last couple of months, the people would eat this story up. It would do wonders for changing our image with many of them."

"That sounds good and all Frankie, but do you really think that Pete wants that kind of publicity towards our business?" he asked.

"Of course we don't want any unnecessary publicity, but this would be great public relations for us if they can make Sal sound like a local neighborhood hero. However I am a pessimistic and realistic person and I know that won't help us in the end. Pete's mind is more than likely made up. I think our family will be broken up and some of us aren't going to be around to see the new regime," he replied.

"Well you're the leader Frankie and I have been with you this long, you tell me what you want me to do and I'll do it."

"I want you to do what I said and go home for now. When we get back here later on tonight will go over our future and maybe we can come up with something together."

Teddy was on the phone with Jeff making their final arrangements for tonight. Teddy was a firm believer in pre-planning all jobs and scoping out the area where a hit was going to take place.

"I'll pick you up around nine o'clock tonight and we'll head to the alley and check the place out. I lied to Frankie. I told him that we would drive the car down the alley and do a drive by and take the money from Bull. However, I was thinking that I'll have you stationed somewhere in the alley and after Dan's car leaves, you'll go over to Bull's car, shoot him and run out of the alley. Everyone else in the car knows that there is going to be a hit, they just think that we will be coming by car. Instead you'll be on foot and take them by surprise, just in case Frankie has any ideas about trying to do a double cross. I don't want anything happening to you."

"If you don't want anything happening to me, why don't you go down the alley and I go up on the roof and be the lookout with the rifle?"

"Well smartass, you are six years younger than me and in much better shape, but I am a better shot with the rifle. I have more confidence in my ability to shoot you out of a jam than trusting you on saving my ass if something went wrong," he explained to Jeff.

"Yeah and don't forget, I wouldn't have as hard a time concealing myself in a dark alley as you might have, considering our size difference."

"Keep it up you little fuck and see who has your back if something goes wrong," Teddy replied.

Tami and Anthony were in the living room when Kevin walked in the door around six-thirty. "I thought we weren't going out until later tonight? Why are you here already?" he asked Anthony.

"Well, Tami and I did a little shopping this afternoon, and then we grabbed a bite to eat and got home earlier than expected. Don't worry about us, go get yourself something to eat because Tami and I are just fine sitting here talking," Anthony replied.

"Where did you go shopping?" he asked curiously.

"Tami made a suggestion that I should get my mother a new dress for her to be buried in, so we went and got a dress and took it down to the funeral home. Tami also showed them the colors of makeup that she thought would be appropriate for my mom and after that we went to Taco Bell for a quick dinner. I suggested a nice restaurant, but your sister insisted on tacos and Pepsi. How could I argue with that?"

"Sounds like the two of you had a busy afternoon. Tami, I hope your school work isn't being affected by all the time that you are spending helping Anthony."

"My school work is fine. I only have a little homework tonight, and when you guys go out I will start it. I also made you a steak with some green beans and a baked potato. It is in the oven. Just put it in the microwave for twenty seconds and it should be ready to eat."

As Kevin headed to the kitchen, Nicholas came into his mind. "Hey Anthony, did Nicholas call you?"

"Yeah, I talked to him for a few minutes while Tami and I were shopping. He seemed to understand what I needed him to do."

"What about the cost? Did he ask you about that?"

"I told him that wasn't a problem. In fact, if he succeeded I told him I would throw in even more money depending on how we make out tomorrow night. A little extra incentive can't hurt."

Kevin was surprised at how nonchalantly Anthony was about sending this kid to Cornell, but that was Anthony's problem not his. All he was concerned with now was eating his dinner and satisfying his stomach, which still was bothering him. Kevin believed that his stomach wasn't going to be the same until this was all behind him and things got back to normal. He wasn't as optimistic as Anthony was about the plans, so having a beer or two with dinner might be a good idea.

"You never did tell me where you and Kevin are going tonight."

"No place special, your brother is just keeping me company on a few errands that I have to run," he answered.

"So why couldn't we have done them earlier today while we were out?" she questioned him.

"Why are you trying to spoil a nice afternoon with twenty-one questions, Tami? Save those inquires for the time when you are married and your husband comes home late and you aren't happy about it. Kevin and I have to take care of some small details about tomorrow and it's the kind of help that I need another guy for, not a teenage girl. It's really no big deal, so drop it. Now back to our conversation before Kevin came home. Where do you want to go next year?"

Tami put down the plate of Oreos that she was eating and looked at the kitchen door to make sure Kevin wasn't listening before she answered Anthony. "You can't say anything to Kevin about this because I haven't thought of a way to tell him yet. I applied to three schools in the South because I want to get as far away from this City as possible. I hate this place so much that I decided I needed to go to a large university in the South that has a beautiful campus with fresh air and trees everywhere. I want to witness the Fall with the leaves changing in a country side instead of this City. I want to bask in the sun on a Saturday afternoon while studying under a tree in the middle of the campus.

"What about Kevin?"

"I know this is going to break Kevin's heart since it is just the two of us, but after my parents' death I knew I had to make a change in my life or I was just going to go crazy staying here. I don't know how Kevin can do it but I hate coming home from school everyday to this empty house. The memories hurt too much and it is starting to take a toll on me. I need to get away and see what else is out there in the world. Maybe when I'm done school I'll even get to travel around the country before settling down and starting a career. There are just so many opportunities that are out there for me to experience, and I would be a fool to waste the chance to accomplish them by staying here like Kevin has decided to do."

"I totally understand your decision Tami, but did you ever think that Kevin stayed here because of you? I mean, he could have opened a shop anywhere once your parents passed away. Maybe he thought it was best for you to finish school with your friends that you have known your whole life. Can you imagine your reaction if he told you that he was moving the two of you somewhere new?"

"I know he has always put me first, but I still think it will hurt him."

"Your brother loves you too much and has sacrificed a lot for you. Believe me when I tell you that I think he would be disappointed if you decided to stay home to go to college. You have the chance to meet people from all over the country and see how different you all are from each other. And as for Kevin,

I'm sure deep in his heart he will be extremely happy for you, and will support whatever decision you choose to make."

"You really think so? I would hate like hell to go away to school and have things never be the same again. What if I make new friends and start fresh somewhere else? I couldn't handle Kevin not being a part of my life anymore. He's all I have left."

"You are too young to be worrying about your future after college. You need to worry about finishing your senior year before anything else, so stop worrying and just enjoy this last year of high school. These are the years that you can never get back, and the people that you are going to miss the most."

"So what are you guys talking about?" Kevin asked as he entered the room with his dinner in one hand and two beers in the other. He sat down on the couch and handed one of the beers to Anthony.

"Tami and I have just been going over all the details for the viewing tomorrow night and the funeral on Saturday. I am just amazed how she got all this accomplished for me and still had the time to go to school each day. See, if you applied yourself a little more like Tami, you would be more than just a grease monkey down at that shop."

"Hey, fuck you man. For your information, I am no grease monkey. I am the assistant manager and I like what I do. And one day I will have my own shop, so stop putting me down just because Tami is the smart one in the family."

"And the good looking one too," Tami chimed in.

"I second that, Kevin is definitely hard on the eyes," Anthony added.

"If I wanted to be double teamed like this, I would wish for Mom and Dad to be alive. Since they aren't and I am the head of this house, Tami say good night to Anthony because I need to go over a couple of things with him before we head out tonight."

"Typical. Kevin pulls rank when he is on the losing end of a conversation. Anthony, thank you for dinner and the talk today, it was nice to get out with someone new for a change. Everything should be in place for tomorrow night and I will call you if I hear otherwise," she said as she walked over to him and gave him a gentle kiss on the cheek.

"No, I am the one who should be thanking you for all your help. I couldn't have done this on my own, nor could I have counted on anyone other than you," he replied as he gave her a hug goodnight.

"If you need me before you leave or when you get home, I will be upstairs in my room studying alone. Mrs. Collins said Sydney has been spending too much time as it is over here this week."

"Well that's good," Kevin replied. "Maybe now you can get your homework done without any interruptions."

"Yeah, unless I just talk to Sydney all night on the phone or chat on-line with some forty year old pervert. Who knows, my choices are endless," she responded back smartly to Kevin's sarcasm.

"Just as long as you do your homework first, you can talk to whomever and have a blast later on."

After Tami's went upstairs, Kevin turned to Anthony and asked, "Did you notice the car parked outside of my house?"

"Oh, you mean the cop car with my two new detective friends in it? Yes, I did and yes, they have been following me all day. Why do you ask?"

"Well if those cops have been following you all day, how the hell do you expect us to go to the alley and check out the layout if they are tagging along?" Kevin asked.

"This gives us a chance to see if I can sneak out the back window without someone witnessing me. Actually, I need to see if I still have the balls to sneak out of the house and get back up and inside. If I can't do it tonight, then we are shit out of luck for tomorrow night. This will be better than a regular practice run, considering I will have the added pressure of knowing that there are cops outside watching the house."

"You know, you are right, they should add to the fear factor."

"I figured that they would and that's why I wanted to stay away from the shop. And having Tami along with me all day shopping is a good excuse as to why I was here. This should draw away any suspicion that they might have about you and me."

Anthony took the last gulp of his beer and got up. "Alright, I am heading out. I'll see you in less than two hours, and please don't forget to wear what you intend to use tomorrow night. And make sure that it is all black. I need to see how well you blend in."

"I have an old, black leather jacket and black jeans, but I didn't have time to get a ski mask so we are going to need to go to a sporting goods store on the way tonight," he informed Anthony.

"I'm sure we can find one on the way. Try to be on time because I want to get to the alley as close as possible to the same time as tomorrow night. We need to make sure that all the businesses are closed and that no one stays behind to empty the trash or something crazy like that."

"No problem, I just need to finish this plate and take a quick shower. And don't worry about me because I'll probably be waiting in the car for your ass to find the courage to climb down the drain pipe, asshole."

"Whatever, I'll see you in a little while," Anthony replied as he let himself out the door.

It doesn't look that far down, Anthony thought to himself as he stared out his old bedroom window. It wasn't so much the distance down to the ground that concerned him, rather than the distance from the window to the drainpipe. He believed he could do this; he just needed to trick his mind into believing it.

All those times he had ventured out to meet the guys for some beers and a joy ride or when he met an old girlfriend in the park for a quickie, fear was never in his mind. He just climbed out the window and went down the drainpipe and that was it. But now that he stood here and thought about it, his brain fought against it. However, too much was at stake and he had to get going. Standing at the window trying to rationalize this was taking up too much of his time.

Getting his first leg out the window was the hardest. It seemed to take forever for his foot to reach the drainpipe and once it did, he couldn't convince himself that it was stable. He clutched the windowsill tighter as he hoisted his second leg out the window, and it found a spot on the other side of the pipe. Okay he thought, the hardest part was done, all I need to do now is tighten my legs around the pipe, let go of the windowsill, and put both hands on the pipe. "Very easy, no problem," he said out loud.

The cool November wind was blowing against him from behind. It wasn't enough to move him in any way, but just enough to send chills and fear up and down his spine. It was creating havoc for him to let go of the windowsill. The pipe between his legs was cold and wet and it started to play mind games with him. The longer his legs were wrapped around that pipe, the more he had to piss and the more he thought about having to piss, the less of a chance he had of convincing himself to let go of the windowsill.

Anthony stayed frozen in place for only a minute, but to him it seemed like a lifetime before he finally found the nerve to let go of the windowsill and latch his hands onto the pipe. Once he felt secure on the pipe, he had no trouble sliding down. Yeah, just like riding a bike he thought to himself. He wasn't surprised to find it difficult to get his legs under him after his feet touched the ground. After he got his nerves under control again, he looked up at the bedroom window and realized that if it took him this much effort to get down the drain pipe, how long it was going to take him to climb back up? How the hell I accomplished this half drunk when I was in high school I will never know, he thought to himself as he shook his head back and forth.

When he came onto Terrace Avenue, he didn't see Kevin's car. Like most streets in this city there were many cars parked along them, and since it was night it was hard for Anthony to see Kevin's car among the twenty or so cars. Anthony had walked halfway up the street still looking for Kevin's car when he heard a car horn from the end of the street. Anthony looked over and noticed a red Trans Am with dark tinted windows.

"Looking for someone asshole?" he heard as the window was coming down.

"Why didn't you tell me that you weren't going to be in your car? You scared the shit out of me, jerk-off!" he yelled at Kevin as he got to the driver's door.

"I forgot to tell you that I got this car for tomorrow night and since we are doing a dry run tonight, I thought we should go in this car. We can test out the noise of you racing away from the alley and see if the sound distinguishes itself from most cars. We need to make sure it sounds close enough to Bull's car."

"Do you have any more fucking surprises for me tonight?" Anthony asked as he got in the passenger side.

"Actually yes, I found this ski mask on the floor in the back of this Trans Am when I got the car from the shop tonight. That's fifteen less minutes we have to worry about tonight," Kevin replied.

Jeff and Teddy were just entering the alley when they came upon a fire escape ladder.

"You going to try to get up this one or do you want to see if there are any others down the alley?" Jeff asked.

"No, this one should be fine. I just need you to give me a boost to reach that bottom rung of the ladder."

Jeff put his hands together in a grip and Teddy put his left foot in them. Jeff gave him just enough of a hard surge that Teddy was able to grab onto the last rung of the ladder. "Come on, pull yourself up you fat bastard. How hard is it to do one pull up?" Jeff yelled at him.

"Do you know how long it's been since I had to do a pull up, you little fuck? Just shut the fuck up and let me concentrate."

Teddy was a very big man and extremely out of shape for his size and weight. He was not what you would expect the city's most notorious hit-man to look like. But his weight never got in the way of a job. Teddy had made over fifty hits for the mob and he had never missed his target, which was why he was the best in the business.

Jeff on the other hand was almost the complete opposite of Teddy. He was an athlete throughout his school years and was still in great shape. He was six inches taller than Teddy and weighed about a hundred pounds less. But, he was still new to the business and was under Teddy's guidance until he thought Jeff was ready to be on his own.

After struggling for over a minute, Teddy was able to get himself onto the fire escape and he climbed to the roof. When he got to the top and onto the roof he spoke into the headset and asked Jeff if he could hear him okay.

"Yeah, I can hear you loud and clear. Do you have a clear path up there on the roof to follow along with me?" Jeff asked back.

"It looks clear enough. Do you see that trash dumpster on your left half way down the alley?"

"Of course I do. What about it?" Jeff responded back.

"I want you to go to it and see if that is as good a place as any to hide out. If not, look and see if you could blend into a doorway. It looks to me like most of these stores don't have their back lights on or they don't have them at all. Why don't you try to squeeze into one past the dumpster further up the alley?"

"I don't want to be behind one of those fucking things smelling that shit for an hour while I wait."

"Fine, the cars can't get past the dumpster, so find a doorway and signal me when you get there. I will look through my scope to see if you stick out or not and if you do, then it's behind the dumpster for you."

"Alright, I'll try an unlit doorway as soon as I pass the dumpster. Let me know if you can't follow along the roof," Jeff replied back.

"No, it looks clear up here on the roof. I shouldn't have a problem walking along up here," Teddy answered.

Jeff stopped at the dumpster to see if he could possibly fit behind it if that was his only alternative. The dumpster was huge and took up a lot of space but there was just enough room between it and the wall for him to fit. Teddy was right; there was no way that two cars were going to get by the dumpster.

Jeff looked from every angle and came to the conclusion that the only possible way to use this dumpster to block someone's view was if he squatted down on the opposite side of it, and if he did that he would then run into the problem of not being able to see them.

"It looks like the only way to use the dumpster is by squatting down behind it," he relayed to Teddy.

"You can't stand up behind it?"

"There's nothing to conceal me if I stand up."

"I will be up here watching them, you really don't need to be able to see what's happening. You aren't going to make a move until I give you the signal anyway. I will be your eyes and let you know what's going on the whole time," Teddy answered back.

"That's fucking easy for you to say while you are up there watching what's taking place. Meanwhile, I'm on my knees next to a stinking trash dumpster filled with God only knows what. Now if it's alright with you, I think I am going to stick with plan A and see about that doorway that you talked about."

"Fine, try and find one without a light."

"Light or no light, I don't think they will be able to see me unless they are looking for me in the first place. It's awfully dark down the alley once you pass this dumpster."

"That's fine, wherever you feel most comfortable. Just stay on the…Wait a second, get into the doorway quickly, here comes a car," Teddy yelled into the headset.

Jeff stayed low to the ground and scrambled into the first doorway he came to. The reason Teddy started to freak out was because this was a dead end alley, and no one would be driving into this alley unless it was a delivery or a garbage truck. Neither one of them would be coming into the alley this late at night.

"Just stay still, Jeff, until I tell you to move. It looks like a Trans Am or Firebird. I don't know who the fuck this could be at this time of night."

"Maybe some kid made a wrong turn," Jeff answered.

"I highly doubt it. He would have stopped as soon as he made the turn and right now they are about ten feet from the dumpster," he notified Jeff.

❧   ❧   ❧

Frankie looked at the clock on his nightstand and couldn't believe that he had taken a three hour nap. He didn't realize the toll that the stress was taking on his mind and body. The nap was a help to him physically, but mentally the stress was not going away. He had acquired a nagging headache earlier in the day and the sleep didn't relieve it. Frankie still had two hours before everyone would get to *The Club*. That was enough time for a shower and some dinner, which he believed would help with the stress.

Frankie was a wise man who had been in this business long enough to know that tonight's meeting was more than likely their last as a family. Pete was going to intervene and clean up this mess his own way. Frankie understood that Pete had to do what he needed to do, and Frankie would do the same. But what was killing him was that his own nephew was the cause of the family's demise, all because of a lousy thousand dollars. He was only kidding himself because he realized it wasn't about the money; it was Bull's egotistical attitude that got in the way of business. This was why he was going to choose Al to take over the family when the time came and not Bull.

It wasn't until he looked at the clock for a second time that he realized he couldn't lay here in bed beating himself to death about Bull. His decision was final and he needed to concentrate on what he was going to tell the rest of his crew. "What's done is done, and there was nothing I could do about it," he said to himself.

He was going to wait until he came back home tonight to tell Ellena everything that had happened in the last couple of days and what it meant to them. The family was in trouble, and more than likely they were going to have to leave the city and go into hiding. This was going to be hard to do because he and Ellena had lived their whole lives here. He couldn't bear to imagine her reaction once he told her. She would never love him the same way again.

This he could get over. Ellena would eventually come around and forgive him. But how was he going to break the news to Anita that her dreams of graduating from an Ivy League school were over? That's the kind of news you don't do over the phone. It meant he was going to have to sit down face to face and have a father-daughter conversation, and this was something he wasn't accustomed to.

Ellena handled most of the talks when it came to the girls. Frankie wasn't really involved with that part of their upbringing because the girls were very well behaved.

Frankie feared the results of this speech more than any other conversation that he had had over the years, including the one last night with Teddy deciding Bull's fate. He never let his emotions get in the way of the business at hand, but breaking his little girl's heart was something that he never expected to have to do. Frankie knew that Anita was a great kid who deserved better from him, but he still had to tell her that her days at Cornell were over. And this was going to make her hate him forever.

Frankie reached for the phone on the nightstand and dialed Anita's number. He called her at least three or four times a week even though Ellena over-did it by calling her almost everyday. Like most fathers, Frankie missed the little things, like listening to her tell him about her day. The one thing that separated him from most fathers was that he listened to his teenage daughter when she spoke to him. He wasn't one of those dads that just nodded his head to please her; he actually cared when she talked and that was what made their relationship special.

On the fifth ring the answering machine picked up. "Hi, this is Anita and I am either in class or at the library so leave a message and I will get back to you when I can and if this is mom, no nothing has changed since the last time you called."

Frankie absolutely hated answering machines and always froze after the beep went off. "Hey Angel, it's Dad and I really need to talk to you about something important so call me once you get in tonight. Thanks and I love you." Frankie was surprised that she wasn't in her dorm at this time of night. But this was Cornell and not some state school, so Anita was most likely studying hard at the library.

Kevin made a K turn right before the dumpster and pulled the car over along the same side of the alley as the dumpster. "How's this?" he asked Anthony. Anthony looked out the front windshield to see how far they were from the street, then turned around and looked out the back window and had a full view of green dumpster.

"I think this is exactly where they park every time," he said as he got out of the car.

"Once you go past the dumpster it isn't that far to the end of the alley. They would never expect anyone to come up from behind them and we are far enough from the street to be out of view from any car that drives by the alley," Anthony informed Kevin as he pointed to the back of the alley and then the front.

"What now?" Kevin asked as he closed his door.

"We'll both take a look around. It is darker in this alley then I expected. It makes no sense for you to go further up the alley, so why don't you go behind the dumpster and let me stand outside the car and see how well you blend in with the darkness."

❋   ❋   ❋

As Anthony and Kevin were trying to see where the best place would be for Kevin to be waiting tomorrow night, neither of them were aware of the two men that were both pointing guns at them.

Teddy was watching through the scope of his rifle with caution as the two men got out of the car. He couldn't make out the face of either man because of the lack of light in the alley, but the one man was extremely big and Bull's name popped into his head. "Jeff, I can't make out their faces, can you see them or hear what they are saying."

"No, not really. All I can make out is that they are looking in both directions and pointing. To tell you the truth Teddy, it looks to me like they are doing the same thing we are doing. I think they are scoping the place out."

Teddy didn't respond back to Jeff right away. He was trying to focus in on their faces, but he couldn't get a clear look. The darkness, which they were going to use as an advantage tomorrow night, was now a disadvantage for him.

"What do you think? You think they are doing the same thing or what?" Jeff asked as he broke Teddy's concentration.

"Yeah, I think they are. If I am right, I think the big guy is Bull."

"The same guy we are supposed to take out tomorrow night?" Jeff asked surprised.

"I think we are being double-crossed, but it doesn't make sense. Frankie said Bull was in Vegas and I confirmed it. He couldn't have gotten back here that soon," he explained to Jeff.

"Well, what the fuck should we do? Do you want me to go up to these guys and find out who they are and what the fuck they are doing here?"

Teddy started to think it over. He believed that it couldn't be Bull down there. So who was this guy and was it merely a coincidence that he just happened to be as big as Bull? As important as it was to find out this answer, it wasn't nearly as imperative as learning who was setting him and Jeff up. Did Frankie believe that Pete came to him first and he was only covering his ass, or did someone leak the hit to Bull and he left Vegas early to plan an ambush for tomorrow night? That scenario didn't really make as much sense as the first one.

Teddy firmly believed that Frankie thought he was being double-crossed and the two men were down there making sure that there was no possible way for Frankie's men to be ambushed. Frankie wasn't worried about a single hit on himself, no, what he was worried about the most were the remaining good men in his crew being wiped out at one time. If Frankie felt that Teddy was given the orders to take out him and his crew, then tomorrow night in this alley would be a good start. Teddy could get at least three or four of them and a shit-load of money while he was at it.

"What the fuck Teddy, are you going to tell me what to do or not?" Jeff complained into his headset.

"Can you wait a fucking minute, Jeff? I want to see if I can get a visual on the big guy. If I can, then I will tell you what to do. It won't benefit us to have you walk up to them right now. I think its best that we should just wait and see what they do. So stay in that doorway out of sight and don't make a move until you hear from me first. If they happen to spot you and try anything, then they will be both dead on the ground with half their heads missing before they even knew what hit them," Teddy answered.

"Christ, it sure is dark in this alley," Anthony said to Kevin.

"Yeah, I don't think it is going to be a problem concealing myself. Why don't you go back to the car and get in the driver seat and pretend that you are a driver staring at over two hundred thousand dollars."

"Why the driver's side? I want you to break the passenger's window since he will be the least likely person in the car to see you." Anthony questioned him.

As the two of them came around from the other side of the dumpster Kevin pointed to the car. "Which side of the car is along the wall Anthony?"

"Oh fuck me. The passenger's side is, but does it really matter?" he asked as they both looked to the other side.

"We backed into this spot because we were the only car here and it was common sense to turn around and face the front of the alley. Frankie's crew will be running late because they will have been waiting for Bull at the airport, which means the other car will get here first. They would be more inclined to do exactly what we did and turn the car around to wait for Bull's car."

"But either way, I don't think it will matter who parks where because both car's passenger's sides will be along the wall," Anthony answered.

"True, but if Frankie's guys are the second car then they will be over there and not in front of the dumpster which will make it a hell of a lot harder to try and sneak up on them," he explained to Anthony.

"Shit, you are right. It won't matter who gets here first, you are going to have to hit the driver's window. If you think about it, this might be better because the driver is the key and now it will be a closer shot for you to hit him in the shoulder or leg."

"Yeah, but he will have a much better chance of seeing me if he isn't looking at the money the whole time. It's hard to say. I mean, it's not like he hasn't seen that kind of money before. Maybe he will be smoking a cigarette and staring out the window or we could get lucky and he and the others would still be pissed and concerned about Bull."

"Ok, we will try from both sides then," Anthony answered.

Anthony got in the car and drove out of the alley and turned around to park along the other wall. He gave Kevin the signal to start and Anthony acted like he wasn't paying attention. It only took a moment, and Anthony let out a little yell as Kevin slammed his hand hard against the window.

"Holy shit! You scared the fucking shit out of me, and I was aware that you were coming. I'm telling you, tomorrow night, whoever has the misfortune to be sitting in this seat is going to piss himself when that glass breaks and you open fire," he told Kevin with a shaky voice.

"Did it seem to take a long time? Because I was taking my time and crouching down as I got to the car," he told Anthony.

"No, and that's why I think I yelled. I mean, it didn't seem more than ten seconds after I gave you the signal," he replied.

"It's nice to have some comforting news from you for a change. Now this time, stare directly at me and the dumpster, but try to do like you said and pretend you are smoking a cigarette and looking around. This time I am going to get more of a running start," he told Anthony.

"Can you see any of this down there Jeff?"

"Not at first, but once the car came back into the alley on the other side I can see them. It looks like the one guy was creeping up on the car after it parked, but I am too far away to really have a clue as to what is going on over there. Can you make out anything from up there?"

"No, not really, I basically saw the same thing that you did. Two times now the big guy has gone from the back of the dumpster to the driver side of the car, while the other guy sits in the driver's seat. It looks almost like a practice. I definitely think that these two will be back here tomorrow and they are going to be in for one hell of a fucking surprise when I get done with them," Teddy responded.

On Kevin's second approach, Anthony saw him coming, though it would still be to late for him to be able to do anything about it. There was not enough time for him to pull a gun out of his jacket if needed. If Kevin was this quick tomorrow night, whoever was in the driver seat wouldn't have a chance to react before Kevin would break in the window.

"I counted and it only took me six seconds to come around the dumpster and get to the window. Did you see me right away or not?" he asked Anthony.

"I saw you about two or three seconds before you reached the car, but there just wasn't enough time to react. Even if he already has the gun in his hand, and I don't think that will be the case, his natural instinct will be to duck for cover instead of taking a shot at you," Anthony replied.

"I think this could actually work unless they park past the dumpster, but I don't believe that they would try to squeeze two cars back there. If another car or a cop car came down the alley they would be trapped. I think the dumpster is our best bet, and they aren't going to have a chance to react as long as I pick the right time to make my move. Let's just hope I have the balls and can pull the trigger when the opportunity presents itself," he told Anthony.

"I think this is enough for now. We both feel comfortable about our advantages—the darkness of the alley and the element of surprise. The last thing I want to do before we leave is have you stay here as I go back to the car and speed away down the street. I want you to see if you can distinguish the sound that the car makes. Between the smashing of the windows and the after-effect of the gunshots, I'm sure their ears will be ringing and they won't be able to tell if the car is a Trans Am or a Volvo. All we need is the squeal of the tires to be loud enough for it to stand out when Frankie starts asking more questions about Bull."

Anthony went back to the car and drove out of the alley. Once he got to the point where he expected to park tomorrow night he floored the pedal and the car took off with the tires spinning, smoking and squealing. Kevin caught up to him three minutes later at the end of the street. "Well, how did it sound?" Anthony asked.

"I got to admit, it was definitely loud. They should have no problem realizing that the get away car was a high-powered sports car," he replied.

"Great, one more reassuring detail for tomorrow night. Now, why don't we end this evening on a positive note and get out of here," Anthony responded.

"That sounds good to me because, no thanks to you, I am so fucking tired. Ever since you showed up the other night, I haven't gotten a good night's sleep, and I highly doubt that I will get one tonight. Want me to drop you off where I picked you up?"

"Shit, I never even gave that a thought. I have to try to get back into the house yet. Man, it took me forever to get the nerve to come down that drain pipe. I can't imagine trying to get back up it," he informed Kevin.

"Well don't look for any sympathy from me. I'd rather have to climb a fucking drainpipe than try to shoot two guys, steal a couple hundred thousand dollars and get away with it. But why bitch about the little things?"

All of Frankie's crew was gathered in the back room of *The Club* except for Sal and Bull. There were speculations amongst them as to what this meeting was about, but no one wanted to say it out loud. For the first time in many years, most of them were in fear of what was going on, and what was most likely going to take place. Down to a man, they felt this would be the last time that they would all gather together as a crew.

As soon as Frankie walked through the door, there was total silence. Usually the talking, laughing and bullshitting would continue, but tonight was different. Even the television wasn't on with the horse racing, to help Vincent keep track of the bets. There weren't any bets tonight because Vincent had unplugged the phone. If someone needed to get through they had his cell phone number, but he had that turned off too.

"I want to get this meeting started right away. I have to go over many important issues tonight and I don't have the time to repeat myself, so everyone pay attention," he announced to them as he sat down.

"I'm sure by now most of you are aware of what happened with Sal. After we found out that he and Bull were responsible for the deaths of Anthony's parents, it was my decision that Sal needed to go. My decision had nothing to do with the fact that it was Anthony's parents, but rather for the heat that I was getting from Pete. And before you start murmuring to yourselves, I haven't decided on Anthony's fate."

This didn't sit well with some of them.

"The kid has done a lot for me that none of you know about. I can't just go and whack him. Do you realize how much more heat that would bring down from Pete? Not to mention the local and federal authorities that are working on this case, and we don't need any more of that bullshit."

As Frankie continued to talk to them, Joey brought him a seven and seven from the bar.

"Here you go Frankie," Joey said.

But Frankie paid him no mind and continued talked. "In case any of you are not aware of this, a lot of shit is going down tomorrow night and I want everyone to be on the same page as to what I expect to be done. Bull will be arriving home from Vegas tomorrow night, and Victor and Carmine will pick him up at the airport along with Rossi." Frankie turned to Rossi, "Make sure you are here at *The Club* on time to go. Victor is going to replace Al as the driver, so I need you as the third man. Do you have a problem with that?"

"No Frankie, whatever you need done, you know that."

"Good, that's what I want to hear tonight from you guys. Charlie and Al will be here taking care of things while Vincent and I pay our respects at Anthony's parents' viewing. Paulie and Jimmy, you two will continue to shadow Anthony all day tomorrow and stay at the house tomorrow night and keep an eye on things, not that I am expecting anything to go down, but I want our backs to be covered just the same. Once Vincent and I are done there, we will meet back here. As for the rest of you, I don't want to see or hear from you until Vincent or I make contact with you. Now what I have to say next is not going to go over well with many of you because I don't know how Pete is going to react."

Frankie had to be hard and stern with his men. He couldn't let them see how worried he was about the events that were most likely going to take place over the next couple of days. He wasn't concerned about most of them, but for guys like Al, Victor and Charlie, who were his lieutenants, Pete could make an example out of any one of them.

"There are two more things that I want to bring up before we call it a night. This may not come as a surprise to some of you, but since Sal had to go, the orders were given today that Bull has to go as well and there is nothing I can do about it. I don't want to hear any questions or bitching about this. What's done is done and he deserves what he is getting."

No one needed to say anything after Frankie announced that Bull was going to be whacked—their faces said everything. Many of them were in total disbelief that Frankie was actually going to have Bull whacked.

"The second issue which I want to discuss with everyone is to stay in this room tonight. No one says anything to anybody. No matter what happens or what orders are given, after tomorrow night I am stepping down as head of our crew. All the signs are pointing for the worse and I think the end has come for me. These last few days have been a disaster and the last thing this city needed was a story like this to come out."

"Come on Frankie, you can't blame yourself for what those assholes did," Al started to explain.

"You're wrong Al, I should have seen something like this coming from Bull a long time ago."

"And you are leaving just like that?" Al questioned.

"I believe Pete has other plans for me and Vincent, so what I am asking is that you guys take the money that you have made and go away. I know this crew hasn't made the greatest of money and most of you have pissed what little you made away, so I have decided to give each of you an envelope as a going away gift. There is enough money in those envelopes for each of you to do what I suggested: start a new life and get out of this business."

"Don't you think that maybe you are over reacting a little, Frankie?" Vincent asked from his usual chair by the phones, which weren't plugged in and ringing off the hook with bets, as they normally would have been.

"I have been in this business too long to think otherwise, guys. Now if there are no questions of what I expect from everyone, I want to thank all of you for your loyalty and services. On your way out, take the envelope with your name on it from the basket at the end of the bar," he told them.

The back room of *The Club* had never been as somber or quiet as this before. It was like a funeral, only without the corpse. Some were upset about Sal and Bull, but they knew that this kind of shit came with their line of business. Even they had to agree that this was the right decision. What concerned them the most was the fact that Frankie had just broken up their crew and now they needed to find work somewhere else. Even worse, some actually had to go into hiding and that would be a new lifestyle all together.

On their way out everyone took their envelope from the basket at the end of the bar, and each of them gave Frankie a respectful hug and kiss on the cheek as they left *The Club*'s backroom for the last time.

After the last of his soldiers had left, Frankie stayed for another ten minutes with his lieutenants to go over tomorrow night's instructions one more time. Once the last of his men had left, he and Vincent had one last drink alone together before they left for the night.

Anthony stood looking up at his old bedroom window in amazement. Fifteen years ago, he was able to climb up this drainpipe without even a second thought. The pipe was now wet from the coldness of the November night, and to make matters worse his eyes weren't as sharp as they had been back then. It was too dark for him to see where to get a good grip to start his ascent.

After slipping off the pipe three times, Anthony started to get frustrated. If everything worked out to plan tomorrow night, but he was unable to get up this pipe, he was going to be extremely pissed at himself.

"Jesus Christ, how the hell could I have done this time and time again, but not be able to get up this fucking pipe now? God, I was even drunk or stoned half the time. If I don't get up this pipe tomorrow night and Frankie doesn't kill me, I am going to kill myself for this," he said to himself out loud.

Before his fourth attempt, Anthony closed his eyes and tried to relax. If he was about to get on a bicycle for the first time in fifteen years would he stand there and think about it, or would he just pick up the bike, hop on and start peddling? He was over-thinking the situation when in reality all he needed to do was what came naturally for him. Start climbing and don't think about what you are doing.

Anthony was half-way up the pipe before he ran into a problem. The pipe was wider at the top, and it was too wet and slippery to get a good grip. He had to reach into cracks and small holes in the bricks to pull him up a little further until he reached a section of the pipe that was secured to the house with a bracket.

He only paused two more times before he reached the point where he needed to grab the windowsill. Almost every muscle in his body was screaming at him to end this pain. He was cold and tired and his mind was telling him that the ledge was out of his reach.

The minutes were passing quickly and his body tightened more as he continued to stare at the windowsill and tried to muster up the courage to go for it. Anthony took his right hand off the pipe and made the sign of the cross and then dove for the ledge. As he hung there, he let go of the ledge with his left hand and pushed the window up as far as he could reach, then he pulled himself up and into the room.

Anthony laid on the floor staring at the ceiling with his heart beating out of control; he realized that he was too old for this shit. He was only twelve years old when he accomplished this little feat for the first time, and the sensation was overwhelming. Unfortunately, this time he only felt glad to be alive and not dead on the cold blacktop of the alley.

When he finally had gotten his head straight and his breathing under control, Anthony got off the floor and noticed that the old fashioned travel clock on his night stand read ten minutes to twelve, which meant it had taken him close to an hour to make it up that pipe: much longer than he had thought. He made a mental note to himself to leave a towel at the window for tomorrow night. He would put the towel in a plastic bag and leave it at the base of the pipe. This way, he could dry the pipe before he started his climb back up tomorrow night.

Anthony couldn't believe how much of an appetite he had worked up climbing that pole, and even though he was tired and wanted to get to bed, he couldn't get the thought of those steaks in the refrigerator out of his head. He knew he needed to get as much sleep as he possibly could tonight, because tomorrow was going to be the longest day of his life. Still, he couldn't bear to let those two steaks go to waste.

It was just before midnight when Frankie got into bed next to Ellena, who was lying there watching Jay Leno. This was the earliest that he has come home in a long time.

"Wow, what's the special occasion? You're coming home to me at a descent time? Usually I don't see you until I wake up in the morning."

Frankie couldn't look her in the eyes at first. He understood that this was going to be a crushing blow to Ellena and the rest of their family, but she was a devoted wife and he believed that, in the end, she would realize that their safety came first over her needs and wants.

Frankie hadn't decided yet exactly where he was going to move them, but the first thing he was going to do tomorrow was liquidate all his stocks and holdings and have the bank and Merrill Lynch wire his money to his off-shore account. After he was done with the bank, he was going to get the ball rolling with the sale of *The Club* and their home.

"Do you mind turning off the TV and putting the light on? I need to talk to you about a couple of things and this isn't going to be a quick conversation."

"Oh God Frankie, what happened? Are we in trouble? Did you finally get caught? Please don't tell me we are losing the house and restaurant because you are going away," she said as she started to sob.

"Now it's not like that, but it is serious and our lives are definitely going to change. By the way did you happen to talk to Anita today?" he asked her.

"No, why do you ask? Is there something wrong with her?"

"Will you relax? I am only asking because I called her earlier and got her voice mail, and I was wondering if she had called back yet," he informed her.

"No, she didn't, but she's been up there now for over a month, and I think she is getting tired of reporting in to us every day," she answered.

"You are the one who calls her every day. I only call her when I feel that she needs to hear a friendly voice. There's a difference between the two," he replied. "But that's not what I need to talk to you about, so please let me get back to what I need to say."

And with that, Frankie brought Ellena up to speed about everything that had happened and what still needed to be done.

Anita returned to her dorm from dinner with Christie around eleven-thirty. Christie decided to head to the lounge to finish her studying and let Anita have the room to herself so she could get some sleep. After spending close to three hours with Christie, Anita had realized that she led a boring life and if she wanted to fit in here and enjoy her college stay, she was going to need to make some changes.

After she turned on the light and threw her coat over the chair at her desk, Anita noticed the light on the answering machine was blinking. Knowing that it could only be her mother calling wondering why she hadn't called home today, she hesitated to play it. But, since it was Thursday and the weekend was tomorrow, she had a feeling that it might be her father wanting to get a hold of her before it started.

When her father's message was completed, Anita sat on her bed totally scared for one of the first times in her life. The message didn't sound right to her. Actually it wasn't the message that didn't sound right, but the tone in her father's voice. She couldn't put her finger on it, but she thought that he actually sounded desperate. That was something she wasn't accustomed to hearing.

Anita believed that Frankie was probably still at *The Club* with Vincent and the others waiting on her call, along with all the other calls that he dealt with on a nightly basis. But, waiting was what he was going to continue to do, because Anita had no plans to call him back. She knew there was nothing good that was going to come out of this phone call. This was the call that she had feared once she came to this school and had been on her own for the first time.

Ever since Anita was eleven years old and found out what her father did for a living, she feared a call like this one, or maybe a visit from the police in the middle of the night, or one of his men coming to the house with news that was going to break her mother's heart. Anita was tired of living like that and when she got to Cornell, she decided that she was going to put herself first and enjoy her life for a change. This was her life now and not his to control.

Anita continued to sit there on the edge of her bed staring at the phone, trying to convince herself to just let it go until tomorrow, but she couldn't do it. Suddenly, Christie's story came to her. Why couldn't she live that carefree fun lifestyle that Christie did? They weren't that much different, really. The only real difference was in the experience department, and Anita wanted to change that, and soon. And as that thought came to her, so did Christie's suggestion about the magazines in her bottom drawer. Anita thought to herself, "If I am going to fit in like everyone else, then I am going to that party tomorrow night, find a boy and forget about the consequences for a change."

As Anita walked over to Christie's drawer, her father's phone call was the furthest thing from her mind. She bent down and picked the top magazine and went back to her side of the room. Anita turned off the rooms light, switched on the reading lamp attached to her head board, and opened her first porno magazine.

♣   ♣   ♣

CHAPTER 4

The River
(4 of Clubs)

Bull was happy to be on a plane that was heading back home. He still didn't know exactly what he was going to do, but if he was going to take the fall, he would be damned if he wasn't taking everyone who was involved down with him. As he clutched the bag on his lap that had Frankie's money in it, he wondered if he was ever going to get the chance to deliver it to him or if they planned on killing him first? Either way, Bull was determined that he was going to be ready for whatever surprise they had intended for him. However, it would be Anthony's surprise at the airport that would be Bull's downfall.

Nicholas reached Cornell campus with the fall sun starting to set just around six o'clock. He had never been to a major university's campus before, and was surprised to see so many students running around enjoying the start of their weekend. The last of the afternoon classes were now over and most students were heading back to their rooms to get ready for their weekend, while others were heading out to get some dinner before the cafeteria closed for the night. As Nicholas looked around, he realized he could enjoy this lifestyle. But for now, he had to finish his two years at community college before he could get to a place like this.

He got out of his car and headed straight for the center of the campus, where he hoped to find the Campus's map. Nicholas figured the best place to start would be to head to the cafeteria and get a bite to eat. While he was there, he would listen to the buzz from the students to see where they were heading tonight.

There were two long lines disbursing out the front doors of the Garzone Funeral Home. Just like in the months of September and October, when people from all over the city had come to pay respects to the families of the fallen victims of 9/11 at various viewings and ceremonies, citizens from various neighborhoods were in line to give their condolences to Anthony and his family. Regrettably for Anthony, he was not expecting this kind of outpouring from all of these strangers when he had first added the time to his equation.

He had gone to many of the police officers that were there to control the crowd to start sending these people home because it was a private viewing, and it was now out of control and becoming a circus. But his pleas fell on deaf ears, as most of the officers were more concerned with their strict orders of being on the look out for Frankie Feliciani and anyone else from his crew who might have ideas of showing up tonight.

It wasn't until his Aunt Bernadette went up to one of the officers asking for them to consider the family's pain, that he took his bull horn and notified the people in line that this was a private viewing and no one was going to get in the door unless they were recognized by Anthony's Aunt Marian, who stood by the door next to two police officers.

When he felt things were getting under control, Anthony went back to his place in the greeting line next to his parents' coffins. And to his surprise, Sandra and Kimberly had arrived and were sitting in the first row right in front of him. As he smiled at them, he could only think that this was a sign that everything was going to go his way tonight.

"What the fuck is taking him so long in there?" Rossi asked the rest of them in the car from the back seat.

"I know that the security has tightened over the last month but this is fucking ridiculous," Victor added from the driver's seat. "Why don't you go in there and see what the hold up is, before anther cop comes up behind us and tells me to move the car again," he told Rossi.

"Like I am going to be able to find him in that zoo in there. Why don't you go instead?" Rossi told Victor.

"If you are going to be a little bitch about it, I will go in and see what the fuck is taking so long. I'm fucking tired and hungry, and I want to get going before it starts getting too late to be able to stop and get a bite to eat before the pick up," Carmine said to Rossi as he got out of the passenger door.

Just as Carmine was walking into the airport, another cop car pulled up behind Victor and flashed his lights, signaling to him that he needed to move his car from the pick up lane.

"These fucking cops are getting on my nerves tonight," Victor yelled as he pulled away.

"What does this make it now? Three laps around the airport? Unfucking real. I'll bet you a C note that they won't be outside waiting for us before we make it around the place," Rossi claimed.

"You're on for that C note because Carmine isn't a fuck-up like you," Victor replied as he started their lap around the airport.

Nicholas was just finishing up his french fries when he heard the girls at the table in front of him start to talk about the party they were going to tonight. By the looks of them, two out of the four seemed pretty hot and would be the kind of girls that only attended the good parties on campus. This was as good a chance as any to find the big party on campus that was going down tonight.

"I can't believe Phi Kappa Sigma is throwing another party this week considering what happened at last Fridays' party. That party was, like, so out of control, it had to be the greatest ever," said Jill, who was the best looking girl of the bunch, and the one who seemed to be the leader of this little group.

"Can you believe it took ten campus security guards to shut it down?" Jennifer, the other good looking blonde asked.

"Why do we even bother going to these fraternity parties anyway? They are over crowded, with too many people, not enough beer and they are always broken up before we even get a chance to get more than two beers. I would rather just go into town and let a couple of the locals buy us drinks all night," Erica, who seemed to be the group's rationalist, said.

"Because everyone who is anyone on this campus will be there tonight, and I would rather be seen at the party than in town with a bunch of fat drunks trying to pick us up all night," Jill stated and then paused to make that look that says why do you doubt me? "We could always go into town after the party, but I think we should go to the Phi Kap house first," she finished making her point.

The fourth girl agreed with the other two making it a three to one vote, so it looked like Nicholas would be seeing them later on tonight at the Phi Kap house once he found it. He just hoped that there weren't more than one or two parties on campus tonight, or his chances of finding Anita would be slim to none.

"Sir, please put your hands in the air and step out of line," the security guard told Bull as he put his hand on the outside of his gun. Alarms went off when Bull went through the metal detectors; scattering some of the people who were in line with Bull.

"What's your fucking problem?" Bull answered back.

"Sir, I am not going to say it again. Now please step out of the line."

Before Bull had a chance to do what the security guard asked or became truly aware of what was going on, four guards and police officers were on top of him and had him pinned to the floor and were cuffing him.

"Jesus Christ, what the fuck are you assholes doing? Do you have any idea who I am?" he yelled at them from the floor.

"No, but we will before you leave here tonight," one of the officers replied to him as they picked him up off the floor and dragged him towards a plain yellow door that led to the interrogation room.

Once they got Bull into the room, two of the officers sat him in one of the two chairs that were at the table, while the third un-cuffed Bull and the forth stood guard at the door. The officer who had un-cuffed Bull took Bull's bags and placed them in the middle of the table and opened them. The first bag that he opened was Bull's carry on, which contained Frankie's money.

"Holy shit, look at what we have here guys. It seems our boy over here is carrying a hell of a lot of money with him. I can see why you needed a bag. I mean when I carry this kind of money around, I never use a wallet," he said sarcastically.

"How much money is in your bag, Mr. Colaiezzi?" Allen Doll, one of the two police officers that were standing behind Bull, asked him as he went through Bull's wallet to get his name.

"A lot more than you make in a year, you fucking douche bag. There's a receipt in there from Caesars Casino. Taxes were paid and everything, so if I was yous, I would zip that up and not think about it again because once you find out who that money belongs too, you are going to regret this," he informed the officer.

"Listen to me Mr. Colaiezzi, I don't give a flying fuck who you are out there on the streets or who the hell you work for. I can assure you right now in here, that your ass is in a world of trouble," Officer Christopher Donlon replied. "All we need to do is find the weapon that set off the detectors that you have hidden on you."

"Weapons, are you fucking kidding me? Do you think I am that fucking stupid to walk through JFK airport with a weapon on me after what just happened less than two months ago?" he asked the four of them. FBI agents Lawrence Kelly and Dennis McCarty walked into the room before they had a chance to answer him.

"Don't worry Mr. Colaiezzi, we know who you are and who your employer is and what your relationship with him is. We know that you are what they consider "muscle" for one Frank Feliciani and that you go by the name Bull instead of Michael. But right now we don't give a shit about all of that."

Agent McCarty pulled up the chair next to Bull, turned it around, and sat in it backwards facing Bull. "Now, since we know who you are, let me introduce meself and my colleague to you. I am agent Dennis McCarty and this is agent Lawrence Kelly, and we have you in this room tonight because airport security got an anonymous tip that you would be coming through the gate tonight with weapons and a bag full of money. Now if you cooperate with us we can make this as painless as possible, but if you want to play hardball with us, I can promise you that this will be the longest night of your life, you piece of shit."

"Fuck all of yous. The money is legit and I don't know what the fuck you are talking about when you keep referring to weapons. I just flew back from Vegas after picking up my uncle's World Series winnings, which the last time I checked was legal, and I was on my way home to celebrate until these fucking douche bags decided to gang tackle me and drag me into this room," he shouted at them but not achieving the effect that he was hoping to reach on them.

"Bull, may I call you Bull?" Agent Kelly asked.

"I don't give a fuck what you douche bags call me, but I will tell you this: for this huge fuck-up by you guys, I know I will be calling my lawyer. I can't believe you treat innocent American people like this."

"Calm down Bull," Lawrence began. "If the money is clean like you say it is and we don't find anything in the second bag, you'll be free to walk out of here without any more hassle. I guarantee you this though, you grease ball, God help you if we find something in that bag."

"Well, well, well, look at what we have here boys," Officer Donlon raised his hands to show the other officers and Bull what he had found in the bag. To Bull's horror, Agent Donlon pulled out a switch blade and a pizza cutter. The second item was far worse than the first considering what the 9/11 hi-jackers had used to overthrow the crew and pilots on the four planes that crashed on that fateful day.

"You either must be the dumbest fuck in this country, or a true threat to national security. You mind telling me what the fuck these items were doing in your possessions?" Lawrence asked Bull as he leaned over and screamed in his face.

In the end, Phillip came through for Anthony. He didn't really plan on going through with it, because he didn't want to bring that kind of heat down on him and his family if something went wrong. The last thing anyone who lived in this city wanted was to be on some mob member's shit list. But once he saw Bull coming out of the runway dressed in his Adidas jump suit, looking like the absolute piece of trash that he was, Phillip didn't need to think twice about trying to have this guy put away for a long time for killing Anthony's parents.

Phillip took his walkie-talkie off his belt and called down to Bob who was waiting for his instructions. "Yo Bob, go ahead with plan pizza, plan pizza is a go for passenger Colaiezzi, I repeat, plan pizza is a go for passenger Colaiezzi."

Two seconds later, the voice on the other end came back, "Roger that Phillip, plan pizza will be delivered to a Mr. Colaiezzi."

"You got to be shitting me. Why the hell would I have these items in my bag?" Bull demanded to know.

But of course, he already had a clue as to how they got there. Somehow between boarding the plane and picking up his bag from the baggage claim, Frankie had someone plant the weapons in the bag. He began to think as he ignored their questions. The more he thought about it, the clearer the answer became. Instead of Frankie whacking him once he got home, it would be easier and more convenient setting him up to be arrested. That way, Frankie could have him whacked once he got to Federal prison. The bosses would be satisfied and their problems would be solved.

"I'm not going to ask you again, Bull. What the hell were you planning on doing tonight with those weapons?" Agent Kelly asked him as he grabbed Bull by his shirt with both hands.

"You know for being a Fed, you really are fucking stupid. Did you ever think that I was being set up? How did I get them on the plane in Vegas in the first place, and why would I bring them on if I wasn't going to use them? Has it occurred to any of yous that they were planted in my bags after I landed? There are many people that would be happy to see me go to jail for a while. In fact, I am pretty sure that I was set up and I have an idea as to who did it. Why don't we take a ride down town, and we can discuss a plea bargain for some valuable information about some very important people."

It didn't take long for Agents McCarty and Kelly to agree.

"What the hell Bull, let's take a ride and maybe you can enlighten us with some useful information. If we can use this information, more than likely, one day you are going to have to testify in court and if that's the case, your life in organized crime will be over forever. You will be an outcast and a hunted man from that day forward," Agent McCarty explained.

"Why the hell do you think I am in this room to begin with? That day has already arrived. I am as good as dead if I walk out of here with or without yous," he informed them.

Thirty minutes after he walked into the airport, Carmine was back at the curb, opening the passenger door after Victor pulled up in the pick up lane. "Man, it is a fucking zoo in that place. There are police and security everywhere and the lines look to have hundreds and hundreds of people in them. I checked the monitors and his plane landed forty minutes ago. I went as close as I could to the baggage claim area, and there were only a couple of people still there and no bags on the conveyor belt. I checked the nearest men's room and the two bars, and there was no sign of him. I take it he didn't come back to the car?"

"Boy, look who just got up to speed. No he didn't come back to the car," Rossi responded.

"Listen to me you little fucking side kick, one more crack from you tonight and two people will be getting whacked. Am I making myself clear?" Carmine responded.

"So what do you suggest we do now?" Victor asked the two of them. "I am getting tired of driving around in circles and eventually this cop is going to write me a ticket and I don't want that fucking hassle," he told them.

"Well I can honestly say he wasn't in line, so where the hell could he be? You don't think he got wind of what was going on and he stayed out there in Vegas?" Carmine asked.

"I wouldn't be surprised if someone leaked it to him, but Frankie didn't tell us until real late last night and that didn't give them a lot of time to try to get a hold of Bull," Rossi said.

"Even so, if he ain't here, my guess is he somehow got the word and is out on his own. I think we need to call Frankie and find out what he wants us to do," Victor informed them as he pulled out of the pick up lane.

"Why are you driving away before I have a chance to call Frankie?" Carmine asked as he was dialing Frankie's number.

"Because you stupid fuck, don't you see the police lights on behind me?"

As Victor drove them for another circuit around the airport, Carmine dialed Frankie. "Frankie it's Carmine, listen we have a little problem. Bull hasn't come out of the airport yet and I went in looking for him and there is no sign of him anywhere. How long do you want us to wait for him?" he asked.

"Are you sure you are at the right terminal?" Frankie barked into the phone.

"Of course we are, boss. I went to the monitor and saw that his plane landed on time. Then I went to the baggage claim area and there were only a couple of people left there and no bags were on the conveyor belt. And after that I went to one men's room and two bars and he wasn't in any of them," he informed Frankie.

"Well, I want you guys to wait a little longer. He's got to be there."

"I hope you don't get offended boss, but do you think that someone possibly got the word to him that there was a hit on him?" Carmine asked cautiously.

"That's possible, but I highly doubt it. There just wasn't enough time to reach him out there. Knowing Bull, he was either at the crap tables all night or in bed with some whore," he replied back.

"You don't think he stayed out there on his own do you? I mean, maybe he started to put two and two together and realized his ass was on the line."

"Carmine, what is Bull's purpose in this family?"

"He's one of our muscles, boss," he replied.

"Right, so thinking isn't one of his strong points now is it? I don't think Bull is smart enough to think of that on his own and even if he got wind of a hit, he wouldn't run. With his temper, he would be here to take out as many of you as he could, including me before he went down, so I don't think he went into hiding."

"Can I make one more suggestion boss?" Carmine asked tentatively.

"Yeah, go ahead."

"Do you think that maybe he made a deal with the Feds about the kid's parents' murders to save himself and take you and the family down?"

This thought never even crossed Frankie's mind. Bull would be the last person in this crew to ever become a rat, but if push came to shove and his back was against the wall, Bull would do what everyone else would in that position and save his own ass from going to jail. No matter what oath they swore when they became a made man—when someone in this line of work was given the chance to save their own ass they would talk, but even if they didn't talk, either way they were dead.

Bosses couldn't trust them one-way or the other. If they kept quiet during their interrogation and during the first month or two behind bars, there would still come a time when being locked up in a cell started playing mind games with them. If given the chance, they would talk to get out. Because the longer they were locked up in a cage like an animal, the more likely they would talk to be free again. As for the bosses, it was just as easy to have someone whacked on the inside as it was on the streets.

Frankie was still thinking about this idea as Carmine was asking him what he wanted them to do. What if Bull did go to the Feds? Once the word got out, no one was going to be spared by Pete. There would be no questions asked and no way of talking their way out of it. Pete would have everyone whacked and that was that. If it was true and Bull was in their custody right now, Frankie figured he had two days max to get the girls and Ellena the hell out of the city.

"Frankie," Carmine yelled into the phone. "Are you there?"

"Yeah, I'm here. I want you guys to wait about another twenty minutes and this time send in Rossi, because maybe a second pair of eyes might see something different. Call me in twenty with a report and let me know if you got him or not," he replied and then hung up the phone.

"Frankie wants you to go in, Rossi, and see if you can find him. He wants me to call back within twenty minutes, so hurry the fuck up in there because Frankie is really pissed," he told Rossi.

❧   ❧   ❧

"Is there a problem Frankie?" Vincent asked as they tried to find a place to park near the funeral parlor.

"I don't know what to think about this just yet, but they can't find Bull. He hasn't come out of the airport yet. Carmine went in there looking for him and couldn't find him."

"You don't think that he stayed out there do you? If he had a hunch that something was going down back here at home, three hundred thousand dollars is a lot of money to go into hiding with," Vincent replied.

"Jesus Christ, I never thought about the fucking money. Carmine put that thought into my head of Bull going to the Feds about the murders to cover his own ass, but now that you brought up the money, three hundred thousand can get him far, especially if he keeps going south to Mexico. It's not like we have people down there, so that's a good a place as any to hide for a long time without running into trouble."

As they circled the home for a second time, Frankie was getting even more furious. "Fuck this. There is no way we are going to find a spot to park. Let's just go to the kid's parents' house and pay our respects there," he told Vincent.

"Whatever you want Frankie. What about Teddy and his brother? Are you going to call Teddy and let him know that Bull won't be at the pick up? If he shows up and Bull isn't there, he might think that he is the one being set up and God only knows what he will do to our guys."

"I am going to wait until Carmine calls back from the airport before I call Teddy. I don't want to jump the gun just yet. Who knows, maybe Bull is at the airport and they haven't seen him yet because of how slow security has become since 9/11."

The cops and Anthony's Aunt Marian had the crowd under control for the most part and it was only friends and family that were getting into the funeral home. Anthony was still greeting people halfheartedly as he kept checking the time on his watch. It's amazing how time slips away when you are chasing it, and for Anthony, on this night, he was far behind. He realized that he had to get back to his parents' house soon and make as many appearances as possible before he left for the night. Even though there was still much to be done yet, he had to give his parents their respect and console their friends and family. However, he was running dangerously behind schedule and he didn't want to think about Kevin all alone in the car panicking. The sooner he could get these people out of here and back to his parents' place, the better.

Nicholas arrived at the Phi Kappa house around nine-thirty and once he walked into the party, he knew that he was definitely at the campus's best party. He couldn't imagine another party on or off campus that was better than what he was seeing. There seemed to be more girls than guys, and for him that was much better than what he was used to at home. Eight or nine guys hanging out at the local bar on a Friday night chasing after the same three or four local tramps from the neighborhood.

The thing that surprised him the most was how diverse the crowd seemed to be. There were all kinds of people at this party. Jocks, geeks, hot chicks, ugly chicks, the average Joe, black or white—it just didn't seem to matter. Even the fraternity brothers were spread throughout the party. It didn't look like there were the typical clicks of people hanging out in one spot. Everyone was mingling with each other. These kids didn't care about their differences. Their only concerns were how drunk they were going to get and who they were going to go home with, and Nicholas was fine with that.

It didn't take Nicholas long to get through the crowded living room, reach the keg, and get his first beer of the night. As he drank his beer, he looked around and thought to himself that there had to be at least two hundred people on the first floor. He had absolutely no shot at finding Anita in this crowd.

❦   ❦   ❦

"What do you think? Should I call him now, or do you want to give Rossi another five minutes?" Carmine asked Victor as they both stared at the sliding doors.

"How long has it been?" he replied. Carmine didn't need to look at his watch to know that it had been longer than twenty minutes, and Frankie specifically said to call him in twenty minutes. When Frankie gave an order, it was to be executed to the exact detail.

"It's been at least thirty minutes, and where the fuck is Rossi?" Carmine replied.

"This isn't good, you know. We got to call Frankie and tell him that Bull isn't here. It's getting late and we have to make the pick up," Victor said.

"Great, just fucking great. I'm the one that gets to tell the boss that Bull fucked us."

As Carmine was dialing Frankie's number, relief came over him as he saw Rossi come through the doors, but it soon turned to horror as he realized that Rossi was alone. "Fuck, here comes Rossi and he's alone," Carmine announced to Victor.

"Make the call," Victor replied.

❦   ❦   ❦

"Are you positive that you checked the airport inside and out?" Frankie asked.

"If Bull took the flight you said he did, then yeah, Rossi and I checked the whole terminal and there's no sign of him. What do you want us to do now?" Carmine asked.

"I want you to go pick up my money and meet back at *The Club* like scheduled," he responded.

"All right boss."

"And one more thing Carmine, just be extra sharp tonight because Dan isn't stupid, and when he realizes that Bull isn't making the pick up he might think something is going down, so just be careful."

"No problem boss, I'll make sure everyone keeps their eyes open for something funny to happen."

"Are you going to call Teddy and let him know that Bull isn't going to be in the car?" Vincent asked Frankie once he hung up the phone with Carmine.

"Can this fucking night get any worse?" Frankie asked. "If I call Teddy now, he'll suspect something and God knows what he'll do. Even if he isn't in with Pete already, he'll imagine that I think he is if I call this hit off and that I am trying to cover my own ass. Either way I can't call him. I just have to let this night run its course and hope to God that someone knows who the fuck tipped Bull off before Pete finds out that he didn't come back."

"Do you still want to go to the kid's parents' house or do you want to get back to *The Club*?" Vincent asked.

"The kid is the least of my worries now. Bull is never going to come back for him and I sure as hell ain't sticking around waiting for my fifty g's. I guess the kid finally got lucky. Hopefully he'll realize that something good came out of his parents' death and he'll turn his life around."

Frankie closed his eyes because he could feel one of those migraines approaching, and that was the last thing he needed on top of everything else that has gone wrong tonight. "Just take me back to *The Club*," he told Vincent.

Nicholas was already on his fourth beer and had gone through all three levels of the house, and he still hadn't seen Anita. The longer the night got and the more he drank, he began to think that there was no possible way that he was going to find her. The house was jam packed, and he could have been standing right in front of Anita and he still might have missed her.

This reminded him of the time last year when his brother Charlie had told him to meet him in front of Yankees stadium before game three of the World Series. If he didn't have his ticket on him, he would have never gotten in because there were just too many people outside the stadium partying and having a good time, even if they didn't have tickets to the game. The odds of Nicholas finding his brother in that frenzy crowd were just as impossible as him finding Anita tonight. There were too many kids crammed into the house and it was hard for him to stay in one place and look through the crowd.

Nicholas looked at his watch and realized that he had been here for two hours already; it seemed hopeless. He was going to have one more beer and then go grab something to eat and try to come back later as the party wound down. At least by then he would have a chance to work off his buzz and, with the crowd lessening, it would be easier to spot Anita if she was still there.

As Nicholas was in line at the keg, he noticed one girl standing by herself, looking out of place as she drank her beer from the red plastic cup in her hand. He couldn't clearly make out her face, but by the way she was standing there, looking out of place and nervous and hardly drinking her beer, he thought that it could be Anita. This girl seemed to fit the profile that Anthony had told him about her.

He looked down at his cup and saw that it was still half full and decided that he would get out of line and head to the girl standing alone in the corner of the room. Nicholas was astonished that he was now standing within two feet of the girl that he came up here to find. He couldn't believe that he had actually found her, and the funny thing was that he wasn't prepared to talk to her because he never believed that he was going to meet her.

"Anita Feliciani, is that you?" Anita turned around stunned that someone at this party had called out her name.

"Do I know you?" she asked the stranger back.

"No, not really, but I recognized you from the neighborhood. You graduated from Little Flower last year."

"Yes I did, but how do you know me? I don't recognize you. Do you live in the same neighborhood?"

"Yeah, I lived on Agusta Street and went to St. Joseph Prep. My name is Nicholas Hance," he replied as he stuck out his hand to her.

"Hi Nicholas, I'm sorry but you don't look familiar to me. Then again, I really didn't socialize with a lot of the kids from the neighborhood. How on Earth do you know me?" she asked.

"Do you want to know my reason, the real reason or a lie?" he responded.

"Well if you want to start off with a good impression, I would like the truth," she replied.

Nicholas took the last gulp of his beer before he answered her. "If I give you a good answer, do you want to get out of here? I'm not one for crowded parties and from the look of it, you don't seem to be having a lot of fun standing here by yourself."

"My friend Christie left me standing here thirty minutes ago. She told me she would be right back, but I think she is trying to see if I can mingle with other people. In case you can't tell, I'm not the social butterfly type, and when you don't have a lot of confidence or looks, it's hard to break out of your shell. But from what I can see about you, I don't think you ever have that problem."

Nicholas had to laugh at that. He wasn't used to a girl like Anita. The kind of girls he socialized with were easy and had no problems coming up to him and telling Nicholas what they wanted from him or to do to him.

"Why would you think that? You are the first person I approached tonight, and the only reason I came up to you was because I recognized you. But you made it awkward for me by not knowing who I was, so I guess I am not as popular or as good with the opposite sex as you made me out to be," he replied.

"I highly doubt it, but ok, we can go hang out somewhere if you give me a satisfying answer to my question," she told him.

"Good, you've got yourself a deal," he said. "Ok, here are my three answers for you: first, which is the real answer, I know you because if I come from the same neighborhood, I obviously know who you are because of your father and what he does for a living."

"Boy I guess you didn't have to put much thought into that answer," she replied.

"Alright, fair enough," Nicholas replied. "My second answer, which is a lie I must confess, is that I saw a lonely girl looking out of place in a crowded party, and since no one else was standing in line to talk to her I thought I'd give it a shot and see if I could get into her pants."

Anita giggled after she heard that. "Ok, that one was more creative."

"I'm glad you approve of that one," he told her. "But the third and honest answer is that I always thought you were very attractive and since I didn't know that you went here and you were all by yourself, I thought I'd come over and try to talk to you. If you don't take chances, how else are you going to meet someone like you?"

For the second time in two nights, Anita was absolutely stunned by what someone had said to her. No one her age had ever said something like that to make her feel special. Hell, who was she kidding; no guy ever said anything to her at all unless they were trying to get to know her because of her father.

"So, you don't want to get into my pants? At least we got that out of the way. Where do you want to go?" she asked.

"Now I didn't say that, I just said it wasn't the reason I came up to talk to you. However, the lady has the honor of picking the place to go. Personally, I am starving and could go for some breakfast food. Would you like me to take you out for a bite and a cup of coffee?" he asked.

"That sounds nice, but I have to warn you, I'm not much of a talker, so I hope you can keep a conversation going," she said.

❦   ❦   ❦

"Hey Hon, it's me. Things aren't going well tonight and I need you to please do what we talked about last night and have all your necessities packed. We might be leaving late tonight or first thing in the morning. Have you heard from Anita yet today?" Frankie asked her.

"No, I haven't. She never called last night or tonight. Frankie, please tell me nothing has happened to her. I swear to God, I will never forgive you if something did."

"Ellena, nothing has happened to her. What kind of animals do you think I deal with that would bring a guy's children into his problems?"

"I don't know, the same animals that might kill two helpless senior citizens?" she replied.

"That fucking animal is why I am in this mess, and we are trying to get rid of him and rectify this whole mess. Unfortunately, he got wind of what was going down," he informed her.

"Frankie, we've been together for so many years, please grant me this favor and tell me which one of your men has put our lives in jeopardy by killing those people. You owe me that much if you expect me to just pack up my whole life and put it in a suitcase and leave all of this behind."

Just when Frankie thought his night couldn't get worse, it did. He made it a point during their marriage not to lie to Ellena. There were many times he wouldn't tell her the specifics of his affairs, but if she asked him a question and wanted an honest response, he would give it to her. However this was too sensitive of an issue to let her know the truth. He just hoped that in the end, she would never know that it was Michael.

"Right now that's not important. The only things I want you to be concerned with are getting all of our belongings together and keep calling Anita until you get a hold of her. And eventually when this is all over with, I will tell you the truth about what happened. Can you just do that for me?"

"You know I have always been a good wife to you, so I will do this, but please keep your word and let me know who is ruining not just our lives, but Anita's as well."

❦ ❦ ❦

Anthony couldn't believe that this many people were in his parents' house at one time. There had to be at least two hundred people. Some were close friends and family, and many of them he recognized as other storeowners from the market district. He also noticed the four undercover cops that were there for his protection in case Frankie had planned on showing up or sending some of his crew to pay Anthony a visit. Anthony didn't notice any cars with people in them, but that didn't mean that Frankie didn't have his guys planted somewhere outside or, for that matter, in the house. No one said it had to be a man that was in the house from Frankie's crew. If the police can use women in undercover work, why couldn't Frankie?

Obviously Anthony didn't know Frankie as well as the police, because they were prepared for something to happen tonight. But Anthony just couldn't comprehend that someone in his or her right mind would try to cause an unfortunate situation at a viewing. However, as cautious as the cops were, Anthony did believe that Frankie would show up tonight because Frankie had always been a straight-up guy with Anthony, and it would be the right thing to do. Unfortunately, he knew they would never let him in the house and he just hoped that things wouldn't get out of control.

Anthony greeted as many people as he could before he couldn't take it any longer. He was being a hypocrite standing there listening to their sympathy for his loss, but most of them didn't have the slightest clue that he and his parents had not been close for the last two years and he had meant nothing to them in their lives. It was hard to look these people in the eye as they stood and cried in front of him or gave him a long hug.

Anthony never felt so ashamed of himself. He just didn't have the same grief as these people had. He had too many things on his mind to be grieving at this moment.

"How are you holding up?" Sandra asked as she handed him a glass of wine. "I would have gotten you a beer, but I figured since you haven't eaten yet wine would be better for your stomach. Plus, it's a little classier standing here greeting people holding a wine glass, instead of a bottle of beer," she told him.

"You always were the smarter one out of the two of us," he replied as he took the glass.

"How much longer before you have to get going?" she asked.

"Actually, I've got to get my ass out of here as soon as possible. Do you think you can get Kimberly so we can go upstairs?"

"If I can get her away from your Aunt Bernadette, I think I can meet you back here in two minutes," she replied.

"Great, I'll see you in two minutes," he said.

As Sandra started to walk away he called her back. "Sandi, just in case I haven't told you yet, thank you for your help tonight. I know you probably took a lot of shit from Chad, and I just want to make sure you know I appreciate what you did to make it here tonight."

"You have no idea what kind of shit I had to do, but you are still welcome," she replied.

"Have you gotten an impression of me yet?" Anita asked Nicholas as she ate her french toast.

"We've only talked for an hour, what kind of an impression do you expect me to have?" he asked.

"I don't know, but are you having a nice time? Please, be honest, because you don't know what it's like to be me," she said.

"What do you mean?" he asked.

"You have no idea what it was like for me growing up. My life wasn't normal and I know that I am not normal and to make matters even worse, I have no self esteem or confidence when it comes to talking to people," she replied.

"Ok to be honest, I have been secretly taking notes on how you act and what you say and I hate to tell you this, but you seem to be perfectly healthy. And unfortunately, I can't write you a note to excuse you from your classes next week."

"That's not funny. I am trying to open up and be honest with you and you're making jokes. I can't tell if you are interested in what I say or if you are sitting there thinking to yourself, 'what the hell did I get myself into'. I have never been in this situation before."

Nicholas couldn't help it, but he started laughing out of control. "I'm sorry, I don't mean to laugh. And please believe me when I say that I wasn't laughing at you. Why are you being so serious? We are only sitting here, eating breakfast and talking. Why are you putting so much pressure on yourself?" he asked as he tried to stop laughing.

"Because," she yelled back. "I have never even been on a date before and I don't know how these things are supposed to go and I want to know if it's going well. Is that so much to ask?"

"Settle down Anita. It was going just fine until that little outburst. Just take a couple of deep breaths and keep eating your food before it gets cold."

"I'm sorry, I know you must think I am crazy. You can leave if you want and I'll even pick up the tab," she said.

"Don't be silly, I'm fine. Come on, just be yourself and let's keep talking, because I still haven't given up on the idea of getting into your pants," he said with that charming smile of his while he continued to laugh.

"I hate to break the news to you Nick, no one has ever gotten there before, so don't get your hopes up," she replied.

"Great, because I am one for a challenge," he said, which made both of them laugh. He now believed that she was his for the night.

Frankie walked into *The Club* to see Al and Charlie sitting at one of the poker tables playing knock rummy. "I'm glad to see that the two of you are relaxed enough to be playing cards while everything is getting fucked up tonight," he yelled at them. "Has anyone called other than people placing bets?" he asked them.

"No, Frankie, the phones have been quiet all night. What's going on that things are getting fucked-up? Did something happen?" Charlie asked.

"Yeah, you could say that. Bull didn't show up at the airport, which can mean many things, with the worse being that he went to the Feds to plea bargain about Anthony's parents' death. Or, another scenario is that someone in our family betrayed me and tipped Bull that there was a hit placed on him. No matter which of these is the case, Pete is going to put an end to this problem. We are all fucked, but I promise you one thing: if someone fucked me and told Bull about our plans, he better pray that Pete takes me out first because he has no idea what kind of fucking torture I will bring down on his ass."

"Frankie, before we start panicking, are you sure that Bull wasn't tied up at the airport? You know how crazy things are at all the city airports right now after 9/11, he could still be stuck on the plane for all we know," Al stated.

"Both Carmine and Rossi went into the airport at separate times. His flight landed on time, and there were only a couple of people at the baggage claim and no bags. I have tried his cell phone for the last forty minutes and he isn't answering. My heart is telling me that he wouldn't be stupid enough to go to the Feds, because he knows that we could still get to him if we really wanted to. I am more confident that he went somewhere else, and let's hope that we got lucky and he flew there because the airline can at least tell us that much. Now make yourselves useful and get on the phone with USAir and see if he got on that flight or if he switched to another destination," he barked his order at them.

Anthony walked up the stairs with Kimberly asleep in his arms and Sandra behind him. He had attended to the people that he had to, and if Frankie happened to show up it really didn't matter, because the police weren't going to let him in anyway. As for the others that were still there, he announced that he was taking his daughter upstairs to bed and wouldn't be down for a while.

For most of the people there, including the police, this didn't seem out of the ordinary, considering he had just lost his parents and his ex-wife was there with their daughter. Maybe they were going to be up there for a while to catch up on the lost time between them. Some of his family even wished to themselves that maybe this tragedy would somehow bring them back together, but only Anthony knew that that was never going to happen.

Anthony put Kimberly in the middle of his old bed and pulled the covers up to her chest and tucked her Barney doll in right next to her.

"Do you think you can sleep in this bed for a night?" he asked Sandra.

"Don't worry about me, I believe I have slept in a lot worse. Will you be coming back tonight, or is this the last time I am going to see you?"

"I plan on coming back tonight, but I can't promise anything. If I am not back in a couple of hours then you will have your answer and, if that's the case, I want you to go right home tomorrow morning, and then go to the mass and burial. If you don't show up, people might think that you were aware of what I was doing tonight," he told her.

All at once Sandra felt fear creep into her. "Why would someone think I was involved in whatever you planned to do tonight? Are you jeopardizing Kimberly and me, Anthony?" she demanded.

"Sandi, nothing is ever going to happen to the two of you. For God's sake, you are a woman and Kimberly is a child. All I meant to say was that someone might question you one day," he told her.

"Please promise me, Anthony, that everything will be fine and that you will be coming back tonight. I don't want the last image that I have of you to be you climbing out of your childhood bedroom window," she said as two small tears went down the sides of her cheeks.

"And what image would you rather have?" he asked.

"I don't know, but I was thinking it could start with you holding me naked in your arms as we slept," she replied.

Anthony wasn't expecting that for an answer. He believed that Sandra still had feelings for him, but he didn't think that they were of the romantic kind.

"I guess you just gave me plenty of incentive to come back home tonight," he told her as he walked over to her and gave her a kiss on the lips for the first time in years. God, how he loved the taste of her lips, especially when there was the hint of wine on her tongue when he kissed her.

Anthony went over to the window, opened it, and took one short look down. Tonight he couldn't waste any time thinking about how he was going to get down the pole. This was the real thing, and he couldn't waste time worrying about breaking his neck. He bent down and threw the bag with the dry towel in it out the window for later. He then went over to the bed and started to get changed into his black jeans and black leather jacket with his black army boots. When he was done, he walked over to the bed and kissed Kimberly one more time, and then went over to Sandra. This time, he kissed her on the head and told her, "for good thoughts" and then proceeded to climb out the window.

♣   ♣   ♣

"As boring as that was for you to sit here and listen, you now know my life story. Now what's your deal?" Anita asked.

"My deal, what do you mean?"

"As I sat here and talked your ears off for the last two hours I couldn't help but think that you don't seem to belong here at this school. Don't get me wrong, I'm not passing judgment on you, but when I first came to this school, it didn't seem like the kind of place that a lot of the city kids would go to even if they were accepted and could afford it. There are plenty of schools there in the city or just outside of it, including St. John's, NYU and Syracuse. Why did you pick Cornell? It doesn't seem to be the place for you."

Nicholas sat back for a second and thought to himself that she was definitely much smarter than he was. He wasn't going to blow her away in an intellectual conversation, nor was it going to be easy to use his regular charm on her. She was much too good for that. It only took him two hours, but he started to realize that even if he wanted to date this girl after tonight, she was way out of his league.

"What are you trying to say? I don't look like the nerdy Ivy League type? Come on, why wouldn't I want to come to a jumping place like this?" he asked with a laugh.

"I thought you were going to be honest with me tonight, Nicholas," she said.

"You are right, I am not the Ivy League type. I didn't want to come here, but my father forced me. Are you happy now? You're not the only kid that has parents that force the way they live their lives you know."

"Good, we have something else in common."

"My father graduated from here and ever since I was born, my life and schooling were structured around me getting here. That's why I am surprised you don't know me. I was the star quarterback from St. Joseph's, and I led our team to the City Catholic Championship game my junior and senior year and now Cornell expects me to win the Ivy League title this year."

"I'm sorry, but I didn't follow sports at all in school. You could say I was the book worm type."

"Unfortunately, I didn't get here because of my grades. But when I graduate, my dad hopes that the Dallas Cowboys draft me. Well, that's been his dream for me my whole life, but it's not mine. I never gave it any thought considering he did all my planning for me. My only concern is graduating from this place," he told her.

"My God, why wouldn't you want to be a NFL quarterback? That would be the greatest. The fame, money and traveling, plus all the hot women I know you wouldn't mind meeting, that would be an incredible career choice," she said with an envious smile.

Nicholas couldn't believe how that story came so easily to him. Once he started it, the rest just came naturally to him. He wasn't a good liar or storyteller, but there was something in Anita's eyes that made it seem so easy to tell.

"That's easy for you to say, but do you know what it is like to live your life by your parents' demands and wishes ever since you were in grad school? Where you went, what you did, who your friends were and what schools you went to? I can tell you this, it was no joy."

But he already knew what Anita's response was going to be because if her father was the crime boss that everyone believed him to be, then she knew exactly what it would have been like even though Nicholas's life was nothing like what he had just explained. He had the typical set of parents who were mainly concerned that he stayed away from the lore of the streets, finished college and got married one day to start a family of his own, but Anita didn't need to know that right now.

"Ready to get this show started?" Anthony asked Kevin as he sat down in the passenger seat. They were both dressed all in black, but Kevin looked the part much more convincingly than Anthony. Kevin could be the poster child for a professional mugger.

"I don't know if ready is the right choice of words, but I'm willing to go through with it, so let's get this over with," Kevin replied.

"If it makes any difference to you, Frankie didn't show up at the viewing or my parents' house and that's not something that he would have done unless there was a problem. Don't get your hopes up just yet, but maybe he already got the word that Bull didn't arrive back from Vegas and he was back at *The Club* making new arrangements. It's all a guess, but even if that's not the case I still think it's a good sign."

"Well maybe it is and maybe it isn't, but I need more than a few signs to get my nerves under control," he said as he patted the brown bag sitting on the seat between him and Anthony that contained the 9mm.

"You sure you still want to do this, Kevin?"

As Kevin drove them to their fate, he thought about it again before he answered Anthony's question. "I guess it really doesn't matter what I think now, I guess it only matters what I am willing to do later on when I am confronted with the task that is in front of me," he replied.

Teddy was in place on top of the roof while Jeff was getting in place on the ground, heading to the same doorway that he stood in last night.

"Can you hear me ok down there?" Teddy asked into his headset.

"Yeah, I read you loud and clear big boy," he radioed back.

"Listen, I don't want you to move from the doorway unless I give you the go. I want to be sure of what's going on before you jump out at start shooting up the place," he ordered.

"Don't worry about me, just make sure you have my back the whole time. If I don't get out of this alley because you didn't react in time, I am never going to forgive you for that."

"Jeff, I don't think it is going to matter to you if that happens, now will it?" Teddy asked.

"Good point, I guess it wouldn't," Jeff answered.

"How much longer before these guys get here anyway?" he asked Teddy.

"It's hard to say, but then again we are here a little earlier than normal. Now keep focus and look down your end of the alley. Make sure no one is trying to sneak down from the rooftop behind you," he barked into the headset.

"Chill out big boy and stop treating me like a fucking kid. I got my end under control, so stop sweating me," Jeff answered back.

"Shut up for a second Jeff, someone is coming down the alley." Jeff peeked out of the doorway, but it was too dark and he was too far back to be able to see who was coming down the alley.

Teddy had Kevin in his scope from the moment that he entered the alley. He still couldn't make out the face but he was very sure that he didn't recognize him. After this stranger showed up last night, Teddy made some phone calls and asked around the streets to see if anyone had heard of a big man that might be in town on a job. But, all the reports came back negative and Teddy assumed that this guy had to be an amateur looking to score on a big heist, even though he didn't have a prayer in the world of pulling it off. And even if he did, he would regret it for the rest of his short-lived life once the word got on the street that he had just stolen from Frankie Feliciani and Pete Ferrigno. This would surely be the last job that this punk would ever attempt.

"He's heading toward the dumpster again. Can you see him?" he asked Jeff.

"Shit, I can't see anything. What's he wearing? I can't pick him up yet."

"He's in all black and he is one big S.O.B. He's about to reach the dumpster," Teddy answered.

"I still can't…wait a second, I got him. He's crouching down behind the dumpster in front of me. Can you still see him from up there?"

"No, I lost him once he went behind the dumpster. Do you have him in your line?" Teddy asked.

"Yep, he's in perfect view."

"Good, just let me know if you lose him or not," Teddy responded.

"Don't worry about that, our friend here isn't getting out of my view."

After Kevin got out of the car and went down the alley, Anthony noticed a parking space across the street just outside the view of the alley and decided that would be as good a place as any to park and wait for Kevin. He turned the car around and backed into the spot so that he was facing the alley and would be able to see when both cars arrived without having to stare into his rear view mirror. But more importantly, he would be able to see Dan's car leave and he figured that Kevin should be right behind him three or four minutes later.

Christ, he didn't know if it was fear or excitement that was taking him over, but the feeling was overwhelming. There were the high and low feelings when he gambled, and he had believed that there wasn't a drug out there that could make him feel any better than the action during a game. However, sitting here in the car alone without being able to watch what was happening in the alley was the worst torture he could imagine going through.

There were a couple of times that he had placed huge bets on games and had been unable to watch or listen to what was happening because he was out with Sandra. And that was a living hell for him because the ending was always the same. They would come home from wherever it was and Sandra would be pissed at him because Anthony wasn't the greatest of company during their evening. If they went to a movie or to dinner it didn't matter, because he wouldn't pay attention to her or the movie. He was in his own world wondering if his team was winning or losing and nothing else mattered to him.

But tonight, sitting in his car waiting and wondering about the possible outcomes, was more terrifying than anything he could envision. Anthony didn't have a contingency plan in place if Kevin didn't make it out of the alley. His only concern was getting him and Tami out of the city and never looking back even if it meant not seeing his parents' bodies laid to rest. That would be a pain that Anthony would have to live with the rest of his life, and at this point he had no other option.

Kevin didn't know what was worse: being the hunter or the hunted. He thought, at least if he was the hunted he would know it and could prepare himself for a confrontation. But as the hunter, staying still in his hiding place behind the dumpster, he couldn't control his excitement. The anticipation of the attack was killing him. He just wished that the two cars would get here and make their delivery so he could get this over with, but they couldn't get here quickly enough for him. Kevin hadn't felt like this since the day his parents' killer was set free because of a technicality and he stood there helpless in the courtroom. This time, he wasn't going to stand there helpless; this time he was going to make a stand for his and Anthony's parents.

Kevin had put the gun in between his pants and his back underneath his jacket. He held the crow bar in his left hand and the ski mask in his right. He didn't want to put it on too early, because it made him too hot and itchy. Plus, it reduced his vision and hearing and he wanted to make damn sure that he heard and saw everything that was happening in front of him.

It seemed like a life time to Kevin, but in reality it had only been four minutes since he crouched down behind the dumpster. Kevin noticed the first pair of headlights appear in the alley, however it was only a few seconds before the car backed out of the alley and onto the street again. Kevin's heart almost exploded; he couldn't take much more anticipation. Just when he thought he was going to go insane, he saw a different set of lights head into the alley. These lights were red—brake lights of a car. It backed into the alley until it was two feet from the dumpster.

Unfortunately for Kevin, the car parked directly in front of the dumpster and he could not see inside. He didn't know if it was Dan or Frankie's guys. He had to just sit and wait until the second car arrived. Once it parked on the other side of the alley, Kevin would be able to get a clear look.

"Jeff, Dan's car just pulled up next to the dumpster, do you still have our guy in view down there?"

"Yeah, he is still crouched down next to the dumpster. He has some kind of pole in his one hand, some kind of towel or cloth in the other. I can't make it out in the dark," he answered.

"Do you think it's a gun?"

"Nah, I would be able to see a reflection coming off it if it was a gun or some other weapon. I'm pretty sure it's a black cloth of some kind," he replied.

"Just let me know when he makes a move. I have the car in perfect view and it's just Dan in the back and two guys in the front. They look like they are on the up and up. Frankie's boys should be arriving any minute now. Just hold your position until I give the go or our stranger makes a move," Teddy told Jeff.

"I ain't moving until whatever is supposed to go down, does," he replied.

It wasn't until Anthony noticed Victor's car pull in minutes after Dan's car that he became nervous. He opened the driver's door and puked up his dinner. He didn't understand why his nerves were so out of control, considering all his poker playing and gambling experience. He guessed that this time there was too much on the line, and it wasn't just his head, but that of Kevin, Tami, Sandra and Kimberly.

When he was done, he wiped his mouth with his sleeve, closed the door and focused on the alley again. It should only be about five or ten minutes before Dan's car would be coming out of the alley, and then hopefully another five or six minutes and Kevin should follow. Anthony prayed that Father John was right and that if he believed; he would still see his parents someday. If things didn't go well tonight; he was going to get that chance.

Kevin was a little more in control of his nerves than Anthony, but he also had a gun and if things went wrong, he would at least have the opportunity to shoot his way out of the alley. It wasn't until Victor pulled his car up next to Dan's that his nerves got just as bad as Anthony's. He saw the headlights the whole time, but Kevin didn't see the front of the car until it was too late. The car pulled up a little further than he was expecting, and now the driver had a good view of Kevin behind the dumpster. Luckily for Kevin, the driver was only interested in keeping his eyes on the other car and never looked over to see if anyone was hiding behind the dumpster.

Without even hesitating, Kevin forced himself backwards as fast and as hard as he could. There was a loud thud as Kevin's head bounced off the wall. He had never had the chance to see just how close to the wall he was. He heard himself yell, but he didn't know if he did it out loud or just in his head. Kevin could only pray that it was in his head and that no one had heard him. Everything in his vision was going black and he could feel himself falling into a faint. He tried to sit upright against the wall to get some fresh air, but it wasn't working. Unless he stood up, he wasn't going to stay conscience much longer.

"Jeff, there are only three people in Frankie's car. There should be four, and the one that's missing is our target. Can you tell if the guy in front of you is Bull?" Teddy asked.

"No, I don't think it is, but get a load of this: when the second car pulled up, I guess our guy thought he was in the driver's view because he jumped back fast and I could hear his head hit the wall. He is sitting there with his back to the wall and hasn't moved for the last couple of minutes."

"Be extra careful. If it is Bull, he might have known that you were there and is playing hurt to decoy you. Don't take your eyes off him," Teddy answered. But Jeff wasn't going to need to worry about him, because Kevin was unconscious.

Dan could see from the back seat when Victor pulled up next to them that there were only three people in the car, and Bull was missing. During the many drop offs and pick ups over the last year or so, Bull was the only person involved in the transactions.

"Where's Bull?" he asked Victor as he was rolling down the driver's window.

"Your guess is as good as ours. He was in Vegas picking up Frankie's World Series winnings and we couldn't find him at the airport. That's why we are running behind. Have you been waiting long?"

"Not too long, maybe five or ten minutes, no big deal. So what's the scoop? Rumor on the street is that he did those two old folks the other day. You don't think that's true and he's skipping town with Frankie's money, do you?" Dan asked.

"Look, I'm only driving the fucking car, they don't pay me to think. If he is on the run, he'd better not still be in Vegas because once Frankie makes the call, he wouldn't last another two hours out there."

As Dan flicked the cigarette he was smoking to the ground, he looked into the back of Victor's car to make sure no one was planning to do something funny. The word was already out on the street about Bull. Dan knew that Frankie was aware of Pete's anger and that Pete might have planned on using Dan's meeting for a hit. Aware that Frankie might have already considered this,

Dan was ready for an ambush. But as he looked at Rossi in the back and then at Carmine and Victor in the front, he believed this was going to go as planned.

Carmine tried to get out of the passenger's front door to go take the bag from Dan, but between his inexperience with driving down the alley and how dark it was, Victor had parked the car too close to the wall and Carmine couldn't get out of the car.

"You dumb fuck, you got me boxed in against the wall and I can't open the door," he yelled at Victor.

"What do you want me to do about it?"

"You can start by getting your ass out of the car and getting the money from Dan," Carmine told him.

As the two of them were bitching back and forth to each other, Dan reached into his car and took out the bag of money.

"Hey, I want you guys to have your hands close to your guns, something doesn't seem right about this. It just dawned on me that Al isn't driving and Victor never mentioned that to me."

When Dan turned around, Victor was standing outside of the driver's door.

"I just realized, where's Al tonight?" he asked Victor.

"Frankie wanted him to stay back at *The Club* because of all the shit that has been going down lately. He's got Charlie, Al, and Vincent all back at *The Club* making calls and answering the phones. Frankie believes something might happen tonight and Bull not showing up just added to his concerns. However, I just think that Bull is stuck at the airport because of all the new security measures since 9/11. Who knows, we might have walked past the dumb bastard and not even realized it."

"I guess it's no concern of mine, since I am the one handing money over to you tonight and not the other way around, but if I was you, I would watch my back. The word is already out that Pete is not a happy camper and you are far too familiar with how he can be when he ain't happy," he told Victor.

"Yeah thanks, I'll keep that in mind," he replied as he took the bag from Dan.

"I guess our business is done here tonight, but take my advice and watch your backs when you leave here," he told Victor as he got back into his car.

Once he was in the car, Dan's driver pulled away and Dan turned around to give one quick wave to Victor. Little did he know that this would be the last time that he would make a drop off or a pick up with any of Frankie's men.

"Bull isn't there, the driver is making the pick up with Dan," Teddy spoke into his headset. "If this was a set up by Frankie, it must have been called off because the other car is pulling away. So we can rule out a double cross against us and Dan, but I still want you to stay put and wait to see what that other guy is up to," he told Jeff.

"It just doesn't make sense that this dumb ass would be here as a pure coincidence. I'm telling you he hasn't moved the whole time. Wait a second, he's starting to make some movement but he's going really slow. I swear to God, this jackass knocked himself out when he hit the wall. I can tell by how he's moving now," Jeff answered back.

"Well stay put until he tries something," he told Jeff.

Kevin started to regain conscience when he heard the engine start and the car pull away, but he had no idea as to how long he was out or if anyone had noticed him there. He wasn't even quite sure where he was at first, but once he felt the crow bar in his hand and smelled the nearby dumpster, it all started to come back to him.

He looked around and saw the ski mask on the ground next to him, and he finally remembered what it was that he was in the alley to do. As he pulled the mask over his head, he could feel the dampness on the back of the mask. At first he didn't know why it was so wet, but after he touched it with his fingers, the pain shot to the spot on his head that connected with the wall and he realized that he had split the back of his head open.

His legs wouldn't support him as he tried to get up and he swayed backwards and fell on his ass. Kevin was now concerned with the fact that he had lost a lot of blood. Even if he could get up on his feet, he wondered if he was going to be able to break the window and remain steady enough to fire the gun accurately. And then there was the other issue of remaining conscience.

On his second attempt to get to his feet, Kevin used the dumpster to pull himself up. Between the sudden move and the heat being generated from wearing the ski mask, Kevin leaned forward and threw up not once, but twice. Once again Kevin got lucky, because Victor had all the windows rolled up and never heard or saw him. If any one of them had a window cracked to smoke a cigarette, Kevin would have been heard and that would have been the end for him.

As he leaned over, he started to get his legs back under him. He started to straighten himself up, and suddenly the world rushed back into him. He could feel his strength return and his confidence started to build. He took two deep breaths and clutched the crow bar in his hand as tight as he could, because it was now or never.

"He's moving," Jeff yelled into his headset not caring how loud he was.

"I know, I can see him, don't move but keep your gun on him just in case," Teddy answered. "I want to see what the hell he is up to before I take him out."

"What do you want to do now?" Nicholas asked Anita.

"I don't know. Are you sure I haven't bored you enough? You're not obligated any longer because we went Dutch on the bill," she replied.

"I can't believe you are still this negative about yourself. If I didn't want to hang out with you, I would tell you that I had to go back to my dorm and study for my history test on Monday or that I had to write an e-mail to my girlfriend, but I didn't. I asked if you want to do something and go hang out," he replied.

"I'm sorry, I can't help it. Ok, if you aren't bored with me, then yes I would love to hang out. What do you have in mind?" Anita asked.

"Unfortunately, we can't go back to my dorm because my roommate gave me strict instructions not to come home early tonight. His girlfriend took the train in from Indiana today and they are spending quality time together. I told the cheap shit that if he really loved her, he would have taken her to a hotel for the weekend, but you know how these Ivy League guys are. Always saving money when they can," he told her.

Anita couldn't believe what she was about to do, but she never felt this sure about anything in her life. "We can go back to my dorm room if you want. My roommate Christie is more than likely still at the party, and she'll pass out somewhere and never make it home. She is one crazy girl from West Virginia."

"As great as that offer sounds, I must decline. No offense, but I like what we have going here and I would hate like hell to ruin it by going back to your room and having you think that you owe me for this evening. But I do have a better idea. Since it isn't that cold out, how about I walk you back to your dorm and you get a nice warm blanket for us. I will drive us someplace nice where we can continue to talk and see if we can't stay awake long enough to watch the sun rise," he said.

Anita reached over and touched his hand. She couldn't believe that this was happening to her. Nicholas seemed too good to be true, but she didn't care because she had never watched a sunrise before and there was no place else that she would rather be at this moment.

Once they got back, Anita raced around her room looking for a blanket to bring while Nicholas stayed downstairs by the elevator because guys weren't allowed past the first floor in the girls' dorms. She found a blanket that they could use, and was about to head out the door when she decided that she should make a few changes to her outfit. She went into her closet and took out her heavy sweatshirt and most comfortable pair of blue jeans.

As she was about to put on the jeans, she decided at the last second that maybe she was willing to take that last leap into adulthood. She went over to her underwear drawer and found the nicest and newest pair that she owned. They weren't anything to write home about considering what the other girls here probably had in their drawers, but she had never expected to have a sexual encounter right away either.

Anita took one last look around the room to see if she had missed something, but she couldn't think straight because she had never been this excited before. She reached over to turn off the light and noticed her answering machine was blinking the number five. Anita believed that at least four of the calls were from her mother and the other might be her father again. If she took the time now to call them, it wouldn't be a quick conversation. She didn't need her mother ruining this moment for her by lecturing her for a half an hour. She would just call them when she got back in the morning. What was so important that it couldn't wait until the morning, she thought?

Kevin peeked around the dumpster and saw that the driver and the front passenger were looking down at whatever they were doing in the car. He couldn't see if anybody was in the back seat, but by the time he got to the car it would be too late for them to react anyway. Kevin took one last deep breath, counted to ten and then raced over to the car.

Victor never saw him coming and didn't react until after the glass had hit him in the face. Rossi, on the other hand, had caught a quick glimpse of Kevin as he was swinging the crow bar. His natural instinct took over and he took cover by ducking his head behind the seat.

There was a loud crash as the glass shattered everywhere. Both Victor and Carmine were cut in the face and Victor took a lot of the glass in his eyes. He couldn't see Kevin standing in front of him.

"What the fuck was that?" he screamed, his eyes on fire with excruciating pain from the glass.

"Was it a shot?" Carmine asked, as he started to put as much of the money back in the bag as he could.

Anthony was right; there was total chaos in the car after Kevin smashed the window.

"Give me the fucking money, you douche bags," the man in black yelled as he pointed his 9mm at them.

"You must be out of your fucking mind buddy," Carmine told him as he continued to put the money back in the bag. "Do you have any fucking idea who the fuck we are, you asshole?"

Just before Kevin could yell at them again, Rossi made the fatal move of getting out of the car with his gun drawn.

"How about you choke on this, you stupid son of a bitch," Rossi said as he tried to aim at Kevin. But his reaction time was too slow and Kevin put his first shot in Rossi's gun arm and the second one into his right leg.

Rossi screamed in horror as he flew back into the side of the car, then hit the ground where he continued to roll around in pain.

"I'm not going to say it again you fucking douche bags, now give me the fucking money or I am going to shoot someone else," he demanded.

Victor turned towards the direction of Carmine, "I can't see him and it sounded like he shot Rossi, just give him the fucking money, my eyes are killing me and we got to get Rossi and me to a hospital."

"Fuck you and fuck him, I ain't going back to Frankie without this money," he replied as he tried to get out of the car and confront Kevin. Unfortunately, he had forgotten that Victor had parked too close to the wall and he was trapped in his seat.

Kevin saw that Carmine was about to turn and open fire on him. His instinct kicked in again and he fired into the car through the broken windshield. But unlike the first two shots that he had fired at Rossi, this one hit Carmine in the chest and was a fatal hit. Carmine flew back into his seat and then slumped forward until his head hit the dashboard. His body fell off the seat and onto the floor, where he took his last breath and died in a pool of his own blood.

Victor could only cry out to Carmine after he heard the shot. "Carmine? Carmine, you ok? Are you hit?" he screamed. Even though he couldn't see him, he already knew the answer.

This time Kevin was standing right at Victor's door, "Douche bag, give me the fucking money or I'll give you more to worry about than just your fucking eyes," Kevin said to him as he leaned into the car.

Victor couldn't see Kevin or the bag, but he fumbled around the front seat and got his hands on the handle of the bag and pulled it close to him. "Here, take it you fucking asshole, but remember this, you are a dead man. You hear me, you are a fucking dead man."

"I guess we will just have to see about that now, won't we? No pun intended," Kevin replied as he took the bag and started to run down the alley.

♣   ♣   ♣

"Why didn't you fire?" Jeff screamed into the headset. "He's getting away."

"He's not our problem. How the hell do you know that Pete didn't set this up? You want to take out one of Pete's men and get us both killed? Fuck that! I'll call Frankie and let him know he's got to get his ass down here now because the way I figure it, he has only twenty minutes or less before the cops arrive. Someone was bound to have heard those shots."

"Well, what the hell do you want to do now?" Jeff asked.

"Head back to the car and I'll be right down. I'm going to call Frankie and let him know that he's got a big problem."

♣   ♣   ♣

Frankie stared at the phone as it rung. Was this the first of many troublesome phone calls of the night? Or could he get lucky? Would it be Anita telling him that she just got his message because she had been out meeting new friends for a change? But, he wasn't a fool; he knew that on this night there were only going to be upsetting calls.

"This is Frankie," he answered.

"Frankie its Teddy, would you like to tell me what happened tonight?"

"Bull never showed at the airport and I am working on finding out where the fuck he is. I didn't call you because you would have thought that something was going down. Just in case Pete or someone else had made other arrangements, I didn't want you thinking I was collaborating with them," he replied.

"Well unless you were trying to take out more of your own men, I don't think you have to worry about me thinking that."

Frankie hesitated for a second before he answered. "What do you mean by that?" he asked.

"Even though Bull was a no show, Jeff and I stayed around to see if it was a double cross or not. I was on the roof and Jeff was on the ground in the back part of the alley, and we witnessed your guys getting shot up by a single gunman in a ski mask after Dan's car left the alley."

"You mean to tell me that you thought I was going to set you up with just one man?" Frankie asked.

"How the hell should I know what your intentions were tonight? But anyway, the guy was hiding behind the dumpster and before you ask why I didn't get involved, I just want you to know that if he was sent by Pete, than Jeff and I would be dead men for getting involved. So, my hands were tied on this one. However, I do suggest you getting down here and getting your men out before the cops arrive or they'll be answering a lot of questions once they are patched up. They haven't moved yet and it's been over five minutes. I counted at least three shots, but I can't tell who all was hit."

Frankie was aware that the shit was going to hit the fan tonight, but this was getting out of hand and he had no idea how much worse it could get. "By any chance did you get a good look at the guy? Did he look familiar to you?"

"What I am about to tell you might not help matters, but I am going to say it anyway. Even though I couldn't make out his face, I could tell that he was a very big man. But, his physical description isn't as important as what he said. I couldn't make out everything that was being said down there, but I caught a couple of the words that he said and I thought they might be familiar to you. He repeated the words douche bag at least three times. Does that ring any bells for you?" Teddy asked, already knowing that Bull was famous for saying those words over and over again. It was his calling card.

Frankie was wrong, his night had gotten much worse and now he realized that his empire was crumbling down around him. Not only did Bull have the audacity to steal his Vegas winnings, but he came home to collect the rest of the money and to seek his own sick justice before leaving for good.

"Teddy, are you sure that's what you heard?" Frankie asked, but he didn't know why. He was only insulting Teddy by asking this ridiculous question.

"Do I really need to answer that or are you going to get your ass moving and take care of your wounded men down here?"

"I'll never get down there in time. Do you think you and Jeff can take them to the address of a doctor I know and I'll meet you there?" he asked.

"Last time I checked, Jeff and I aren't running an ambulance service. What if it wasn't your boy Bull, but someone from Pete's organization? I don't want to get any more involved than I already am. I still have to make a living as a cleaner in this city, and I don't want to jeopardize everything by interfering with whatever shit is going down," Teddy replied.

"Teddy, I am asking you as a favor to me and my men. If the cops pick them up, they are good as dead anyway. Please just get them out of there and take them to 511 West Street, Apartment 311. I will call and let them know you are bringing in three men, all of who might have gun wounds. And if you do this for me, I will double what I was giving you for the hit. It's your call. It could be a hell of a payday for you considering you didn't have to kill anyone."

"If I do this and my name is mentioned, I don't have to make any open threats to you Frankie. Because all I have to say is that you will be in the ground a lot sooner than I will if the heat comes down on me."

Teddy hung up the phone and never spoke to Frankie again. However, three days later he received an envelope in the glove compartment of his car containing his earnings for taking care of Frankie's men.

Anthony raced out of the parking space after he heard the first two gunshots. It was loud, but on a cold November night like tonight, most people would have their windows closed and might not have heard them. Anthony only heard it because he had the car windows down to let the cold air in and keep him alert. He stopped just short of the alley entrance and waited for Kevin to appear out of the darkness, but instead of seeing Kevin he heard a third shot fired.

In his mind he started to calculate what that could mean. Kevin was only supposed to shoot the driver and maybe the guy in the back seat, so why did this third shot come so late? He started to hyperventilate after he concluded that one of Frankie's men must have shot Kevin. He was aware that his crazy plan might not work, but he wasn't prepared for the consequences. What the hell was he going to say to Tami? There were no words possible that he could say to her to ease the pain.

"Go, go, go, get us the fuck out of here," Kevin yelled as he jumped in the car.

Anthony looked at Kevin in between shifting as he took off. "Son of a bitch, you scared the fucking shit out of me. What the hell happened back there? I heard the first two shots and I pulled the car around. Then I heard a third shot and I thought that one of them got a shot off at you."

"No, whoever was in the passenger seat tried to shoot me, but I got my shot off first and I think he's dead. He slumped forward and wasn't moving when I left. I shot the guy in the backseat in the arm and leg, and he was still on the ground crying and screaming in agony. It looked like the driver was bleeding from his eyes. I guess the glass from the windshield got into them and cut him because he couldn't see me or the bag of money. After I took the money, I just ran the hell out of there. Now floor it and let's get going," he demanded.

"Do you think they thought you might be Bull or was it total chaos back there?"

"I don't think they know what the hell hit them, but I did keep saying douche bag over and over. At this point, one guy has two bullets in him, one might be dead and the third can't see. I don't think we have to worry about the witnesses," Kevin answered.

When Kevin took off his ski mask, Anthony noticed the blood throughout his hair.

"What's the blood from?" Anthony asked.

"I stupidly fell back against the wall of the alley and whacked my head pretty good. I think I lost a lot of blood," he answered.

"Do you want me to take you to the E.R.?"

"No, just get back to the house and we'll take a look at it then. If you think I need stitches, I'll take myself there. You need to get back to the house and mingle with whatever people are still there," Kevin replied.

"Are you sure? Christ Kevin, you look like shit," Anthony said.

"Well how the hell would you look after shooting two people and blinding a third?" he responded.

"Good point, I'm sorry for being inconsiderate."

"Don't start getting all emotional on me Anthony, you fucking wuss."

The rest of the car ride they rode in silence. Kevin passed out from either the amount of blood he lost or the emotional stress that he had just put himself through. Either way, Anthony wasn't going to wake him until they got back to his parents' house.

They made great time and Anthony believed that if he could get up the drain pipe quickly, he might still be able to see a few people that were still mingling at the house. He was even going to try to make an appearance or two outside on the front porch as people left, just in case any of Frankie's boys were still scoping the house from the streets or if one or two of them were still inside his house.

"Come on, be honest, when was the last time you used this trick on a girl?" Anita asked Nicholas as they snuggled under the blanket in the front seat and talked.

"Trick? I don't have the slightest idea what you are talking about. What do you mean by trick? We are just sitting here, talking and having a nice time. I didn't even bring any alcohol to get you drunk, so obviously you are mistaken," he replied.

"Oh, you would need alcohol and not just your good looks to seduce me?" she asked, laughing.

"Listen, I don't know what kind of guy you think I am, but one day when I was out riding my mountain bike I passed by this place, and I thought it might be nice to watch either the sunset or sunrise with someone who might appreciate it as much as I would. That's why I brought you here. You seem to be the kind of girl who enjoys the simple little pleasures in life, so I asked you if you wanted to come here. Now get your mind out of the gutter and let's get back to my questions," he responded.

Anita put her head back on Nicholas's chest and smiled to herself. She was never as grateful to anyone as she was to Christie right now for having that talk with her last night. Two days ago, Anita would never have had the courage to talk to a strange boy, let alone sit in a parked car with him in the middle of a field, waiting for the sun to come up. This was truly turning out to be the greatest night of her life. But she was unaware that in less than twelve hours, her whole world was going to be turned upside down.

♣   ♣   ♣

Frankie and Vincent arrived at the address he gave Teddy forty minutes after they got off the phone. He left Al and Charlie back at *The Club* and told them to be on the look out for anything. Tonight was going bad, and Frankie wanted them to know that he believed it was only going to get worse.

Jeff greeted Frankie as he walked in the front door. "Listen, your boy Rossi was shot twice, once in the arm and once in the leg, neither wound is life threatening. The doctor said he can patch him up without any complications, and he would be fine staying here recuperating for the next couple of days."

"How's Victor?"

"Victor, on the other hand, needs to go to a regular hospital because he needs a specialist to look at his eyes. There are little fragments of glass that they could find a lot easier than this guy, and since he wasn't shot the hospital wouldn't have a problem with the answers Victor would give them about what happened. And now for the bad news: Carmine was shot one time in the chest and he didn't pull through. He was dead when I got to the car. Sorry to have to tell you about that."

"Did you leave him there?" Frankie asked.

"No, I took their car and drove it to an abandoned lot and we put Carmine in the trunk of Teddy's BMW. What do you take us for, a bunch of amateurs? Why would we leave the body? And second, we weren't prepared for this little problem of yours and his body is bleeding all over the trunk of Teddy's car. You can take Teddy's car and dispose of his body however you see fit and once you are done, take his Beamer to a professional that you can trust and have the trunk cleaned out and looking like it did when he bought it," he told Frankie.

"That won't be a problem. Vincent here will take care of that as soon as we leave here. You can take my car back to *The Club* and either Al or Charlie will take you home and I'll return Teddy's Beamer no later than Monday," he responded as he handed Jeff the keys.

"What about our payment?"

"Your payment will be in the glove compartment of the car when Teddy gets it back. If he has a problem with that, he can come back down to *The Club* and discuss it. Now if you don't mind, I need to go talk to my men," he responded as he headed to the back room where the doctor was working on Rossi and Victor.

"It might not seem like it, but Frankie is grateful to you and your brother. You can understand that he has been under a lot of pressure lately and there is a bunch of shit going down tonight that has him too preoccupied for conversation," Vincent informed Jeff.

"Yeah, Teddy let me in on what was happening. You think you guys are leaving town or are you going to confront Pete about all of this?" Jeff asked.

"Right now the only thing I am concerned about is getting Carmine's body to a funeral parlor so his wife can have him buried in a dignified way. Now if you don't mind, please take me to the car," Vincent told Jeff.

❧   ❧   ❧

"Yo Kev, we're here. Wake up. You are right?" Anthony asked as he shook Kevin back and forth.

"Yeah, I'm fine. I'm just so tired and light headed," he answered.

"Do you want me to take you to the hospital?"

"No, you got to get in there and make an appearance. I should be fine, really, don't worry about it. I'll just take myself to the ER and get some stitches. It's only a ten-minute ride and I'll drive with the windows open. Really, I'll be fine. Just get your ass up the drainpipe and get back to your family. I'll see you at Mass tomorrow," he answered.

"Ok, if you are sure that you can make it, then I'm out of here. I already split up the money and I left your cut in the trunk. Once again, I can't thank you enough for going through with this, but don't think that we are out of the woods just yet, it all depends on how Frankie will react to what happened tonight. Now go get that head of yours looked at and don't forget to call the house once you get home."

Anthony opened the driver's door and got out and Kevin slid over to take his place behind the wheel. Anthony closed the door and gave one last wave to Kevin before he turned around to race back to his house.

Anthony was surprised at what adrenaline can do to one's mind and body because it didn't take him more than ten minutes to make it up the drainpipe and back into his bedroom, even with the added weight from the bag of money that he had strapped to his back. The first thing that Anthony saw when he hit the floor was Sandra sitting in his old rocking chair with a blanket wrapped around her as she slept. He walked over to her and picked her up and laid her in bed next to Kimberly, who didn't appear to have moved from the spot that he had put her in before he left. He was happy that both of them were able to fall asleep in this strange room without a problem considering what he had put them through.

Anthony stared at the both of them while they slept and he changed back into his suit. When he was finished getting dressed, he went over to the mirror to fix his hair and tie and made sure that there wasn't any dirt from the pipe on his hands and face. After a quick once over, he was satisfied that everything was in order and he went back over to the girls and gave them both a kiss before he went back downstairs to the remaining guests. If it weren't for him, they would have stayed the night if he didn't announce that it was now time for them to leave.

Frankie was prepared for the worst when he headed into the back room. It wasn't the first time that he had brought one or two of his men here, but the shock was still traumatic as he saw Rossi's near-lifeless body on the table. Rossi was unconscious with tubes sticking out of both arms, an oxygen mask over his face and still wearing his blood-soaked clothes.

"Give me the scoop Doc, how are they?"

Doctor Mike Toresco, who wasn't a certified doctor anymore after his trial, jumped when Frankie spoke to him because he had never heard him come into the room. Mike was an alcoholic, and he looked the part. He looked like he hadn't shaved or showered in days. This was not a man that you wanted to trust with a scalpel in his hand.

"You're a big boy Frankie, so I'm not going to sugar coat this. The one on the table unconscious is in pretty bad shape, but if you leave him here for a couple of days to stabilize he should be able to pull through. Unfortunately, he lost a lot of blood and I don't have the kind of supply that he needs here. I am going to need you to make some calls and get me a couple days worth of supply."

"And Victor?" he asked.

"As for Victor, I cleaned his eyes out the best I could and I gave him some morphine for the pain, but you need to take him to a hospital to have them look at him. If you don't, he might end up blind for life."

Frankie looked at Rossi and was disgusted that this had happened. He vowed that he was going to make sure that whoever this lone gunman in the alley was, he was going to pay for this ambush before Frankie left town.

"Did you have a chance to see what make the slugs were that you pulled out of Rossi?" Frankie asked.

"I don't see how it matters because they did their job, but if you need to know they were your standard 9 mm's," he answered Frankie. And the doctor's response didn't surprise him at all.

"Can I talk to Victor or is he knocked out?" Frankie asked.

"He's in my room lying down, but if you need to talk to him he isn't in a deep sleep," Toresco answered.

Frankie walked past the doctor and went into the bedroom where, to his surprise, he was greeted by the sight of Victor sitting up in bed smoking a cigarette.

"I can't see you boss, but I heard you when you came into the apartment. This was some fucked-up shit. What the hell happened tonight?" he asked Frankie.

"I don't know, that's why I came back to talk to you because I was hoping that you might be able to shed some light on what happened in the alley," Frankie responded.

Victor took another drag from his smoke and laid back down on his pillow as he exhaled.

"All of a sudden it happened out of nowhere. Dan's car had just pulled away no more than two minutes prior. Carmine was counting the money and I was watching to make sure everything was in order and all of a sudden there was a massive crashing sound of glass and then I couldn't see a thing. The next thing I knew someone yelled for us to give them the money and a minute later I heard Craig yell back at him as he opened the door. And then, two shots were fired and I could hear Rossi screaming from the ground."

"You only heard one voice and not two? Are you sure it was just one man?" Frankie asked.

"Yeah, from what I could tell it was just one voice. The guy once again told us to give him the money and I think Carmine tried to get out of the car but I had parked us too close to the wall and he was pinned inside. Then I heard a third shot and the next thing I knew Carmine slumped over and hit the dashboard. I don't know if he tried to shoot the guy from inside the car but if he did, he never got a shot off. After that, the asshole leaned into the car and demanded the money and took it. I swear to God Frankie, there was nothing I could do, I couldn't see a fucking thing," he said as he started to cry in anger.

"What the hell would I have expected you to do Victor? If you did anything stupid I might have three of my men dead instead of just one," he replied.

"One?" he questioned. "Who didn't make it, Carmine or Rossi?"

"Carmine took one in the chest and he died in the car. Rossi is in the other room and the doc here thinks he is going to pull through if I can get some blood here quickly enough for him."

"I can't believe this Frankie, I swear to God, none of us saw it coming. He must have come out from one of the stores or behind that dumpster because he was on us quickly," Victor said.

Frankie went over and sat on the bed next to Victor. "Victor, I need you to listen to me carefully. I know that you are in a lot of pain and good ole doc over there gave you some strong medicine for it, but you have to make an effort to answer these questions the best you can for me," Frankie told him.

"You know I will, Frankie," he replied.

"Is there anything about this guy that you might be able to tell me, what he looked like, what he might have said? And I want you to think hard before you answer."

"Honestly Frankie, I never got a look at him even before I was hit in the face with the glass," he answered.

"What about what he said? Did he say anything to you that might be important?"

"No, not really Frankie, he just demanded the money from us."

"Are you sure there weren't any key words in his demand?" Frankie asked again.

The medicine was fogging up Victor's mind and he couldn't concentrate well enough to think about Frankie's question. "I'm sorry Frankie, I'm not sure what he said..." as he started to fade back into sleep.

Frankie leaned over and lightly slapped Victor in the face. "Victor, stay with me for a second."

Victor shook for a second and then faced the direction where he heard Frankie's voice.

"Yeah, I'm still awake Frankie," he answered groggily.

"If I ask you if you heard these specific words do you think you can remember or not?" Frankie asked as he leaned closer to Victor.

"I'll try Frankie," Victor replied.

"Good, that's what I want to hear from you. Now really concentrate before you answer me. By any chance did you hear this guy say douche bag more than once?" Frankie asked.

Victor didn't even need to answer Frankie because Frankie noticed the way his face changed once Frankie mentioned those words.

"Jesus Christ Frankie, yeah he said it a couple of times. It never dawned on me that he did. You don't think it was Bull, do you?" Victor asked.

"I don't have to think about it anymore, I already know that it was him. Do you think you can get out of bed with my help and make it to the car?" Frankie asked.

"Yeah, I think so, why?"

"Because I'm concerned about your eyes and if I don't get you to a hospital, you are going to go blind. Let's get going, we are running out of time," Frankie answered.

Frankie helped Victor off the bed and they managed to make it into the other room where the doctor was still working on Rossi.

"I need your car keys," he told the doctor.

"They're over there on the kitchen counter. When am I going to get my car back?" he asked.

"Come by *The Club* one day next week when Rossi is doing well enough for you to be able to leave him alone."

"I still need that blood for him. Are you going to get me some?" the doctor asked.

"What type do you need?"

"O negative and as much as you can get," he responded.

"I'll make some calls and hopefully someone will drop off enough for you to get by for the next couple of days."

Frankie picked up the keys from the counter and put them in his coat pocket and replaced them with an envelope.

"This is for your trouble and cooperation with keeping this hush-hush. Unless you hear from me, no one is to know that Rossi is here," he told the doctor as he led Victor out of the room and to the front door.

Anthony was surprised to see that there were still at least twenty people in the house as he walked down the steps. As he combed over the crowd, he noticed at least two of the undercover police officers were still there and doing a good job at mingling with his friends and family. Father John Jordan greeted Anthony as he reached the bottom of the steps.

"How are you holding up, Anthony?" he asked.

"I'm doing the best than can be expected," he responded.

"After all these years, why would you try to play dumb with me Anthony? You know what I am referring to and I wanted to know if you still had intentions of seeking restitution for your parents' deaths."

"I know what you were referring to Father, and I took your advice. I want to see them again but not just yet. However, after tomorrow I am still planning to leave the city and try to make a fresh start in a better place," he answered.

"I noticed that Sandra and Kimberly were here and that you have been upstairs with them for quite awhile. I hope you didn't do anything that you would regret in the after-life Anthony, because you know that she is still a married woman," he explained.

"Father, I have loved you to death ever since you entered my life, but I just lost my parents and I don't need someone to take their place when it comes to telling me how to live my life. Now if you don't mind, I have to start getting these people out of here because it is getting late and I am tired," he said as he excused himself and walked away.

He scanned the room until he saw his Aunt Marian standing next to Tami. On his way over to them, he noticed two younger women sitting on the couch talking. They had had their eyes on him ever since he started to talk to Father John.

"Hi ladies," he said as he kissed Marian and Tami hello. "Would the two of you mind helping me get these people to start leaving? It's getting late and tomorrow is going to be an even longer day."

"Anything for my favorite nephew," Marian replied.

"Great," Anthony responded.

Anthony started to walk away and head to the kitchen to grab himself something to eat, because in all the excitement of the night he had built up quite the appetite and needed a drink to calm his nerves.

"Hey Anthony," Tami called out as he walked away. "Have you seen Kevin tonight? I didn't see him at the viewing nor here yet, have you?" she asked.

"He was outside the funeral home helping the police keep the crowd under control, but that was the last time I saw him," he answered.

Anthony hated to lie to the people that he loved, but some habits are hard to change. This time it hurt more because Kevin had risked his life for Anthony tonight, and Tami had been so helpful all week with the arrangements that he knew she deserved better than that.

"Well if he doesn't show up, I'm stuck here tonight because I don't have a ride home," Tami replied.

"If he doesn't show up, I'll take you home myself after everyone leaves," he promised her and then turned around to get that drink and some food.

As he came out of the kitchen, Anthony saw that some of the people were already making their way out of the house with a little help from his Aunt Marian and Tami, but what caught his eye the most were the two girls who were still sitting on the couch talking. Anthony casually walked over to the couch and sat on the other end away from the girls and started to eat his sandwich. After taking a couple of bites, he put his plate down on the end table, picked up his drink, and then slid across the couch until he was just inches from the first girl.

"How long have you known Frankie?" Anthony asked the brunette in the short black dress.

"I'm sorry, who is Frankie?" she responded.

"Oh come now, you can do better than that. You obviously are too young to be friends of my parents, nor are you any missing relatives that I may not have known about. You are too beautiful to be an undercover cop, which means that the two of you were sent here by Frankie."

She just had to give him a little smile because Frankie had warned the girls that if Anthony's mind was still sharp, even with all that happened to him over the last couple of days, he would still be able to notice them in the house.

"Emily and I have been doing some work here and there for Frankie for only a year or two," June answered him. "My name is June, and I'm sorry that we are here tonight disturbing you in your time of sorrow. Frankie needed to make sure that nothing funny was going down and we did try to stay out of everyone's way the best we could," she explained to him.

"Obviously, Frankie must think that I am some kind of David Copperfield that can be in two places at one time, because in case you haven't notice I have been at my parents' viewing and here trying to entertain my guests as best that I can considering the circumstances. What the hell would he expect me to do anyway? Is he so afraid of me that he doesn't give me the respect or courtesy to show up at either the viewing or the gathering?" he asked.

"That's where you are wrong Anthony, Frankie tried to go to the viewing but between the cops and your family, no outsiders could get in to see them. As for why he didn't show up here, I really can't answer that."

June stood up and tapped Emily on the arm as she excused herself to Anthony. "I'm sorry that we had to be here tonight Anthony, but when Frankie calls and tells us that a job needs to be done we don't have a choice about the matter," she said as she touched Anthony on the shoulder. "Frankie does give you his best and let me say that we to are sorry for your loss and the circumstances surrounding their deaths," June said to him and then proceeded to walk away.

Emily on the other hand just gave him a sympathetic smile and followed June out the door.

Anthony waited a minute and then went to the front door where his Aunt and Tami were saying their goodbyes to the people who were leaving. He walked by the group gathered at the door and went to the front porch to see where the two girls went. Anthony didn't have to look too far as he saw Emily get in the back seat of a black Lincoln that was parked halfway down the street, which drove off as soon as she closed the door. As they passed the front of the house Anthony couldn't make out who was behind the wheel, but he did notice that both the girls were in the back seat, so whoever was driving was also acting as a look out the whole night.

"Please let me know somebody has figured out where the hell Bull is?" Frankie asked as he and walked into the back room of *The Club*. Charlie and Al could only shake their heads no.

"I fucking can't believe this. What the fuck else could possibly happen next?" he asked to no one in particular. "Did Vincent get back yet?"

"No, but he did call and said he took care of that business with Carmine. He didn't say, but I guess Carmine didn't make it?" Al asked.

"No, Carmine died and Rossi is banged up pretty bad and Victor might end up blind for life in his left eye. I just dropped him off at "Our Lady of Lourdes's" E.R. and the doctor told me it was too soon to tell, but it didn't look good. Talk about a mad house on a Friday night. That place is a fucking zoo with all the people in that waiting room trying to get in. Luckily for us there were only three other people in the trauma unit and they took Victor as soon as we got there," he told them.

"Frankie I think it might be best if we call it a night and get the hell out of here. Most of the crew has left or gone into hiding. We have one dead and two badly injured, and I don't think we need to add to those numbers. You said you had a plan to get out so I think the time might be now to use it," Al said.

Frankie walked over to the bar and poured himself one last seven and seven and sat down at the table with Al and Charlie.

"I can't believe it is going to end like this, but I guess you are right. Why don't the two of you leave and I will stay and wait for Vincent to get back, and then we'll leave the same way we opened this place, together," he told them while he downed his drink in one gulp. "You guys up for one last drink together?" he asked.

"Yeah, sure boss, but let me get them," Al said.

Al walked over to the bar and had the honor of pouring the last three drinks that were going to be drunk by Frankie and his crew. The end of an era was upon them, but Frankie really wasn't that upset about it because he wanted out of the business. He wanted to do it on his terms and no one else's, but in this business you rarely ever get what you want.

Al returned with their drinks and the three of them stood up as Frankie made a toast. "To good fellas like us, there is no other way I would have wanted to live my life. *Salude,*" he said as they clanked their glasses together and drank their drinks.

Five minutes later Frankie was alone in his back office, wondering what was going to be his next plan of action. Frankie looked at the clock and saw it was close to one in the morning. Vincent should be getting back in any minute, and he would go over the last little details of what needed to be done before they said their goodbyes for the last time.

Vincent has been in Frankie's life forever and he didn't know how he was going to get by without him. There were the girls of course, and his new life of retirement, but it was the little things that he was going to miss the most- like coming into his office listening to the guys while they played cards, bullshitting about last night's game, making a deal that was going to bring them a good amount of money.

His favorite moments were him and Vincent sitting in his office on a Monday afternoon, eating the lunch that his mother had made just like childhood friends would do, and going over Sunday's football figures, either rejoicing over their winnings or bitching about what team had fucked them on a last second back door cover. Those are the times that he would never have again with his long time friend and no matter what he did from now on, nothing was going to fill that void.

❦   ❦   ❦

It was just past one in the morning when Anthony got back from dropping Tami off. He had never felt as sick with guilt as he did during that ride back to her house. Tami wouldn't leave him alone about where Kevin had disappeared to, and since he was aware that she wasn't naive there was no way he was going to be able to lie to her. Over the last few days the one thing that Anthony admired the most about Tami was how much of a young lady she was turning out to be and how smart she was for her age. And lying to her would only make him look like a jackass.

It was only after the third time she asked that Anthony finally gave in and told her about everything that they had done, and what still could possibly happen to them if the word got back to Frankie of what they did. He ended up informing her that after the funeral tomorrow she was going to have to go to a friend's house until Monday when Kevin thought it was safe for her to come back home. But the worst part of their conversation was when he told her that there was a good chance that Kevin might not make it out of this mess and she might end up having to pack up everything and end up on the road with him. And she didn't take to that idea very well.

"How could you do this to me and Kevin after all we've been through? We are all that each other has in this world, and you jeopardize that. How could you possibly think that I would leave with you if your actions had killed my brother? I'm telling you right now you bastard, God help you if something happens to my brother because I will make it my life's mission to get back at you for it," she told him.

There were no words that came to him to be able to respond to her outburst. She was absolutely right and there was no sense in trying to argue that fact, so they remained silent for the rest of the car ride. When they pulled up to the house, Anthony tried to thank her for everything that she had done for him but before he could say a single word, Tami had gotten out of the car and slammed the door behind her. He waited until she was inside before he left, because he noticed that Kevin's car wasn't in the driveway and he thought that Kevin might still be at the hospital.

When he walked into his old bedroom Sandra was sitting up with her back against the bedpost, waiting for him as she drank a cup of tea.

"Did everything go ok tonight?" she asked.

"I guess. We won't know for certain, but the next three days are going to be the key. If we can make it through the weekend, then we should be alright," he told her.

"Are you still planning on leaving after the funeral tomorrow?"

"That was the plan. No matter what had happened here tonight, I intended on leaving after the funeral because if I don't go right away, I might not ever find the courage to go through with it. If I stayed here, I would only end up dying a slow and meaningless death trapped in this city," he responded.

Sandra had put down her tea on the nightstand and then let the covers fall off of her so Anthony could she that she was naked. "Why don't you come lay down next to me Anthony, and maybe we can talk about your plans."

Anthony could only stand there, frozen in place staring at her bare breasts. It had been such a long time since he had seen her like this and he had forgotten how great of a body she had. There was nothing in the world that he wanted to do more than sleep with her again but Father John was right, if Anthony truly wanted to start a new life he needed to do it now. Sleeping with Sandra would be a step backwards and that's not how he wanted to end his night. He was grateful to God for the first time in a long time that everything went well tonight for him and Kevin, and he didn't want to slap God in the face by breaking one of his Commandments.

Anthony took off his jeans and sweater and was down to just his tee shirt and boxers as he got into bed with Sandra. She gave him a big hug as he got into bed and then tried to kiss him, but Anthony had pulled away.

"What's wrong?" she asked.

"It wouldn't be right Sandra. You are married now, and Kevin and I just did the unthinkable tonight and I really am trying to start my life over again. If we do what I want to do then I would just be a liar to myself and I won't ever change," he said.

Sandra leaned over again, and this time Anthony couldn't move away or he would have fallen off the bed. She kissed him as passionately as she ever had in her life, and then said, "I have never respected you as much I do now, more than I had in the whole time we were together, and you have convinced me that I want Kimberly to be a part of your new life. Chad and I don't belong together and we both know it. After you left the other night he pulled his usual macho act with me, telling me how he was the head of the house and that I was lucky to be with him and he forbid me to help you tonight. Needless to say, I told him otherwise. When that happens, he usually forces me into a sexual act that I have no desire to do to make up for my insubordination. I can't live like that anymore. What if I promise to divorce him, would you allow me back into your life Anthony?" she asked.

Anthony couldn't help but look at her breasts before he looked back up to her eyes. "Sandra I would love to have the two of you back in my life but I don't know where I am going, and I don't have a plan for finding a job, buying a house or living in one place—and that's no way for a child to live. I left you a ton of money for Kimberly. If you want to use it to leave Chad, than I will call the bank Monday morning and give them permission to add you as guardian of the money. And the day that I decide to settle down, I will call you and let you know where I am. If you still want to be with me, then I would love to start being a husband and father again," he told her.

"How long do you think it will take you to finally decide to settle down somewhere?" she asked.

"I really don't know now, but wherever it may be, I will know when I am there. It could be in a little town in Nebraska or Kansas, maybe Arizona, I just don't know. My plan is to get in my car and drive South and West and when I am finally at peace with a place and it feels right being there, then that will be my home and I will get in touch with you," he answered.

"Try not to make it too long, because I don't want Kimberly to be without her father," she replied.

Anthony leaned over and kissed Sandra with the same passion that she did moments before and he let his hands roam over her breasts and then lower, until he was making her feel the way they did when they were first dating. As Sandra pulled him on top of her to help guide him into her, Anthony pulled away and rolled back onto his side.

"How about I just hold you until you fall asleep, and we'll continue this at another time when we'll be living in our own home and sleeping in our bed and not my childhood one," he said as he kissed her lightly on the lips.

"That's sounds beautiful," she replied as she rolled over and then up against him, where she was asleep within minutes. But it took sleep a lot longer to come to Anthony, as he lay in bed awaiting Kevin's call.

Frankie was sitting in his office drinking his third seven and seven of the evening and wondering when Pete's men would come in and end this anticipating hell. He was quite sure that Pete was aware of Bull's absence by now, and it was only a matter of time before two or three of his men would be paying Frankie a visit. He had already left Ellena with instructions as to what to do if he didn't make it home tonight, but he still felt optimistic that he had one more night before Pete would order the hit.

Noticing that it was getting later and Vincent hadn't arrived yet, Frankie needed to hear Ellena's voice for some comfort. It wasn't until about the fourth ring that she answered.

"Hello," the sleepy voice on the other end answered.

"Hi honey, it's me. I'll be home in an hour or two. Are you all ready to go in the morning?"

"For the most part I guess. My car is totally full and the rest of our things are at the front door. What are we going to do with all the furniture, televisions and anything else that can't fit in your car?" she questioned.

"Hon, trust me, we have more than enough money to buy three or four of everything that you are leaving behind. Just pack only the necessities and keepsakes that you can't leave behind, because I don't know yet where we are heading," he told her.

"I did and we still need to fill up your car."

"Alright, I'm not in any mood for arguing. When I get home I'll load my car before I come to bed."

Before he asked Ellena the next question he had to convince himself that he was worrying about nothing, but in this profession over the last five or ten years people hadn't minded going above their laws and committing the unthinkable, just like Bull did three days ago. But that was an isolated incident that was committed without orders, and people who were responsible for those acts were punished in ways that the regular judicial system would never dare to do. However, he was still petrified that neither he nor Ellena had heard from Anita in two days, and the fear of her safety and whereabouts wouldn't leave him.

"Has Anita called back yet?" he asked, knowing that if she did Ellena would have called to let him know since he was very concerned.

"No, not yet," she answered. "I keep getting her answering machine, but sometimes in the past her roommate has picked up to tell me where she is. She hasn't after all the messages that I left tonight, so maybe they are somewhere together. You know you kept encouraging her to meet new friends and get out of that room, so maybe she did just that and they went to a party or something. Please stop worrying, because you are making me sick thinking about her and I know she's just fine," she told him.

"You're right, I am just being an over-protective parent. I'm sure she'll call tomorrow morning when she wakes up. Why don't you go back to bed and I'll be home shortly," he said.

"I still love you Frankie, no matter what happens to us. I still love you," she said.

"I love you too and trust me, nothing is going to happen to anyone in this family," he replied before hanging up the phone.

"Hey sleepy head, are you awake?" Nicholas asked Anita as he looked out his windshield at the sun rising up in front of him. He couldn't believe that he had actually spent a night with a girl in his car and not taken the opportunity to get laid, or at least get a blowjob out of it.

"What? Why did you wake me?" she asked.

"I thought you came out here to see a sunset," he responded.

"Oh my God, it's morning already? I don't even remember falling asleep. Did you stay up the whole time?"

"No I went out right after you did, but I couldn't sleep much because I am so uncomfortable in this position," he answered.

"I'm sorry. I guess sitting straight up with someone lying across your lap wasn't the best for your back and neck, huh?"

"No, no it wasn't, but that's ok because I enjoyed watching you sleep the whole time," he said.

"You watched me sleep? Why would you do that?" she asked.

"Well, what else did you expect me to watch? The windshield doesn't get that many good channels you know."

"That's your best response? You couldn't have thought of something more romantic than that?"

"Of course I could, but I didn't want to sound too feminine this early in a relationship," he responded.

Anita lifted her head and upper body from his lap and sat up in her seat. "Relationship? What do you mean by that?" she asked sounding surprised.

"I don't know. I guess I thought you had a good time tonight and maybe you might want to pursue it a little further, that's all."

"Yes, I had a great time tonight, in fact it was probably the greatest night of my life, but I thought that it would have been really boring to you, considering

I'm sure you are used to much more satisfying outcomes, if you know what I mean," she replied.

"Well I won't lie to you and say no I haven't the slightest clue what you mean however you are right, I have had many nights like that. But, tonight was much more satisfying than many of those typical dates because it was refreshing being with someone who has great morals and wasn't out with me just for sex. You know guys get used too, and don't deny that."

"Really, women use guys? I didn't know that," she said with a laugh.

"I'm not stupid, I have been with many girls who were only with me because they wanted to be able to tell their girlfriends later on in life that they slept with a NFL quarterback before he made it to the big times," he told her.

Anita was taken back by that response. Nicholas was the complete opposite of the stereotypical handsome jock looking to score with the average girl. "Did you want to?" she asked. "I mean, do you think I am attractive enough to be with or am I not your type? Be honest, I won't be offended." she asked.

"Of course you are. Why would you even need to ask that question," he replied. She leaned over and kissed him hard. It was only the second time that she had kissed a boy like that.

Nicholas was surprised by her sudden aggressiveness but he wasn't going to complain about it. Anita let her hands roam all over Nicholas's chest and through his hair and when he started to do the same she didn't stop him.

"Wait," he said as he pulled away.

"What's wrong?" she asked.

"This isn't right," he replied.

"I'm sorry, am I doing something wrong? This is all new to me," she answered.

"That's the problem, this is all new to you and I don't won't your first time to be in the front seat of my beat up car. Wouldn't you rather wait until we could go back to your dorm and make it more special for you?" he asked.

"Trust me, I am as ready as I am ever going to be, and I want to do it now because this place and time will always be special to me," she responded as she started to unbutton her jeans.

"Are you sure?" he asked one more time, but before he got an answer Anita had her pants off and was already on top of him unbuttoning his pants.

Two hours later they were both still naked under the blanket holding each other as they talked. Anita had experienced the greatest moment of her life and continued to hold onto Nicholas hoping that time might skip them over and this date would never come to an end. But in less than five hours from now it would come to a crashing end because her father was about to drop a bomb-shell on her.

Frankie kept looking over his shoulder every time he came back to his car with more items from the house that Ellena couldn't leave behind. It was just a little past seven o'clock in the morning and Frankie realized that he needed to get him, Ellena, Angela and his mother on the road. The longer he waited, the more his chances of making out of the city diminished.

He barely got any sleep and was running on pure fear and adrenaline alone. Frankie didn't leave Vincent until four in the morning because the two of them had to go over the final details, including what Vincent had done with Carmine's body and giving him a new cell phone in case Frankie decided he might stick around and see this mess through.

The girls were gathering up the last of their things, and he figured two more trips back and forth and the car would be loaded. On his way back to the house his cell phone rang. He had no intentions of answering his phone again until he was well out of the city limits, but he recognized the number and was wondering what on earth Lieutenant Joe Brown would want with him this early in the morning.

"Frankie, it's Lieutenant Joe Brown. I have some interesting news I thought you might want to know before it gets out to the public," he said.

"Joe, no offense, but now is not a good time and I am in kind of a hurry," Frankie responded.

"Trust me, I think you might want to take a second and listen to the news that I have for you," he insisted.

Frankie could only think that this was even more terrible news about another one of his crewmembers. He just hoped that Joe wasn't going to tell him that they had just fished Vincent out of the river around sunrise.

"So, what do you got for me that is so important?" he asked.

"I know this is a stupid question, but have you ever heard of Perna's Pawn Shop on 5th Street?"

"You're right, stupid question. What does that place have to do with me?" Frankie asked sounding frustrated.

"Bear with me for a second, because what I am going to tell you about what took place in that store yesterday might have an effect on you or some members of your crew," Joe responded.

"Alright, I'm listening," Frankie answered.

Joe believed that if this information turned out to be vital for Frankie, he was going to be rewarded handsomely. "It seems that the owner pissed off the wrong person and they axed him in his store late last night. It looks like Larry Perna was into child pornography because a ways back a couple of parents tried to bring charges against him but a case couldn't be brought against Larry. But we came up with new material and when our boys went down there last night to pick him up, well, we won't have to worry about needing evidence anymore. Now before you go jumping down my throat asking why the hell you would care about a pedophile getting killed, let me tell you what else we found in his store," he told Frankie.

"I'm glad you can read my mind Joe, since I told you that I am in a hurry and I don't have time for this right now," Frankie answered.

"Oh, I think you can spare five minutes, Frankie, for this information that I am about to lay on you," he said. "Fortunately for Larry, he was smart enough to have a surveillance camera in his store and the killer's face was all over the video, and it turns out to be one of the two parents that tried to press charges against Larry earlier. My men happened to go through the whole tape from beginning to end and would you like to know what else they saw, or should I say who else they saw?" he said as he gloated to himself, knowing that he had Frankie hooked.

Frankie didn't have to take too long to think about the answer. There was only one person that he knew of that frequently went to that place, but why did Joe think Frankie would care that Anthony was there on that day? Anthony needed to come up with fifty g's and Perna's was the place that he always went to when he was in a pinch for money.

"If you are going to tell me Anthony Albergo, then that isn't earth shattering news Joe," Frankie told him.

"No, that wouldn't be considering that Anthony frequently did business there by depositing most of his belongings, but this time he made an unusual withdrawal."

"Withdrawal, what do you mean?" Frankie asked, now intrigued.

"It seems that Anthony was Larry's first customer of the day and let's just say that things got out of hand and there was a skirmish and Larry pulled a shotgun on Anthony. The tape doesn't have any audio with it so we don't know what was said, but it looks like the kid talked his way out of it and then they went ahead and finished their business," he told Frankie.

"What did he purchase?" Frankie asked.

"That's the funny thing. The tape doesn't show Anthony giving Larry any money, just Larry giving Anthony a gun," he replied.

"He gave him a gun?" Frankie questioned.

"Yeah, Larry gave the kid a gun and after an exchange of words, Anthony left. What do you think about that?" Joe asked.

"Did Larry happen to give him a 9mm?" Frankie asked.

"Funny you should ask but yeah, it was a 9mm. Why, does that mean something to you?" Joe asked.

"No, but its good information to know just in case," Frankie responded.

"Just in case of what?" Joe had asked but Frankie had already hung up.

It couldn't have been Anthony, Frankie thought to himself. Teddy told him that he thought it could have been Bull and even in the dark, Anthony couldn't wear enough clothes to make himself as large as Bull. And how the hell could Anthony possibly know that Bull wouldn't come home from Vegas? Both the girls and Jimmy had reported back to him that Anthony was at the house the whole night.

Nothing was adding up, and it would be pure speculation on Frankie's part to think Anthony was involved in any way. If Frankie was in Anthony's shoes, he too would have gone and purchased himself a little protection. It was only a coincidence that it happened to be a 9mm.

But no matter how hard Frankie tried to make himself believe it couldn't have been Anthony, that nagging little voice in his head kept telling him that he should take a chance and pay Anthony a visit before he left for good.

Ellena had come back outside with another box. "Your mother is sitting in the living room ready to go. Just give me another ten minutes and I will be ready to leave also," she said.

"I hate to do this to you, but I have to make a change in plans. I want you, Angela and Mom to take your car and go to Cornell and I will meet up with the three of you later on today. There is one thing that Vincent and I have to take care of before I can leave. I promise by the time you and Anita get done arguing about where she's been over the last two days, I'll be there breaking it up," he told her.

Ellena could only shake her head in disbelief. She couldn't believe that Frankie was sending her upstate alone with his mother to break the horrible news to Anita that they were there to take her out of the school that she had dreamed her whole life on attending. This was the kind of shit that Frankie always made her do so that Anita wouldn't hate him. Daddy was always the good guy and Ellena was the hated one, but she wasn't worried about it any longer because Anita was bright enough to know that her father had fucked it up for all of them.

Ellena didn't bother saying a word to Frankie before she turned around and went back into the house. When he was certain that she wasn't going to come back out and argue with him, he took out his cell phone and called Vincent. Vincent had already been on the road heading to Canada for the last twenty minutes when Frankie called.

"Hello," he answered, surprised to hear his new phone ring.

"Vincent, its Frankie, how soon can you be at my house?" he asked.

"Sorry Frankie, but I have been on the road for awhile already and I'm already out of the city heading north, why what's up?" he asked.

"I just received an interesting phone call from our friend, Joe Brown and I need your help. Can you meet me at Oakland Cemetery by eleven o'clock?" he asked.

"Sure, but I thought you wanted to get out by this morning. I hope that this is worth me coming all the way back, because you are jeopardizing both our lives," Vincent responded.

"All I can tell you, Vincent, is my gut is telling me that it will be."

The day turned out to be sunny and on the warm side for early November. The cemetery was packed with hundreds of cars carrying people who were there just in hopes of getting on television from one of the many news stations that were there, trying to get the burial on film for their audiences. And with all of those cars came the police escort, which was there to enforce that this burial be kept private for Anthony and his family.

Phil Engman and Joe Fishman made an appearance as they stood guard on both sides of the gatherers. Neither one of them had attended the viewing last night because they had received a phone call on the incarceration of Bull down at the airport. They spent most of the time listening to his confession about the killing of Anthony's parents, and all the other bullshit that he tried to sell the Feds about Frankie to save his own ass.

Father John Jordan read a passage from the bible as Anthony sat in his chair in front of both coffins, with Sandra and Kimberly on both sides of him. Tami and Kevin were seated in the row directly behind them. Anthony hadn't spoken to either of them since last night and he desperately wanted to speak to Tami now that it looked like everything was going to be okay, but that wouldn't matter to her because Anthony had still jeopardize her brother's life and their future.

"You mind telling me what we are doing here?" Vincent asked Frankie as the two of them stood by an old weeping willow tree, standing out of view of the mourners.

"Like I told you in the car ride, I am hoping to get a little lucky. I know it's a long shot, but it's a shot that I need to take. I would hate like hell to be beaten by a low-life degenerate gambler who finally got lucky and broke even," he replied as he looked through his binoculars.

"Well you tell me when that happens because right now you and I should be long gone instead of standing in this cemetery. You know the longer we stand here, the better chance we have of becoming permanent residents," Vincent responded.

Father John turned to Anthony as he finished the passage and signaled to him to take one of the many roses that were in the three baskets beside him and for Anthony to come forward and approach the coffins. Anthony stood up and took two roses and stood over his parents' coffins and said a little prayer before laying a rose on each of them. Sandra took Kimberly in her arms and was the next to approach the coffins. The rest of the gatherers followed her lead.

"Motherfucker, I know him. I know I have seen him," Frankie said.

"Who boss, I can't see who you are talking about?"

"Wait a minute, I need to see something," he replied.

Frankie stared at Kevin as he stood in front of the coffins. "Come on and turn around for me," Frankie whispered. After Kevin placed the second rose down, he turned and went back to his chair.

"It is him. I'll be a son of a bitch, we just hit the fucking jackpot," he told Vincent as he handed him the binoculars.

"Who am I looking at?" Vincent asked as he started to comb through the people in line.

"Look at the big guy sitting one row behind Anthony to his left."

"Yeah, what about him?" he questioned.

"Well, last night when I was with Victor in the emergency room there were only three other people in our area of the emergency room, and he was one of them. I thought he looked familiar. I remember that he was bleeding from the back of his head and sure enough, there he sits right behind Anthony with a patch on the back of his head."

"So, what the hell does that have to do with us standing here?" Vincent asked impatiently.

"Look at him. Does he look like anyone we know?" Frankie yelled.

"No, I don't recognize him Frankie."

"Jesus Christ, you fucking amaze me sometimes. What did Joe tell me this morning about Anthony and what did Teddy tell me about last night? If you put two and two together, that scum bag who is sitting behind Anthony is the same guy that Anthony gave the 9mm to and who shot up our guys last night," he informed Vincent.

"My God, now that you say that, he is almost as big as Bull, maybe even bigger. And in the dark of an alley with a ski mask on, who could tell the difference?" Vincent asked.

"I don't have any idea yet as to what happened to Bull and I'm not sure that these two do either, but you and I are going to follow this asshole and get us some answers," he told Vincent as he turned to head back to the cars.

Anthony was saying his goodbyes to Sandra and Kimberly as Kevin approached the car.

"Are you sure we can't come with you?" Sandra asked one last time.

"I swear to you, I will contact you once I am settled. It could be as soon as next week, just have a little patience," he answered as he kissed them both goodbye, not realizing that he was making a liar of himself again because this was the last time that Anthony was ever going to see his ex-wife and daughter again.

"You got a second, Anthony?" Kevin asked as Anthony was still hugging Kimberly goodbye. Anthony turned around to see Kevin standing in front of him with a look that could kill. It didn't take Anthony long to realize that Tami had confronted him when he got home last night.

"Sure, just let me put Kimberly in her car seat," he answered. He gave her one last kiss before Sandra drove the two of them away and out of his life forever.

"Before you get all pissed off at me, I had to be honest with her. She's an adult now and I didn't want to insult her by being dishonest with her. Tami is too smart for me to bullshit her Kev, so I am sorry but she wouldn't stop insisting until I gave her an answer. I gave her what I thought she deserved," Anthony told him.

"Do you know what that could have done to her if I didn't make it home last night? Did you ever think about that before you went off and told her everything that we did?" he screamed at Anthony.

"I didn't go into all the details with her Kev, just that you did me and my parents a great deed. If you told her more than that is on you, I only told her where we were and nothing more," he informed Kevin.

Kevin didn't know what else to say. He felt betrayed after all he had done for Anthony and wanted nothing more than to punch the living shit out of him, but this was not the time nor the place for that.

"When are you leaving town?" he asked Anthony.

"I am going back to my parents' place and pack up a couple of things, shower, get a quick bite to eat and hopefully I'll be on the road before dark. Where is Tami going to stay?" he asked.

"She's staying with her friend Sydney for the rest of the weekend and I am actually looking forward to staying in bed and getting some sleep for the next forty straight hours," he replied.

"Did you hide the money?"

"Yeah, it's back at the shop in the trunk of an old Ford Taurus that has been sitting on the shop's lot forever. I'll move it Monday once the banks open," he answered.

Anthony could only imagine how much Kevin hated him at this moment for making Tami aware of what they did, but he wasn't going to be able to talk any reason into Kevin.

"Once again, thank you for everything that you have done for me over the last couple of days. I'll contact you early in the week to see how you and Tami are making out and after that I don't think you'll hear from me again. If I want to start a new life, I have to cut all ties to my old one," he said.

"Well I hope you use this opportunity wisely and get your life turned around," Kevin responded, and then he turned and walked away from Anthony and headed towards his car, where Tami sat waiting for him. Tami had no intentions on saying goodbye to Anthony after last night.

Kevin drove past Anthony and Anthony gave him a wave that Kevin returned, while Tami ignored it.

"You could have at least waved back and acknowledged him Tami, you know better than that," Kevin said.

"Why, it's not like I am not going to see him again?" she asked.

"I hate to argue with you, but he's leaving today for good and isn't coming back."

"We'll see," she replied. "Strange circumstances seem to follow Anthony wherever here goes."

Kevin gave her a quick look, but she didn't acknowledge him. She just stared out the window, as she couldn't help thinking that this wasn't over and, unfortunately for her, she was right.

❧   ❧   ❧

Anthony's two favorite people decided to pay him one last visit before he left the cemetery.

"It was a beautiful ceremony if that helps any," Phil Engman said.

"Gentleman, I guess you got what you wanted, because I didn't see Frankie or anybody else from his crew last night or today," he replied.

"It's not just what we wanted Anthony, it was what was best for everyone. Did you really want to take a chance that something could have happened if they showed up?" Joe Fishburn asked.

"No, but that's where the three of us disagree because if Frankie had shown up it would have only been to give me his condolences. I guess he won't have the chance because I am out of here in a couple of hours, once I finish packing some last minute items," he told the two of them.

"We figured as much, that's why we came over here to give you some information before you leave," Phil said.

"I can't imagine you have anything too important to tell me before I leave, but go ahead," Anthony answered.

"I guess you haven't had the time to read the paper or see the news yesterday or today, but an acquaintance of yours was found dead in his shop yesterday. It seems that one of the parents finally got sick of his behavior and cut off his privates while he bled to death in his store," Joe informed him.

Anthony didn't want to start playing now this close to being able to leave town and not looking back, so he thought it best to just cooperate and make this as easy as possible for the three of them.

"I can only imagine that you are referring to that model citizen, Larry Perna," Anthony said.

"See Joe, I told you he was going to make this easy for us today," Phil said.

"Hopefully Anthony can answer a couple of our questions and not make a liar out of you," Joe responded.

"Not Anthony, I can tell by the look on his face that he wants nothing more than to get the hell out of here, Joe. He'll answer them," Phil remarked.

Anthony realized that they wanted something from him but he really couldn't imagine that he could offer them any help with their investigation. Christ, he was in the store and saw what Larry was reading and watching, it should be an open and shut case. Anthony believed that they should pin a medal on the guy that killed Larry.

"I haven't the slightest clue as to what information I could shed on the case to help you out. I know he was a low-life and it doesn't surprise me that someone would want him dead. Look at the line of work that he was in, it's not the kind that makes you a lot of friends," he said.

"Oh, it's an open and shut case on our end and we are going to do everything in our power to help the guy who did it because he had tried to bring charges against Larry for child molestation. Needless to say you know how the law works most of the time, the bad guys usually win. But that's not what we are here to talk to you about. It seems that Larry had a surveillance camera in his store and we saw the craziest thing on tape. There was a confrontation between the two of you first thing in the morning and after that he gave you a 9mm. Mind telling me what that was all about?" Joe asked.

If Phil and Joe were already aware of what took place in the alley last night, they wouldn't have been first to pay Anthony a visit because more than likely Frankie would have been tipped off and he would have gotten to him before these guys.

"Can't a guy go in to a pawn shop and get himself a little protection? Maybe I believed that you guys were right and Frankie was planning on taking action, what's the harm in protecting myself?" he asked the two of them.

Joe realized that this was a bullshit answer, but it really didn't matter because they had nothing on Anthony. They were only hoping that maybe he would reveal a little more than he needed to, but of course Anthony didn't. Anthony was on a different playing field than most of the perps that he and Phil were used to dealing with on a daily basis.

"It didn't look to us like the usual transaction that takes place in a pawn shop. I mean I'm sure Larry didn't point a shotgun at all of his customers, but then again the two of you have built up a good relationship over the last few years," Joe replied.

"I wouldn't go so far as to say that it was a relationship, but I'm not going to lie to you: yes, I did a good amount of business with him because that's what happens when you bet and lose a lot. Yesterday I was tired of the asshole ripping me off and things got a little heated and he took out the shotgun thinking

I was going to attack him, but in the end I was able to talk him out of it," he told them.

"Yes, we saw that, and we also saw that you didn't pay him with a trade or any money. Can you tell us why?" Phil asked.

"I don't know, maybe he saw the evil of his ways and decided to do something nice for a change to a person in need. I guess Larry is the only one who knows the answer to that but you can't ask him now, can you?" Anthony asked them in a cocky manner.

Both Joe and Phil knew that this was all over. If Frankie or Bull were planning anything against Anthony, their window of opportunity was closing quickly and they both believed that Anthony was on the up and up about leaving town. They didn't have a charge to hold him on and they had actually started to like and admire him, so they felt it was in their best interest to just let him go on his way and get the hell out of Dodge.

"I guess there's nothing else to ask you then, Anthony. I wish you luck on your new venture and let's hope we never have to see you again," Joe said as he stuck out his hand to Anthony.

Anthony took it and replied, "I don't think you have to worry about that. I'm history within the next three hours," he said as he shook Phil's hand next.

"Take care of yourself Anthony," Phil said as he and Joe watched Anthony get into his car and drive out of their lives. Neither one of them ever saw Anthony again, nor was the case of his parents' deaths ever solved. It still remains open to this day, since Bull never got the chance to testify against Frankie and his men.

Kevin was out cold in his bed and never heard Frankie and Vincent enter his bedroom. He had dropped Tami off at Sydney's house directly from the cemetery and when he got home he fixed himself a drink and was asleep fifteen minutes later. He was so exhausted and overwhelmed from everything that had taken place over the last couple of days, he didn't even have a chance to dream before he was awoken by a sudden blast of pain in his jaw.

Kevin didn't even have time to react when he opened his eyes, as Vincent brought the butt of his gun down a second time, this time connecting with Kevin's nose, completely breaking it beyond repair. The pain registered instantly and Kevin screamed, but no one other than Frankie and Vincent were going to hear him.

"Hello asshole, do you know who we are?" Vincent asked as he put his gloved hand over top of Kevin's mouth to quiet the screams.

Kevin had never met Frankie or Vincent before, but he didn't have to because who else would be here in his bedroom about to kill him? Kevin shook his head yes as he splattered blood on the other side of the bed.

"Good, asshole because we want this to be over quick and the more you cooperate, the less pain I will have to inflict upon you before we leave. Now I am only going to ask you each of my questions one time and if I don't like what you tell me, then I am going to break something else on your body to go with your jaw and nose," Vincent told him.

If it wasn't for the excruciating pain, Kevin might have thought that this was just a bad dream brought on by mixing alcohol with some medicine, but that was only wishful thinking. He understood that he wasn't going to leave this bedroom alive no matter what he told these guys and he could only pray that they would get Anthony too.

"Last night did you and your little shit cousin go to that alley and take something that didn't belong to you?" Vincent asked. Kevin wasn't like Anthony when it came to playing games. He realized the best chance for a quick and merciful death would be to tell them everything and hope that they would just shoot him quickly, so he shook his head yes.

"See Frankie, I told you that without a gun and the element of surprise, this piece of shit wasn't that tough and we could get the answers for our questions," he said as he turned to Frankie for approval.

"I am an honest man. You gave me the right answer, so no new pain to a different part of your body," he said to Kevin.

Kevin could only lay there in agonizing pain and fear because the thoughts of what they could do to him raced through his mind, keeping him in absolute horror.

"Next question for you asshole, where is our money?" Vincent asked as he put his other hand on the raw flesh that used to be Kevin's nose.

Kevin tried to wriggle free, but Vincent was a big man and he put all his weight into both his arms as he pressed on Kevin's nose and mouth. The pain was so intense that Kevin started to black out. Vincent, who had been witness to this kind of behavior numerous times over the years, eased off of Kevin's nose and jaw and slapped him hard across the face.

With Vincent's hands now removed, Kevin screamed as he sat upright in his bed. He had never screamed like that before in his life, but then again he had never experienced this amount of pain at one time either. Vincent punched the unbroken side of his jaw and Kevin's head immediately fell back onto the pillow.

"Stop your crying you little bitch, and answer the question. Where's our fucking money?" he yelled.

Frankie stood up from the chair that he was sitting in as he watched Vincent work Kevin over. "Enough, leave him alone for a while Vincent, as I talk to him. If you fuck him up too much too soon, what the hell good is he going to be to us?" he asked.

Vincent stepped back from Kevin's bed and Frankie came over and took his place. Frankie didn't stand over Kevin; instead, he sat down on the edge of the bed like he had done a million times in the past with Anita and Angela as he kissed them good night.

"Look Kevin, the three of us know that this obviously wasn't your plan. You just happened to be the right size to pull off an attempt to pass for my nephew Bull. Now I am not going to lie to you and tell you that if you explain everything to us we are just going to disappear and leave you alone. That's not how it works in our business when someone steals from us. However, I do have the power to make sure that your death can be swift and painless if you choose to cooperate with us and tell me where my money is and what the hell happened to Bull," he explained to Kevin.

Kevin could only believe Frankie when it came to the fact that he was going to die and that Frankie had the ability to make it a quick death. And if he was going to die, he wasn't going to give up the money. He realized he wasn't leaving this room, so why tell the truth about the money? Last night he wrote a letter for Tami containing instructions about the money and put it under her pillow. So screw Anthony, he was going to tell them that Anthony had all of it and hadn't split it up yet. Why would that be so hard to believe considering that Anthony still had the gathering and burial to deal with last night?

Kevin struggled to get the words out because his jaw was swelling on both sides and he couldn't move his mouth well enough to speak clearly. "It was all Anthony's plan," he started to say as he coughed out some blood and two teeth. "Anthony has the money hidden somewhere and I don't know anything about your nephew," he answered.

Frankie stared at Kevin's deformed face and into his fear-filled eyes, and knew that he was lying to him. "Kevin, you really don't want me to have Vincent work on you some more, do you? The way your face looks right now, I would recommend a closed casket to save your friends and family the pain that they would suffer by having to look at you like this," Frankie answered.

Kevin sat back up only to be pushed back down by Frankie.

"No one told you that you could get up. Just lie there and bleed some more and think about your answers. Now if you don't give me the answer that I want to hear this time, I am going to head downstairs and go out to the car and wait for Vincent to finish with you. I might be a Mafia boss, but that doesn't mean I enjoy the sight of some guy getting the shit kicked out of him before he gets whacked. In my old age, I just don't have the stomach for it anymore," he informed Kevin.

"I swear I don't have any of the money. Check the house if you don't believe me. I am supposed to meet with Anthony later today to pick up my share of the cut before he leaves town. And as for Bull, Anthony never mentioned a word to me about him. He only discussed the hold up with me and that was all. We didn't do a thing to your nephew," Kevin replied.

Frankie patted Kevin on his chest as he got up from the bed. "Find out what the hell they did to Bull, Vincent, and hurry up because I don't know how much longer we have before Anthony takes off. I'll be waiting in the car," he said as he walked out of the room.

"Please, I swear to God I don't know anything about your nephew," Kevin tried to scream, but it was too late because Frankie had already made up his mind and had left the room.

"What part of the body should I start with next?" Vincent asked as he approached the bed.

"How did everything go last night and this morning?" Chad asked as Sandra carried a sleeping Kimberly in her arms into the house.

"How do you think it went? It was a funeral," she responded, irritated by this question.

"You know what I mean. If I didn't ask the question you would have gotten pissed at me for being insensitive for your loss. I knew no matter what I said or didn't say, you would act like a bitch. This is the thanks I get for letting you go last night. Well from now on you can kiss my ass if you want something from me. I'm tired of your shit, Sandra," he said.

Sandra walked past him and went into the family room and laid Kimberly down on the couch. When she was finished with tucking Kimberly in with a blanket, she went back into the foyer, where Chad was still standing.

"I'm glad you feel that way, because it is going to make it a lot easier on me with what I have to talk to you about," she told him.

❧   ❧   ❧

"Do you want him in the trunk or the back seat?" Vincent asked Frankie as he got to the car with Kevin's body draped over his shoulder.

"It's your car, your call, but if you don't want blood on your back seat, throw him in the trunk," Frankie replied.

"I think there's enough air in the trunk for a twenty minute ride to Anthony's, so fuck it, in the trunk he goes."

Vincent popped the trunk open and threw Kevin's unconscious body into the trunk. Vincent hadn't beaten a guy that bad in almost ten years, but he still enjoyed the satisfaction from it even after all these years, especially when the guy deserved it and Kevin deserved the beating that he received.

"What happen to Bull?" Frankie asked Vincent as he got into the car.

"You're not going to believe this but what he told me is going to blow you away," he replied.

"After all that has happened this week do you really think that what he told you could possibly amaze me at this point?" he asked.

"Oh, I think it will," Vincent said as they pulled away and started their ride to Anthony's parents' house.

Frankie saw the look on Vincent's face and realized that Vincent wasn't kidding—this news was going to floor him.

"So is he dead or alive? What the fuck happened to Bull?" Frankie asked impatiently.

"Supposedly Anthony knows someone at the airport and this guy planted weapons in Bull's luggage and the locals most likely detained him until the Feds arrived. God only knows where he is being held now, but you got to believe that he's talking and selling all of us out. If I was him, I would have believed that you back-stabbed me too, and I would do the same thing. It wouldn't surprise me if the Feds were at your home right now waiting for you to get home," Vincent answered.

Frankie could only shake his head because Vincent was right; this hit him fast and hard right between the eyes. That was the last scenario that he would have ever dreamed up.

"When we get to Anthony's house, I don't care how long it takes, I want him to die slow and have it last for days. If I have to go back to Toresco's place to get morphine to keep him alive longer I will, because this death will last until I am fully satisfied," he said.

"What's wrong with you? Are you still upset about the funeral?" Sydney asked Tami as the two of them were reading the newest "Seventeen" magazine. "Hello, Earth to Tami, are you going to answer me?" she asked.

"What?" Tami asked not aware that Sydney had been talking to her.

"What's wrong with you today?" Sydney asked again.

"I just have a lot on my mind right now, and I was just wondering what would happen if Kevin decided to sell the house and make us move out of the city," Tami responded.

"Why would Kevin do that? I thought he was doing well with the shop," she replied.

"I don't know how to explain it, but I just have this bad feeling that I won't be staying around here to finish my senior year," she answered.

"Now you're just being silly. If Kevin did do something that ridiculous, you can stay and live with me, you know my mom loves you and besides you are eighteen and an adult now, so he can't force you to go if you don't want to live with him," she told Tami.

"I don't think that matters Sydney."

Anthony was putting the last of his mother's belongings in the suitcase when he was startled by the doorbell. He wasn't expecting anyone, and the people who needed to know were aware that Anthony was leaving. Anthony went back into his room and took the 9mm out of his bag just in case he needed it. He was keeping it until he was safely out of the city and on the road. During his trip he would eventually toss it into the woods along the parkway.

As Anthony descended down the stairs, he couldn't completely make out the figure through the stained glass window of the front door. Considering the size of the figure in the glass, Anthony believed it had to be Kevin and that he was here to finish the conversation from the cemetery.

Anthony didn't see anyone else in the glass, but the front door was mostly made of wood and it would be easy for someone else to be hiding out of his view.

"Who is it?" Anthony asked as he reached the door.

"It's Kevin," Kevin answered in a voice that Anthony could hardly recognize from the other side with his back to the door.

Anthony cracked the door open and could see that it was Kevin, but he didn't look right. "Kevin, why are you...", but before Anthony could finish his sentence, he was blinded by all the blood and brain fragments of Kevin's head.

Anthony was thrown to the floor by the force of Vincent slamming into the front door and, before he could react or comprehend what had just happened, Vincent struck a blow to his head, rendering him unconscious.

"Busy little boy last night, weren't you?" Vincent asked Anthony as he slapped him awake. Anthony was still groggy and unclear as to what was happening. He wasn't even aware that he was tied to a chair in the middle of his parents' living room.

"What?" he responded.

"A college kid like you knows not to answer a question with a question," Vincent replied while delivering another sharp slap to the other side of Anthony's face.

"I said you were very busy last night. I mean the viewing, the gathering and driving the get-away car. I would say that was a lot to take care of in one night, wouldn't you agree Frankie?" Vincent asked.

"I would say so," Frankie responded.

Anthony's head was spinning and he had just now realized what was all over his face and in his eyes as he saw Kevin's lifeless and headless body lying on the floor where it landed.

"Jesus Christ, you didn't have to kill him," Anthony cried.

"On the contrary, Anthony, I think we did. In case you weren't up to date with the facts, he killed one of my men and critically wounded two others. The two of you have stolen roughly two hundred thousand dollars of my money. And let's not forget the whole airport fiasco with Bull. That was priceless, I must admit. Now just be happy that it's me that's going to kill you and not Pete, because Pete wouldn't show you the mercy that I am going to if you cooperate and let me know where you put my money," he told Anthony.

How the hell could Frankie have figured this out so quickly, Anthony thought to himself as he ran his plan through his head over and over again?

"I know what you are thinking," Frankie told him. "I can see it in your stunned eyes. You are wondering how the hell I knew it was you that fucked me last night. I'll tell you what. I am going to be a nice guy and enlighten you since

I am feeling a little generous today," he told Anthony as he approached the chair.

"First off, I received a call this morning from a police friend of mine saying that he had you on surveillance tape taking a 9mm from Larry Perna's pawn shop. At first I thought no big deal, because you always went there and you were getting yourself a piece for protection, but I was still a little curious so I went to the burial this morning, and a lovely burial it was, you should be proud of yourself for that."

"Thanks, but I can't take the credit for it," Anthony responded.

"Anyway, back to my explanation. While Vincent and I were there this morning, I noticed your cousin sitting behind you and I knew I had just seen him somewhere," Frankie said as he pointed to Kevin's body lying there in a pool of blood.

"And just like that, it hit me where I saw this guy. Would you like to know where and when I saw him Anthony?" Frankie asked with that smirk that Anthony was accustomed to when they played cards on Friday nights and Frankie was holding the winning hand.

Anthony didn't want to give him the satisfaction, so he shook his head no.

"No, you don't want to know? I'm surprised, most guys would love to know where they failed but I guess you are so used to being a fuck-up that it doesn't matter. I really don't care that you don't want to know because I am going to tell you anyway because I think your cousin's and my paths crossing has to be a one in a million coincidence. While I was sitting in "Our Lady of Lourdes" emergency room with Victor, to get his eyes checked out, you remember Victor, he's the one that your cousin fucking blinded last night, the same guy that you played cards with a thousand times in my club," he said as he punched Anthony dead center of his chin, sending a bolt of pain right to his head.

"There were just three other people there in the trauma center and your cousin was one of them. At the time I had no idea who he was and never gave him a second look because I was still too concerned about my crew members being shot up," he screamed as he punched Anthony in the gut.

Anthony couldn't move or breath as the wind was knocked out of him. He tried to gasp for air, but he couldn't and he started to vomit.

"Look at what you did on yourself. That's going to be hard to get out of the carpets too, but I don't think you need to worry about that, let the people who buy this house next worry about that. You should be more worried about getting the blood stains out over there, because that is going to be a much more difficult job," he said as he laughed and pointed to Kevin.

Anthony was finally able to get his breath as the pain subsided. "Fuck you Frankie," he said.

"I'm glad to see you have a little fight in you because I would have been disappointed if you would have been a total pussy about all of this. Where would the fun be in that?" he asked.

"Would you think it would be fun, Vincent?" he turned and asked.

"No, boss, not at all. I was hoping for a good struggle myself, the kind that his cousin put up before he cried like a bitch for his life," Vincent answered.

"Just for the record Anthony, we promised Kevin his life if he turned you in and led us to the money, but I guess he didn't realize the kind of people that he was dealing with before he agreed," Frankie told him.

"You don't have to worry about me putting up a fight Frankie, I intend to," Anthony answered.

"Great, then let's get on with the questioning," Frankie said.

"Before I answer your questions, I have one for you Frankie," Anthony replied.

Anthony realized the only shot he had at getting out of this alive was that Nicholas had come through for him and Anita was with him. If not it wouldn't matter what kind of poker face he put on when he asked Frankie the question, but it was his only hope.

"How's Anita doing, Frankie?" he asked and was instantly relieved to see that tell appear on Frankie's face. Anthony had hit a nerve because Frankie, for the first time in Anthony's presence, looked nervous.

"What the fuck do you mean by that question you little fuck?" Frankie asked as his voiced quivered a little.

If Anthony was going to pull this off, he was going to have to put up the bluff of a life time. He only had one chance to sell Frankie that Anita was in danger and it all depended on his delivery.

"It's really a simple question Frankie. How is Anita doing?" he asked as he stared at Frankie and didn't let his eyes move from his.

"You motherfucker, God help you if anything happens to her," Frankie screamed as he lifted Anthony and the chair off the floor.

"I take it, then, you understand the circumstances that you are facing, now untie me and let me go," Anthony demanded.

"Untie you? You are lucky that I don't cut your fucking throat open. You are bluffing and you know it. Do you really think that I am that naïve to believe that you were that stupid to bring family into this, no less a child," Frankie answered.

As much as Frankie tried to call Anthony's bluff, Anthony knew that it was fear taking over Frankie and not rationalism.

"Bring family into this? That's a laugh. Correct if I'm wrong but, if I'm not mistaken, I was the one who just buried two parents. So fuck your code of ethics when it comes to your business because I am new to all of this and you were the one who forced me to. Besides, she's an adult now," Anthony replied.

"I told you that we were going to take care of the situation, all you had to do was sit tight and let everything work its way out, but you had to go and pull this stunt. Now enough with the games Anthony, where the fuck is my money?" Frankie asked.

"I don't think you are taking me seriously about Anita, Frankie. She was what you call my ace up the sleeve on getting out of this if you happened to get to me before I left. If you don't believe me, why don't you call her? Or have you already tried calling her?" he asked.

Frankie played cards with Anthony long enough to know that he wasn't bluffing. He knew that if Anthony was clever enough to get to Bull than he was clever enough to get to Anita, but he couldn't let Anthony know that. Unfortunately for Frankie, it was too late and Anthony was already aware that he had the upper hand in this confrontation.

Frankie got up and walked out of the room and into the kitchen where he called Ellena's cell phone, knowing that she was only going to tell him that she hadn't heard from Anita yet.

"Hello," Ellena answered.

"Hi it's me. I'll be leaving in a couple of minutes and I was wondering if you ever got a hold of Anita yet because I was thinking that maybe it would be better to show up together, instead of her walking into her dorm with her mother and mom-mom sitting there waiting for her with the surprise of a lifetime."

"I'm glad you said that Frankie because I was really pissed at you for making me look like the bad guy as usual," she replied.

"Ok, then just wait for me at the hotel and we'll go together," he told her. "By the way you never answered me, did you get in touch with her yet?" he asked.

"No, I haven't tried since I left the house, but that was early and she's probably still out from last night," she answered.

"I guess that will be something we will have to talk to her about," he said.

Frankie realized it was pointless to call her room but he had no choice and after the fifth ring, Anita's machine answered. Frankie hung up his phone and put it back in his coat. Vincent took one look at Frankie as he walked in and knew right away that the kid wasn't lying about Anita.

"Are you fucking kidding me?" Vincent yelled as he leaped towards Anthony.

"Vincent, leave him alone," Frankie ordered, but Anita was his God daughter and he was just as upset as Frankie, but with less control of his emotions.

Anthony's long shot had come through. Nicholas must have found Anita because Frankie no longer looked like a man in charge of the situation.

"Like I was saying, untie me and let me be on my way and as soon as I am out of the city you will hear from Anita. However, kill me and you'll never have closure on her disappearance," Anthony said.

"Anthony, I am only going to say this one time to you. If one hair on Anita's head is harmed I am going to make it my life's mission to find you, and when I do your ex-wife and little girl will die a slow death in front of you before I finish you," he told Anthony as he nodded his head to Vincent to cut him loose.

"If I was you, I would be more worried about me finding you than Frankie, because once I get a hold of you I am bringing your body back here and putting you in the ground right next to your parents so you can all be one happy family again," he told Anthony as he cut the ropes around his wrists and ankles.

Anthony stood up and walked past Kevin's body as he reached the front door. "Like I said, I didn't start this mess and I only did what I had to do to ensure my safety. Anita is fine and you should hear from her within the next two hours. I am sorry that it had to come to this, but you left me no choice," he said as he opened the door, hoping that there would be no more confrontation before they left.

"Mark my words Anthony, this is far from over," Frankie said as he now stood directly between Anthony and the doorway. "Far from fucking over," he said one last time, pointing his finger into Anthony's chest before he walked out.

Vincent's exit wasn't as pleasant as he sucker punched Anthony in his left side. Anthony found out a day later that the punch had broken two ribs. Anthony dropped to both his knees gasping for air for the second time that morning. Vincent bent down so he could talk right into Anthony's ear. "Frankie's right, this is far from fucking over you little prick and I promise you that we will one day see you again," he whispered into Anthony's ear.

And then Vincent pushed him over and Anthony landed on the same side that had the broken ribs.

Anthony couldn't remember how long he laid there in pain before he was able to get up, but he believed it must have been awhile based on the shadows the furniture were casting in the living room. He was still very dazed and now he had to deal with the new and extreme pain that was coming from his side, along with his head from Vincent's original blow.

As he stood in the foyer trying to get his thoughts under control, he noticed Kevin's lifeless body was still in the same position. Anthony had no idea what he was going to do with it because he had never had to dump a dead body anywhere; this was Frankie's line of work. But a thought even worse than that rushed into his mind; what was he going to tell Tami? She already hated him for bringing Kevin into all of this, but now he was dead and it was Anthony's fault.

He had time to worry about Tami's emotions, but right now he was running out of time to get out of the house and the city before Frankie realized that Anthony didn't have Anita. Plus, he was sure that one of his neighbors had to have heard the shot and yelling coming from the house when Frankie and Vincent were there, so it was only a matter of time before the police would arrive and fuck up everything.

It was just past three in the afternoon when Sydney answered the doorbell. "Hi, can I help you?" she asked.

"Hi, I'm Anthony, may I please speak to Tami?" he answered.

"Well, isn't this the strangest thing," she replied. "Tami has been expecting you, hold on one second while I get her," Sydney answered.

Sydney turned around to go back upstairs to get Tami, but, to her surprise, Tami was already at the bottom of the steps with her bags.

"I guess this is good bye," she said to Sydney as she embraced her for a hug.

"Why are you going to go with him when you know you can stay here with us? Why do you want to turn your whole life upside down again when you are only months away from graduating next year? Please reconsider this before you walk out that door," Sydney begged Tami.

"He already turned my life upside down and I don't have a choice, but don't worry about me Sydney, you know no matter what life throws at me I always land on my feet. I promise I will call you when and wherever we settle down," she replied as she gave Sydney once last big squeeze before she let go.

Tami headed toward the front door where, waiting for her on the other side, was her new life with Anthony: living on the run and always looking over their shoulders, which she did not want, but at this point she didn't have a choice.

Anthony could only stand there in silence because, even with an hour of preparation, he still didn't know what to say to Tami.

"Don't even bother telling me what happened Anthony, because if you are here then that means my brother is dead and I am alone in this world without any family left. And now I am stuck with you. Whatever pain that you may have suffered after your divorce or just this week with your parents' death doesn't even come close to what I am feeling right now about Kevin. Our lives were just getting back to normal until you showed up and fucked it all up. You know something? You seem to be really good at that, fucking up other people lives," she said as she walked by him and went to his car parked in front of the house.

Anthony got in the car and didn't say a word to her as he drove towards Kevin's shop. Frankie never mentioned if Kevin had given him his share of the money, but Anthony believed that Kevin hadn't because if he had, he would have killed Kevin at his own house and not at Anthony's. As they approached the lot, Anthony saw the Taurus parked alone next to the left wall of the garage. Kevin was right: no one in their right mind would want to steal that car even if they needed the parts. The car had cancer throughout most of the body, two front flat tires and a missing windshield.

"Just wait here for a second, I have to get something out of that car," Anthony told Tami, but she didn't say a single word to him.

Anthony popped open his trunk and lucked out and found a crow bar. He walked over to the Taurus and began to work on the trunk. Within two minutes Anthony was able to get inside and, with luck still seeming to be on his side, he saw Kevin's bag, which was hidden underneath an old blanket. Anthony took the bag, slammed down the trunk's lid and went back to his car, where he put Kevin's bag with his in the back compartment, which used to house an old spare tire.

It wasn't until they were across the river when Tami finally spoke. "God, I never thought that the sight of New York's skyline could look so heartrending. It used to be such a magnificent sight and now it just makes you want to cry," she said.

Anthony looked out her window and saw the sun setting just behind the skyline. He thought that he had seen this sight numerous times but not since 9/11 and Tami was right; there was a hurtful pain in his heart as he looked at it. New York would never be the same, and neither would they.

"Yeah, you are right, it is heartbreaking how everything looks different. The city will never look the same no matter what they do to replace those buildings," he responded.

"Yep, the way we live will never be the same again," she said and that was the last time they spoke until they reached the Mississippi border.

Anita and Nicholas walked into her dorm room just after five o'clock and were greeted by a relieved Christie, who had been sitting on her bed waiting nervously for Anita to come back or any news on her whereabouts ever since her parents arrived. Frankie and Ellena were sitting on Anita's bed and she hadn't seen them when she walked into the room.

"You mind telling your mother and me where you have been for the last two days? We have called and left messages numerous times and you haven't returned any of them?" he asked in a tone that Anita was not accustomed too.

"Oh my God, what are you guys doing here? I wasn't expecting you," she replied in a startled voice.

"Well maybe if you would have found the time and had a little consideration and returned our calls, you wouldn't be that surprised. And is this the guy that you have been out with all night?" Frankie asked.

"Mom and Dad this is Nicholas, and don't insinuate what we did last night, it wasn't like that at all."

"It wasn't?" Frankie asked sarcastically.

"I ran into Nicholas at a party last night and he recognized me from the neighborhood and since neither one of us wanted to stay at the party, we went to a diner and got some breakfast. After that we went and took a ride and spent the rest of the night talking about our high school days and the neighborhood and before we knew it, it was already morning. We came back to campus early and spent the rest of the day at the library because I have a paper due tomorrow and that's where I have been all day. You make it sound like I have been gone for a week. You know I am in college now and I don't need to be treated like a little girl anymore," she answered.

Frankie got off the bed and walked over to Nicholas, who was aware of who Frankie was and what he was capable of doing to him if he found out that he was paid to be up here with his daughter.

"It's Nicholas, right?" Frankie asked and he stuck out his hand.

"Yes sir, Mr. Feliciani," he responded.

"You're a student here at Cornell, Nicholas?" Frankie asked.

"Yes sir, I am a freshman," he answered without even thinking about what the consequences would be for lying directly to a mob boss.

"I would like you to do me a favor Nicholas. I want you to take Christie and go for a long walk. Mrs. Feliciani and I have to talk to Anita for a little while, and I would take this as a good gesture on your part to do me this favor considering that you have just been out the whole night with my daughter and I really don't like you that much at this point," he told Nicholas.

"Certainly sir, I would be happy to do that for you." He turned toward her and asked, "Christie, you want to go over to the café and get a quick bite to eat?"

Christie still showed signs of fear all over her face, and Nicholas couldn't imagine what it must have been like to be her and have to sit in this room waiting for Anita to come home while trying to entertain them by answering their many questions.

She jumped up right away and answered, "Sure that sounds like a good idea. Nit, I'll see you in about an hour," she said as Nicholas led her out of the room.

"Mr. and Mrs. Feliciani, I hope you enjoy your stay and maybe the four of us can go somewhere and spend some time together," he said, but neither Ellena nor Frankie even bothered to acknowledge him as he left the room.

"I can't believe how rude you were to him. Nicholas is the first guy I have ever met in my life that actually wanted to talk to me. We had such a great night together and the two of you treated him like he was some typical guy from the neighborhood who would only be interested in me for sex or because of who my father was, instead of just caring about me," she said.

Frankie walked over to Anita and took her by the hand and sat her on the bed next to Ellena. "I think caring about how we treated your friend Nicholas is the least of your problems right now, Anita," he told her.

❦   ❦   ❦

CHAPTER 5

A New Deal
(2 of Spades, 7 of Diamonds)

Anthony stood in front of the refrigerator and looked at the calendar, which had today's date circled in red marker. The date was Tuesday November 10th, exactly one year ago to the very day that he and Tami had arrived in Oxford, Mississippi to start their new lives. And what a better way to celebrate than by telling Sandra that he was ready for her and Kimberly to join him?

Even though she was within driving distance from the University, Tami lived on campus in the freshmen dorms. Anthony agreed that she needed to have her own space and that living at school would be best for her. Anthony had found part time work helping a local CPA get his business off the ground. The pay wasn't the greatest, but then again Anthony wasn't doing it for the money as much as to kill the boredom that was controlling his life. Anthony missed the excitement of his old life, but that was behind him now and trying to adapt to the slow paced, friendly, southern living was more of a challenge than Anthony had prepared himself for when he came to Mississippi.

The date on the calendar was also circled for Anthony's eight o'clock Gambler's Anonymous meeting down at the Kennedy Middle School, which would mark a whole year for Anthony in which he hadn't gambled. He could only smile as he looked at the calendar, because today was going to be a great day in his life.

♣   ♣   ♣

"You coming to French class or not?" Veronica asked Tami from the doorway. Tami was still sitting at her desk holding the same envelope in her hand as she had for the last hour.

"I'm not in the mood to listen to French today, besides, this is a big day for me today and I don't want to waste it by sitting in French class," she responded.

"Fine, I'll go by myself, but if you expect me to take notes for you, you better think about going to my eight-thirty Accounting I class tomorrow," she informed Tami.

"That sounds just lovely, accounting first thing to start my day tomorrow," Tami answered.

"Great, I'll catch up with you later and you can tell me all about this big day of yours," Veronica said before she darted off to class.

Tami didn't pay her any mind because all that she cared about at that moment was Kevin and what he left her in the envelope that she had been holding for over an hour. Tami always believed that Kevin was much smarter than people gave him credit for and he proved that by leaving her all the information that she would need in case anything happened to him. She wanted retribution, and today was going to be that day.

Kevin had left Tami a name and a phone number to call in case she wanted to start the process of avenging his death, and with the number was a note attached to it stating, "This is only a long shot, but it can't hurt to be lucky once in a while." But lucky wasn't the exact word that Tami would have described her fortune when she made that call four days ago. Blessed would be more like it, because only God or a guardian angel from above could have somehow kept Nicholas and Anita together after a year, considering how much of a long shot it was that Nicholas had ever found Anita in the first place.

The phone number was Charlie's from the shop, stating that she should call him about Nicholas, who could hopefully help her. But it wasn't Nicholas that had helped her—it was Charlie. Charlie informed her that Nicholas was now living in Arizona and attending the University with his girlfriend Anita. He asked Tami what the chances were of two neighborhood kids meeting together one weekend and just packing up everything and moving all the way across the country. Tami had informed him that fate has the craziest plans for all of us, and thanked him for their phone number as she hung up the phone.

But where fate or God really made Tami feel like she was blessed was after she made the second phone call. Anita was aware of her parents' whereabouts and promised that she would relay Tami's message to her father.

Yes, sitting here at her desk with Kevin's envelope still in her hand, Tami felt exceptionally blessed, and why not? For all the shit that she had been through, she believed she deserved to be for a change.

Anthony was still beaming after his phone call with Sandra. He had kept the dream alive every day for the last year that there was a chance that he and Sandra were going to get back together, but he was a realist and he didn't expect it to come true. They had talked on the phone for over three hours and she assured Anthony that no one from Frankie's crew had been looking for her and Kimberly and nothing peculiar had happened to her since she left Chad. Sandra had also promised Anthony that she and Kimberly could be down in Mississippi within a week.

Anthony was so caught up with his happiness from the phone call with Sandra that he had totally forgotten to call Tami and let her know about his intentions. Even though Tami didn't live with him all year round, he still wanted to be considerate and give her a heads up, because Fall break was only a month away. Anthony looked at his watch and saw that he still had time before he had to get going for the G.A. meeting, so he figured he would take a shot and see if Tami was in her room.

"Hey Tami, its Anthony, how's everything going with school?" he asked.

"Everything is going well. I am just sitting here catching up on some French homework," she replied, but in reality she was laying on her bed counting down the minutes until her day would become truly perfect.

"I hate to bother you on a school night and I really didn't want to talk about it over the phone, but you never have a set pattern in your days and I don't know when you are going to have a chance to come home," he said.

"If you want you may talk to me now, because I have some free time and the rest of the week looks bad," she replied, which was also another lie.

Anthony looked at his watch and realized it was getting close to seven. He didn't want to walk into the meeting late because he was up for becoming a sponsor, and it wouldn't look good to set a bad example for the new people, who were there for their first night.

Each meeting there was usually one or two new people, mostly consisting of older people who were blowing their pension and social security checks on lottery tickets. With the casinos in Mississippi, these G.A. meetings could get crowded with the hard addicts.

"I really wasn't expecting to get a hold of you and I was only prepared to leave you a message on your machine. How about I call you once my meeting is over? Will you still be awake?" he asked.

"I'm sorry Anthony, I totally forgot about your anniversary tonight. Congratulations on making a year," she replied.

"Thanks Tami, that means a lot to me," he said.

"I really won't be around later, but you can leave the message on the phone and maybe I'll come home over the weekend and we can talk," she responded.

"That would be nice because I do miss you and I would love to hear what has been going on with your life," he answered.

"Ok, then I will try my best to come home," she said.

"Great, then I will hopefully see you this weekend," Anthony replied.

"I want to ask you something—one last thing Anthony, before you go to your meeting."

"Can't it wait, Tami? I really have got to get there, you know how they react when you walk in late," he responded.

"Well, I think they can wait for you for five minutes, considering I have been waiting a year to know what happened to Kevin and what you did with his body," she said.

This completely threw Anthony off-guard. He was not prepared for this question. Tami had never brought up the topic before, and he was hoping that it would be something that she lived with and would never bring up. But that was not going to be the case.

"Tami, you know that is something that is going to take a long time to explain and it would be best if we saved it for the weekend, when I can tell you face-to-face," he replied.

"Anthony I really need for you to tell me tonight, this can't wait. I figured a year was long enough to wait," she responded.

"Tami, this isn't being fair, please just wait until the weekend and I will go over every last detail with you about what happened to Kevin."

"Be fair? Is that some kind of poetic irony? Because of you I don't have a brother anymore and you want me to be fair? That's asking a lot, don't you think?" she asked.

"Tami, I'm sorry but I've got to go. However my offer is on the table and if you want to come home this weekend, please do," he said, and then hung up the phone.

Tami laid there for a moment listening to the dead line before she finally put the phone back down on the handle. She wasn't going to let the disappointment from Anthony ruin her day. It really didn't matter to her if she heard it from Anthony or not: she was already aware of how Kevin had died from one of the other three people who were there when he was killed. She was sure that after tonight she was going to know what Anthony did with his body, because, after all, this was her special day.

Matthew Cocco had already started tonight's meeting when Anthony walked into the room a little after eight. They both acknowledged one another as Anthony sat in his normal spot in the front row.

"Looks like tonight's guest of honor decided to join us after all," Matthew announced as Anthony noticed the congratulations sign taped to the blackboard and the cake and refreshments on the table next to the wall closest to the door. "As most of you know, tonight marks Anthony's one year anniversary in our program and we will have a little celebration for him once everyone is done speaking tonight," Matthew announced.

Anthony turned and gave a little bow to the rest of the group to acknowledge their applause.

"Now, let's get back to the meeting. I see we have most of the usual crowd here tonight and if I am not mistaken, I see a couple of new faces. Since it is customary to start with the fresh faces, how about one of you stand up and tell the group something about yourself," Matthew said.

All the new people were sitting in the back, which was usually the case because they either wanted to hide from everyone else or they wanted to be able to see everything that was going on in front of them. Matthew kept half the lights in the room off during the meetings to ease the new people's fears. This also had the effect of obscuring their faces, preserving a certain amount of anonymity for them. Both of the first timers looked at each other, and finally one of them stood up and addressed the group.

"Hi, my name is Francine DiNardis and I have a gambling problem. With the help of my friends and family I decided to come here tonight to see if I can't lick this addiction. I have been taken prisoner by slot and video poker machines, and I don't want to be under their spell any longer," she announced to the room.

"Well Francine, hopefully tonight will be the first step on your way to recovery and, if you continue to be honest with yourself and continue to come to our meetings, we can make your wish come true," Matthew informed her.

"Those were the words that I wanted to hear," she replied as she sat back down and started to shed tears. The rest of the group applauded her.

The gentleman who let Francine go first stood up, faced the group and introduced himself. "My name is Frankie and I have been a professional gambler for about forty years. Even though I have been extremely successful over the years, my wife thought it was time for me to change my way of living. I came here tonight hoping to get a little help from the group to accomplish my goal," he said as he sat down.

And like Francine, the members in the group applauded him.

"If quitting gambling and making your wife happy is what you want Frankie, then you have come to the right place because we have some great sponsors in our group who would be willing to see that you accomplish your goals. After everyone has their turn speaking tonight, you and Francine can mingle with the others and we'll see if we can pair the two of you up with one of our existing sponsors. If either of you would like, Anthony, who now qualifies as a sponsor, would be happy to work with one of you," Matthew said to the two of them.

"That would be great," Frankie responded. "That is why I came here tonight, so I can start to get closure on my problem."

Epilogue:
Almost One Month Later…

Veronica was standing at the door with her two bags in her hands as she looked at Tami one last time. "Are you sure you don't want to come home with me and spend the Christmas Holiday with my family and me? I would hate to spend my Christmas worrying about you being stuck in this room for a week all by yourself, eating soup out of a can."

"What makes you think that I am going to be here alone? You never know, there might be some other losers on this campus that don't have any family to go home to and I might have the time of my life with one of them," she replied.

"I really wish you would reconsider my offer, Tami," Veronica answered.

"You don't have to worry about me, I won't be staying here for the Holiday, because I decided to get out of this place and take a trip," Tami answered.

"Really? Where are you going on such short notice right before the Holiday?" Veronica asked, surprised that Tami had actually planned on going somewhere.

Veronica knew Tami hadn't been the same since Anthony's sudden disappearance. It had been almost a month and Tami still hadn't heard from Anthony. No email, phone call or even a postcard telling her where he was. It was like he had vanished.

"I decided that you were right and I would have to be a fool to spend my Holiday here alone in this dorm room, so I was thinking of taking a little road trip to kill a couple of days," Tami told her.

"Well that's great, where did you decide to go? It wouldn't be back to the big city would it?" Veronica asked.

"You know I swore that I was never going back there again. Actually, I decided a trip to the West coast would be nice, with maybe a stop in Arizona."

"Why Arizona?"

"I have a friend who attends the University of Arizona and I thought I would pay her a visit because, like me, she doesn't have family to visit during the Holidays either," Anita replied.

"Oh my God, are her parents dead too? What happened to them?" Veronica asked.

"No silly, they aren't dead. Her parents retired to Monaco or Monte Carlo, I forget which, but like me she'll be all alone and I figure the visit would do wonders for the both of us."

"That sounds great. Did you guys make any plans yet or are you going to play it by ear?"

"This is a surprise visit. She has no idea that I am coming to see her," Anita informed her.

"Really? How come?" Veronica asked.

"Because everyone loves an unexpected surprise," she replied.

978-0-595-41309-6
0-595-41309-9

Lightning Source UK Ltd.
Milton Keynes UK
UKOW02f0855080716

277903UK00002B/311/P